# MACHINE DREAMS

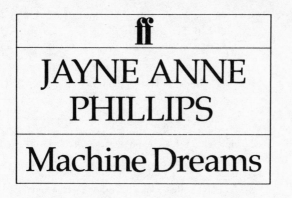

**JAYNE ANNE PHILLIPS**

**Machine Dreams**

*faber and faber*
LONDON · BOSTON

First published in Great Britain in 1984
by Faber and Faber Limited
3 Queen Square London WC1N 3AU


Printed in Great Britain by
Thetford Press Limited
Thetford Norfolk
All rights reserved

Portions of this book have appeared in the *Atlantic Monthly* and in *Grand Street*. *The Secret Country: Mitch* was published as a limited edition by Palaemon Press Ltd.

Any resemblance to persons living or dead is purely coincidental.

*British Library Cataloguing in Publication Data*

Phillips, Jayne Anne
Machine dreams
I. Title
813'.54[F]   PS3566.H479
ISBN 0–571–13398–3

FOR MY FAMILY,
PAST AND PRESENT

# Contents

# Acknowledgements

*The author wishes to express her thanks to The Ingram Merrill Foundation, The Bunting Institute of Radcliffe College, and The Fine Arts Work Center in Provincetown for support during the writing of this work. She also wishes to thank Rick Ducey, U.S. Army, Retired, and Geoffrey M. Boehm, helicopter pilot, First Cav., Vietnam, for their time and consideration.*

"Here is the story of flying, from the dreams of ancient Greece to the wonders of the present day, presented in brief, authoritative text and superb watercolor paintings. It is a fascinating story of people and ideas, of adventure and daring, and of flying machines."

MELVIN B. ZISFEIN,
*Flight: A Panorama of Aviation*

"The Greeks believed that their heroic dead appeared before the living in the form of a horse. . . . The soul of the deceased was often depicted in horse-shape."

NIKOLAS YALOURIS,
*Pegasus: The Art of the Legend*

"Now he (Pegasus) flew away and left the earth, the mother of flocks, and came to the deathless gods: and he dwells in the house of Zeus and brings to wise Zeus the thunder and lightning."

HESIOD,
*The Theogony, vv. 284–86*

"And the voice said:
Well you don't know me,
    but I know you
And I've got a message to give to you.
    Here come the planes
So you better get ready. Ready to go. You can come
    as you are, but pay as you go . . .
They're American planes. Made in America.
Smoking or non-smoking?"

LAURIE ANDERSON
"O Superman"

# MACHINE DREAMS

# REMINISCENCE
# TO A DAUGHTER
## Jean

It's strange what you don't forget. We had a neighbor called Mrs. Thomas. I remember reaching up a long way to pull the heavy telephone—a box phone with a speaking horn on a cord—onto the floor with me. Telephone numbers were two digits then. I called 7, 0, and said, "Tommie, I'm sick. I want you to come over." I can still hear that child's voice, with the feeling it's coming from inside me, just as clearly, just as surely as you're standing there. I was three years old. I saw my hands on the phone box, and my shoes, and the scratchy brown fabric of the dress I was wearing. I wasn't very strong and had pneumonia twice by the time I was five. Mother had lost the child before me to diphtheria and whooping cough, and stillborn twins before him. She kept me dressed in layers of woolens all winter, leggings and undershirts. She soaked clean rags in goose grease and made me wear them around my neck. Tommie would help her and they'd melt down the grease in a big black pot, throw in the rags, and stir them with a stick while I sat waiting, bundled in

3

blankets. They lay the rags on the sill to cool, then wrapped me up while the fumes were still so strong our eyes teared. I stood between the two women as they worked over me, their hands big and quick, and saw nothing but their broad dark skirts.


I was so skinny as a kid, and had such big brown eyes. In the summer I was black as a darkie and Mother called me her picka-ninny. She used to say I was the ugliest baby she ever saw; when I was a few days old she lay me in the middle of the high walnut bed and stood looking. The neighbor woman at her elbow said, "Just you wait. She'll be the joy of your life." Mother would tell that story as I was growing up—I don't know how many times I heard it—then she'd smile at me and say, "And it's true, you are."

Later you look back and see one thing foretold by another. But when you're young, those connections are secrets; everything you know is secret from yourself. I always assumed I'd have my own daughter. I picked out your name when I was twelve, and saved it. In a funny way, you were already real. I never felt that way about your brother. You were first-born; then he arrived and made a place for himself; I'd had no ideas about him. Maybe it's that way with boy children; maybe they're luckier.


I was like an only child, growing up alone with my mother. She'd lost those three babies before me, and my brother and sister who survived were ten and twelve years older—out of the house by the time I needed someone to talk to. They had grown up very differently—Dad had money then. Mother's furniture was new; the house was kept up; the street, with all those big trees shading the sidewalk, was referred to as Quality Hill. Dad had the biggest lumber business in the state at one time. He was twenty-five years older than Mother and she was his second wife; at the time they married, he had grown children nearly her age. Even though he was rich, her parents hadn't wanted her to go with him—I guess he had quite a reputation: an eccentric, a womanizer. Her family ran a small hotel in Pickens. That town is a ghost town now but the building, the old hotel, is still standing. Did I ever take you to see it? He stayed there on business trips and Mother had seen him come and go. One night she was clerking at the check-out desk and he suddenly noticed her. She was seventeen; he must have seemed worldly and dashing. After a few months of courtship and presents—mostly by mail—they eloped and went to Niagara Falls for a wedding trip. It was her first time away from home since childhood; all her clothes were new and they stayed in a suite of grand rooms. Mother told me how she'd sit up at night, writing letters back about the steamer boat and the spray of the Falls; how the spray turned colors in the sun but was cold even in summer and smelled to her of mint or violets. She begged her mother to forgive her, but the letters weren't answered; it was a year before they'd let her come visit.

Dad brought her home through Hampton to impress her. Now it's just shacks bought out by the mines and fallen to ruin, but then it was a town of forty frame saltboxes he'd built by the river to house his workers. The mill hands lined the tracks and cheered as the train pulled in.

They lived there near the mill in the master house for the first couple of years. She was a help to him in the business, though he never admitted as much and pretended not to take her advice. Soon he moved her to the big house in town and was home every other night; he was accustomed to doing just as he liked and had a succession of "secretaries" out at the mill. My sister told me she remembered a big row between them when she was thirteen or so. I was just a baby. He'd hired a manager that summer and was going to be in town most of the time; he said there was a lot of work to do and he was going to move his secretary into one of the spare rooms down the hall from his. Mother said she'd sooner march down the street naked than take one of his women under her own roof. He said by God it was his roof, he'd paid for every inch of it. He did move the girl in for a few weeks—daughter of one of the mill workers. She wasn't very bright and Mother ended up being nice to her, but my sister hated Dad from that time on and never spoke to him again except when threatened. But what toys she had as a child! China dolls and a dollhouse with a circular staircase. I think of those times as grand because they had no money worries, but Dad was always hard to live with. Still, he was a shiny figure, dapper, and gone from home enough that they were often left in peace.

By the time I was seven the mill was lost and he was a terror, sentimental or raging. He'd always been a drinker but he drank more; he'd extended credit to Easterners and what we called Gypsies—Italians from the upstate river towns. He liked being owed and flattered, begged for more time. He thought he was doing good works by letting his buyers go further and further into debt, and the Depression finished him.

We got along, but just barely. Mother had kept every stitch my elder sister hadn't worn out, and she made those clothes over to fit me. My dresses were always mismatched affairs of good fabrics, twelve years out of style. I liked them and thought I looked grown-up. We kept a big garden and canned for weeks— she had a full pantry and those cloudy jars fed us through the winter. Any money we had came from the sale of milk or cream or butter—we had four cows in the barn, up the hill back of the house. Mother did the work year-round but I remember the cows especially in summer. We seemed to spend the long days in attendance to them while Dad sat on the porch or disappeared into the unused room on the stifling third floor of the house. He was totally unpredictable and talked to himself. Sometimes he fed the cows or walked out in the evening to inspect the barn, to knock on the falling boards with his fist and listen as though testing the wood. But he did chores as a whim. Usually I fed the cows and chickens. It used to occur to me at the age of seven and eight how stupid those cows were—like big warm rocks. Though we came to the barn every day at regular times, they didn't recognize us except as they'd recognize rain or snow. They didn't even have the nervousness and greed of the chickens, but ate placidly, like machines. The only time they seemed at all human was at calving, and that was terrible to watch. They bawled in pain and seemed bewildered, as though they didn't know what hurt them. Then the calf was out on the straw, blinking.

Mother milked into a quart cup and dumped the milk in a can. When the can was full she pulled it to the house in a hand wagon. We had the coolest cellar, like a still tomb, with stone walls and a stone floor. Rough shelves along the side were lined with mason jars sealed full of tomatoes and beans and beets. The jars were just jars but you were always aware of them in the dimness, dense and weighted. The milk crocks were on the floor, white earthen urns. Mother wore a long man's apron over her dress and skimmed the cream off the milk with a wooden spoon shaped like a small flat spade. We dipped the milk back into cans with a gourd dipper and carried them up the stone steps, across the yard into the kitchen. The bottles had to be boiled and the milk strained through a sterile cloth. She set some of it aside and let it curdle to frothy clumps the size of popcorn, then poured that heavy yellow cream over it and ground fresh pepper on top. Her cheese was famous but I wouldn't touch it, and they had to beg me to drink milk. I guess I didn't like it because we were always fooling with it, from dawn to dusk, the cows and the milk and the bottles.

Mr. Hardesty delivered for us and I helped him in the summer. I could see him driving the cart along from way down the street. He had an old barrel-chested workhorse named Gus, and that horse knew every stop by heart. Gus was well known around town. Mr. Hardesty did landscaping and plowing as well—Gus wore blinders then and pulled a big double rake by harness; they graded yards for seeding or turned gardens. When we delivered milk, I met them at the top of the hill and handed up our four metal racks of four bottles each. Then I rode beside Hardesty and jumped down to take the orders to the doorsteps. The horse always waited just long enough. There was one customer who'd died a couple of years before I'd ever started helping, but Gus stopped at that house anyway. We sat waiting the time it would have taken me to run to the door and back.

My father got worse as time went on. When my friends stayed with me, he used to stride into the room, pull the sheets off us, and tell them to get dressed—he didn't want strangers in his house at night. One autumn we were burning trash on the hill. He picked up a pitchfork of blazing leaves and chased Mother around the fire. After that we had to have him put away. A couple of weeks later, a guard knocked him down and that was all. I was fourteen. My mother and I turned on every light in the house that evening and sat on the porch, looking at the street. October, a clean moisture in the air. We both felt such relief. We'd been ashamed to send him there, but we'd gotten afraid of him and had no money for anything better. I didn't know until he was gone what a shadow he'd cast. Partly because we were free of him, the next few years were good. We took in roomers, students from the college. I had a part-time job and lots of friends; I was eager to know people. You may not like me to say so, but high school was the best time of my life.

On Sundays in the spring, the kids in my crowd got all dressed up and walked downtown to the drugstore for sodas—that was our big thrill. But Tomblyn's was beautiful then—as grand, everyone said, as any soda fountain in Washington or New York. The big mirror was beveled glass, and the fountains themselves were brass. The floor was marble tiles with a black border, and the deep booths, mahogany. Only the high carved ceiling and bar wall are left now, and the store is half as large as it was.

We girls took pains and were high style, but really, all the young women then dressed like matrons—silk shoulder pads in our dresses and those big hats. We got the shoulder pads from our mothers, and silk lingerie at rummage sales; you couldn't buy silk during the war. The war influenced everything. We were the Class of '43, and all the boys worried the fighting would stop before they could get overseas. Rummage and church sales were War Benefits; all the women's clubs rolled bandages and collected tin. High school girls wrote to boys who'd graduated five and six years before, boys who'd driven their cars past them as they stood on the sidewalk playing hopscotch. Three letters a week to Europe on blue onionskin stationery; letters to boys who'd been our heros, and boys who hadn't. We tacked Kodak snapshots on our walls—small black and white pictures the size of six postage stamps. A soldier in a graveyard and on the back: *All these Germans are dead ones.* You've seen your father's war album—airstrips, everyone in khaki; how it was. Easy to tell good from evil.

There was one boy I went with off and on through high school. He wanted to go to medical school instead of to war, and be a doctor like his father and two of his older brothers. The Harwins: they were a family of four brothers and one sister, grew up in one of the fine old turn-of-the-century houses, and were well-off. But Dr. Harwin had died when Tom was fourteen, and his mother died two years later, both of heart attacks. Tom was the youngest and Peggy, the sister, was in her twenties and taught phys. ed. at the college. One of the brothers—the oldest, I believe —was a sort of ne'er-do-well; he had a traveling job and then joined the navy. The other two were studying at Duke. They sent what they could, but the mother's death took the last of the family money. Tom and Peggy had to sell the house his senior year, and the college bought it, just as they'd bought several of the other old homes. Shinner Black was Tom's best friend and Shinner's mother ran a rooming house, so Tom moved in for the summer. He didn't really want to, but Peggy said he'd spend half his time there with Shinner anyway, and they couldn't take a chance on losing the offer. Peggy was very practical and steady. She used to go along as chaperone when the high school kids went on picnics out by the river. Yes, we had chaperones, can you believe it? But Peggy was like one of us. I remember her lying on the rocks at Sago, wearing a black one-piece with a pleated bodice, and smoking cigarettes. . . .

Sago was lush before mine drainage ruined it; the river so quiet, isolated. We went to Blue Hole—clear water circled with massive flat boulders, like a stone beach. We walked a long train trestle to reach it, a shaky old trestle high over the gorge, then down a trail by old tracks and over a wooded bank. Once we broke through the trees and a colony of butterflies, big yellow monarchs, were dipping their wings at clear puddles collected on the rocks. Forty or fifty of them, so silent. And the water was cool and clean then, twenty feet deep at Blue Hole. We swam and got lazy on beer, ate dinner, and went home. Peggy always took a wristwatch and hung it on a bush; we left at seven, before dusk. She'd tell us to wake up, children, and she yelled some hide-and-seek chant into the woods for the ones who'd gone off together. We walked back in a warm exhaustion, watching our feet on the trestle ties; trash, broken toys, trickle of stream in the weeds far down. Peggy said not to look—if you stared straight ahead you could be sure of every step and run to meet the train. She was a beautiful girl, fair, with honey-colored hair. She and Tom resembled each other; the other brothers were dark.

Tom's father died before I really knew him, but I'd seen his mother. She dressed her gray hair in a chignon and always wore gloves in the summer. I have a photograph that must have been taken the summer after the father died: Mrs. Harwin in the garden with her children, wearing a long black-lace dress, a gold brooch, three strands of pearls. The sons flank her, all in black suits, and Peggy is directly behind her mother, peering between black shoulders. Must have been an occasion, a wedding, the men wearing boutonnieres, morning coats, cravats. The wide trellis is behind them, and the shaggy trees. Tom is fifteen and pleased with himself, the kid brother dressed in his first tuxedo. Considering what happened, it's a scary picture. Only Peggy is still living —all the rest died of heart. And Tom was the youngest; we were seventeen, had just graduated from high school. Now it seems to me he died as a child, before anything touched him. But that's not really true. He'd already lived through the deaths of his parents, not easy at any age. He was one of the boys, popular, but he had such a presence, a gravity. Everyone respected his family and he grew into that same respect. Sure, he fooled around sometimes— once he and Shinner Black dressed in drag on Class Day. Bobby sox, sweaters over C-cup bras stuffed with apples, head scarves, and lipstick. Pretty Peasants, they called themselves, and played it up all during the ceremonies. Another time they somehow got a bull into the chemistry lab. It must have been difficult to lead that animal up three flights of steps; it was nearly impossible to lead him down.

Tom was different because he was mannish and independent, but not afraid to be attentive the way a woman would be. He never forgot anything I told him, and he was proud of me. Sometimes when we were at a dance or out with the crowd, he'd nod in my direction and say, "Look at her. Isn't she the prettiest thing you ever saw?" Probably sounds silly to you, but it wasn't really about being pretty. He wanted everyone to know he loved me.

I'd gotten a job at the telephone office that spring. "Number please" a few hundred times a day, plugging and unplugging the connections. The operators knew everything that went on in the town—if you weren't rushed, you could listen in by leaving the key open. But you didn't need to, there was plenty of information in who called whom and what they said to the operators. We could always count on Mr. Lee, who owned the dry goods store, to be tight drunk by noon and curse us out for answering too slowly or for getting him a busy signal. A lot of the girls knew which married men were seeing whom by the calls they made at odd hours. I never worried about all that and was glad to be getting a paycheck. I only minded our supervisor, a red-headed spinster named Lindstrom. She watched our work shifts to the minute and called us her chickens, as if the clicks and scratchings of the board were *our* sounds. She thought we were brainless, trying to take advantage. And I was so scrupulous, the perfect employee. Like a dumb kid, I was glad to work long shifts and have a lunch hour like a grown-up.

Tom wasn't working yet. He and Shinner Black had decided to paint houses for the summer and were looking to buy a cheap truck. But they were in no hurry, and it was around then that Tom started getting sick. He would walk me home every night from the telephone office, and we'd have to stop twice on the way up the hill for him to rest. He had chest pains and shortness of breath. After a few days he went to Doc Jonas at my insistence and was told he had gas on his stomach, to take some antacid pills and exercise. But he couldn't; he had no stamina. He'd played sports all his life and suddenly he couldn't run up the hill. I think he knew all along, though he may not have thought it actually possible—at seventeen. The last week, he stayed in bed most of the time. I would go by after work and make supper for him in Mrs. Black's kitchen. One night he lay in bed sweating and would barely talk to me. I went home crying to Mother that he was going to lie over there and die if nothing was done. So she called Mrs. Black and told her to phone Tom's brother Nate in Chapel Hill. Nate, who was a fifth-year med student, recognized the symptoms right away, and drove all night to get to Tom by morning. He examined him and hired an ambulance, made arrangements for surgery down south. Tom said he would only go if I went with him, and Nate agreed. Mother had my bag packed and they were to pick me up from work. . . . Tom got out

of bed to comb his hair and dropped dead by the bathroom sink.
That quickly. I put the call through from Black's house, recognized
Nate's voice, and kept the key pressed down. He was calling
Peggy, told her to come at once, that they were all too late, and why
hadn't she known Tom was so sick? Then he hung up and called the
undertaker. I put that call through too, then left the board and
went into the bathroom. I sat there dry-eyed and stared at the
brooms and mops propped against the wall.

Outside, the other girls were talking. One of them was sobbing and Lindstrom was saying there was no one to take over, I
would have to finish the shift. I went back out. None of them
looked at me and I finished: thirty-five minutes. I started walking
home and Mother had someone meet me at the bottom of the hill,
in a car. Who was it? Oh yes, Shinner. He'd been there when it
happened and had seen Tom lying on the floor, then had gone to
my mother in a panic. She sent him after me but he stopped the
car at the hill and waited; he couldn't be the one to tell me. We
went home and sat on my bed and wept for hours. He said Tom
lay there in his pants and no shirt or shoes, on his side, his feet
reaching into the hallway. His face just empty, like you wouldn't
believe anything could look.

They asked me to plan the funeral and we buried him with
his parents. All of that is a blur. I've almost no memory of it. A
few days later Peggy and I went down to North Carolina for a
month, to visit Nate and his wife and their new baby. In pictures
from that time, I look like somebody's grandmother, my face
puffy, my hair tied in a kerchief. And Peggy is so blond and
bright, too bright, her hair perfectly curled, light blue eyes
straining above a set smile. She looks perpetually surprised, but
scared and insincere, like a play actor. She felt guilty because
she'd insisted they sell the house; Tom was off with his friends
all the time and there she was with the cleaning and the upkeep
and her teaching job as well. But the fact was he'd had to move
out and she hadn't, since the college turned the place into a
girls' dorm and Peggy stayed on, in her own room, as house
mother. She and Tom had argued and three weeks later he was
dead—she hadn't even known he was sick. She thought I blamed

her but wouldn't say so. I did blame her some, but with such a resignation there was no anger. It was all muddled. I kept thinking Tom and I might have broken up anyway when he went off to college, and said so, but they all denied that, as though his honor were at stake. We talked about him endlessly. Finally I sickened of the whole thing and told myself it was his business, his death. We all seemed to have so little to do with it, and no right to such feelings. I suppose I was stunned. All the days were like some repetitive dream—sometime next week I would wake up and be in the real world.

Mother said, "You're young. Your life's not over." A girlfriend of mine moved in with us and Mother gave us the whole top floor of the house. We moved the Victrola upstairs, played records loud, and practiced dance steps. "Fascination" is a song I remember from that time: *I might have gone on my way empty-hearted*; every jukebox had two or three versions. I wore anklets and heels and did the furniture in gaudy colors. Took one of Mother's beautiful antique vanities, painted it pink and black, and hung a starched white ruffle around the legs. Wow, I said, isn't it pretty; Mother said yes, it certainly was. Anything I did was fine with her. My girlfriend and I had jobs as checkers at the grocery, and clothes, and dates—I never went out with the same boy three times. I forced myself to be happy and flip. Really, I was mad at all of them, and mad at Tom for leaving me. There in town with all the same people and sidewalks and buildings, it was as though he still existed but wouldn't come near me. Like he was watching me all the time, disappointed and sad-faced. What had I done wrong? Nate and Peggy had made copies of all their snapshots of Tom, then given me the originals and the negatives. Envelopes of those stiff dark negatives, squares that rattled when I shuffled them. I kept them in my high school scrapbook. Sometimes I took them all out and held them to the light one by one. We all glowed up like angels. The smiles and unsuspecting gestures made more sense, full of a secret everyone ignored, but what was it?

So the time went on quietly. I worked, took classes at the college. Life wasn't like it is now. Look at you—born here and think you have to get to California, go so far, do so much so fast. Crazy situations, strange people—all this I hear about drugs. We had the Depression and then the war; we didn't have to go looking for something to happen. And the things that happened were so big; no one could question or see an end to them. People died in the war and they died at home, of real causes, not what they brought on themselves. Living with that was enough.

Late in '44 I enrolled in the Cadet Nurses' Program in Washington, a special accelerated course subsidized by the army. My mother's trouble, the cancer, had started the spring before—but she wasn't ill except when she had the treatments, and she so wanted me to have the training, some security. So I went. I lived in a dorm at American University. The food was terrible and we all smoked cigarettes to cut our appetites. Washington was exciting in wartime, choked with soldiers and service people. And I loved the classes. But I only stayed four months; Mother got worse. My brother was in the service, my sister was divorced and had a child to support—there was no one to help but me. At that time we still thought she'd recover, but I didn't want her to be alone. I was twenty years old, almost an adult, and felt I should earn the money to support us, the money to get her whatever treatment she needed. And that's what I was doing two years later, just barely, when I met your father.

How did I meet him? I met him at a VFW dance. Veterans of Foreign Wars had fixed up an old house down near Main Street. There was a bar and jukebox and no furniture in the parlor so couples could dance on the hardwood floor. He was there with Marthella Barnett—she was wearing a purple sweater with cheap pink glass buttons down the front—and he left her and asked me to dance. I don't remember who I was with; I was dating Bink Crane and Jimmie Darnell at the time. I was always going out with older fellas, but not as old as Mitch Hampson, and I was a little scared of him. What year was it? 1947. And he was thirty-eight, a man about town since the war was over. He was so much older that even though he'd gone to high school in town I'd never heard of him, and no one I knew had heard of him, except he was related to the Bonds who owned the hospital. He was wearing a nice suit and drove his own car, and asked me to lunch. I said no; I didn't have enough time, my lunch hour was too short.

But we must have had lunch, because we certainly started going out. I remember him then as very patient, a perfect gentleman, none of the cussing and bad temper he was full of later. Of course it's not hard to be a gentleman for a three-week courtship. Three weeks, and we were married! Drove to Oakland, Maryland, with a wedding party of eight people. I wore a white suit I'd bought on sale and altered, and a white broad-brimmed hat I'd done in pale blue net and sprays of silk honeysuckle. What little fool would marry a man after three weeks? I should have had my head examined. But it seemed the right thing at the time. Mother said from her bed, "What's your hurry?"

She and I had been through a lot those years she was sick. Mitch and I were married in June and she died in December. He really was good to her. Every evening he went down to the drugstore to get the paper, and he'd go into her room before he left, sit and talk to her about the weather or the news, ask if she wanted anything.

She was bedfast about the time I started seeing him, and I guess I felt the ground going under me. We were alone in that big house, living mostly on my salary. I did office work for Maintenance at the State Road Commission; I balanced the payroll, answered phones. . . . I kept a telephone on her bed so she could call me if she got in trouble. The cancer had gone clear through her and her body just didn't work. She was so afraid she'd offend people. She'd drag herself to the bathroom every day and wash herself out with a syringe. I kept a big bowl of gauze pads on the table right next to her, gauze cut to measure from long strips I bought at the hospital. She kept herself clean with them all day, and every night I washed them along with her sheets.

Sometimes I wonder how things would have turned out if she'd never gotten sick. I didn't want her to die thinking I was alone. It seemed the least I could do for her, but really I suppose I was scared for myself. I had no idea what I would do without her.

o   o   o

I'll never forget the day she found it. One of those first warm days in early April, and a woman had come from Winfield to measure the couch for slipcovers. She'd spread material samples a yard wide, five yards long, all around the living room—a bright blue and a pale blue, a green floral, a beautiful off-white cream they called "oyster." I was standing in the dining room doorway looking in at the colors. Mother came out of the bathroom and said she was spotting. She was fifty-one then, just past menopause. She said she would call Dr. Jonas just to be safe. The seamstress had opened a window and there was a smell of mown grass from across the street. . . . We chose the cream; it really was lovely, textured with raised threads and very rich. A little more expensive, but Mother said the material would make the room seem lighter, summer and winter—and later we could have the chairs done in a print, maybe the floral.

Those slipcovers were the last thing but necessities we bought for three years, and the last housewares I bought until she was gone and the house was sold and I was buying for my own house. You never see the everyday the way you might.

She did call Dr. Jonas that very day and made an appointment. He diagnosed it and said there was no problem at all, not to worry, they could cure her with radium at Baltimore. So she went to Kelly Clinic by train. They told her it was a spot the size of a pinpoint on the mouth of the uterus. She went every three months, always by herself—we couldn't afford anything else. Sometimes they wouldn't find a trace in her whole body. The disease seemed to come and go like a shade. For a long time she had no pain, she would just get terribly tired.

Once she hemorrhaged and I took her by ambulance to Baltimore. They gave her radium and deep X-ray, and she was so quickly recovered that we walked to the hotel. The room was depressing—two little single beds on steel frames, no rug on the floor, dusty, like the place was never aired. I was upset to see this was where she'd been staying all those times, but she seemed accustomed to it and talked about all the fine people she'd met at the clinic. She said the doctors and nurses were generous and kept her informed; that the patients were interesting and came from all sorts of places.

She had every amount of hope.

Even after the disease metastasized, she wasn't as afraid as most people would be. Her life hadn't been easy but she was never a downhearted type. In an odd way, I suppose she was prepared.

The last eight months she was good and bad; then she was bad. She stopped the treatments and I kept her at home and kept her comfortable and clean. What did we give her? I don't know, I don't remember—whatever they gave then. Morphia, maybe. Why do you ask me all these questions? Living through it once was enough, and I hate for you to know her through these kinds of stories. I live with the fear of it, I'll tell you. When I had the hysterectomy, I woke up in that bed in the recovery room and thought—even through the terrible pain—"good, now there's nothing there to go wrong."

Right before she died, she seemed to come to herself. After two days of drugged sleep, she opened her eyes and looked all around the room. It seemed she saw everything at once without looking at any one object. She was perfectly calm, and the air of the room went still. Only for a moment . . . as if the room had detached from the house and come clear, the way light looks when a hard rain suddenly stops. Then she turned her head and was gone.

I felt the difference in her hand. Her body was empty; it lay there, familiar and strange. So many months we had tended it. Then I absolutely felt her absence, and left the room.

It's true the body turns empty as the shell of an insect, or like something inflatable but flattened. You don't know that until you're present at a death. And if it's someone whose presence is so known to you, so specific—you feel their movement, a lifting —you recognize them in what moves. Not ghostly, but amazing and too much to understand.

That winter, my breath caught each time I heard a sigh of heat from the register in the hall. Small, silly things. I did sometimes talk to her in my mind, and answered myself with memories of things she'd said or particular details. An hour before her death, I'd given her a drink of water from a teaspoon. Months

afterward, I felt us frozen in that instant, the spoon at her mouth.
She was semiconscious and I had the feeling, as the wetness
touched her lips, that I was only taking care of things—the house,
the rooms, her body. Then or later, I wasn't aware of any anger
toward her, or even toward the disease. But there was so much
sadness, and constant measuring up. Those cold months, I sewed
or read in the evenings. Her sayings seemed present in the walls
of the house—*between* the walls, as unseen as the supports and
beams. Alone, without her sense of humor, the words were pray-
erful and heavy. *Anything worth doing is worth doing well. Sit
down and collect yourself. Look until you find it and your
labor won't be lost. Hitch your wagon to a star. The Lord helps
those who help themselves. Lay it in the lap of the Lord.*

She thought funerals were barbaric. We had talked it all out.
She wrote her own service and wanted to be cremated. The service? I really don't remember. She didn't pretend to be educated;
it was only a poem she'd written, a list of quotations, two hymns.
Very simple. We'd thought the cremation would be simple as well,
but it was more difficult to arrange than you'd think. Not a usual
practice then, not here. Some of her friends disapproved and tried
to dissuade me. Maybe she'd made such a choice, they said, but
she wasn't herself. Legally, I had to get permission from the State
and from each County whose lines we crossed in transporting the
body. Then we took her ninety miles, my brother and sister and
I, in a rented ambulance. The place was a plain one-story building
with a cellar and no sign outside but THOMPSON BROTHERS. We
arrived in the evening and were to come back for the ashes the
next morning. The man who spoke with us was very kind. I
wanted to know everything; he explained the whole process. He
said the words "white heat" and showed me the crematorium,
three long ovens built back into the wall. There was a strong steel
mesh, very fine, with a sort of flat tray below, "so the ashes stay
pure and are contained." He seemed to want to reassure me about
that.

I knew it was only her body, and I hadn't let myself open the
casket except once. Still, it was strange to leave her there. Walking out of the building was physically hard, as though I were
moving against a wind. That night in the hotel I didn't sleep. I

can't describe my feeling. The others slept, or seemed to, but I sat
up and kept a light on. If I lay down or closed my eyes, I felt so
far away, as though the bed rested on air. When we could afford
a stone, she'd said to put simply her name, the years, and *It is
over.* That phrase ran in my mind all night until it lost its meaning.

We went for the ashes very early, seven A.M. When I saw
them I felt a first easing, a release, handed me like a gift. They
were more like sand than ashes. Irregular grains the color of
ivory; soft and rough to the touch. So clean they smelled of nothing. I kept them all winter in a small brass box. One day in the
spring, I scattered them in the garden at home. Must have been
March. Jonquils had budded early and the wind moved across
them in a swath.

I thought my marriage would work. Maybe you always think
that, you have to. Times had been so hard for everyone. When the
war was over and when the thing with Mother was finished, all I
wanted was to have a family. Not just for something to do, but
because I knew what family meant.

People had lost whatever was taken in those years and survived, and a lot of them married, had children, quickly. It was
denying what had happened in a way, saying life had started
again and you could trust it. For me that feeling was delayed, as
if the war didn't really stop until my mother died. She had first
gotten sick in wartime; we had always struggled—with the sickness, with money, in the shadow of the war— and then suddenly
the war was over and the men were home, but we were just
starting the hardest part, that last six months. I married and
Mitch moved in with us. His presence helped but he wasn't directly involved; it wasn't his job to be. Mother and I saw it
through. Then I took a year, some time for myself, and I *wanted*
my children; she had wanted them for me.

And family wasn't just who you were married to, not here.
Late forties, the end of that decade, people were relieved. There
were jobs and money and no more catastrophes. People knew each
other, they helped each other. A lot of people around town were
good to me, good to us. Family was more than blood relation.

○ ○ ○

Your father and I lived with Gladys Curry while our own house was being built. We'd sold Mother's place to get the money to buy land, and Gladys let us stay in her spare bedroom. What a pistol she was—still working at the dress shop then, hard as nails and took no truck from anyone. We weren't paying rent and I did a lot of work around the house, or tried to: I could spend all morning scrubbing the kitchen floor; she'd come home, get down on her knees right in front of me, and do it over to suit herself.

But she was a lot of fun and said outrageous things—especially considering she'd known me since I was a little girl, and her daughter, Jewel—her one child—had married my older brother. They'd lived with Gladys awhile too, before moving to Ohio, and we filled the space they'd left. Gladys was a widow, one of those women three times stronger than the man she married. She'd tell me that every woman should have a husband and a lover; it took at least two men to stay this side of the desert; no one man had sense enough to take care of things and it was useless expecting him to. She'd had her daughter at seventeen, and her husband had died in a mine accident when she was thirty; she never did marry again but had a boyfriend for years. He kept a room downtown but spent most of his time with her—she cooked and cleaned for him and cajoled him and entertained him—she said she was no fool, she owned her house and her car and why on earth should she marry again.

We'd moved out to the other house by the time you were born, but Gladys was around a lot all those first few years. When you and Billy were toddlers, we'd dress you both up every summer afternoon and take you somewhere. You were like two dolls, done up in matching blue and white piqué sunsuits. We'd show you off to her neighbors in town. Mrs. Talbot, across the street from Gladys, would sit on her leafy porch and shake her head. She thought I took too many pains keeping my children so clean. Especially Billy. "You wash that child too much—you're going to sap his strength. You're washing his strength away."

Gladys and I would take you both down to the train station. The trains were still running then. Patchen, the engineer, would hold Billy on his lap and drive the engine back and forth across the yard. Then he'd hand him back to me covered with soot and crowing. Those engines were coal burners, dirty and loud. You were three. While Billy rode, you stood without a word and never took your eyes from that square of filthy window in the cab. I remember Patchen's old striped hat and those yellow gauntlets he wore—elbow-length padded gloves covered with coal dust. He would say to me, "Best let that boy alone. A boy can raise himself." Gladys said she'd never raised a boy, but she doubted they could fix their own meals or mend their own clothes any more than a man could.

She was there the night you almost died of pneumonia—you were five months old. Your father was out of town and there was a blizzard; the phone lines were down and the car was drifted in. You couldn't seem to breathe if we laid you down, so we kept you awake all night, upright, to keep your lungs from filling—took turns walking the hall and holding you. You were so small but you'd open your mouth when you felt the spoon near your face; you wanted that bitter medicine. By dawn we were giving you whiskey with an eyedropper, a drop at a time. Gladys walked a mile through that deep snow to get to a working phone, and the doctor came by seven. Somehow you were better and he said just to keep you at home, it would only be worse to try to get you to town.

Stayed way below zero that whole December and January, one storm after another. If you hadn't been breast-fed from the beginning, I don't think you would have made it. Several people lost young babies that winter—influenza and pneumonia. Adults got sick and didn't get well till spring.

I was always afraid when you were sick because you couldn't take drugs—you never could—allergic to sulpha and penicillin, and almost anything affected you badly. You were always so strong, but if you really got sick it was a matter of luck that you didn't get worse and worse.

You couldn't even take motion-sickness pills. Once in summer Gladys and I took her old Plymouth up to Ohio to visit Jewel and my brother—you were a little over a year old and Billy would be born in two months. Gladys did all the driving because I was too pregnant. We weren't on the road an hour before you went crazy on those pills—thrashing and screaming, throwing yourself against the dash. "We've got to stop," Gladys said. "She's going to bounce that baby right out of you." So Gladys walked up and down the road with you while I sat and sweated on those prickly car seats; they were wooly and as full of springs as an overstuffed chair. When she brought you back, you had quieted and your eyes were glazed; you went into such a sound sleep that I was worried to death.

You were always too sensitive. Everything that passed through you showed. That's why I don't know how you can take the kind of life you have, always moving around. You've got too much guts for your own good, and one of these days you'll come to a dead halt. Sometimes I'm afraid for you; I feel responsible. I stayed married all those years until you and Billy were grown —I only kept going to make you safe. It turned out I couldn't keep anyone safe. Not you. Not Billy.

Still, you and I will go on and on, despite whatever differences, whatever quarrels. For me, we are what's left. How are we different? Body and soul, I know—but some things don't change.

You were late getting born. I drank a bottle of castor oil to start my labor. I remember leaning out the door, still holding the bottle, yelling to the neighbor woman across the road that I'd drunk it all. August, ten in the morning, already hot as Hades. Then there were twenty hours, on and off the delivery table three times that night while other women had their babies and got on with it. I thought you were a boy for sure; no girl would cause such trouble. But when I knew I had a daughter, I was so thankful —like my own mother had come back to me.

# THE SECRET COUNTRY
## Mitch

I was born on the farm in Randolph County, 1910, lived there until I was six. Then went to Raynell with my aunt and her husband. He was a conductor on the railroad—big business then, everything went by rail. It was a new job for him and not traditional in the family; they had all been household farmers and worked the mines. Mines weren't like they are now. Then, there was no automation, mostly crawlspace, and the coal hauled out by mule. Three of the brothers died in the mines, including my father, but I never really knew him, never even remember seeing him. I know he was there sometimes in the summer, because there are photographs.

My mother lived at the farm during her confinement and left right after I was born. The birth certificate gives her name as Icie Younger, but no one ever told me anything about her. Her people were from down around Grafton and she went back to them. When I was selling road equipment for the State I used to travel

through there. Asked after the family several times but no one
had ever heard of them.

I grew up living always with one or another of the sisters. In
the beginning there were twelve kids in that family, seven boys
and five girls; and the farm was five hundred acres. Bess was the
youngest, twenty when I was born, and she took care of me. The
boys, my uncles, worked all over the county once they were
grown, but the sisters stayed home until they married. Even after,
they came home in the summers—the sisters and the wives of the
brothers, with all the children. The men came for a few weeks and
made repairs, helped the old man. They grew their own food but
didn't farm much on the rest of the land—too mountainous and
rocky—but all those hills were rich-timbered. The family had already started selling timber to the Eastern businessmen, who
came in and clear-cut and paid a fraction of what the trees were
worth. Later the mineral rights were sold as well. Hampsons had
been in that valley a hundred years with just their neighbors, and
didn't understand much about business.

The farm was beautiful, two big white frame houses cross-
pasture from each other, the smaller a guest house, and a plank
sidewalk built up off the ground so the women wouldn't dirty the
hems of their dresses on Sundays. The houses had full circular
porches with fancy trim, and a black iron fence to keep the barn
animals out of the yard. The women held church socials and picnics. They picked berries near the barn and used their big hats for
baskets, then were all day making pies.

Church was the only social life, and Coalton Church was a
half hour's wagon ride away; in warm months there was something going on nearly every night. Don't ask me what. But my
uncles had built that little church for the town, and the family
gave the land for the graveyard. It's still called Hampson Cemetery, and most of them are buried there: the grandparents, the
parents, all the brothers but Calvin, who left home at seventeen
and disappeared out West, and all the sisters but Bess, who is
ninety now and the only one left living after Ava died.

Ava died at a hundred, think of that. You remember her
funeral. That was the old family plot. Snowing so hard no one
could drive past the gate and they had to walk the casket up. Bess

took the death hard. The old house was just down that road, out
the Punkin Town turn-off. Foundation still standing, but that trail
is steep mud in bad weather.

All those winters the family stayed put, just ate food they'd
dried or put up in pantries, and venison the old man shot. They
kept one path shoveled through the snow to the barn, and the
walls of the path were as high as a man's shoulders.

I know all this because I heard about it, growing up—I was
too small to remember, really. Just a few things.

I was lying in the grass and watching my uncles hammer
slate on the barn roof. They were all big men dressed in broad-
cloth shirts. They swung the hammers full circle, from the shoulder, as they drove the nails. Tall pine ladders lay against the barn
walls and thick yellow ropes hung down. The slates were shining
like mirrors.

And once I looked out a window at snow. Snow as far as you
could see, pasture fences covered and trees gone, so their top
limbs fanned out of the snow like spikes. Nothing but snow. Snow
like an ocean.

In the winter, I was the only child.

I was with Bess at first. We were in the big house by ourselves, except for the old parents, and at times the brothers stayed
a few days. The wagon was hitched on Sundays, and not even then
in January, February. Snow too deep for the wheels. When Bess
was a girl, she'd gone to finishing school for a year in Lynchburg,
so she'd been farther from home than any of the other women.
She was the youngest, and pampered. The older sisters would tell
a lot later how she'd been sent away to learn to ride a horse like
something other than a savage.

Bess had been married once before; she was young and it was
kept secret in the family. Divorce was rare then. The first husband? He wasn't from around here. Seems to me his name was
Thorn. She probably came back from finishing school and had big
ideas at eighteen, nineteen. Left with this Thorn and went out
West; I don't think she knew him very well. Just within a month
or so, she wired home from St. Louis—he'd taken off and left her

out there. It was my father, Warwick, went to get her. He was
closest to Bess in age and had warned her against leaving in the
first place. They booked passage back on the train, but it was near
Christmas and a winter of bad blizzards; they were weeks getting
home.

Afterward Warwick was very protective of her. All this was
before I was born and no one ever talked about it. Why would
they? What's the difference, it don't matter.

Bess stayed there on the farm for seven years then, and
helped—putting up food, companion to her mother. Maybe she
felt chastised, but the family would not have said a word to her.
She was like a mother to me.

The brothers all had parcels of the land but were twenty, fifty
miles distant. They farmed or mined and drifted by the homeplace
every few weeks, on horseback, alone; women and children didn't
travel in the winter. My father, Warwick, was the only brother
worked in towns a while and wore a suit. Later he went back to
the mines, but then he was a wholesaler for a dry goods company.
Just a few weeks after he brought Bess home from St. Louis,
Warwick brought this bride of his to the farm and moved her in.
Then he left, as Bess tells it, and was only back twice the months
the girl was there. She was a girl he'd met in his work, a working
girl. She never gave any facts about herself, Bess says, and went
away after I was born. Went away as soon as she could travel, and
sent no word to anyone again. *Warwick paid for a wet nurse half
the winter, but there is more to a baby than feeding it.* I never
saw my father, not really. *You did see him, you don't remember.
He had the new wife, but by then you were accustomed to us.
Then he died when you were still in skirts. . . .*

They gave the impression it was his new wife didn't want me,
but I knew it was him. I don't remember what he looked like,
except from pictures. I just remember him yelling at me once or
twice. He never did a damn thing for me, never noticed me. One
summer—I was real young, at the farm—I had a baby coon. My
father had his rifle and was standing over me. It was out at the
edge of the fields, away from the house, where the grass was tall.
He said go into the field and let that coon go, you can't keep a wild
creature. I held the coon and walked in. The grass was over my

head, deep and high. He started shooting. The gun made two sounds, a big crack from behind, like thunder, and a high zing close by, like a stinging fly close your face. The grass was moving and he was shooting where the grass moved. I· stayed still for a long time. I don't know what I thought. Years later I asked Bess about it and she said wasn't Warwick did that at all, was a neighbor man, because it was a danger to have coons when there was rabies in the county.

I don't know. He was well liked. There is an old homemade album Bess must have pasted together. The pictures are taken outside the old house, and everyone is dressed in their best. My father is wearing a woman's big hat and posing like Napoleon.

They had his funeral there at the house. The brothers made the casket out of pine board, and the lid was kept shut. That was the practice in that country; if a man died in the mines, his coffin was closed for services, nailed shut, even if the man was unmarked. They would have put Warwick's coffin on the long table in the parlor, the best room. The window shades in that room were sewn with gold tassels. Silk tassels, and children weren't to touch them. The parlor was seldom used, but it was dusted everyday, spotless, and the floor was polished once a week with linseed rags fastened onto a broom.

It was soon after Warwick's funeral Bess left the farm.

She came to Bellington because it was the closest good-size town, and started working as secretary to Dr. Bond. Bess would have been in her late twenties, an old maid. She met Clayton because he was Doc Bond's younger brother.

Doc Bond and Doc Jonas were the only two doctors here besides the veterinarian. Clayton was in the construction business, always was, so the three men started the hospital. Bought two houses; Bess and Clayton lived in the smaller and built onto the bigger one. Knocked down walls inside, built wards. The modern addition that stretches out from the back now wasn't there then; the place was much smaller. Didn't need to be so big; most people birthed and died at home. And Bess has lived here, in this house across the alley, for sixty years. She sold the hospital twenty years ago, but they still get mail addressed to her. She learned a lot about nursing by working for Doc Bond, keeping the office, helping with examinations. Doc Bond died a few years after the hospital got going, and Clayton was building roads, so Bess ended up doing most of it herself—ran the hospital, the kitchen, hired nurses, did the books. Katie Sue and Chuck grew up running back and forth between the house and the hospital.

There was so much talk about Doc Jonas in the later years that Bess didn't like to let him use the hospital, but for a long time hers was the only one in town and she couldn't turn his patients away.

Some swore by Jonas, others said he was a scoundrel. I grew up with his son, Reb, who we always called Doc after his father. Doctors' sons then became doctors as well, inherited their fathers' patients same as another boy would inherit a farm or a storefront. Reb never cared much for doctoring, but he liked being called Doc and he liked not having to go to war when the time came. He and I had some scrapes, all through high school while I was living with Bess and Clayton.

But that was later. Right after Warwick died, I was sent to live with Ava, my aunt ten years older than Bess, and her husband, the train man.

I lived with Ava and Eban eight years but was gone every summer, to the farm, to one cousin or another. Eban was a railroad porter, then a conductor. We lived at Raynell, down near the Kentucky border. That town has nearly disappeared now, but when the trains still moved goods and passengers, Raynell was a big junction for Southern Rail. There was a pride about the railroad then—a railroad uniform in the '20s had almost as much respect as military dress. Eban wore blue trousers, suitcoat and vest, and a visored hat trimmed in braid. He wore white shirts with cuffs that Ava was always ironing. She would stand at the ironing board, a broad wooden one, while the iron heated on the stove.

If Bess was the youngest and prettiest of those Hampsons, Ava was the most stubborn. She was spirited and tall, a handsome woman even if her face was plain. Knew her mind and fought plenty with Eban. They had two little girls, just babies when I went there. Ava kept me out of school all she could, to watch them and help her do the garden. Train ran right back of the house, right the length of the town. Houses shook when the train passed. Kids always played on the tracks, tag and roughhousing. Ava had a fear about her kids getting too close to the trains. The younger girl was slow, never said a word till she was three or four, and collected things the way blackbirds will, shiny things. That was my cousin Emily. She would always be going down to the tracks to pick up pebbles or bits of glass. She never really learned to talk but would sit and stare at anything bright, a gas light or a coal fire. That child died young. Just took sick and died suddenly. They stood her coffin up against the wall; the box wasn't very big, about as high as a man's waist, and it was narrow at the foot the way homemade coffins were. The church at Raynell gave a velvet altar cloth, deep red, to put inside.

Ava arranged the flowers all around. Seems to me she asked the children who lived near to come to the service and sing a hymn. Yes, she did, and the shortest ones were in the front, closer to the coffin; I was nearly ten years old by then and stood in back.

Ava was distracted for weeks. A neighbor woman came in to look after the other daughter and me.

Near that time the B&O Railroad discovered they had employed a leper and, for want of any other plan, deposited the man on forest land by the tracks near Raynell. Townspeople were alarmed. It was said this man was a Chinese known as Li Sung, banished by his own government because of his disease. He had a brother in Washington, D. C., who was a tailor, and he traveled to that city to work in his brother's shop. He wore gloves to cover the lesions on his hands, but somehow his brother discovered the secret. Or maybe Li Sung confessed. Anyway, he was turned out and wandered for a time, then finally got a job maintaining track for the B&O. The railroad often hired laborers who didn't speak English, and paid them very low. Li Sung never removed his gloves and co-workers became suspicious, so the rail superintendent sent him to a doctor well-known in that area. The leprosy was confirmed. B&O had no policy for such a case, so they isolated Li Sung in a boxcar at the rear of the train and transported him all over the state, asking privately after hospitals. No hospital would accept him, and passengers began avoiding the railroad. B&O lost

workers on all lines, since no one knew which train pulled the car
where the leper was kept. Finally it was decided to put Li Sung
in some isolated place with supplies and make him stay there. The
railroad sent the B&O surgeon and a caretaker out to prepare a
site near Raynell. They found a grassy knoll near the river and
put up a World War I army tent with a stout pole in the middle,
then camped to await the leper's arrival. The B&O brought him
in by night. Employees stood aside as Li Sung was ordered to the
tent, then they burned the boxcar and left on the train.

The surgeon stayed behind in the town to arrange for Li
Sung's meals, and offered a small subsidy to any widow willing to
prepare his food. The food was to be delivered once a day in
disposable wooden trays provided by the County, and Li Sung
himself was to burn the trays at his campfire.

Ava had done nothing for weeks but mend and starch all the
dead child's clothes, smoothing each piece and packing them away
in clean boxes. She'd ironed even the handkerchiefs and undergar-
ments, but it was all done and now she volunteered to cook for the
leper. Eban tried to talk her out of it, but for the first time she
seemed more herself, so he signed a paper saying he allowed the
endangerment of his wife and family and would not hold the
railroad accountable.

In just a day, the County delivered six months' supply of
wooden trays and stacked them like firewood on the south wall of
the porch.

The appearance of the trays got the town talking. There were
fears Li Sung would bathe in the river and contaminate the water.
The railroad surgeon walked with Ava and me to show us the
route to the tent, ten minutes' walk along Ransom's Ridge. We
put the tray (bread and cow cheese and cold grits, as it was a
warm day) on a stump fifteen feet from the site. And the surgeon
yelled for Li Sung to come out.

He did, and stood by the tent pole, barefoot, dressed in a
white button-collar shirt, suspenders, and the wool trousers of a
winter rail uniform. The trousers were too large for him and he
wore bulky work gloves, tied to his wrists with twine. He was
slight and looked younger than Ava, who must have been in her
late thirties then. Not many people in those parts had seen an

Oriental. His black hair was long like a woman's and hung in one thin braid down his back. His eyes were slanted, almost like slits, and hid any expression. He stood politely and waited for us to talk. The surgeon yelled—as though the leper was deaf—not to go into the river or touch the water, to fill his bucket by holding to the handle and dipping the bucket in, and to burn all his trays and the paper used to wrap his food. He was told to eat with his fingers, as no one could solve the problem of utensils. To each instruction, the leper called back, "Yes, yes," in an accent. Anytime I heard him talk, he had a tone of question in his voice. He understood some English. The surgeon said, "Do you see the bucket?" and the leper pointed to it.

The first month, Ava put up his food every morning and carried it out herself. She would be gone about an hour and watched to see that the leper ate. She spoke to him a bit and he talked back, though sometimes only repeating what she'd said to him. He was cheerful and often waiting outside the tent when she arrived. She took him a tin coffeepot, a supply of tea and coffee, a mirror, scissors, needle and thread, and a comb. She gave him some of Eban's old clothes, but Li Sung never wore them; he wore only his railroad uniforms, which he laundered himself with soap provided by the railroad. After Li Sung's death, it was discovered he'd saved Eban's shirts and trousers and sewn them layered onto his blankets during the cold. But that was later.

Early on, Ava tried to give him a dog for companionship, but he chased the animal back to her as though afraid he would infect it.

*He was grateful for the smallest kindness; the railroad men must have been very brusque to him. I took no liberties and addressed him as "Sir" or "Mister." I would put the tray down and back up to the edge of the woods; he would nod and bow, pick up the food, and then sit cross-legged by the tent, eating. He seemed to feel he showed thanks by eating in silence with great concentration. I went closer again. Later we spoke briefly or sat without speaking. He knew some words but understood the ideas behind many more.*

*I hadn't been outside my house in weeks. Early mornings in the woods were so quiet and green, all the wildflowers bloom-*

*ing and the sounds of the river so cool. The clearing was like
a church, the sky arched over and deeply blue. I think I talked
aloud because I knew he didn't understand all I said. I told him
my little girl had died and showed him in motions. She was
. . . this tall, etc. He knew someone had died and folded his
hands, then pointed to his eyes and touched his cheeks. When
I describe these simple gestures, I don't mean to give the impression he was not smart. I believe he was quite intelligent, and
wishing to comfort me. He gave me to understand that he also
had children, two, in his homeland. He would not see them
again. I explained he might send letters, messages, but he said,
"No, no," holding his finger to his lips.*

*I wanted him to see Emily so badly that I took him a
photograph of her, knowing once he touched it I could not take
it back. I put the picture on his tray. He understood at once and
looked at the image carefully; then he bowed his head to me in
gratitude and put the picture in his breast pocket. He placed
his hand there and said, "Yes, safe. Safe." "Yes," I said to him,
and knew she was, when before I'd felt only the injustice.*

*Safe. He knew that word because the railroad men had said
it loudly, many times, about the woods and the tent, and where
they were taking him.*

By July Ava was much improved and began keeping house
again. I was sent with the trays; Ava went with me on Sundays.
She told me always to call out to the leper and make a remark or
two that required answer. This was important, she said. The man
could go crazy if he never spoke with anyone.

Some boys from the town tormented Li Sung that summer,
but he didn't know they were making fun. A few threw apples at
him and he picked them up, nodding his head like the fruit was a
present. If anyone came too close, he stood in the door of his tent,
holding his arms over his head and calling out in his accent, "Unclean, unclean!"

Winters were hard in that country. A lumber company
donated wood, and some rail workers arrived in September to
build a shack. Li Sung sat at a distance and watched the work. The
old tent was burned where it stood after the leper transferred his
belongings, and a low fence was strung around the shack. The

people of Raynell donated a wood stove, feather tick, and ax, and allowed the leper to gather and chop his own wood from near the shack in early morning.

Snow was deep for five months. I walked out once or twice a week, pulling a sled of provisions. Ava sent a cache of preserved foods, canned vegetables, jams, and meat jerky. The leper constructed a rabbit trap and used it with some success.

He got through the cold weather but wouldn't talk anymore in the spring. I came with the trays every day again; he would only look out and pull away. Ava was concerned and walked out with me. She had dressed as though on a social call and stood talking in front of the shack. *Mr. Li Sung? I know you are listening. Won't you come out?* He never answered, so we hid in the woods to watch for him. He looked just the same, though shabbier, peering from the door. Then he walked out and stood beside the tray. He stood for a full five minutes, looking down the ridge like he was trying to see trace of us in the distance.

Ava insisted I keep talking to him even if he didn't talk back. I felt damn stupid standing in front of that shack every day and yelling. I had nothing to say and was in a hurry to get to school, so I would call out whatever was on the tray, tell him the weather according to the almanac, and say the date. Since I never saw him, I started being afraid of seeing him.

In May he didn't pick up the tray at all, and Ava sent word to the railroad doctor. He found Li Sung dead in his cot. Heart attack, the doctor said, but I doubt he examined the body very close. Some men from Raynell, Eban among them, went out to put an end to the whole thing. They wore kerchieves over their faces, dug a grave, filled a casket with quicklime, and raked the leper into it. They covered the casket with lime and dirt. The shack was doused with kerosene and burned, and the ashes covered with lime. The men camped out there the whole day to be sure no one stumbled onto the contaminated ground unawares. It was the first time Eban had seen the leper or the leper's house. He wouldn't say anything when he came back home, though some of the other men talked around the town. They said it gave Eban a start to see his long-worn clothes sewn on those blankets, the sleeves of the shirts and the trouser legs spread out like one body on top of another and another.

Bess and Clayton let me come to Bellington when I was thirteen so I could go to high school there in the town. Bess seemed a lot older when I saw her again, and I called her Aunt. Clayton probably didn't want me at first, but I became an older brother to their kids. Katie Sue was a pretty little girl and Chuck was moody like Clayton, thin as a rail—they were just tykes. The town looked like a big city to me. It was prosperous in 1924: several lumber mills were going, and the Methodists had started a college. Most people had automobiles, and the streets were paved with bricks.

That first day, Clayton took me for a ride in his Studebaker, up Quality Hill past the Jonas house, and he stopped to talk to the Doc. That old house is a wreck now, broken up into cheap apartments, but it was pretty then—a big white elephant on the hill back from the street. All those round cupolas in white shingle and a circular drive planted with boxwood. The drive went right up past the front porch under a latticed arch. There was Doc Jonas in his white rocker, and there was Reb, with green eyes like a snake's. Fourteen, and drove his father's car like a bat from hell. Brand-new Pierce Arrow coupe. You could see yourself in the running board. Reb tended that car like it was living, and thought of it every minute. His father said he was love-struck.

In those days most people didn't bother to get a license, just bought a car and drove. Cars were like toys; nobody thought they were dangerous except people who couldn't afford them. There had been a few wrecks in the town, but no one ever killed or hurt bad. Streets were wide. Seldom more than a few cars on any one at a time, and nobody went very fast by today's standards. Reb and me would tow the mark in town anyway, because everyone was looking.

But after dusk you could get outside the city limits and go like the wind—not meet a soul. Road between here and Winfield wasn't paved, but in the spring it was smooth dry dust that flew up behind like a cloud.

You went along, river on one side hidden by trees, and along

the other side were shanty houses where the white trash lived.
Men and women would be out on their ramshackle porches, kerosene lamps lit on tables and bannister rails. The lamps were the
old hand-held glass ones with reflectors—tin discs behind the
globes that shone and made the light waver. The lights blinked
and quivered like a long broken streak, and we could see them, see
them all. A Pierce Arrow coupe was high off the ground, with
windows all around like you were in a cockpit.

Aunt Bess liked Reb and felt sorry for him. She would lecture
him about getting good grades and getting into a medical school
out of state, where they wouldn't pass him through because his
father paid. Reb would slump in his chair, dejected, and say maybe
he'd just join the army. You're joking, Bess would say, all serious.
Reb could get her going, pretending to want to do right.

She did dislike Doc Jonas and was only civil to him. *We got
a few of those girls down here. How many times did I walk
across the alley in the dead of night . . . then had to give them
my own skirt because their clothes were ruined.* Jonas and Clayton were in a hunting club that rented a lodge at Blackwater every
winter. The whole week Clayton was getting ready to go, Bess
made noises. Clayton said her own thoughts had gone to her head
and anyway, the whole business was complicated. *Of course he
never gave them any anesthetic but a shot of whiskey, or they
couldn't have gotten up and walked out fast enough. We had
one who walked from the Jonas house to the hospital, two
o'clock in the morning.* Clayton cleaned his deer rifle and she
mended by the light. Would she rather have those girls jump
through the ice, like the one over at Milltown? They talked so low
they were almost hissing. It was night. *There's going to be a
judgment on him, a trail of blood straight down the hill for
everyone to see. And you know where that trail ends? Right
here across the alley. He's not so good at it that he doesn't make
a mistake about once a year, or let one beg him into it when
she's too far along.*

Doc Jonas had a lot of stories told on him, and some of them
were lies. He was not an addict of any kind, I'm sure. And he was
the only surgeon at the hospital in all those years who never lost
a patient on the operating table. His wife had to be taken care of

like a child; that was why the sister lived in. Mrs. Jonas had hair
like a young girl's, long and done up. Her sister, Caroline, brushed
it in the evenings. *That woman doesn't know who she is half the
time. Neurasthenia. Now, it's not neurasthenia. Never seen out
unless it's in the car with Jonas, and then she looks at you like
we're all afloat on suds. How could her own sister allow it, for
years* . . . Reb and me sat in the living room. Mrs. Jonas played
the Victrola and drifted like a feather. *I'll tell you how.* . . . Mrs.
Jonas was thin and her sister baked burnt-sugar cakes to tempt
her into eating.

　　*She was a beautiful girl and came here with a whole trous-
seau from New York City. Such dresses as you've never seen.*
Reb's mother really was like a child, wandering around in the
house. She was wakeful at night and stayed in her room, then
slept all morning while the sister, Caroline, worked in the office
with Doc Jonas. Then Caroline took her breakfast in, and I suppose gave her a shot. I don't know, none of that was ever mentioned. By late afternoon, when Reb and I were there after last
classes, she was up and dressed and happy in her vacant way. She
wore clothes that women wouldn't wear on the street, evening
clothes—kind of lavish, like the clothes of a rich young girl. She
used to remind me of the farm in Randolph County, because her
dresses looked like what the women wore there on Sundays.

　　The widow sister, Caroline, looked like Mrs. Jonas in the face,
but she was different. Like a thin dark rock, moving through the
hall in her brown dresses. She did all the work around there but
seemed to do it invisibly; I ate dinner with Reb and the Doc pretty
often, and she never sat at table with us. Reb's mother was nervous about eating and took her meals in her room. Maybe Caroline
sat with her. Doc would leave for the hospital on evening rounds,
and Reb and me would go to the parlor to steal ourselves a glass
of brandy.

　　I remember Reb dancing with his mother once, on a winter
night.

　　She came into the room very animated and turned up the
radio, and was dancing by herself until she noticed we were there.
Reb stood up and made a deep bow, then danced her all around
the room. Made a big show of her, turning and dipping and lifting

her all past the big windows, with the chandelier lit up and throwing shadows across the walls. You could see by how Reb moved how light Mrs. Jonas was; they were both laughing. It was a nice picture, with the dark outside. Then I felt something behind me —I knew it was the widow before I even turned around, and it gave me a chill. But when I looked she wasn't even watching them. She was standing, real still, looking out the window at the snow.

Marthella Barnett fell in love with Reb his senior year, and she was no match for him by most standards. She came from a big family and had no upbringing. Barnetts owned the pool hall next to Shackner's Store; the families were related and both had bad names. They were from Coalton and Bess would warn Reb about the girl, say Shackners were trash back then and hadn't changed. They'd moved the store when the Coalton mines shut down and come to Bellington the way a lot of people did. Marthella was a pretty girl and met Reb in the pool hall—she was fifteen and had a beau she broke off with to go for a ride in the Pierce. Reb didn't take her seriously at first, called her Tarbaby.

She looked even younger than fifteen because her father didn't allow her to cut her hair or braid it or use rouge.

Barnett was known to marry his daughters off before they could graduate from school, but he thumped the Bible as he shoved them out the door.

Marthella was a dark little thing—the family had guinea blood, or Indian. Reb let her follow him around awhile; then he started taking her out; Reb driving and Marthella sitting way over on her side against the door, touching the dash with one hand.

*I wouldn't for a long time, when I did first chance with any other girl. Turn a corner and she's standing there, trying to give me presents—cigarettes, an empty watch case. She told me she never had but she would, she wanted to. I laughed her off, told her she wasn't legal. Drove fast to scare her, but she never scared. Her black hair hung to her hips. She would pull it over one shoulder so as not to sit on it, and look straight into the road, the black hair in her lap like some kind of animal. She would, she said, do anything, and her father wouldn't know, no one would, she would never tell. For a long while we did other things. Holding off got to be a game, and she did what I said, no matter where, fast or slow. Then she'd kiss my wrists like I was all that gave her any peace. Once we went in her father's bedroom while he was sleeping; she leaned against the wall by the foot of his bed and I was kneeling—she tasted like sour honey, small and tight and she bit her own hands to stay silent. She didn't do these things for me, do you see? It wasn't natural, she was only a kid. Like being a kid, a girl, was a disguise, and I saw her, I was the only one. I didn't understand, I didn't know what I saw.*

After Marthella began to shadow Reb, the older girls were a little cruel to her. She wore white nurses' stockings because Shackner's got them in at the store. The girls asked her where her bedpan was, when would she get her cap and make an honest living.

I was courting Dot Coyner, and the four of us went to the river once that spring. Dot thought Marthella was odd, the way she would say things that had no bearing on the conversation and do anything Reb told her. Reb told her to climb to the top of the rocks in two minutes, in her shoes, and started counting out loud. Marthella jumped up and ran, held her dress up and climbed like a boy. Only reason she didn't fall was because she moved so fast. Then Marthella was standing on top, and Reb said take off your dress and jump, jump in. That water was cold, freezing in early April. Dot stood up and said we were leaving, that Reb was disgusting and made anyone ashamed. Okay, all right, Reb told her, and yelled at Marthella to come down. But before anyone could do anything Marthella did jump, holding her arms out like a circus tightrope walker. She was lucky she hit in deep water, dropped and sank like a stone. *One night I was looped and got so twisted, for a second I really did think she was my mother. Then she was Marthella again and I hit her, I told her she smelled like something burst open, too sweet and dirty, not my mother, not my mother, and she cried and begged me to forgive her.* She came walking out of the water, embarrassed at the looks on our faces, and we had to wrap her up and get her back to town before she caught pneumonia.

Wasn't so rare then for girls to marry at fifteen, especially country girls, but everyone knew Reb Jonas wasn't about to marry a Barnett. There was just no one to stop them; Doc Jonas let Reb do as he pleased and no one supervised Marthella. She didn't really even have many friends; she was a strange girl. Reb was truant a lot and barely graduated in May; word was he and Marthella had been to Pittsburgh to the Carlyle Hotel and to the ocean, the beach down at Newport News.

It wasn't till July that everything blew up. Dot and I pulled into the parking lot out in front of the dance hall. The Pierce was already there, Reb and Marthella sitting in the front seat arguing. Dot and I went in. After a few minutes I went out to have a cigarette and they were still there. Reb was yelling at her and rammed the Pierce into reverse, like to back out of the lot. Then he stopped the car, leaned across, and opened her door, told her to get out. She pulled her door shut; he revved the car and drove fast into the street, going out toward the river. Something was going to happen. I left Dot and drove out the river road after them. I drove way out past the shanty houses, where nobody much lived and the river was deepest, but there was no sign of the Pierce. On the way back to town I saw a glimmer through the trees on the river side, and the rutted soft grass where Reb had pulled off and driven toward the water.

I parked and walked a short distance through the trees. The Pierce was there, lights on and motor running, maybe a hundred feet back from the drop-off.

I yelled at Reb, and damned if he didn't put the car in gear. I thought he was going to back up, but he floored the gas. The Pierce lunged up, tires spraying dirt, then rolled fast over the harder sand. I saw Marthella twisted round, looking at me as the Pierce rolled forward, but she made no move to stop Reb or get out of the car. It was like something in a dream. The Pierce was shining in the moonlight and they hit the drop-off and sailed out. Seemed like they stayed in the air a long time, but I remember too well how it looked. There was still light in the sky and the car's headlights looked like candle glow playing across the river. Then they hit, as water came up all around. The car sat a second and went under. *I didn't know I wanted to hurt her. How bad did I want to hurt her? If I had wanted to, I would have had the windows rolled up, wouldn't I?* I couldn't move, it happened so fast. But I jumped in after them pretty quick—the water was still moving on top and I came back up and swam toward the ripples.

Don't know what the hell I thought I was going to do. I couldn't have gotten them out. The water was deep. I dove down and saw the Pierce, big and black, still sinking way below me. It looked huge in the water, a big block, and the headlights were still on. Then I saw Reb swimming up like in slow motion, drifting up through the water, and he had Marthella by the arm. She looked like a rag doll in the gray water, not moving or helping him. I thought she was dead. I swam toward them and surfaced right after. They were gasping and coughing water. I held them both up and then we swam back, Reb and me holding Marthella. We got to the rocks—that rock ledge under the drop-off. *Mitch, get her out of here for me. Take her to my father.* We were all shivering and spitting water. I took her, pulled her up over the rocks, and Reb lay down where he was, didn't move, didn't watch us go.

I took her to Doc Jonas. He and Caroline were standing at the back door, looking at us through the screen. Doc was behind Caroline and he had his hands on her shoulders. Caroline came forward and let us in. All three of them went up the stairs.

I went to Reb's room and put on some of his clothes and went home; I didn't see Marthella after that. She was gone in about two weeks, to a beautician school that boarded girls. Maybe it didn't turn out so badly for her—she probably ended up better than she would have otherwise. I did see her a few times years later, after the war. She was dressed too stylish for around here and had her hair cut short, managed a milliner's shop in Toledo. She liked Ohio and she liked the work. She only came back to visit her mother and didn't ask about Reb, though I guess she knew he was a doctor long since, living in the old Jonas house with his own family. Old Doc had retired and gone to Florida soon after Reb's mother passed away. *I couldn't marry her and I couldn't let my father touch her. She'd gone to his office and told him that afternoon*

*in front of Caroline; it was all arranged, Marthella said. I just
wanted her to disappear, all of it, disappear with her face the
way it was when we got out of the Pierce and walked into the
ocean. She had never seen ocean.*

Fourteen years between high school and the war. Time
passed like lightning.

Why didn't I ever get married? Having too much fun, I guess,
wasn't ready to settle. And it was the '30s too. A peculiar time.
You worked for nothing. Everyone did.

I went to college a year and dropped out, then worked in
construction with Clayton. He got me on at Huttonsville. Max-
imum-security prison there used to work chain gangs and they
needed foremen. I worked crews awhile. Those were rough men,
but I never had trouble, never held a gun on them. Worked all but
a few without leg irons and never had a man run. Prison labor was
an accepted thing in this state for many years. But I did better
working on my own—lived in Morgantown, Winfield, working for
various companies. Clayton and I didn't start the cement plant
until after the war. Earlier I traveled a lot and stayed in boarding
houses, moving with the work crews on the road jobs. Between
times, I stayed at Bess and Clayton's in Bellington, in my old
room. It was good to have a man there: Bess was busy at the
hospital and Clayton was gone a lot; I helped with the kids in his
absence.

Every spring we went out to the cemetery at Coalton. Even
after the land was sold and deeded to the mining companies, Bess
insisted on taking the kids every year. *Our people are there and
as long as I'm breathing those graves will be tended. It's anyone's duty. One day we'll be lying there ourselves, miles from
anything.* Clayton was away, working at Huttonsville most
likely. Bess had Katie Sue and Chuck ready. We were in a hurry,
wanted to get there before the heat of the day came up, and Katie
cut a fit. She got sick in cars when she was little and dreaded
riding any distance. Seven or eight and high-strung as an old lady.
She hid in the house and wouldn't answer us. I got damn mad and
switched her with a birch switch. Don't you know I regretted it
for years. Only hit her a couple of times across the legs but she

hollered like she was killed. I guess it bothered me too that these
kids didn't care anything about the farm—to them it was just a
deserted old place. I still liked to go there. House and land were
empty, but otherwise it was all the same—mining companies
didn't work that property till after the war.

I went to the farm before enlisting, one of the last things I
did. Took a good look. Went out with Reb. We sat on the porch
of the old house and drank a few beers. I wasn't real happy about
the army, but they were going to draft me. Reb had a wife and
children, but they wouldn't have helped if he hadn't been a doctor.
He said if all the docs in town hadn't signed up on their own, he'd
have paid them to enlist so he could stay home and deliver babies.

The farm looked pretty, wintry and frosted and quiet. I enlisted in March—March 2, '42—so must have been late February.
Grass in the fields didn't sway, didn't move in the wind. Everything was chill and clear. Reb finally said it was time to leave and
not sit any longer in the cold like fools.


The war swallowed everyone like a death or a birth will,
except it went on and on. I was gone three years. They dropped
the atom bomb on Japan as our troop ship steamed into Oakland
harbor. No one really understood what had happened at first;
soldiers got on the trains and went home.

I had my thirty-fifth birthday on the train—cake with candles,
and ice cream. Red Cross girls kept all that information on us,
must have been their idea to celebrate. They were nice girls. The
men got a kick out of it and joined in with the singing. The train
was hitting rough track about then, and one of the girls (she was
from Ohio, I believe) came walking down the aisle carrying a big
square cake, lurching from side to side and trying to keep the
candles lit. The way the car was jolting and shaking made me
think of the boat crossing to the Philippines . . . April of '45, how
bad that night storm was. Raining and blowing, gusts of wind till
you couldn't stay on deck. Not a star in the pitch black and the
boat tilting so you couldn't keep food in a bowl. I looked out the
train window as they were singing; we were crossing the Southwest. Flat, yellow land, and the sky was sharp blue, blue as it was

in Randolph County the summers on the farm. I thought I would go back there even though the farm was gone—just to see it. Go back to look at the fields.

But I didn't go back for a long time, even though I wasn't far away. When I was married and had my own kids I was down that country—selling cranes and bulldozers for Euclid to a strip-mine outfit. The land was all changed, moved around. There were a few buildings left from the Main Street of Coalton, used as equipment shacks and an office. But out where the farm was—almost nothing. Heaps of dirt, cut-away ledges where they'd stripped. Looking at it made me think I'd been asleep a long time and had wakened up in the wrong place, a hundred miles from where I lay down. Like I'd lost my memory and might be anyone. Only thing they left alone was the wooden church, all falling in on itself, and the cemetery.

I walked up by the stones, between the rows of names. Warwick. Eban. Ava.

Icie. What kind of name is that for a woman. You always asked why I didn't try harder to find her. Why should I? She left me.

The cemetery was still and clean, though the grass was ragged. You know I thought of the leper; hadn't thought of him in years.

I never saw the inside of that shack. What did he do all day. No country, no family, no job. No one. Maybe he wasn't sure anymore who he was. He was a secret. I was the only one ever saw him. He could have stopped talking because I didn't seem real either, only another sound he heard in the woods. A sound in his head. During the war I used to dream of him, walking toward me on one of the tarmac landing strips we laid in New Guinea. I'd wake up in a sweat.

I was a secret myself. I used to lie awake nights when I was a kid, before I slept. I grew up in different places: with Bess, with Ava, with cousins at the farm. I'd fall asleep and hear a voice I'd never heard. I was called Mitch, or nicknames like Cowboy. But this voice said, "Mitchell . . . Mitchell . . . Mitchell . . ." with no question, till the sound didn't seem like a name or a word.

# WAR LETTERS
Mitch, 1942–45

Physically the Japanese is a mixed race of all shapes and sizes. He is intensely patriotic, aggressive and stubborn. He is mostly an ignorant villager drilled to fight to the end through years of teaching. While of an inferior type to the civilized Western nations he believes himself to be immensely superior to everything on earth, so he does not surrender freely and is eternally disgraced if taken prisoner. He is liable to run if surprised or rushed by a determined attack and on these occasions you will hear him utter loud squeals. He is entirely treacherous and has no sense of a sporting instinct. He will attempt any number of tricks.

—*Soldiering in the Tropics*
(Southwest Pacific Area),
prepared by the General Staff, LHQ., Australia,
and issued under the direction of the Commander,
Allied Land Forces Headquarters, SWPA.
(Revised edition, January, 1943)

## FORT WARREN, WYOMING

March 31, 1942

Dear Aunt Bess. Was glad to hear from you, got all five letters at once. So far I have not been able to see much here because we have been under quarantine ever since we arrived, measles and scarlet fever, some fun. We have classes and daily drill anyway but we are not allowed out at night. Maybe it is just as well. They keep us on the jump and by the time night arrives I am ready for bed. The sun comes up every day but there is always a strong, steady cold wind and it carries a lot of dust. I am 2 miles south of Cheyenne and about 500 miles from Yellow Stone Park, don't know how far from Sun Valley. On the train out I didn't see much —we traveled at night a lot—but what I did see was just level flat land and once in awhile I could see a house. The boys were looking for Cowboys & Indians but we didn't see any. Guess that has all passed. Everyone says they will never go to another Western Picture. People live here just like you do at home. Give Clayton my best and I wish I could come East before I leave this country. I look to be sent to the West Coast and then on across, where I don't know. However I have at least six weeks more here. Well Bess, hope you are taking care of yourself. Tell Katie Sue and Chuck the Twister hello from Old Man Mitch.

Love to all,<br>Mitch

## OAKLAND, CALIFORNIA

Pvt. M. Hampson
Company C
327th ZMC Bn (Port)
Subport of Oakland, CA
May 26, 1942

Dear Clayton. We hope to go across soon. Have been issued all our clothes and helmets and lack only our rifles—I understand we are getting a short, 30-cal. rifle, carbine type with lever action, something like the old 97 model Winchester shotgun. Everyone is anxious to get across. Of course none of us know what we are getting into, I expect we will find out soon enough. I am classified a labor foreman and have been made a corporal and might be a Sergeant before we sail. I am getting $54.00 a month now, new pay. You asked how it is here. I had always heard that it was hot in this state of California but it is not as warm as home, people wear coats in the evenings. Would like to have seen you and Bess and the kids but it won't be possible. Would be an expensive and hard trip out there and I can't get off to come home, so it will have to be put off who knows how long. I hope you like the new job at Reeder, I was there a couple of times while working at Wheeling. Clayton, stay in good health and keep the kids straight. Thanks for everything you have done for me. Maybe I could have done better but we all have one way to learn—experience. Good luck and I will see you.

Mitch

June 9, 1942

Dear Aunt Bess. I have just a few minutes to write this so it will be short. The alert is off for today, for how long no one knows—saw a shipload of troops leave here Sunday afternoon, a lot of workers for Pearl Harbor were aboard. Not a sound as the boat pulled away from the dock, no cheers or good-byes; it gave you a funny feeling. I am not worried about the car, it is yours & Clayton's to do with as you please, I owe you both a lot more than I could ever repay. Have to close now. I will send the kids a birthday telegram if I can, hello to Clayton. A lieutenant said we would be on the high seas by July 4, but can't tell. Don't fret about me.

Lots of love,<br>Mitch

## AUSTRALIA

Brisbane
August 14, 1942

Dear Aunt Bess. We did not have a bad crossing though it seemed long. I am lucky to have an apartment, in town here with another lieutenant for a few weeks (Lieutenant Estimatakis—he is from Ohio, up near Youngstown). Word is the outfit will go by train across Australia to Townsville, then somewhere in New Guinea. For right now I have no complaints, I have a place to go always, which is good because everyplace else is so crowded and expensive. Liquor is very hard to get except on the black market and is very costly. I get a weekly ration, 1 bottle of spirits and 6 bottles of beer. It doesn't last long. When I go to town it's on the electric train, takes thirty-five minutes. The city is alive with men on leave and of course the Base Section Commanders are always present. If you know the right people and places—and have plenty of money—you can have a very good time. Transportation is the big problem but when you learn the trick you are all right. The girls here are very nice (mostly) and there must be 40 for every man. They all want to marry a Yank so they can go to the States. Do not worry about Lorraine—the rumor about us getting married before I left of course was not true. I don't know why anyone would get married before going to a war. If I had of wanted Lorraine I would have done something (as you thought) about it before enlisting. I am surprised she didn't find someone before this. Now, I will not be getting any mail for quite awhile, until the outfit moves north, and so you will not hear from me much. But I am well, keep writing letters, they will all catch up with me at once when base camp is established at our next Post.

As ever,
Mitch

# NEW GUINEA

APO-929, New Guinea
November 15, 1942

Dear Reb. Letter from you in the first mail delivery though I have not heard yet from anyone else. Tell them all I am all right, have not had time to write, also there is not much to say. I left Townsville, Australia, with my outfit (am still with 41st Engineers) and arrived at Port Morsby, New Guinea, then we moved by truck to Ora Bay. Tell Clayton I have a 10-yd. dragline and two dozers working now and several cranes. Patched or built them all with junk. We have established a good Base camp here, built tarmac strips for a landing field, etc. I am in charge of the motor pool and all equipment. A week after we got to Ora Bay the Japs landed at Morsby, about 200 of them, but they were surprised by about 60 infantry with machine guns. It was open beach and all the Japs were killed. I was sent down with some men and dozers to bury them—the heat here is infernal, hot as hell, and such a stink as you have never smelled. We wore masks and buried them in pits. Of course you will not say anything about this to the family. It is the worst that has happened as yet, though shelling is sometimes bad—mostly we are kept busy loading and unloading the supply ships, patching the loading machines with scrap, and building more airstrips. We get little news and scant mail. I am well but awfully tired. It's very difficult for me to sleep but that is the way this climate affects you—nothing to worry about. You are lucky Doc that you did not get pulled in. Take care of yourself and let them know you heard from me.

Mitch

APO-929, New Guinea
January 3, 1943

Dear Katie Sue. I had a letter from Mother today and she told me that you have both gone to Columbus to the doctors there. If the pneumonia has gone to rheumatic fever, you must be very careful.

I am praying for good news from you. You should be back home by the time this letter reaches you. Are you being good? Doing any romancing and are you still practicing the piano? You better be and so had Twister. That brother of yours should be pampering you now you are sick. I hear I am getting a picture of you, how about one of Twister too? Are you going to stay in school this year? I know it would be a bad break not to, but if it is necessary you wouldn't mind too much, would you? You must do what Mother and Doc Reb and the other doctors say, so you will be there, right as rain, when Old Man comes back. Will you do that for me? Well, Honey Bunch, write me soon. The snapshots are for you and brother.

Lots of love,
Old Man Mitch

APO-929, New Guinea
March 1, 1943

Hello Darling. Thank you for the very nice pictures of yourself and Twister. You don't look like you've been sick at all. And both so grown-up, I would not have recognized either of you. Boy, that brother of yours will surely be a ladies' man. I am glad you are popular, however don't let it go to your head—and don't grow up too fast or I will never catch up with you. We do a lot of work here but some play—I have been hunting three times, killed a 9-ft. snake, and some Wallaby. (Small edition of the Kangaroo. One had a little one in its pouch. The natives eat them, and when you go out hunting you always take a guide. You pay them by shooting a few Wallaby for them.) Still summer here and it is hot and muggy. I'm glad you got everything you wanted for Christmas, I was thinking of my best girl on that day and now I am so glad you will be all right and Doc Reb has said you can start school again. You are a very Good-looking dame and I suppose you know it—I am glad you are, and I'm sure you will be a joy and the apple of your father's eye. Take care of yourself Honey, and stay in love with me—

Love & Kisses,
Old Mitch


PHILIPPINES

Philippine Islands
April 19, 1945

Dear Reb. Thanks for writing, yours is the first letter in weeks. I sure hope to get out of here soon. Though it is an interesting enough place, I am tired of being away. A great number of the little boys and girls go stark naked—a lot of them have been to school or will go this coming year. The pigs and chickens live in the house with them. I went into a house the other day (am drawing up leases on buildings the Army used, and finalizing payment) and the house started to crack, so I jumped out—they all laughed & said "too Big." Most of the houses are made of Bamboo (floor and framework) and Coconut leaves woven into mats (called Nipa) for the sides & roof. I want to send some things back if I can get the boxes to mail them. However as for most of what you can get over here, the five and ten store at home has much better ones—surprising but true. I believe it is worse here than New Guinea, hotter, damper, and the water is terrible, the chlorine comes off in waves and you taste it very strong even in tea and coffee. But we are beginning to make improvements, existence here should pick up. You say Lorraine is expecting; I am not surprised. She must be a sight, she isn't very big. Well, I wish her the best, she will need some luck. So long, Doc, you say you are tired of tonsils and rationing, but I would gladly trade places with you. See you, and we will have a drink on it all.

Mitch

Philippines
June 10, 1945

Dear Aunt Bess. The news continues to be very good and I believe
the war will be over by the 1st of next year. Weather here is even
hotter now, especially until noon, then we have heavy showers all
afternoon and the ground steams till dark. Then it becomes cool.
The moon and stars are beautiful, people who wrote of these
places must have gone out only at night and then let their imagi-
nations run on. Bess, Reb wrote me that you are working too hard
at the hospital again and that you may have had rheumatic fever
when Katie had it. Quit working so much and take care. I still have
the note you put in my bag when I left. I have read it many times
and it always helps. I hear that the lights came on again in the
States and that more gas will be had soon. One thing I know, no
more of these places for me, when I come back it must be to stay.
Am sending a pair of Filipino native shoes for Twister, a mesh bag
for you, flight jacket for Clayton (if it fits) and two native arm-
bands for Katie Sue—I washed them, clean them good before you
handle them. Just now the evening shower is on us. Another
month half gone, these months really roll around. It is cool—the
evenings are lovely after the terrific heat of the day.

Love to every one of you,
Mitch

# MACHINE DREAMS
## Mitch, 1946

The smell was bad, horrible and terrible and full of death, he couldn't think of a word to say what the smell was, it rose up underneath and around him and he turned to get away. Behind the smell someone kept crying, weeping like a child on and on as the smell broke in the heat, ten in the morning and hot, already hot as hell and the sky a seering bright blue mass over the dried rust red of the bodies. A twisted khaki of limbs and more he didn't want to see clearly opened flat and mashed and rumpled, oh, the smell, like a deadness of shit and live things rotted, some gigantic fetid woman sick to death between her legs had bled out her limitless guts on this sandy field flattening to the green of Ora Bay. Nothing to do but go ahead, hot metal seat of the dozer against his hips, vibration of motor thrumming, and that kid still crying, some island kid, get a detail over there to keep those kids away, got to get pits dug and doze this mess. The smell blew against and over him; he felt the whole awkward dozer tilt, rolling on the ocean of the smell as on the slanted deck of a transport. Bad seas, it was a bad, bad sea, he looked down over the metal dozer track to his left and one of the bodies lay closeby, the rear of the trousers torn open, the small hips yellowish and mangled like the crushed halves of a peach. The shirt had caught fire and burned nearly off, the splayed arms above the head were sleeveless past the shoulder and one arm was a blackened stick with the hand still curled at the end. The hands, all small and delicate like the hands of big children, and the averted faces smooth and beardless. He tightened his mask and realized the dozer blade was already down, when had he lowered it? What the hell, he was losing his mind, he shoved the gear into forward as the smell assailed him, pushing, pushing back. He felt the give of the earth, just earth, had to think it was all just earth like at Wheeling, working on the Reeder road with Clayton. But the crying was louder and he couldn't hear the motor of his own machine anymore, just the rush of a big wind and then distinctly, in the empty air, the discreet soft latching of a door, and footsteps on a wooden floor. He was falling and falling toward the quiet of those steps, the throbbing shift of the dozer still rattling in his hand, and he woke with his fist clinched beside his jaw. The footsteps continued past his door toward the kitchen at the back of the house, and when he opened his eyes he saw, very near, the round white face of the alarm clock, its black numbers afloat like fragile, meaningless shapes. Bess had been up with Katie Sue again; only those red shoes of hers made that quiet sound on the floor.

Now she would be making coffee in the tin pot; yes, there was the rattle of the stove drawer where she kept the pans. He heard water running. Quietly, she would dispose of the bottle Clayton had drunk empty last night, easing it into the garbage where it made no sound against peels and meat scraps and leavings, never putting it in sight beside the pail and the empty cans, the glass jars washed compulsively before being saved or discarded. He could nearly see her, standing beside the sink in one of her seersucker housedresses and her red wool sweater, her long straight body, her back and shoulders erect as always but taking on now a slightly brittle aspect. How old was Bess? He lay motionless, figuring slowly, watching the cold March light fall from the window across the polished bureau top. He was thirty-five, since

September on the transport train from the coast: that made Bess fifty-five the month before he'd come back. No wonder her hair had gone gray, a steely, peppered gray that was bluish and strong and sad. And the war. Keeping the hospital going with the rationing, Katie being sick, and Clayton hitting the bottle a little more. Katie was ten now; she'd just started school when Mitch left. Twister had been eight—Mitch remembered him as sociable, a chatterbox, always wanting to tag along. Now he was an independent, silent kid who went his own way, paid mind to his sickly sister only when he thought no one noticed.

Wasn't the first rheumatic fever in '43, and then pneumonia, and she was out of school that next year? They'd all tried to make light of it in their letters. But Katie was almost an invalid, a kid invalid. Strange sometimes, how when she lay in bed in the dimmed child's room he remembered, sheets pulled up to her shoulders, she looked so much like the smaller girl he'd left— maybe even younger, her features more frail because her face had lengthened and paled. When Mitch had first come back in the fall, she'd been up and back in school, though restricted by Bess's regimen of naps and liver oils and hot soaks. But the winter had been long and now Bess would take her out of school for the rest of March, waiting for warmer weather. They'd told her last night; must be why she'd cried and hadn't slept.

It was good he'd come home. This thing with Katie had about driven them crazy. Wasn't like they were a young couple; Clayton must be sixty. Nearly four years Mitch had been gone, and they'd all got old. Four years. He sat up on the edge of the high bed and felt for his slippers. Jesus, what a dream he'd had. He hardly ever thought of the bad things, although he thought of the men, Warrenholtz and Strauss and Wilson, and the base camp, alien the two years in New Guinea but now more familiar in memory than this house he slept in. As though he went back to it every night—the thatch-roofed buildings and steamy air, the scrap heaps and tin shacks of the motor pool—looking at every detail but seeming just to live there as before, complaining with the rest of them, sweating in the grime of it and looking up to watch the slate sea while the natives touched the machines with their palms. They'd taken them out to open beach to teach them to drive the dozers and trucks, and the black men had touched the machines hand-over-hand, seeming to measure them as horses are measured, then touched all the gears and pedals, saying Papuan words for the parts. The enlisted men had laughed openly at such reverence, laughing more at themselves than at anyone since the machines were serious jokes, most of them built and repaired with scrap, metal welded in approximate versions of whatever parts broke down, the machines evolving further and further into jumbled mismatched puzzles that still worked. Worked and moved, groaned and rumbled according to some other logic of mechanics than what held in Cincinnati or Topeka or Wheeling.

New Guinea trees flared straight to the sky and splayed their fronds; their shapes looked from the tents like intricate sprays held still by the humid night. The sea glared flatly and was warm in January and had no winter in it ever. Wind blew up hard before storms and the trees tossed their fronds all of a piece, like women throwing skirts over their heads, and the clouds boiled up as though poured out of a spigot, filled the whole flat horizon impossibly and completely and it was an angry show. He'd longed to see an oak tree, a big oak with layers of limbs and summer leaves moving in wind with that deep rippling that is deep as the rippling of water. He'd wanted to see that, and women in dresses and stockings and heels. The palm trees were strangest at night because they were so big and womanly, tossing themselves and sighing, while the women in the camp wore fatigues and boots. 41st Engineers had arrived to construct the camp and the airstrips, and the native men had still worn grass skirts. The skirts rustled as the dark men walked, their flat-footed storkish gaits rustling the grass in a way that was stern rather than girlish. Later they wore long swatches of cloth held in at the waist with army belts, and their bracelets were strips of cloth wrapped round their forearms and tied. The natives were in the camp at all hours and the skirts came to seem natural above their nearly hairless, muscled calves, natural on them rather than on the women, so that the outward things distinguishing men and women lost meaning. You noticed instead the wrist of a Red Cross girl, narrow and flat in the masculine greenish cuff of a fatigue shirt. The whole world was turned around like that—the sky arched so high up that it seemed lost, and they were all floating: the white beach and the guns and the natives, the creaking machines, the officers' club with its sling chairs and regulation cots for couches, its reception desk bordered by palms in pots and built in the shape of a horseshoe to look transplanted from the lobby of some American hotel. But the bar top was plyboard and rough and splintered, and the boy serving drinks stood shirtless in his rumpled dirty skirt, smiling, his hair a thick dark bush and his metal chain necklace dangling a gold amulet meant to keep the evil of this place from following him back to his village at night. *Someone told someone and someone told you,* blaring of the bar radio, a square '30s-style Motorola whose patchy fabric front showed through to cardboard, *but they wouldn't hurt you, not much,* and the control knobs were off an Australian kitchen stove shipped up by boat. But the thing worked, late afternoons the reception was bell pure and the bar boy turned it up *since everyone spreads the story* as the men came in from showers for mess, scuffing their boots along the plank floor that showed the ground where boards had pulled up, and if there was a storm blowing in later that night they sat hearing it crackle between the lines of USO songs. *Do nothing till you hear from me* * when the bruising rain was still nothing but electric air. Hadn't he heard that song just lately, last weekend? Katie made him play the car radio when he took her out for a ride in the new Pontiac, Bess standing on the walk by the back door, lifting her hands to her throat to remind Katie to keep her scarf pulled tight. *Pay no attention to what's said* and Katie had told him sagely this was a song about gossip, which was all the fourth-grade girls ever talked, and he thought about when the first tarmac strip was finished and the first plane came in. How the native boys had stood at the edge of the field in a bunch and crouched down together holding their arms like they were chilled, talking talking talking, jabbering in low tones as the plane taxied past. They kept their backs to the Yanks, making intricate motions with their hands like words alone weren't enough, and the

only ones who learned any English were the ones who served
instead of worked. The bar boy and the cooks picked up a singsong
lingo and talked in strange mixtures of words whose cadences
were backwards, funny and inside-out. The radio behind them
would splatter a breath of crackling static and Warrenholtz nodded, called it news from the front, Papua tango, excuse me while
I go to Paris, Texas and hoe a row for Mom.

Warrenholtz, back in Texas. Mitch belted the robe Bess had
given him, Glen plaid from Rossings on Main Street, just the kind
of quality thing she'd buy to last for fifteen years. Where would
he be in fifteen years? The time stretched out, and whirling in the
center of the time was a small group of men around a bamboo bar
table while the fans turned and the potted palms moved in the
heavy air, the men olive shades in their fatigues and the green
island air dampening finally with evening. Katie was crying, he
could hear her, had it gone on all this time? Now he would go in
and tell Katie, tell the kid he'd get her some comic books today,
anything, strawberry ice cream right now for breakfast, if she
would keep a stiff upper lip for Old Man and stop that crying.


"Hey, Snickelfritz, what's all this, a man can't sleep with such
a ruckus." He advanced into the darkened room, his voice soft.
"Can't drive a brand-new car with no shut-eye. Don't be mean,
what about it?"

The little girl in the bed half-sat, long sleeves of her winter
nightgown twisted. "I, I'm not mean," she said, gasping, her
breath broken by the crying.

"Pretty mean." He sat down on the edge of her bed. "Your
old dad Clayton is in there watching the ceiling, wide awake, hears
every sniffle. Ears like a cat."

"Like a cat," she repeated, trying to stop, her eyes full. She
looked at Mitch, her face almost stunned with the tension of
sobbing.

"Like a big tiger cat, hears every sound his girl makes. Old
Mitch with that new Pontiac to wax this morning, too, and not a
lick of sleep. After a hard week selling trucks." He opened his own
eyes wide, had to make sure she knew he was joking, kids took
things so serious.

She breathed calmer, sniffling. "Over at Winfield," she said. Occasional involuntary gasps. No talk about the matinee this afternoon: then Bess had said nix to the movies. Take a different tack.

"That's right, Hon, and after I get me some breakfast I'm going upstreet to buy some wax for the car, and some ice cream and comics for you. Whaddya say? Four comics enough? Keep you busy?"

She nodded hopefully, twisting her hands under the covers like a schoolmarm. She'd always seemed old for her age, a little prim, damn cute kid. Smart, too, a shame she'd had it so rough. Her wide, tear-brimmed eyes looked too big for her face, and she held her mouth tense.

"Know where old Mitch was last night?"

Shook her head no.

"Lean back there on the pillow while I tell you, that's right."

She leaned back, so tired her eyelids fluttered, and sighed.

For a minute he was taken aback but talked on smoothly. "Your old Mitch took Mary Chidester over to the big dance at Winfield, and a fella was playing the fiddle to beat the band." A good time, that Chidester girl, no doubt about it, she'd drunk more than Mitch and there was no fight getting her out to the car before the dance was even over. "Everybody danced up a storm and the whole ceiling was full of colored balloons," he told Katie. He could feel her concentrating on the sound of his voice and he talked on, automatically, his thoughts elsewhere. Surprised at Mary Chidester though, she was damned experienced. College for two years over at Lynchburg, that was it. Snap of her sweater as she'd pulled it up over her brassiere, smoke of her cigarette in his eyes, and her brassy laugh like the laughter of the boozy Aussie girls. Warrenholtz weaving in a doorway and Strauss leaning solidly against a wall. First leave in Sydney before they'd shipped out to New Guinea, and they'd roughed up that hotel room a little, Strauss with a bruised face where the girl he'd laid socked him just as he'd rolled off her and she discovered he'd had no bag on, did he want to spread Yank brats all over New South Wales? Mitch looked at Katie and tried to imagine her grown-up, fair prey, couldn't, what did a man with a daughter do?

"Fiddle is like a violin," she said now, sleepily. Her gaze was drifting and she touched his large hand with her small one.

"Sure, Fritzel, that's right. And then we went for a ride in the Pontiac just like you and I did last weekend, but it was night and the moon out bright as a plate. White lines on the road just like silver." Somehow Mary had talked him into letting her drive and they'd ended up in the empty fairgrounds, driving too fast on the dirt roads between the stock pens, zigzagging up and down. She wasn't bad on the turns, fishtailed once but he grabbed the wheel. He was laughing and finished off the bottle as she took off fast, then slammed on the brakes—he was thrown forward and banged his head good on the dash. When he opened his eyes, odd sensation of total blackness: she'd driven straight into one of the big open stock barns and stopped, but in his high from the liquor he thought they were still moving and he looked out into the blackness and didn't know where he was. Didn't know. Then: peal of her laughter, the joke on him.

"Katie?" He said her name but she was asleep, dead asleep, tumbled blond of her curls on the pillow.

In the kitchen, Bess was heating the iron skillet for his eggs. The butter, the clean spatula, the two brown eggs, lay on the sideboard. He sat down and she poured his coffee, put in the sugar and cream, set the steaming cup in front of him.

"Morning, Mister," she said as always. "I hope Katie didn't wake you. Still, aren't you glad it's Saturday and you're home with us, instead of in that rooming house in Winfield."

"The rooming house is fine," Mitch said. He watched Bess tie her apron as she turned to the stove. She hadn't wanted him to get the room in Winfield, but the fact was they really didn't have room here for him; kids getting older, Katie with her own room because she needed so much rest. Bess looked tired. Her glasses magnified her eyes and concealed their fatigue, but her tiredness showed in her shoulders, in how she moved and held her head. Butter spattered in the hot skillet and she cracked the eggs, the sound loud in the quiet house; he had done a man's job in getting the kid to sleep, but Bess would never take advantage of a break and rest. On her feet from six in the morning and never sat down except to eat meals or read to Katie or do handwork while she listened to the radio.

"I dare say you enjoy driving around Winfield in that new car of yours." She turned the eggs expertly and put the bread in the oven to toast. "The office girls over at the hospital were saying how fine your new Pontiac looks and how everything has changed since the men came home—just in these six months. New cars on the streets, the firehall dances crowded again, Main Street full like every afternoon was Saturday. First peacetime spring is coming, even through this chilly weather. I really enjoy going up-street to pay the bills."

Mitch smiled. All during the war, he'd thought of her walking the length of Main Street, ladylike, holding envelopes in her gloved hand. Wartime stockings well mended, coat and hat sensible, neat leather purse over her arm. She paid hospital and personal accounts herself between one and two in the afternoon. Mailing a bill four blocks was foolishness, stamps were money, people ought to speak as they take care of business, it's only civilized, and wouldn't everyone agree a Main Street where people exchange talk is one reason the war was fought, a small but human reason? He pictured her receiving news, tidbits of stories, at the bank, at the mercantile, at the telephone company. *You don't say, Oh, don't tell me, Well I had no idea, The Lord bless us and keep us.* And it wasn't just love triangles, but who would run for the school board, how much loan money the bank had to distribute, should the town establish an annual festival in summers, like the Buckwheat Festival over at Elkton.

Bess arranged the salt and pepper shakers, the jam jar, near his plate. "I was saying to Mr. Chidester at the Hardware—Mary's father, you know—the Pontiac Eight sedan is the nicest car on the market, stamina, not really terribly expensive. And the dark blue, with the chrome and the gray top, is really lovely."

He kept his expression serious. She wanted him to mention Mary, but he wouldn't. And she was funny when she tried to talk about cars. Really though, he was touched that the merchants downtown were discussing his new car. For a moment he thought of leaving the Philippines on the ship, seeing with a last glance the dirty women sitting on the docks, the packs they roped to their

backs made of hemp net, showing their paltry possessions. The
moment passed, the look of their faces receded, and he saw instead the rich dark blue of the car, felt again the shock of its
newness as he'd leaned inside at the salesman's invitation: the
dash, the steering wheel, the silver gray upholstered seats, even
the floors—absolutely clean, shining and private and quiet like the
interior of a big jewel. He'd thought maybe he'd die in the war;
he was seldom in obvious danger, since he wasn't infantry, but
he'd thought his apparent safety somehow made the odds worse:
it would be an accident with the machinery, or a fluke attack on
the airstrip—

He ate his toast and jam. "It's thanks to you I was able to buy
that car so soon," he said. "You and Clayton should have sold the
old Ford, not kept it out there in the garage. You could have used
that money."

"Don't talk silliness. I knew you could sell it to help buy a new
one when you got back. And what good is money in wartime? We
were glad to keep it for you, and I don't want to hear another
word."

"I told you, Bess, I'll take you and Clayton to dinner in Winfield. A night on the town, anytime you'll let me." He waited as
she smiled, pleased, then shook her head in the familiar denial.
"Or maybe I should take those office girls for a ride, all four of
them."

She smiled more broadly, her shoulders relaxed. "I think one
girl at a time is enough."

"I guess I should be thinking along those lines myself," he
answered.

"Now, you know there's no hurry. Plenty of time. You haven't
been back but a few months." She nodded once, conclusively.

He ate the eggs, relishing the heat of the food and feeling in
the kitchen an old privacy. Where did it come from, coming back
as though never broken? Birds outside, tick of a clock. Light on
the big sink, dense weight of the pocked, scoured porcelain.

"Don't you want some breakfast?" he asked her, willing to
say only conversational things, not change the feeling.

"I'll have some later, with Katie." Gravity of the child's name
in the room. "She's asleep?"

"Sure. Tuckered out, fell off while I was talking to her. She keep you up all night?"

"On and off. I should have waited until this morning to tell her about laying out of school, when you were home. She's a little soldier when she thinks you're watching."

"She cried about school?"

"Yes, I suppose, but really she only cried about the movies. She said you'd promised to take her and her heart was set."

"Well, can't she still go?" He sopped up the last of the eggs with the bread, drank the coffee down. "Wrap her in a blanket in the car, movie house is warm, keep her right in the side aisle by the registers." He thought then of her face in the bed, how wan she'd looked, little girl like an old lady, and felt a stab of fear. "But if you think it would make her worse—" He lay his fork down.

She took the empty plate and moved to the sink. "I don't suppose, if she sleeps all morning . . . " And then almost to herself, "We can't let her think she's so different from other children or that she'll always be sickly."

He wondered how much of her life was made of such strategies, tending to appearances, careful shelter of one influence and not another. "Will Katie be sickly?" he asked quietly.

Bess didn't turn or alter her movements. "Of course not. Her heart is weakened. It takes time. One of the main things is that she stay cheerful."

"Then I'll take her to the show. The matinee." He stood and gave Bess his empty cup.

"It's a Disney movie. Three cartoons and she's told me about every one of them—the little Carpenter girl went a few nights ago. You must only stay for the first one. Take the blanket inside and keep her very warm." Bess began washing the plate and the frying pan—that meant she didn't expect Clayton up anytime soon. He'd really tied one on.

"She'll be fine," Mitch said.

"She'll be so happy you're taking her," Bess said. "Katie's your darling, I'm afraid."

He went upstreet to get the wax for the car and was back by ten. Automatic, this work, rubbing onto the long car a substance like cold butter, filming the hard shine of the metal. Methodically, he did the car in sections, beginning with the long front hood, the broad snout of the machine. The deep blue they'd called "royal" was really almost navy, and as he rubbed, leaning into the circular motion of his effort, the color seemed to darken more under the whitish film. His own reflection distorted on the cloudy surface and he thought of unconnected things, no stories, remembered jumbled associations from last night. How in the dark barn, in the sudden sealed quiet before Mary Chidester laughed, pleased with herself and her trick, he'd been momentarily frightened.

That anonymous black, dark like Australian dark, Sydney streets during the blackouts. A leave he'd taken alone soon after he and Warrenholtz had trapped that Nip pilot in the field west of the base camp. Above Coco Mission beach it was, but he wouldn't think of that and remembered instead coming back from the cinema in Sydney where he'd seen *Gone With The Wind* for the second time during the war. Theater full of soldiers with girls from a USO escort service, and he'd gone alone, walked back ignoring the clipped voices of the drab prostitutes. Just as he got to his hotel the air-raid sirens had wailed, drawling their panicky scales. Interior of the hotel lit only with dim green-shaded lights, seemed nearly empty. Eight flights to his room; he counted the landings. The sirens would cut off before long; as he assured himself of this, he came to the eighth floor and the sirens stopped.

He'd leaned against the wall, listening. No sound. It was late. He had the key in his hand but couldn't see a damn thing. Had only checked in before he went out for dinner and they'd taken his bag, said they'd put it in his room and show him up later. He took his lighter out of his pocket and shook it; wet the wick, there, it caught and he held the small flame high. Numbers came up in the dark and he found his room, 808; he turned the key and went in, hit his shin on the metal bed frame. Fumbled on the nightstand with his hand, felt for the lamp and turned the switch, stupid, of course it didn't work, and he touched the bed. Good, a double, the mattress lumpy but not as bad as it could be. The all-clear sounded as he'd known it would, and he lay down, pulled the pillows behind his head, and crossed his feet. Then the strange thing had happened. The power came on, trembling faintly in the walls, and the

room turned bright, startling him. He looked at the room uncom-
prehendingly. It was plain, clean and ordinary, with a water closet
to the left behind a narrow door—but he felt his skin prickle with
an odd, interior fear and sat up on the bed. He put his feet carefully to the floor and gripped the edge of the metal bed frame.

The room was entirely taken up with a plain pine bureau,
luggage table, nightstand and lamp, the bed—his eyes came back
to the lamp. In its angled light he saw the flowered paper of the
walls. The walls were plastered unevenly so that the fanlike pink
flowers of the old paper seemed to ripple. He looked more closely
then and understood. The paper was the same print as the pattern
on his walls at home, at Bess's house in Bellington. He sat, a
stupid Yank son of a bitch. Then he stood abruptly, switched off
the light. Laughed once, out loud. Felt for his suitcase and walked
out. Fifteen minutes later, he had a room in a hotel two blocks
away.

That's why he'd been spooked last night, afraid of what he'd
see when the lights came on. Not scared of the dark, scared of the
light. And what was Katie afraid of? Afraid of that room, he
guessed, being made to stay in it instead of going to school.

He touched the solid roof of the car: that silver gray shined
up real nice with a good waxing but the chrome grill would take
some work. Moving to the front of the sedan, he was conscious of
the office girls in the hospital across the alley. Didn't want to get
to his knees to wax the ample grill, so he bent from the waist. Hold
the can of wax in one hand, rub briskly with the other. Could leave
it to sit and dry while he went inside. Check on Clayton, that's
what. He could take Clayton with him to meet Reb for lunch at
the Elks', make sure the old guy stuck to an innocent beer. Reb
seemed to control his drinking; a beer at noon was his limit,
though he likely drank more at night than people thought proper
for a doctor. Reb could hold the liquor but Bess had said Clayton
was "sick" Thursday, and sleeping in weekend mornings wasn't
like him. Bess pretended not to notice; did she complain in private?
Probably not, those old girls knew their place and were smart: if
a woman told a man not to drink, he'd drink till he fell down.

Mitch looked toward the small white house. Trellis roof of the
little cement porch seemed fragile, overspread by gnarled, naked

branches of the big buckeye. He could bring the porch swing out of the garage and hang it any day now. Though the weather was still cool, the snows were surely over.


Ease the screen door shut—there, the smallest thing could wake Katie. Standing in the kitchen, Mitch heard Clayton getting up—so, finally. A relief not to have to wake him. Could light the gas under the coffee now. Get the bread out of the drawer, put the loaf on the cutting board beside the knife: a setup, make it clear Clayton ought to eat something.

"Well, Cowboy." Clayton stood in the hallway, rubbing the top of his bald head. "Near slept my life away. Surprised you'd let me have such peace."

"Just about to haul you out. Want some coffee?"

Clayton shook his head. "Not yet. Think I'll have a red-eye. Hair of the dog that bit me."

Mitch opened the Frigidaire, surveyed its contents as though he didn't already know Bess had gotten rid of that six-pack. "You're stuck with caffeine, Clayton. Or straight tomato juice."

"Who the hell drank all the beer?"

"Looks like Bess drank it, after she put you to bed last night."

Clayton sat at the table, his arms folded, and chuckled. "I bet you that coffee she left me is black as sin."

"See for yourself." Mitch poured a cup and set it in front of Clayton; they both observed the steaming liquid. It smelled strong, like burnt grounds. "Want some milk, lighten it up?"

"No use trying to dilute it." Clayton held the cup to his lips and took a swallow. "Best drink it when it's so hot I can't taste it."

"Better get some toast in your belly to sop it up."

"No, thanks." Clayton frowned. "Katie wake up yet?"

"Awake most of the night, Bess told me. Sleeping now. I'll take her to the movies this afternoon. Some Disney movie she's nuts about."

"Damn, suppose I kept her awake."

"You weren't loud, Clayton." Mitch said it off-handedly but felt Clayton's relief.

"Right." Clayton smiled, drank the coffee with a grimace. "This potion will set me up."

Mitch watched him, lit a cigarette, and sat back in his chair. Clayton's hands were steady but he was bleary in the eyes, tired, flushed-looking. Didn't seem like himself. Drinking more since Mitch had come home, these last six months—like now there was another man around to help hold things together. Wasn't true though. If Clayton didn't straighten up, the whole situation would go to hell.

Clayton widened his eyes, yawned, then shook his head to clear it. "You seeing Reb for lunch at the Elks'?"

Mitch nodded, then assumed a mock-serious expression. "I don't know Clayton, seems to me you're leading that Reb in bad ways. Doctor needs to be strait-laced. He'll be sewing his clamps up in some poor bastard's stomach."

"Hell, Reb didn't drink much. Keeping me company mostly." Clayton leaned forward, touching the cup with both hands. "How's the new Pontiac running? Get her waxed yet?"

"Nearly. Some of us been up for hours."

Clayton half-stood from his chair, leaning to see out the kitchen window. Mitch didn't look; having already memorized the image of the car, he watched Clayton's face instead. Crazy how men loved cars. Clayton did his characteristic wink and click of the tongue, a gesture Mitch remembered from the first summer in Bellington: fourteen years old and looking up, seeing this big balding man, a stranger who had the power to say whether Mitch stayed or went. Went where?

"She looks like heaven," Clayton said now. "Katie's head will turn—she don't have any other escorts with new Pontiac Eights." The chair creaked as he sat back down. He was still a big man, healthy-looking except for the bad color in his face.

"You be here for lunch with Bess and Katie, or you want to come up to the Elks' with me?"

"Can't do either. Told Twister I'd come watch his basketball practice. That kid is growing like a weed, getting so he looks five years older than Katie instead of two—"

"She'll catch up, Clayton." Mitch put his cigarette out, stubbing it into the ash tray harder than he needed to.

Clayton nodded. "Sure, maybe she will." He was silent a moment, turning the coffee cup a meditative half-circle. "I don't mind how tall she is or how big, or even whether she goes through school—that kind of thing don't matter so much for a girl. But she's got no strength. Doesn't seem to gain an ounce. Smallest thing sets her heart to beating like a drum."

Mitch stood and turned to the sideboard, busied himself cutting the bread. If someone made it for him, Clayton would have to eat it. "You talk to Reb about Katie lately?"

"Some. Reb seems damn optimistic. Can't trust him."

Mitch put the knife down. "Reb would tell you if Katie was in a dangerous way."

"Don't mean that," Clayton said. "I know he's done everything he can." Scraping of the cup across the saucer. "Look at you, cutting that bread when I told you not to. Working for old man Costello over at Winfield must be adding to your cussedness."

"That's for damn sure."

"You still like that rooming house where you're staying?"

"It's all right." Mitch put the thick slice of bread in the oven, feeling the wave of heat on his face as he bent to latch the oven door.

"All right, eh?" Clayton smiled. "I know what rooming houses are. You give Mary Chidester the address last night?"

"Figured I'd give it to her tonight, if she beat it out of me."

"Better not. She'll show up at your door next thing you know, move in." He laughed. "These young ones are really something. She must have heard you're selling a lot of trucks over there."

"Could be." Mitch got the butter from the Frigidaire.

"Costello raise your commission yet?" Clayton drank the coffee and spoke softly to make the question less loaded.

"Not yet. The salary is passable but there's nowhere to go with Costello." Mitch took the toasted bread from the rack. Christ, it was hot. He'd burn himself being a goddamn waitress.

Clayton nodded. "Costello is a damn tight Talie, and crooked besides. But goes to Mass every whipstitch. Here, give me that toast. I reckon I can butter my own bread." He took the plate and heated the knife on the toast before slicing the butter. It was something he did Mitch liked to watch. "Dagos are close-knit. I was surprised he let you have that job."

"He brags how he hired every experienced vet that applied, just so I don't get a swelled head. It's an education, rooming there on Dago Hill."

"Dagos aren't bad people," Clayton said. "They just aren't our people." He ate the bread slowly; Mitch knew he wouldn't finish it.

Jam. Mitch got the jam from the shelf and put it near Clayton's plate. Damn if he didn't get nervous, talking about work with Clayton. Might as well be a teenager again. He leaned back from the table and looked out the window at his car. Now was as good a time as any.

"You know, Clayton, while I was gone I used to think you and me ought to start up a business. A war over and room for new people. Look at Costello—he's cleaning up."

"What'd you have in mind?"

"Oh, a supply business, maybe concrete. Did a lot of that work in New Guinea—and I can keep about any engine running."

He didn't look at Clayton but at Clayton's hand on the tablecloth. The hand was big and finely shaped, the fingers tapered, the fingernails so perfect they looked manicured. And when he raised his eyes, Clayton was watching him with that still, contemplative gaze Mitch had thought about in the war, wondered about.

"We'll see, Mitch," he said. "Things calming down now. We'll see."

They sat while Clayton finished the coffee. There was an easy silence in the room. Only the sound of the clock, and a car going by in the alley.

Mitch hadn't gone to the Elks' much before the war but now he went for lunch nearly every day he was in Bellington. The aura of the back barroom was overpoweringly familiar: smells of tobacco and men, the sound of men's voices. He liked the ritual of the locked door with the triangular window, the card he stuck in the slot beneath the doorknob, the official sound of the buzzer as the door unlatched. The people were always the same, the food modest and cheap. Past the dining room, it was just the men.

Mitch paused a moment at the swinging door to the bar, hearing a low hum of conversation, then walked on through into an ocher, interior shade.

The Elks' barroom was always a little dark, dark enough that the electric beer signs along the back wall shone with a pale night-light glow even at noon. Windows along the single row of booths were draped with dark green pleated curtains that kept the sun out; behind the drapes the window glass was thick and patterned, opaque as bottle bottoms. The wall behind the bar was almost solidly covered with clippings, jokes from men's magazines, newsprint photos. Scattered heroics: twenty years of high school sports wins; service news of local boys; color photos of Roosevelt, MacArthur, Patton. Patton was a favorite of McAtee's, the bartender; a miniature Fourth of July flag bordered Patton's picture. On the far end of the wall, near the mirror, McAtee had tacked up *Life* newsprint of Patton's funeral, wrinkled black and white images of a blurred cortege. Directly below, the plastic Schlitz beer wagon lamp looked like a battered toy, the illuminated horses gone white in patches where color had flaked away.

Mitch and Reb habitually sat at that end of the bar. Reb wasn't here yet; Mitch walked back and sat down as McAtee brought him a draft.

"Cowboy, my favorite bachelor. How goes it?" McAtee wiped the already polished bar top and set the frothy beer in front of Mitch.

"Not bad, McAtee. Where's our Doc? Fell asleep over his operating table probably. Out causing trouble last night."

"Yeah?" McAtee gestured toward the door. "Don't let him get away with that. Here he is now."

"Hey, Old Man Hampson." Reb saluted as he walked toward them, then shook hands as he reached Mitch. His hands always felt cold and dry and clean; the alcohol, Mitch guessed, sterile hands. "Clayton up yet?"

"Just barely," Mitch said.

McAtee grinned as Reb sat down and leaned on the bar, sighing with satisfaction. "Home," Reb said.

Mitch watched the two men; he raised his eyes to McAtee's

jovial face and glimpsed behind him the *Life* newsprint pictures
—they looked almost like enlarged Kodak snapshots, out of focus
and aged. Mitch smiled. "Home is damn morbid lately, McAtee. I
don't know why you have to have those funeral clippings right
here where Doc and I sit."

"I'm trying to get you boys to think serious," McAtee said.

Reb raised both hands to his eyes and peered at the pictures
as though through binoculars. "Fate does play the old trick."

"Damn right. Never can tell how things will turn around."
McAtee set the beers up and gestured toward the clippings. The
glossy paper of the pictures shone slightly in the light of the lamp.
"Look at old Blood and Guts. Liberated the damn graveyard and
then laid down in it. All those battles and then breaks his bastard
neck in a kraut car wreck."

Reb pulled his beer mug closer, turning it by the cracked
handle. "Plenty broke their fool necks for him."

"Right, Doc." McAtee made a show of scowling. "Broke their
necks to save yours."

Reb grinned. "Old Man here saved my neck personally—I
know that for a fact. Isn't that right, Cowboy?"

"That's right, and I'd say you owe me a little sobriety." Mitch
threw McAtee a collaborative glance. "You're an insult to your
profession and to Bond Hospital."

Reb laughed. "He's on me again, McAtee. Reads me like a
book." He took a long drink, draining half the glass. "Damn you,
Cowboy, you know I don't take a drop till one in the afternoon.
McAtee, tell him."

"I got work to do. You two want the special? Yeah, you want
the special." McAtee moved down the bar away from them, pulling his long apron tighter. Behind him the glass bottles registered
the shading of his passage, then shone again with their same dull
sparkle.

Mitch leaned on the bar, his hands touching his cool glass.
"Really, Doc, you and Clayton been keeping some late hours
here."

"Cowboy, I believe you're serious." Reb was quiet a moment,
then tipped the glass and drank slowly. "Clayton's been hitting it
lately."

"He was damn drunk when you brought him home last night. Finished that bottle the two of you started."

"No kidding." Reb took his cigarettes from his suit jacket pocket. "My drinking buddy is getting ahead of me."

"Maybe you'd better talk to him, Reb. Be a doctor, give him a scare."

"Hell, Mitch, where you been? He's already scared, that's why he's drinking so much. He's scared about Katie. Thinks she's going to die and then Bess will go to pieces. Trying to beat Bess to it, fall apart himself before anyone else does." Reb lit a Marlboro. "He's wrong. Bess could stand up under anything."

"Die? Katie?" Mitch felt his stomach tense as though in preparation for a blow.

"Listen, she's not going to die. I just said Clayton thinks she will, though he won't admit it." He took a drag on the cigarette, then looked at Mitch squarely. "Katie's on a daily dosage of penicillin now. She's safer from infection than you or me, but Clayton doesn't believe it. The truth is, Katie scares him every day. She's not the healthy kid she used to be. Clayton can't take it."

Mitch touched the rim of his glass. The edge was blunt and thick. "Katie won't ever be any better, will she?"

"She'll get some stronger, maybe, but she'll always have that heart murmur, tire easily . . . be delicate. No way to repair a damaged heart. We never even knew about that first strep throat. Katie kept it a secret because she didn't want to miss school. Strep symptoms go away, show up later as fatigue, pain in the joints— and by then it's rheumatic. But everyone in town had a flu then, and Bess thought Katie had it too. Kept her in bed and gave her aspirin. I saw her after about a week, heard the murmur, knew what had happened. That was in December. She just didn't have much resistence afterward and got pneumonia in February."

"That was the term she was out of school."

"Yes, and she was ashamed to be home in bed. Bess tried to explain it all but the kid is—over-responsible."

Mitch touched the grooved, uneven surface of the bar. It was true, she had to be perfect, like Bess. Ten years old and would drive herself to a frazzle. "And the second time, she didn't tell you she had a sore throat?"

"She knew she was supposed to, but in the winter of '44 she'd only been back in school a few weeks, afraid we'd take her out again. I'd had her on sulfanilamides, only thing I could get during the war, but she developed an allergy and I had to take her off." He shook his head. "So she was unprotected and went rheumatic again. Bess recognized the weakness right away, but the damage was done. That's why the murmur is so bad."

"But she won't get strep again?"

"No. Katie is real lucky the war is over. Now we can get penicillin. And the heart will get a little stronger, with rest, good food, care. No one could take better care than Bess. She blames herself for not realizing it was something serious that first bout, but no one could have known." He was quiet a moment. "Maybe, if we'd known about the throat that first time, before the strep developed—"

"And the kid did it, kept it secret, to win some school attendance prize. Now here she is. It's a goddamn hell of a thing."

"Yes—lots of hellish things. Holdovers from the war." Reb smiled sadly. He looked up and Mitch watched the ceiling light play across his eyeglasses. Didn't use to wear those; Reb had gotten older too. Now Reb took the glasses off and rubbed the lenses with his wrinkled linen handkerchief.

McAtee brought the plates and moved on down the counter to wash glasses. Meat loaf was good today, and Mitch ate with Reb quiet beside him. Sound of the glasses in water, clink as McAtee set them on the drying rack.

"They say the Nips like MacArthur," Mitch said. "First ruler they've had isn't a direct descendant of the gods."

"What gods are those, Cowboy?"

"Who the hell knows."

They ate then without speaking until Reb pushed his empty plate to the far edge of the bar. "Clayton said you were out with Miss Chidester last night."

"That's right." Mitch looked over and registered Reb's expression without much surprise; of course, he'd been there too. "You old married lech. Then she's a real tramp."

"Hey." Reb did a modest pantomime of throwing up his hands. "Doctors get it easy. And I'm not saying she's a tramp. Be a little broad-minded, Old Man—might be a good idea to marry a girl like her. Lively, young enough to keep her looks awhile. Move her out of town, settle her hash quick with a few kids. You're up to it, aren't you?" Reb finished the beer and faked a right cross to Mitch's ribs. "Then you really got problems."

Mitch stopped Reb's hand and held him by the wrist. "You'll talk to Clayton? I don't want this getting any worse."

"I hear you." Reb pulled his arm away gently and stood from the bar stool, reaching in his pockets for money. "What's more, I'll buy lunch. With Mary Chidester's hands in your pockets, your change won't last long."

Mitch shrugged, smiling. "It's a crime. I keep telling you, Doc, you don't get anything in this world for free."

Katie loved to ride in the new Pontiac. Mitch had first brought the car home the week before, and she'd asked to have her picture taken—a movie star picture, she said. Clayton sat her on the long swoop of front fender, and she arranged her white skirt against the dark blue of the car. Twister stood aside making faces, trying to get her to laugh and spoil her serious expression. Where did she get those expressions? Studied movie posters probably, looked at magazines. Always after Mitch to take her to the matinees.

Today she sat over next to the door like a grown-up, wrapped in a soft cotton blanket from head to foot. Mitch had made a joke of it and said he'd wrap her in the warm cloth like an Egyptian mummy.

"You sure you're warm enough, Fritzel?" He glanced over. She'd assented to the blanket for his sake, but once in the car pulled it down so only her legs were covered. In case anyone saw her in the bright new sedan, she would look like any other kid.

"I'm warm, honest." She smiled, rested one arm on the plush gray armrest.

"Lock your door there. Don't want you falling out before we even get to the pictures." He always drove her around a bit before they went to the movie house; the route was a ritual by now: length of Main Street, up Quality Hill past the big old houses and the school, down around by the grocery and the Mobil station, where he got gas. The Mobil station was a favorite since they'd installed the new sign. Giant red horse with wings: NEW MOBILGAS GIVES FLYING HORSEPOWER. She would sit and stare at that big sign until he didn't know what the hell she was seeing, and he usually bought her a cola from the cooler in the station, so she'd have an excuse to stare longer.

Now she pushed the lock button down on her door and said, adultlike, "The motor still runs very smoothly."

"Sure it does. Only been a week since you heard it."

She nodded. "One week. I told all the girls at school: you got a Streamliner sedan, four doors."

Of course she would tell them. Aloud, he said, "That's right. And why is it called a Silver Streak?"

"Because of the chrome strips. Like right there." She pointed in front of them to the silvered midline of the hood. "Runs right down to the grill. Those are the streaks. But you know too,"—she raised her eyebrows—"if the Pontiac was going real fast, like in a comic, the chrome would shine like lights. The car would look like a blur, but the chrome would be all streaks."

"I guess you're right, Fritz."

She frowned as they turned onto Main Street, pretending to look carefully at the storefronts. "You ought to call me Katie," she said, "I'm too old for nicknames by now."

"Well, is that so." He steered with one hand and lay his arm along the back of the seat. "Don't seem possible you're that old already. Reb is called Doc Reb by the whole town—he's a grown man and most people don't even know his real name. And look what he calls me."

"He calls you Cowboy, I realize."

*Realize?* Where did she get that word? "Around home," he continued, "you all call me Old Man."

She seemed to deliberate. "I think you started calling your-self that," she said softly.

Damn, he supposed she was right. He kept himself from smiling. Quickly, just as he'd intended, she read his response as hurt and tried to make it up. "Men have a lot of nicknames," she said, "but it's different with girls and women."

"I don't know why girls and women can't have some fun."

She shrugged. "I guess they don't need much fun."

Now they were passing the school and he slowed the car so she could take a look at the playground. Good, it was empty. To distract her, he said softly, teasingly, "You sure you're not too old to go to a cartoon show? That's what's on today, a Disney show."

"It's *Make Mine Music.*" She turned her full gaze on him, her smooth pale face close to his hand. "Long cartoons, like stories. I'm going because I've decided to collect comics. I've already got one hundred and forty, before the collection is even started." He felt her delicate breath on his fingers as she spoke. She turned her face forward then, watching the scenery as though she hadn't seen it hundreds of times. "A cartoon movie is the same as a comic except it moves," she said, "and there are thousands of comics one after another." She folded her hands on her lap. "Since I have to stay home, Mama said I could have a new notepad, a great big one. I'm going to draw comics."

"Katie, that's a good idea." He meant to encourage her but she was lost in the idea and barely heard him.

"First I'll trace my comic books with tracing paper—the covers, where things are biggest, until I can draw my own. I'll learn one at a time." She seemed almost to talk to herself, then looked over at Mitch. "I thought of this while you were at lunch with Doc Reb and Daddy was asleep. Mama was over at the hospital and Twister was at basketball. I have my best thoughts when I'm by myself."

"It's always that way," Mitch said. He pulled into the Mobil station and drove up beside the pumps. For a moment he listened to the engine idle—a smooth and satisfying purr—then turned the ignition off. "You stay here," he told Katie. "I'll go in and pay and maybe find you a soda."

Already she'd leaned forward, looking past the high dash of the Pontiac at the billboard. The red horse above them seemed to fly over the cracked concrete of the station lot and the street beyond, a red gleaming horse with powerful flanks, its feathered wings spread to glide. The belly was long and flat and the horse seemed to swim a fast current of wind, mane flying, head lowered, nostrils flared with effort. There was a white streak up the center of the side-viewed head.

"Good-looking fella, your horse," Mitch said.

"Oh, he's beautiful," Katie whispered. "I wish I could draw him."

"No need," he told her. "You wouldn't find a horse like that in the comics." He watched her earnest face and hoped she really could draw a little. She was such a perfectionist, so finicky—she'd stop if she wasn't good. He looked back at the billboard above them, at the blue script in quotes: I'VE BOOSTED BOMBERS AT 60 BELOW. He gazed with the kid at her gleaming, muscled horse and wished things were really like that.

Katie was still reading. "Socony-Vacuum," she said.

He stood holding her in his arms while his eyes adjusted to the dark. Didn't want to stumble holding her; gradually he saw the broad aisles and the crowded rows of metal plush-lined seats. Close against him she smelled of baby powder, the fragile scent specific in the shadows. She said softly, her mouth at his ear, *"Peter and the Wolf*— it's just starting."

Mitch moved quietly down the far aisle: keep her near the heat registers and get out fast when the show was over. He settled her in the seat soundlessly, leaning to pull the blanket around her shoulders.

"You keep this tight around you," he told her. "No one can see you anyway."

She nodded, smiling, her face tinged blue and orange by a shifting of the bright images over them. Mitch sat back in his seat and looked at the theater, the walls painted to look scalloped with draped bunting, layers and layers, and stars up high near a border of blue. How many times had he been in this theater since he was a kid? Silhouettes in the rows of seats looked decorative, part of the painted finery, until they moved; then he noticed faces, their expressions obvious even in shadow. Women and children mostly: he might be the only man here. Funny how the women watched with real concentration, taken in like children. On the bright screen the cartoon kid led a band of animals through snow, deep snow, holding his worthless popgun and menaced by thick blue trees. A popgun, that was about right, and in the comforting crowded dark he shut his eyes and listened. Wind blew on the sound track, realistic wind, billowing; sounded like they'd recorded it in New Guinea, the most deserted place in the world, where no one recorded anything. Now he wished someone had, even movie people; he wished he could hear again exactly how things sounded. Have something more than those little snapshots, so small and colorless they were all alike, less real than the words he'd typed on the backs to say who was who. But that wind—he could hear it now, how it sounded by the sea: beach road wind. He knew that road and where it went; didn't want to go there now, but he had to sit here in this dark and his mind kept falling into the wind: it's all right, go ahead, think about it now. So he kept his eyes shut and heard the palm fronds moving; surf played under the wind like a pulse, and the pulse was Coco Mission. Lee side of the bay. All of it in focus now and they were driving, he and Warrenholtz, in the Jeep. Jap Zero shot into the sea the night before and they drove out to look at it, thinking they'd peel down and take a swim. Motor pool in the morning heat was a caldron of still air, smells of axle grease and gasoline.

Driving along the coast road, Mitch listened closely to the engine, rebuilt just the day before; listened so hard what he looked at was barely seen. Instead he heard the steady growl and occasional miss of the motor and felt the prod of his pistol butt. Shoulder holster a little tight, so the gun pressed the pit of his arm. Rumble of the engine a half-tone off and the timing spotty; he heard it and felt his own shaky gut, off the whole day like something was coming, some sick something that had his number. Warrenholtz had the tremors too, and they stopped halfway for him to shit in scrub bush back of the road, Mitch revving the motor to know exactly how the timing missed, how to put it right. He played the engine like music to put down his own cramps; if you ignored the pains the urge lessened. He'd told Warrenholtz that, but Warrenholtz wouldn't believe it and said not to legislate anyone's bowels, pull the hell over. Afterward they'd kept driving and the sea was flat, barely rippled. Parrots called from the palms, flew in front of the Jeep in dips and glides. Warrenholtz going on about the birds—he had two back at the camp he'd trained to eat from his hand. Mitch ragged on about why the hell a man would want parrots to feed when they were all over New Guinea, thick as rats, and Warrenholtz smiled and said nothing; and then they were close enough to see the Zero. The big wing rose up, breaking water a hundred yards out. The plane had gone in nose first and then tipped in the surf, rolling sideways so the wing reared out of the water, fuselage shredded at the tip.

Farther on, the aluminum ribs were visible, holes blasted in the overlaid structure, the red sun of Hirohito's empire flapping.

Warrenholtz took a picture of the wing and stripped down to swim, but Mitch sat in the shade of the Jeep, smoked a cigarette. He watched the ruined wing and the white floating form of Warrenholtz. Later they drank more paregoric before starting back but still had to walk into hilly brush across the beach road and relieve themselves, with Warrenholtz grousing how it was all good revenge for the Papua boys, see the Yanks with their diarrhea scowls once a month on the average. When they got to the top of the rise above their own Jeep, Warrenholtz saw the Nip, saw the brush move where the Nip was crawling, drew his gun and yelled. Mitch saw then the lobbed grenade flying high into the air but knew it was hopelessly off target; the Nip was hurt and had no aim. The grenade burst off to the right and the sound was deafening; after that, Mitch walked in, the spiky grass to his knees; somewhere Warrenholtz was yelling *"Kosan, Kosan, Tomare,"* the words ridiculous and piping after the burst of the ammo, but the Nip kept crawling deeper in. The tall grass wavered. Mitch saw momentarily the fields behind the farm at home, and he drew his own gun and fired—fired again and again into the grass until the chamber was empty and Warrenholtz stood beside him, staring not at the grass, which had long since stopped moving, but at Mitch.

Mitch saw Warrenholtz's lips moving and heard sounds he knew were words, but the words were like buzzing over a bad wireless, like Warrenholtz had a radio voice and the voice blinked on and off. They stood still and the grass was motionless in the hot sea air; Mitch put the pistol carefully into his holster and could feel the heat of the gun through his shirt, good, then he was fine and the mechanical way things sounded was maybe because of the loud grenade. Probably Warrenholtz couldn't hear good either, but even as Mitch thought so he knew he was wrong: not just his ears were funny but his body was strange to him; he looked at the field with a feeling of total detachment, as though he saw the grass and the swell of the land from a low-flying plane. No part of him. He couldn't feel his feet or the ground under him. He touched the leather holster and his own chest, felt the front of his shirt. Had he been hit and didn't know it, couldn't tell? No, he wasn't hurt, this was something else. Warrenholtz walked forward toward the Nip in the grass and Mitch watched, stood and waited. As he stood, his whole frame of vision rotated once, smooth and circular, the figure of Warrenholtz turning around like the long straight khaki hand of a clock. He must be dizzy but he wasn't; the world turned once, once only. Far away, Warrenholtz nudged the corpse with his foot, bending until he was lost to sight and then straightening, shaking his head as he turned to come back.

They sent a native patrol out to bury the Nip, and later in the warm night they drank PX scotch. They tied up the sides of Warrenholtz's large tent so the tent was only a canvas roof over a board floor; the parrots flew through the space as Warrenholtz whistled, and the two birds perched on his shoulders, cocking their green heads and chortling low-pitched sounds. Soft vibration right into his bones, Warrenholtz said, like an idling of small motors. Mitch asked then where the Nip had been hit.

"He was burned and his gut ripped open," Warrenholtz said, "but not by you. You weren't trying to hit him. I don't know what the hell you were doing."

Mitch got the leave he asked for; Warrenholtz had sway with the CO and interceded to be sure the leave was granted. After Mitch came back, the episode seemed forgotten and Warrenholtz never mentioned it again except indirectly. Sometimes he drawled on about the war in his liquid Texas accent; how the war had a filthy smell and sneaky way of crawling along deadly for years like some endless Guinea python.

Mitch looked over at Katie and then at the screen; the wolf had made an appearance and wore bloodshot green eyes.

"Katie," Mitch whispered, "are you warm enough?"

She nodded.

"Want some popcorn?"

She nodded again, anything to keep him from distracting her, and he was smiling as he walked up the aisle. Felt good, walking that carpeted incline with a big image mixing up the dark behind him, and when he got to the lighted lobby he asked the boy at the counter for a large buttered.

Waiting, he could still see a bit of the screen; as he watched an abstract movement of color, the colors suddenly went silent and flashed, eaten into mottled holes by a racing black edge. "The film's on fire," Mitch told the boy, and the lobby lights went off, the room lit only with what daylight filtered through the double doors from the street. "Hell," Mitch swore, starting back into the dark. Just as he stepped forward, he heard a woman yell, "Fire, fire!" The stupid fool, it was only the film had burnt, but there was the chilling sound of everyone rising at once, and then he was fighting his way through the crowd running past him to the entrance. The goddamn fools, some of the women screaming and kids crying, Christ, he pushed them aside and moved toward Katie, hoping she'd have sense enough to stay put. He reached their places and saw the empty chairs. Grabbed the blanket, that way, the street exit down by the screen, surely she'd gone that way, terrified by now if they hadn't run over her already. He shouted her name and felt himself shoved along, spilling with the crowd into the alley back of the theater.

He saw her then, leaning against the wall of the opposite building, her shoes gone, her coat unbuttoned. Her eyes were big and shocked, and as he pushed his way toward her she waved to him feebly, apologetically, as though afraid she'd done wrong. He thought she was trembling but saw as he reached her that her body was shaken by the pounding of her heart; she was breathless and didn't speak. He picked her up in his blanketed arms and walked quickly across the street to the Pontiac. As he opened the passenger door she looked over his shoulder at the crowd, fascinated, and said in a small voice, "Was that like the war?"

He got her to lie down across the seat and drove home; after he'd put her in bed he tried to phone Reb, who wasn't at his office or at home or at the Elks'. He called Bess at the hospital; she'd gone upstreet, the switchboard girl told him, but she'd get the message to come home as soon as she got back. He went in to Katie then and she was sitting quietly, reading a comic.

He felt her forehead.

"I'm okay now," she said. "It's just my heart beats like that when I get scared."

"Everyone's heart beats faster then," he told her. He thought of carrying her over to the hospital, but he might only scare her again.

"There wasn't really any fire at all, was there?"

"No, just some fool woman yelling."

"I lost my shoes," Katie said. "When I got up and ran so fast, the shoes came right off my feet." She raised her brows for emphasis.

"I'll go by the movie house after your Mom gets here, see if I can find the shoes."

"It was exciting," Katie said softly, "after I got over being scared."

"I know it was, Fritz. Now I want you to lay down and close your eyes. You need a rest."

He sat watching her. In just a few minutes, she was sleeping lightly and easily, her breathing regular. He supposed the best thing was just to sit here till Bess came. He had a presentiment then that he might still hurt Katie somehow, be bad luck for her sitting in the room, so he stood and walked out, crossed the hall into the living room. He sat down in one of the seldom used velvet chairs and felt for the first time the total exhaustion of his relief. He touched his hand to his eyes.

There had never been so many goddamn flowers, so many the sides of the box were obscured by deep waxen petals of the lilies and roses, spider fronds of the mums, and she looked as though she were floating on a fat crescent of blossoms that filled that side of the room, leaving scant space to stand close. After everyone sat down, he looked straight ahead at the minister but felt a ripple of movement from the silent flowers, as though the island of color and the body itself moved on an eddy of current. Jesus, would the bastard minister never shut that book, give us some help here, won't you, and finally he quit with the Scriptures and wandered on, all of them wading in his sonorous performer's voice as the kid floated placidly on her moon of flowers, delicate alabaster stone in her white organdy dress. She'd been supposed to wear it in April for Easter, and remembering that fact made him consider what the hell they would all do now, snuck up on like this, to get through the next few weeks. After that he would be able to think of something, things would happen, even small things like a road job in the south of the state so that he could go away and live in a rooming house in Wierton or somewhere and work all day until he couldn't think except to eat dinner late at a cheap coffee shop and go to sleep—talk to strangers who didn't know anything about this and so would make remarks about the weather or the front page. Front page of what? Christ, time went on and on. He couldn't go unless he felt they wanted him to, leave them alone with it, then they could put it somewhere: *she's your darling, I'm afraid*, but she never had been. Except in how he supposed if he'd got his in the war, she might still be lying in her bed, a sickly little kid whose fingers and wrists swelled. It was like the numbers had got mixed up and Bess had been right to be afraid: somehow after he'd got back from the war, all the numbers changed around and Katie had come out wearing his. All the time had caught up with him, all the floating around since he was a kid younger than her and moving from one household to another; floating around is what it was and there she was now, wearing his number and floating. He saw her on a wide, wide sea, riding the flowers and the words he heard in the room: *at the Rapture the body shall rise, we all shall rise at the Rapture (to be with God in the air), at the Rapture the body shall rise.* But the body only floated, the rug of flowers stirred like a banner from below, so easy, so gentle, and now the whole floor was gently moving, barely but percepti- bly moving, he could feel it himself: they were all floating, restful and lulled, moved according to tides he'd experienced before but hadn't understood. Surely they all felt it; he stood up from his chair as the minister's voice continued, and far off he heard rifle shots. The shots kept on as though in celebration or ceremony, and as he turned toward the open window he felt Bess near him; she was pulling him, pulling him back, her hand cold on his shoul- der, what could she want of him? He tried to ask and her hand became more insistent, shaking, shaking him. Her face was sur- prisingly young, the face of a young woman, and as he awakened the face aged in a flash of seconds. She leaned into his field of vision, filling it totally.

"You must be dead tired," she said. "You've fallen asleep here in the chair."

"Is Katie all right?" His own voice sounded strange to him.

"Yes, and asleep. She woke when I came in and told me about the movie."

"Hadn't you better call Reb?"

"No, he'll be by tomorrow anyway—she really is sleeping. I'm sorry you had such a scare."

Mitch sat up now and rubbed his eyes. "We lost Katie's shoes."

"Those old shoes," Bess said. "I'm glad they're lost; they were completely worn out." She watched his face and realized he didn't believe her. "I've taken Katie's temperature. She's not chilled or feverish, she seems to be fine. Now, would you like some tea?"

He nodded and she turned away; he heard the tread of her footsteps in the hall and saw vaguely the young face in the dream. It really had looked like her; he must have seen a photograph.

Scary how time flew by and you couldn't tell, ever, what would happen. He would get married, he would start thinking of it. Mary Chidester wasn't the one; he would play the field, no ties to bind, but he would look at things differently.

# ANNIVERSARY SONG
Jean, 1948

Jean stood by the window and watched him park the Nash. The car was too big for the small garage and Gladys insisted Mitch park on the street, just to the right of her sidewalk. Gladys was the only resident of the street whose sidewalk was poured cement instead of haphazard bricks. She'd told Jean how she bargained long and hard for that sidewalk in the '20s, when the city had pay-off revenues from stills. *I marched myself down to City Hall,* she was fond of saying, *and I told those jerks that my husband was a City worker—and if they weren't going to pay him well enough that he could own a car like every other Sam Smith, they were going to build me a sidewalk. I sank to my ankles in mud when I got off the bus carrying a baby and two sacks of sewing.* Gladys must have been almost seventeen. *I stood there holding Jewel as I shouted, you bet I did. I tell you, I have a permanent swayback from carrying that baby everywhere I went for nearly three years. There wasn't any baby carriage in this house, and no baby-sitters.*

*Andy Curry was lucky to bring home enough for two meals a day. If I hadn't breast-fed Jewel until she was old enough to ask for it, she would have been as hungry as we were.* Gladys had told the story again just last night, Mitch sitting there as always reading the paper and leaving Jean to listen.

Seemed a long time ago people had things so bad. No one took in sewing anymore, except the poor whites who lived between the feed store and the tracks. Now the war was five years past, people felt rich. The new Nash was wide and high and long; Mitch had bought it even though the concrete company had only been going six months and they were so strapped building the new house. Jean thought surely Gladys would remark how they were staying with her free so Mitch could have luxuries, but she seemed to love the new car and had gone on about it until Mitch was fairly strutting, touching the Nash and showing Gladys how the seats tilted back. Would have been a different story if Jean had gone out and bought a car. Gladys would never sanction foolishness from a woman in anything; despite all her complaints about men, she loved it when they did something crazy.

Still, she'd been kind about helping Jean do a dress over for the New Year's party. It was the sort of thing Mother would have done if she'd been here, and healthy. Jean had turned slowly as Gladys knelt to pin the hem, and Gladys chattered softly about trivial things. Jean was glad not to answer; she didn't feel so sad anymore, except when people were unexpectedly kind. It was just over a year since the death; that's why the last two weeks had been such a strain. A couple of mornings, faced with Christmas vacation from her secretarial job and being alone in the house all day, Jean had actually been sick. Last night she'd stared ahead at the kitchen clock as Gladys folded the wool skirt of the dress, and realized she wanted to drive out to the grave. But Gladys was at work today, doing inventory alone at her dress shop, and Jean would have to borrow the Nash.

If he knew where she was going, he'd offer to drive her, keep from worrying about the car. *Why go out there in all this snow and cold?* he'd say. *You'll just get hung up; that graveyard road isn't even all paved.* But the snow wasn't deep, only a powder really—she'd tell him she had errands. Surely he'd take a nap before the party anyway. He'd been out with Reb Jonas last night at the Elks', and he'd gotten in late.

Jean pressed her face to the cold glass. There, he'd stopped the car and stepped out, shaking wrinkles from his long tweed coat, pulling his hat brim lower as he shifted the sack of groceries. Oh, it was cold outside, too cold to snow hard. Mitch came up the walk and Jean moved away from the window, heard his footsteps, that flat *slap* of a man's shoe on cement. She sat down and picked up the folded party dress, shook it out over her lap. He knew she was fixing it; she'd say she was out of thread. The doorknob turned and she slipped the wooden spool under the soft cushion of the chair.

"My God, it's cold," he said as he stepped inside. "Like hell froze over out there."

"I know," Jean said, standing, "and I have to run downtown to get some thread." She took the sack of groceries and leaned up to kiss his cheek. Under her lips his skin was faintly rough with beard, and cold and sweet.

"You're crazy to go out now." Mitch took off his gloves and blew on his hands. "Supposed to be zero by dark, and Main Street is bumper to bumper. People shopping because everything's closed tomorrow."

"You're right, but I have to wear this dress tonight. I can't finish the hem without the thread."

He looked at her, a little exasperated. "Do you want me to get it for you? I've still got my coat on."

"No, no. Didn't you want to take a nap before the party? I'll just put these away and drive down real quickly."

She walked into the kitchen and he followed her. Oh, did he have to follow her, as though she couldn't even put groceries away without being watched? He unbuttoned his coat as she put the sack on the table and opened Gladys' refrigerator.

"Reb is bringing his wife tonight," Mitch said, confiding in her.

"His wife isn't well, is she? Gladys says she's very nervous."

"I don't know what the hell is wrong with her. Reb doesn't seem to know either." He paused. "Will you be sure and talk to her tonight at the party? Just in case she stays quiet and doesn't speak to anyone."

Jean turned to put the milk away and felt a little ashamed. That's why he'd followed her in here; he really did care about Reb. "Of course I'll talk to her," Jean answered. "But your Aunt Bess will be there. She always helps at VFW parties, and she'll certainly be talking to Reb's wife."

"I know, but Reb thinks Cora needs to know more women close her own age. She's only five or six years older than you."

Cora. Yes, that was her name. Jean had only met her a few times; you seldom saw her. How strange—the last time Jean had seen her had been last summer, at the graveyard. Jean had gone out with some flowers and there Cora Jonas was, sitting on a cloth spread across the grass, as though at a picnic. She seemed a sweet woman, but distant.

Jean shut the refrigerator and moved to fold the paper sack. Where was it Gladys kept these? She'd have to put it in exactly the right place or never hear the end of it. She looked up at Mitch then and realized he was still waiting for an answer. "Don't worry," she told him, "I'll talk to Cora. I'll be sure to."

Mitch patted her shoulder awkwardly in thanks, then turned quickly and left the room as Jean stood with the folded sack in her hands. She heard him at the hall closet, hanging up his coat, shaking it out before he put it on the hanger. She sighed. He certainly was fastidious, even if he talked a little rough. She'd given up saying anything about it—then he only blustered and swore more.

Once outside, she wrapped her coat tighter around her and pulled on bulky mittens. She'd have to hurry; as it was, she wouldn't get back before the early dark fell. The blue Nash looked surprisingly bright on the gray street; in dusk light, the houses and dark cars lost definition, powdered with old snow and shadowed. Jean went around to the driver's side and pulled on the door; heavens, why had he locked it? Now she'd have to take off the mittens, fuss in her deep pocket for the keys. Immediately, her bare fingers ached with cold, but the key fit and she turned it. Nothing. She heard then the dull thud of Mitch's hand on Gladys' living room window and saw him, in his bathrobe, elaborately motion that she should turn the key the other way. Jean waved cheerily, pretended not to have understood, and opened the car door. There.

The car started smoothly and easily—not even a clutch or a gearshift; a child could drive it. She sat letting the engine warm, hugging herself in the cold and smiling. If she tried to take off too soon, he'd be running out here in his bare feet to stop her. She could feel him at the window, still watching, but she looked stead-fastly ahead. Finally the curtain dropped back into place; she was alone. Jean eased the Nash down the street on the soft cover of snow and heard the muffled road under the wheels.

Anniversaries were strange; you felt the important ones in your body even if you tried not to remember—and not just the day of the event but the days before and after. A deep change was a short season of its own; you felt the season come and go for years after. Tom had died in the spring, late May, when they were seventeen. Jean felt it, every spring, before she remembered what she felt. Now she knew they'd been children, but still—not such children. They were in love; maybe they would have married in a couple of years, and grown up. After he died, Jean had felt that now she was like anyone else: it didn't matter so much who she married.

She stopped the Nash at the turn onto Quality Hill; it was such a quiet car that you could drive along with no diversion from your thoughts. Jean looked down toward town and she could see the traffic on Main Street, the lights of the cars. She turned the other way, up the hill toward the country. She'd go right past the concrete company but it wouldn't matter; Clayton and the other men would have gone home when Mitch did. Tonight was the New Year; my God, time passed. Already, she was twenty-three, mar-ried a year and a half. And last summer, she hadn't remembered her wedding anniversary at all—Mitch had told her that morning that his Aunt Bess and Uncle Clayton were having dinner for them. Jean had used her lunch hour to go downtown and buy Mitch a shirt; she'd planned to buy it anyway, to replace one she'd burned with the iron. Anniversaries: maybe she just remembered death instead of life. That was bad. But death wouldn't let you

forget, would it? Life did; life let you go on for long weeks and
never think at all. You just lived, nothing was wrong; those
weren't bad times. Mitch would never have remembered the anniversary if Bess hadn't had the dinner—he didn't remember such
things. But wives were supposed to. Jean frowned and touched
her face; she felt so at loose ends: that was it. In the warm interior
of the car, she unbuttoned her coat. Damn it, she was a good wife,
she knew she was. She kept her temper and was a help to him, and
didn't interfere with what he knew about; she was a good cook and
usually did things right. Being a wife was a job, like being a
secretary or a student. And if you took pride in what you did, you
did things well. Mother had had no illusions about it. Oh, had she
ever really loved a man, and been carefree? Strange to think she'd
probably loved Dad in the beginning, but then she'd loved her
children. Dad had really been a child himself, even though he'd
been so much older: first he was eccentric and successful, then he
was eccentric and broke. Jean could almost hear her mother
laugh, softly and without bitterness. If she were here, there'd be
someone to be honest with, someone to laugh with at how things
went.

I'm strong, Jean thought, I'll pull myself right out of this and
have a good time at the party. She turned onto the rough graveyard road and passed the darkened concrete company. One bright
light burned atop a pole near the trucks and the MITCH CONCRETE
sign was dusted with snow. Making the blind turn up the cemetery entrance, past the stone pillars that looked so forboding, she
felt shaky and ill again. Lord, what was wrong with her? She felt
such a fool. She drove slowly along the narrow road and turned
on the high beams to make herself feel less alone; finally she
stopped beside the family plot. None of the stones had much
meaning to her except the one that was off by itself; she'd just had
it put there last summer. Graves: what did they mean? Her
mother wasn't even here, if people ever were; she'd hated funerals
and left instructions she be cremated. But she'd told them what
to put on a stone, when Jean and her brother and sister could bear
the expense. And there was a wisdom to it; people had to have a
place to make remembrance. Jean looked at the stone. It was
smooth granite the color of pewter and relatively small, not even

waist high. Yet it had a weight, a power: it marked a place. Jean's brother and sister were much older and lived in distant towns. What family did she really have of her own blood, except this stone. She thought of the saying "you can't squeeze blood from a stone" and heard it said in her mother's voice, like a joking and fond reprieve.

She took off her mittens, flinging them down on the seat, and held to the steering wheel of the Nash. Aloud, she said, "Everything is all right. His business is doing well enough. We're building a nice house." Then she looked at her mother's gravestone and began to weep. There was no one here to know; she wept loudly, hearing her own harsh sounds as though they were part of the weather, the cold wind. The Nash shook slightly, buffeted in the dusk, and Jean felt a silly fondness for the car; it was so new and big and blue, and signified such expectation. Somehow that fact made her sadder; she wept harder, and felt ridiculous.

Minutes passed. Snow blew across the stone like a moving veil. She couldn't read the words from where she was, but she could see the writing. Well, yes, so it was over. Now what? She sat quietly, the weeping finished, and watched the passive movement of the snow. It was slow and ceaseless, as soft against the stone as the stroke of a hand. Jean heard a word in her mind, *sleep* or *peace*—she couldn't tell which—and she was tired, so tired. Safe and tired as she hadn't felt for many nights. She turned off the motor of the warm Nash and tilted the seat back. Bulky in her soft coat, she pulled her knees up nearly to her chest and lay her face on her open palm. She was looking at the stone as she fell asleep.

Mother and one of the other women were lifting her out of the car and onto the road. Nearly noon and the day was stifling. The women wore long-sleeved dresses and hats with veils; the palms of their white gloves were damp with sweat. Oh, there was such a crowd, like at church. People were dressed in their best clothes and moved along the dusty road in silence. Far ahead, pickaxes pounded rhythmically on the stone cellar walls of an isolated house. The other two women went on ahead, walking quickly; Mother walked with Jean and held her hand to keep her

from stumbling. She couldn't walk as fast as the grown-ups, and
flies buzzed around her face; the air droned strangely with flies.
The dirt road seemed long. People from nearby towns had been
arriving for hours, and the road was solidly lined on both sides
with shiny cars. High black doors above the dusty running boards
glimmered in the heat. The chrome bumpers shone, one nearly
against the other; between them, Jean glimpsed the overgrown
fields. Mother smoothed Jean's hair and they neared the crowd.
Ladies passed them, walking back toward the paved road; they
held handkerchieves to their noses and walked along wordlessly,
unhurried.

Now the axes rang out.

People stood so close that Jean could see very little, but a
wide pit had been dug along the stone house so that one side of
the foundation was exposed; workmen had chopped big holes
right through it. Stone and mortar lay round about the pit and
there were several stretchers. One stretcher was covered with a
sheet. An old man bent down and said into Jean's face, "Not a
pretty sight, little girl, but history is made here today." "Imagine," a woman's voice intoned, "his own wife, his own children."
Jean felt her mother's arms around her then and was lifted up into
the warmth of an embrace. "Never you mind, Jeannie. Now we'll
go." They had to walk along the very edge of the pit to turn back,
out of the crowd, and there was a terrible cold rising from the
dark earth where the workmen stood. The cold followed Jean and
her mother, even in the bright light of the sun. "When suffering
seems reasonless," her mother's voice said clearly, "people come
together and want to understand." Jean felt herself lowered to
the dusty road. The dust was cloudy and yellow under her shoes.
"We'll wait in the car for the others. Now, hold my hand." They
walked on and the cold grew colder, so cold the light went out.
Jean knew her mother was near but could feel nothing, her fingers
were so terribly cold. She woke touching the slick leather seats of
the Nash and found herself in darkness. She was chilled to the
bone. Dear God, the party—how long had she been asleep?

The keys were still in the ignition and she started the car,
then looked at her watch. Fifteen minutes, and the interior of the
Nash was like an icebox. What a strange dream. What had she

remembered? She pulled on her warm mittens and pressed their wool to her face. No matter. She remembered clearly her mother's voice and the sensation of being lifted up. The heater of the Nash clicked and the fan hummed; Jean put the car in reverse and backed up in the dark; then she turned on the headlights and saw that a fleecy snow was falling. Wet, heavy snow. She must go back right away. Mitch might be sleeping but Gladys would have gotten home and started supper: Jean's job. She didn't let herself look again at the gravestone but simply drove, turning out of the cemetery onto the asphalt road that ran past the concrete company and back to town. From the hill here she could see the lights of Bellington, glowing behind the snow. She recognized in the silent lights something more than home and felt calm . . . as though her brief, deep sleep had been a journey to some lost place still existing alongside this one. This one began a new year, but the other played in the mind, repeatedly, selectively.

Jean passed the Parkette, a drive-in restaurant closed for New Year's, and slowed to cross the railroad tracks. The Nash lurched, bumping over uneven ties. Mitch had never been one for talking. He was good-looking and older; he'd seemed quiet and dependable. He'd been back from the service nearly two years by the time they met at the VFW, a dance like the one tonight, except it had been no special occasion. Once they started going out, they'd seen each other every afternoon and night for three weeks; in the last week, they were planning their wedding. Jean hadn't needed anyone to talk to then. She'd had so much to do—with her job and nursing her mother. Then she'd quit her job, and she and Gracie moved closer to the approaching death as though partners in it. After they realized there was no way out, they'd talked openly and freely about what might happen, how it would be: a mystery.

Main Street was nearly deserted, the street lamps on. Christmas decorations, red aluminum bells and flocked pine, swung heavily in the wind. The street, so familiar, was quiet and empty and clear. It was how every day had been, in every season, since her mother had died. There was no more talking, not really—no one whose past she knew, who knew her.

Even when Mother had been so ill the talking stopped, Jean

hadn't felt alone. Old Doc Jonas, Reb's father, still practiced then. Gracie was one of his last patients: when the time came, just as he'd promised, he gave her drugs to stop the pain. Suddenly, it was as though all the consciousness she'd used to combat her sickness was now free to float forward and backward, witness to all that happened. Oh, Jean had felt things in those weeks that didn't seem Christian, things she'd never tell anyone. Most nights she slept on a cot beside Gracie's bed, and she'd have such dreams, all through the fitful hours, and wake exhausted. She thought she dreamed her mother's dreams, not hers. She'd empty the bedpan, straighten the sheets, give her mother the morphia—then lie down and plummet into a sleep she never owned. She saw her father standing outside a baroque locked door, begging to be let in. He hadn't had a thing to drink tonight, he promised, oh Gracie, this time he'd be gentle. Jean woke with her heart pounding in a rush of heat and panic. She'd check on her mother, whose thin body seemed pressed to the bed, oblivious.

It was a relief then to go downstairs and fix breakfast for Mitch, who by six had shaved and dressed and made coffee. It was a blessing to sit opposite him at the table and talk as though to an acquaintance. They talked about the concrete company, just started then by him and Clayton, or about some harmless gossip in the town. Sometimes, on those still-dark December mornings, they made love quickly in a downstairs bedroom, a small room behind the kitchen, where Mother had always kept household accounts. A tall wooden file cabinet stood sentinel beside the narrow bed; the drawers still held business papers from JT's lumber mill, and sales receipts from the Depression years, after the mill had failed and they'd scraped along selling milk and butter and eggs to townspeople and renting the upstairs to roomers. Jean would turn from those dark knobbed drawers and press herself tight against Mitch as though fighting his weight, and the weight of the sickness above them. The fighting took her in until kissing him was deep and hard and unfamiliar, like kissing a stranger with whom she was trapped, with whom she was drowning. Behind her eyelids she saw the face in the bed upstairs, and she was able to cry. She never realized she'd cried until afterward, when her throat and temples were wet. Mitch and she didn't speak about the crying, as though they'd made some agreement. All their agreements became silent ones. The four months they'd slept in the same bed, down the hall from Mother, seemed another life, and their four-day wedding trip to a hotel in Baltimore seemed long ago. Even then, what had they talked of? Mitch never spoke of his childhood, as most people did, or of the war. And Jean didn't ask about what came between. He'd been thirty-seven when they married—he'd had experiences, of course, judging by the crowd he'd run with—but those years weren't her business. Oh, what was it she wanted from him? What could she have?

Jean turned the Nash onto Gladys' narrow street. The aching nervousness she'd felt all week, with Christmas a tinsel backdrop, had eased. None of her questions had answers. She parked the car and let it run, sitting a moment in the comfortable warmth, and looked with a placid curiosity at the modest, snow-sheathed houses. The houses were lovely, lit with yellow, each one a shelter private and alive.

Jean closed the front door quickly, trying to keep the cold out, and stamped her feet on the rubber mat Gladys put over the rug in winter.

"Hello at last," Gladys said from her chair. She sat quietly, Jean's party dress on her lap. "I was just about to put out an alert for one Jeannie Hampson."

Jean turned to face her and brushed the snow from her shoulders guiltily. "I'm sorry I didn't have dinner started, Gladys."

"Doesn't matter. There'll be plenty of food at the VFW. You know how some of the wives show off at these parties." She smoothed the full black skirt of the dress over her knees like a coverlet. "You'd think they never got a good word from their husbands, and most of them don't."

It was irritating sometimes, the way Gladys talked. "Gladys, for Lord's sake," Jean asked her, "how would you know?"

"I sell women's dresses, that's how." Gladys was matter-of-fact. "They tell me everything, from start to finish, whether I want to know or not."

Jean took off her coat and tried to fluff her dark hair dry with her hands. "I'm glad I work for men at the State Road," she said. "They may be boorish sometimes, but at least I don't get yakked at."

Gladys smiled and held the dress up. "Jean, you'd better try this on so I can press the hem."

"Oh, you finished the hem?"

"Sure I did," Gladys said easily. "Didn't take a minute. Mitch said you'd gone to get thread, but I had a spool of black silk in my desk." She shook the dress out busily, but Jean saw the spool of thread on the arm of the chair. It was the same spool Jean had hidden; of course, Gladys had sat down and felt the small lump under the cushion. My God, she was impossible to deceive.

"Gladys," Jean began, "I didn't really go downtown. I—"

"Oh hush, it's no one's business where you went. You can't tell everyone what you do every minute or you'll have no peace at all."

The two women exchanged a look, and then Jean took the dress and held it against her chest. "I'm sure it's perfect," she said.

"You'll look wonderful. Black wool is so classic, and you have the complexion to wear it." Gladys smiled. "You can show off that little waist of yours while you still have it."

They heard Mitch in the hallway. The bathroom door closed and the spritz of the shower began.

"I'd better hurry." Jean stepped out of her wet shoes and stood for a moment on the heating vent. The furnace blower had clicked on and the floor grate was warm.

"Yes, you had. He'll have a fit if we aren't ready in half an hour." Gladys got up from the chair, rubbing her arms, and stood beside Jean over the heat. "Oh, I'm getting old. Arthritis is next, probably." She fished in the pocket of her wool sweater and held out a small white bag. "Remember that tube of Fire Red you asked me to order at the store? Here it is, just in time."

"Gladys, thank you." Jean was unaccountably, purely happy. "Really, thanks so much." She put her arm around the shorter woman and rested her face against Gladys' stiffly permed red curls. Gladys came to Jean's shoulder and smelled wonderfully of Tabu bath powder and cosmetics: twice a day, she rouged her cheeks with red lipstick and rubbed in the color with tissues. Mitch's proper Aunt Bess would say Gladys was painted, but Jean thought suddenly how perfect Gladys really looked, those red cheeks a brassy declaration of gumption, even in the middle of winter.

Gladys chuckled and hugged Jean's waist. "Here we are, two fools on a heat grate, 1949. Your mother is looking down and having a laugh on us."

"You think so?"

"Of course. Gracie was a Danner, from Pickens, and there's a special heaven for Danners."

"But it's not 1949 yet, not until midnight." Jean watched Gladys' profile. The round, lined face seemed delicate, the powdered skin colored carefully as a doll's.

"Well," Gladys sniffed, "if you want to be a stickler. You Danners are such sticklers."

"I'm a Hampson now," Jean said.

"You're a Hampson legally," Gladys corrected her, "like I'm a Curry. But you'll be a Danner all your life—look in the mirror. You look like all the Danner women, dark-haired, dark-eyed— beauties, every one of them, and such sticklers. Stubborn and mannered as hell. Danners could be poor as church mice and walk around like heiresses."

Jean felt herself smiling. "Gracie was like that, wasn't she? She used to say I'd have no self-respect if my posture wasn't perfect. Drove me nuts, lecturing about such things while we milked the cows."

"Are the two of you going to this party?" Mitch stood in the hallway, his hair still slicked and wet from the shower, knotting his tie. He smelled of Old Spice and pretended to scowl impatiently. Their collective joke was that he, the man of the house, made heroic efforts to keep the two women on an even keel.

"We thought we might go," Gladys said coolly, her brows raised, "if Prince Charming could ever let anyone else in the bathroom."

The three of them rode through the snow in the Nash, seated in their usual formation: Mitch driving, Jean in the middle, Gladys on the passenger side, her window open a crack to vent the smoke of her cigarette. The night was dark and the storm worsening; the car seemed to coast like a sled on the deepening snow of the unplowed streets. Electric candles were triangular dots of light in the windows of houses.

"People ought to leave Christmas decorations up all winter," Gladys said. "Makes the cold more cheerful."

"And the utility companies richer." Mitch pumped the brakes gently as the car swerved around a turn.

"Oh well," Gladys said contentedly, "if they don't get money one way, they'll get it another."

"You should have seen the VFW club in Washington during the war, when I was in that nurses' training program." Jean heard the animation in her own voice, then spoke more softly. "We girls went every weekend. That place was always lit up like a birthday cake—mostly with candles, so as not to waste energy. It was an old hotel, and the floors of the ballroom were marble."

The car was silent. Jean had completed a few months of training, then come home because of her mother's illness. If things had been different, she would have gotten the degree. Maybe she would have lived in a big city. How exciting, to think of Baltimore, Washington, maybe even New York, where she'd never been.

As though in response to Jean's thoughts, Gladys spoke up in her arbitrary fashion. "Being a nurse is no kind of life."

"Oh, I don't know," Mitch said.

Of course, he was talking about Red Cross girls he'd known in the war. They were brave, Jean supposed, and pretty; the men had all admired them. Did anyone, ever, admire a secretary? Well, she wouldn't be a secretary all her life, that was certain. Someday, she'd find a way to finish college. Now, in the gently moving car and snow-blurred dark, the future seemed far away.

"Everyone and his uncle will be at the VFW tonight," Gladys said. "People this town hasn't seen for years. It'll be a madhouse." She waited for her proclamation to take effect, then proceeded. "Marthella Barnett will be there. I wonder how Cora Jonas will like that."

"Hell, Gladys," Mitch said, "it was twenty years ago Mar-thella knew Reb. High school stuff."

"High school stuff is the stuff that lasts." Gladys straight-ened her wristwatch. "I don't care what anyone says."

Jean turned away from Gladys and looked at Mitch. "Didn't you go out with Marthella a little?" she asked quietly. "I mean, the summer we met."

"No, she was in town that summer for the first time in years, and I took her down to the dance. I never knew her so well—she'd been Reb's girl. She left Bellington clear back in '28, the year we graduated." Mitch shifted his weight on the seat and Jean felt his movement.

"*She* certainly never graduated," Gladys said. "Quite a story that was. She must be in her mid-thirties by now, and already divorced twice."

"Gladys," Mitch told her, irritated, "you have a mouth like a bell clapper."

Gladys smiled. "I say what I think, if that's what you mean."

"Hell, maybe everyone doesn't want to hear what you think." He slowed a little suddenly as they came to a stop sign, and the car slid to the left.

"If 'everyone' lives in my house," Gladys said, unruffled, "they're going to have to hear—though of course they don't have to listen."

"I wish you wouldn't argue before we even get to the party," Jean said.

"It's not an argument." Gladys chuckled. "This is how we have fun. Isn't that so, Mr. Hampson?"

"We're here." Mitch was parking the Nash. He looked at Gladys patiently and arched one eyebrow, then shook his head in a parody of fortitude. He put the car in reverse and turned to look back, throwing one arm along the seat behind Jean. The warmth of his body was muffled in his thick coat, but Jean smelled a scent of after-shave, a delicate musk of tobacco and soap. She let her face touch his shoulder as the car came to a stop. Mitch let the engine tremble a moment, then turned off the motor. Across the whitened street, the VFW house was softly illuminated. Snow fell across the swept plank floor of the wide porch, drifting softly and heavily. As Jean sat watching, the snow was suddenly buoyed on a gust of wind. Snowflakes whirled then with a feverish motion, so incredibly fast, like an animated swarm drawn to the light.

Reb met them at the door and bowed from the waist when he saw Gladys. "Why, Mrs. T. A. Curry."

"Oh, you old fool." Gladys passed him by with a wave of her hand, walking down the hallway toward the big kitchen.

Mitch lifted Jean's coat from her shoulders. She felt proud when he did such things; his manners were kind and old-fashioned. "Cora come along?" he asked over Jean's head.

"Sure." Reb smiled confidently. "She's in the kitchen helping Bess set out the food. Don't know why in hell they're setting it out already." He talked to Jean then, trying to include her. "People might want a few drinks first, dance a few times."

"Of course," Jean answered. "Let's go start the jukebox."

"That's the spirit." Reb took a drink from his flask. "But no jukebox tonight—we've got a big cabinet Victrola, and every Ellington and Dorsey record ever made. And the Crooner. Marthella brought the Crooner."

Mitch laughed. "No kidding? She brought all those records of hers?"

Jean smiled uncertainly and Reb touched her arm.

"Would you like a drink, Jean?"

"Just some wine, I think." She gave him a grateful look. Reb was good at smoothing situations; he seemed to see everything so squarely and easily. Maybe it was just part of doctoring. But Old Doc Jonas, Reb's father, had been very different. A bit silent and grave. He'd inspired a secretive confidence rather than ease. Ease, that was it. Reb's manner encouraged an ease that skated along over the tops of conversations and was evasive. Jean watched the two men joking and felt surprised at her own conclusion. But I like Reb, she thought, I really do. He seemed to perform his slight dishonesties for the sake of others, to give up something himself in the inclusive gestures, the arbitrarily friendly voice. Mitch wasn't like that: he was absolutely honest, to the point of being tactless and not getting along with people. Tonight he was in a good mood. She hoped Reb wouldn't influence him to drink too much.

"Cowboy," Reb said, "what'll it be? Have some good brandy here in my flask, or you can start on a fifth of Jack Daniels."

"I'll have to drink fast to catch up with you." Mitch winked at Jean.

She felt his hand, lightly, at her waist. He was so courteous in public; if only he wouldn't get tipsy. She felt shy of him then, a little scared—not of Mitch but of her own discomfort. Well, she'd just have a few drinks herself. After all, it was New Year's. She looked up at Mitch and said brightly, "I think I'll have some of Reb's brandy, he brags about it so."

"Fine," Mitch said in her ear, "but I think we'll mix it in a little water for you."

Yes, there, he was taking care of her. They walked across the hall to the parlor, a big room kept empty for dancing, and music was already playing.

"Jean, have you met Marthella?" Reb gestured toward the woman beside him and began pouring four glasses of brandy. "Cowboy, I insist on at least one toast. This is good, aged stuff, and perfectly mellow. If you try to water it for them, I'll deck you."

"Now, now," Marthella laughed nervously. "Not on a holiday."

She wasn't from good family, Jean thought. You could tell. Her clothes clung a little too tightly and were too bright, but she seemed nice enough, even a bit shy. Gladys and her gossip. "Marthella," Jean said, "hello again. I think I met you a couple of summers ago, probably right here in the parlor. A VFW dance."

"Yes, I remember." Marthella nodded. "But it sure isn't summer now. What a storm."

They stood a little awkwardly, sipping their drinks. Jean looked at the room; she'd helped decorate it that morning. The holly and red candles on the mantle looked beautiful, and the ceiling was hung with real mistletoe and red and green crepe paper.

"Well," Jean said, "I'm glad the crepe isn't red, white, and blue again. As late as last year, they wouldn't let us use Christmas colors."

"Probably smart." Reb sighed. "We may be in another war soon, with this Korean thing."

"I don't think so," Marthella answered. "Everyone is still recovering from the last one."

"Cheers to that," Mitch said.

The four of them smiled and stepped close to touch glasses.

They'd danced for hours, changing partners, joking, showing off. Empty bottles stood in a cluster near the Victrola. Mitch was a good, solid dancer, but Reb liked to try tricks and fancy moves. He swung Jean around in a circle; she laughed, and in the midst of her laughter felt totally relaxed with him, familiar. After all, she'd known him, known of him, all her life, and his father had been a presence in her house. Reb was almost a brother. Now he grabbed her hand and spun her back toward him effortlessly. His hands were like his father's hands, broad and square.

Jean looked down and the toes of his wingtip shoes were polished so bright she saw the reflection of her own slim ankles. When he snapped his fingers and pulled her smoothly near, he was smiling, his eyes were closed. She smelled his cologne. It was tangy, like candied fruit. Too sweet, meant to cover the smell of something else—hospitals, Jean supposed, or the bourbon he'd had before the party. Jean felt too warm, a little feverish.

"Reb," she said, stopping, "I just have to rest. I didn't realize I'd had so much brandy."

"That's what New Year's is for," he said.

She really had drunk too much. She'd go to the bathroom and pull herself together a little. As she turned toward the hallway, Reb got another partner and Jean saw Mitch and Marthella across the room, their heads inclined. They were holding hands. Jean walked quickly into the hall. Well, what if they were? They were old friends. You had to be mature about these things, and about dreams and apprehensions as well. Dreams didn't mean so much. Anyway, what sort of dream could she expect, falling asleep in a graveyard? And she'd been thinking about her father; it was true they'd been afraid of him sometimes.

That was better. Jean shut the bathroom door behind her, relieved. She'd have a headache tomorrow if she wasn't careful. Cold water would help, and then she'd stop drinking. She stepped to the big sink, lowered the stopper on its chain, and ran the cold water. She held her hands under the tap and chilled her wrists, then bent to splash her face. As the cold water touched her skin, sharp, comforting, she remembered the dream again clearly, and understood. Quiet Glade—she'd dreamed of the murders at Quiet Glade. Jean had been four or five; she remembered, growing up, Gracie's telling her how whole congregations of churches had driven out to the country after Sunday services one morning to see the bodies exhumed. A man had killed his family, buried them in the cellar, and confessed weeks later. It was the only such happening in anyone's memory, a sort of myth. Jean reached for the linen hand towel and blotted her wet face, then let the water drain. You could never tell what was in your mind. She was sure she hadn't really been there that day; her mother surely wouldn't have taken a tiny child to such a place. Why had she dreamed of it, up there in the snow? She dried her hands, feeling the rough fiber of the towel and recognizing sewn into it Bess Bond's monogram. Bess had lent her linens for the party. Jean folded the towel carefully, hung it back in place. The fabric was rich and fine and had a sheen; it was probably older than a lot of the girls who were dancing. Jean smoothed her dark hair in the mirror, then stopped primping and looked seriously at her own reflection. She was scared; that's why she'd had the dream. But why should she be afraid? She and Mitch had a chance. He was a good, responsible man—he'd never hit a woman the way Dad had hit Mother a few times, and the age difference was fifteen years, not almost thirty. Marry an older man, Jean and her girlfriends had told each other, not an *old* man. Jean smiled at their foolishness. She touched her ring, twisting it nervously, and saw how the diamond glinted. It was a small stone, but perfect; Mitch had been so careful to get her a nice one. She shouldn't be scared; she'd done the right thing. The Victrola clicked off then in the parlor and she heard the dancers arguing good-naturedly about what to play next.

After her mother had gotten sick, Jean had started going out almost exclusively with older men. When she was with them she felt she was wearing a sort of disguise, being her best, most responsible self. Convincing everyone that she was, at twenty-one, head of a household, nurse to her mother, a working woman. She belonged with older men, not kids her age. The funny thing was, once you knew the older men you realized they were just like the kids, only they had better jobs, more money, and were more polite. When they drank, they got sad instead of happy. She looked at herself again in the spotless bathroom mirror and shook her head; she probably saw things wrong. Mitch and Reb were plenty happy tonight. And it was uncharitable to look at things so hard; still, she didn't see as much to admire as she got older. Pointless, really, a lot of what happened. Didn't people have to do more than just endure? Didn't they have to be smart, as well, and know what things meant? Oh, she compared everyone to her mother: maybe that was what scared her. God, did she hate it— her mother's strength? It was what she loved most and what she hated. Her mother had fought for every minute, and here Jean stood in this bathroom, or on a street in the town, or in Gladys' kitchen, with all the years stretched in front of her. Oh, how had Gracie known so much? Even when JT was craziest, she'd seemed to value him in some strange way at the same time she held her own against him. It was how she'd been with the cancer, too: as though she respected her own assailant because it was part of her; she watched and didn't panic and was somehow guided. How? Where had it come from? In the parlor someone had put on a record. Laughter as an Ellington tune came on so loud the sound distorted—Marthella's laughter, Jean could tell. The volume was lowered a little then and a girl vocalist's sloe gin voice rolled out over the melancholy swing of the music.

Jean couldn't think anymore; she wanted to dance. She opened the door and shut off the light and stood in the dim hall-way. Straight ahead in the parlor Mitch was dancing with Mar-thella, jostled between two other couples. The others moved and Jean saw his hands cupped low on Marthella's red skirt, caressing her hips and moving up to touch the small of her back. He pulled her against him. Jean knew his touch exactly: hard and slow and firm. Oh, didn't they know everyone could see them? She turned away, her face burning, and walked down the hall toward the kitchen. She stopped then and leaned against the wall. Bess, Gladys, Cora: they'd all see her embarrassment if she walked in now. If she said something to Mitch later, he'd tell her she was only being prudish or that she hadn't seen what she saw. Well, she wouldn't say a word, but she wouldn't be coming back to one of these parties. *The things I tell my pillow, no woman should;* over the sound of the music, Jean heard the wind of the storm still blowing, and women talking in the kitchen. A scraping of chairs. Bess must be leaving.

Maybe Jean shouldn't be embarrassed. Cora certainly wasn't; she didn't seem to mind at all. Maybe Jean shouldn't either, but Mitch could damn well respect her and be discreet. Everyone was watching him with Marthella; Jean was ashamed but not really surprised. The truth was she'd never felt she owned him, that he was hers. He'd never belong to anyone the way some men belonged to women. Jean guessed she'd liked that in the beginning: his aloneness meant she could pay attention to other things. Well, here was the price. She'd have to pay it.

"Jean." Bess stood opposite her in the hall, her tall, thin form bundled in her heavy coat.

"Bess, you're going? We hardly got to say hello, with all the dancing. I'm just taking a rest."

Deliberately, they looked into each other's faces and didn't glance toward the parlor.

"Yes, it's late," Bess said, "and Katie has a bad cold. Clayton's not much of a nurse."

"But Katie's done awfully well this winter, hasn't she?"

"Well, she's twelve and says she's too old now to be a sickly child."

Bess touched Jean's arm, and her hand was dry and warm. Jean covered the hand with her own palm. Bess wasn't yet sixty but her hand was the hand of an old woman—soft, like worn silk: the structure of the bones beneath seemed delicate, sprung with tension, as though the whole of her upright carriage was an uncompromised act of will. Bess waited, allowing the moment of recognition, then moved her hand away.

"You know," she said, keeping her voice low, "he and Clayton have sunk all they have into this new business. Clayton has won

and lost before, but Mitch. . . ." She stood so close that no word
was mistaken. "Of course, they've got no work at all in this kind
of weather." She stepped back then and said, in a tone just loud
enough to be heard in the parlor, "I'll be going now, Jeannie."

"Yes, all right," Jean said, "I'll walk you out."

Bess leaned close again. "No need for that. Go sit down in the
kitchen and have some hot tea."


The kitchen was bright, the overhead light nearly glaring.
The women had washed all the dishes and serving platters, and
stacked the clean borrowed plates in baskets. Jean sat down at the
table, across from Gladys; now that the work was done and Bess
had gone, Gladys would probably have a couple of stiff drinks.

True to form, she poured herself a shot of bourbon as Jean
watched. "Join the clean-up crew." She smiled and nodded toward
the parlor. "I expect they're playing musical partners by now."
She sipped the bourbon cheerfully. "Just dancing and teasing,
Jean—I expect you'd benefit by not taking it all to heart."

"Gladys, why don't you hush." Jean put both her palms flat
on the old carved-up surface of the table. Kids had written their
initials for years on the old VFW table; her initials were probably
here, and Tom's, from high school.

Gladys looked over at Cora. "I think she means it. I'd best
shut up. Too much advice on New Year's can wreck the best
disposition."

"Oh, look," Cora answered, pointing to the wall clock. "It's
just midnight. Let's turn the radio up all the way." She leaned
toward both women, her eyes very bright, her expression joyous
and slightly too set. "Al Jolson always comes on just at the stroke
of twelve, 'Anniversary Song,' and tonight he's absolutely right
—it's 1949." She clapped her hands twice, like a child, and jumped
up from her chair to go to the kitchen counter.

"Straight ahead, Cora," Gladys said. She caught Jean's eye
and tapped her temple with a forefinger.

Jolson's booming voice filled the room. Amazing that the old
radio could play so loud. Violins sounded the slow strains of a
waltz, and a melancholy harp built a stair-step preface of chimes.
Jolson's voice, so deep at first it was almost non-melodic, began.

alone: *Oh, how we danced,* the *Oh* deep like the turning of a broad
dark knife, like a man in the dark surprised by his own sharp
pleasure. Cora's lilting, reedy voice rode along on Jolson's bari-
tone, and together they seemed to describe some fairy tale with
absolute belief. *The world. Was in bloom.* It was all so silly. Jean
lifted Gladys' glass to her lips and drank the bourbon down. The
liquor tasted hot, biting. Jean stood a little shakily and walked into
the pantry; if she had to hear the rest of this song, she wanted to
be by herself.

Yes, she could breathe in here. The small room was cold and
lit with an odd, restful light—snow light, and the glow of a street
lamp outside the one window. The walls of the narrow space were
lined with floor-to-ceiling cupboards, old-fashioned ones painted
white, and they were nearly empty. The glass of the cupboard
doors looked lovely and clean, a series of shining windows, one
measured shape after another. It really took Gracie a long time
to die, Jean thought. She hadn't died until she'd taught Jean
everything, but what good was what she knew? No one spoke this
language; it was language you knew in your blood and learned to
hear. Jean stood listening, looking at the bar of kitchen light
thrown across the linoleum from the half-open pantry door; from
here the song was almost pretty. She heard Gladys come in behind
her.

"This isn't a real veterans' club," Jean said. "It's someone's
house they nailed a sign to."

"You shouldn't drink in your condition," Gladys said quietly,
"and you certainly shouldn't drink so quickly."

"What?" Jean steadied herself, one hand on the countertop,
and raised her eyes. In the glass cupboard door she saw her
reflection hover over a single yellow plate.

"You do know what's the matter, don't you?" Gladys' round,
powdered face was earnest.

"No, I don't know anything." Jean smiled. You had to smile,
didn't you? The bourbon was warm in her stomach now, like a core
of heat.

"You're about to know," Gladys said. "I've known for a week,
but I didn't suppose it was my business to tell you."

Oh, what was she talking about? Well, it didn't matter; they could talk about anything, just so long as Jean could stay here in this small, private place with its neatly painted, abandoned cupboards. Aloud, she said, "It's just that I've been so tired lately."

"Of course you have. You're pregnant."

The wind of the storm outside continued to rise and fall. Jean saw snow through the square pantry window, and the round bulb of the street light. "It's true," Jean said quietly. "I must be. I am."

Gladys nodded. She took off her sweater and put it across Jean's shoulders. "There," she said.

Tomorrow she would tell him. Tonight it was too late, they'd been at the party so long. When he lay down beside her, she was nearly asleep, dreaming vacantly of telling him. Unformed shapes and sounds surrounded the words as storm winds rattled the windows of Gladys' guest room. Boards creaked as he walked across the cold floor to the bed. She knew without looking that he was naked and had put his wool robe over their quilt like a blanket. His skin was moist and warm from the shower; as she turned to him he smelled like someone just come from a pool of heat, and the whiskey on his breath was a faint, sweet residue tinged with bitterness. He touched her forehead with his mouth and his warm shoulder pressed the side of her face. Nothing mattered for one moment but this: she took his weight and held him. He moved on top of her slowly and kept one hand under her; the heat of his hand ran in her spine like current. She looked at the ceiling and imagined on its surface the imprint of a dark, delicate body, a body that vanished by degrees. She strained to keep the image in sight, but her eyes closed involuntarily as she moved against him, blind, moving with her own breath until the shadow was closer, nearer, deep inside her, its lines and boundaries blurred. The body disappeared like a shadow or a wish and that was how she gave herself up, all her words gone like sparks burned up in a darkness. She felt his body tense then and brought his mouth to hers; he cried out and the vibration of his voice trembled in her throat, a rush of air dark and full. The sound passed through her, vanishing rapidly.

# CORAL SEA
## Mitch, 1950

This was the Gulf of Papua, the Coral Sea: he knew by the feel of the air and the emptiness of the horizon. Two years he'd heard New Guinea tides, until he didn't hear them at all but lived with the sound like a heartbeat; how had he arrived here again? The sea was flat as a transparent plate, the water still, glowing with a metallic sheen like it was dead and had a clear light under it. The sea had gone strange; Katie was in his arms and he told her to try it again, this time he would take smaller steps. Her face was robust and healthy like before the war; he understood then that the war hadn't happened yet; he was here before the war or it was going on somewhere else. Least he could do before he left was teach her to dance; Clayton was too old to teach a girl to dance right, though he stood watching them at a short distance, beach sand blowing about him like a grainy smoke. That wind was goddamn fierce, a wonder the sea was so calm. He could barely hear Katie's piping voice above the loudness of wind and clattering leaves—sound of leaves crazy since the beach was barren, nothing anywhere. Sand swirled around them, obscuring their feet as they turned: a waltz was always the simplest way to learn. She was eager, excited, her body so light she had trouble keeping her feet on the ground. He had to hold her down as he led and circled, careful not to tread on her shoes. Misstepping once as she drifted upward, he listened for the beat and realized there was only the wind they danced to; that's why Clayton was nodding and looking out to sea. Weather was coming up fast, wind blowing so loud and hard he couldn't look and he turned, alone, shielding his eyes. He looked seaward then and saw Clayton wading in, holding Katie like they were honeymooners, Katie being a kid and kicking her feet, dragging her hand in the water starlet-style. Far out Mitch saw the sea lifting, the whole edge curling and sucking in, piling up and rumbling. He yelled at them, wind crushing the words back. But Clayton turned and Katie was Jean, her black hair blowing. They looked at Mitch, trying to hear, and past them the wave kept building. Jesus, the weight of that hard water: he heard it rattling savagely onto glass, a drenching rain he could smell. Hard rain, sharp and cold, and when he opened his eyes he saw water lashing the windows. He sat up in bed and listened for the baby, but the house was quiet and the lights in the hall were out. Why was she up if she wasn't feeding the baby? The room was drafty; she'd left a window open in the cold March night, and rain had wet the sill and the floor. He got up and closed the window, his skin prickling at the cold, and walked through the L-shaped hallway to the kitchen.

One small light was burning, and she stood there in her robe, pouring milk into a saucepan.

He leaned against the doorjamb, hearing the rain surround the house. "Baby wake up?" he asked her.

"No." She stirred the milk with a spoon. The burner under the pan was bright red and threw a glow against the enamel surface of the stove.

"It's three in the morning," he said. "What the hell is wrong with you?"

Her voice was weak. "I'm pregnant again." She wiped her eyes with the back of one hand and looked into the pan.

He walked nearer and touched her shoulder. The side of her

face was wet, and her throat. "What's wrong with that, now?" he said more gently. "We're married, aren't we?"

"But Danner's only six months old, and you were just saying tonight how slow it is at the plant, and with all the bills from this house—"

"Things will pick up at the plant. Things always pick up in the spring, and it's March already." Mentally, he calculated; he would probably have to fire one man and go out on jobs himself. Damn, he should never have told her the state of things. "You're not to worry. We can afford another baby."

The milk was steaming and she pulled the pan from the stove, one hand at the small of her back. "We have to insulate the attic before another winter, and we just bought the new furniture, and you've picked out a car. We're almost falling behind now."

"The car will wait. If we tune up the Nash, it'll go a while. And I'll do the insulation myself, hire a man from the plant to help. Maybe even Clayton—get the old guy up there to do an honest day's work."

She sighed, moving to get a glass from the cupboard. "Don't talk silly," she said, as though he were serious. "Clayton's not in shape to—"

"Clayton will be all right," Mitch said, his voice sharper than he'd intended. He lowered his tone. "I told you, he went down to this same place once a long time ago, in the thirties, and didn't touch a drop for nearly fifteen years after. When he comes back, he'll be fine." Mitch sat down in a kitchen chair, the chair creaking as he leaned forward. He touched the table and followed the wavery grain of the wood with his fingertips as the rain intensified, pounding the concrete porch in back. Had he pulled those damn porch chairs into the breezeway last night? He'd thought to enlarge the porch in summer and put a roof over it. Well, later, and better for two kids than one. Now only the concrete—if business improved enough—and a fence around it for a good large playspace, keep them out of the road and the fields. Those fields got so tall in summer and autumn; if kids wandered in you wouldn't find them at all. Aloud, he said, "Clayton will be back at work in two weeks, then you'll see I'm right."

She stood holding the warm glass in both hands. "I'm sure you're right."

"Except for Katie's getting sick during the war, he might never have started again. Just came on slow after that."

"They sure kept it quiet he was going away."

"Bess keeps everything quiet. Have to in this town. People always looking for something to gabble about."

They were silent, looking out the kitchen windows. The rain was so thick the narrow road and the fields opposite weren't visible. Even through the walls of the house, Mitch could feel the cold of the water. He heard the rapid-fire pelting of hailstones. So it would turn colder; hail was a sure sign of spring snows. That would keep jobs spare for weeks more. Maybe he should do the insulation now, borrow a little money and go ahead while things were slow.

Jean unlocked the thick breezeway door. "I'm cold and then I'm hot, like before with Danner. I should have known sooner, just from these sweats. Mind if I open the door? I have to have some air." The door swung open and the sound of the sleet rain swept in.

For a moment he thought she was going to walk out into the covered breezeway to the edge of the dark. "Don't get chilled," he said, almost rising from his chair, feeling damned stupid at the flash of fear in his body—not for her exactly, but because the rain was so wild and suddenly present.

She seemed unaware of him. "It's been a long time since we've had such rain," she said, staring into the storm.

He sat back down, settling himself. "You've been to Reb already? When are you—"

"He's not sure, October or November."

"That's just fine," Mitch said. "Some time to put money back. And jobs are always thick in the fall, until November anyway." He kept his tone certain and reached for the pack of cigarettes he'd left on the table after supper. She stood nearly motionless, listening to the storm. Under the pounding of the rain, he heard, faintly, the baby crying: an insistent wailing muted to a shadow of its strength. He waited for Jean to hear, watching her. Her hair and eyes were so dark; she looked pretty in the red robe, and young, without the bright lipstick she wore.

Peering into the dark, she started, pulled back from the cold, and drew the neck of the robe close. "There, Danner is awake." Jean pushed the door shut. "It's raining so hard—flash flood rain."

"The creek will have swollen, but it doesn't matter. That's why I built on a rise."

"She sounds scared," Jean answered, walking quickly back through the house.

"Just hungry," Mitch said, but Jean was too far away to hear over the rain. He got up, lighting his cigarette, to lock the door. Standing, he pulled it open and smelled the full, cold smell of the storm. He hesitated, then walked into the breezeway, trying to see past the rain. The fabric of his pajama pants was thin and he felt almost naked, hugging his arms to his chest. If he squinted, changed how he was looking, he could make out the periphery of the first field and the fence posts. The bulk of the big hill was there but invisible; still, at its foot, he saw a whiteness that glimmered gently in the dense gray shadows of the rain. Puzzled, he walked farther and felt rainy vapor as he leaned almost into darkness. Yes, the stream had already left its banks, and the spreading water was deep enough to dapple like a lake.

# THE HOUSE AT NIGHT
Danner, 1956

In the humid nights her mother let her sleep under one thin sheet, an old one worn soft from many washings, and in the dark of her child's bedroom she turned and sweated until the sheet wrapped her small body like a sour cocoon. Night sounds in the house were shot with lambent silence: rotary blades of the stilled electric fans gathered a fine dust behind the ribs of their metal cages. *Once you're asleep you won't know how hot it is, go to sleep, fans cost money to run;* crickets sounded in the close dark, their throbbing continuous as the running of a high-pitched musical engine. No breeze stirred to break their sounds; Danner drifted, almost sleeping; each shrill vanished faster than the last. She heard faintly her brother breathe and whimper; in these summer days the artificial disruption of school was forgotten and the fifteen months of age separating them disappeared; they existed between their parents as one shadow, *the kids,* and they fought and conspired with no recognition of separation. Doors opened now onto the same unlit hallway; near

Billy's room the hallway turned, lengthened past the bathroom
and emptied into their parents' bedroom. There the high Grandmother Danner bed floated like an island above its starched white
skirt; the row of closet doors slid on their runners, a confusing line
of illusions; and the two big bureaus shone. The bank of windows
was so high no one could see anything but the branches of the
lilacs, branches that now in the August night looked furred with
black and didn't stir. By day the leaves were a deep and waxen
green. *Jean, come and get these kids, don't either one of you
ever stand near the driveway when you see I'm backing the car
out, goddamn it, I'll shake the living daylights out of you:* what
it meant was the State Road construction and the jackhammer,
shaking a grown man's body as he held the handle and white fire
flew from the teeth of the machine. Endless repair of the dusty
two-lanes progressed every summer, but the roads were never
finished; they kept men working who had no other work and
Danner liked to watch; at night she saw those men in the dark
corners of her room, tall shadows with no faces. *Even if there
aren't prisoners anymore the workmen are nearly the same
thing,* and they did look different, dangerous, though they wore
the same familiar khaki work clothes her father wore to work at
the plant. *Your father and Clayton own the concrete company
—they don't work for a wage, do you understand what I'm
saying?* The workmen were from Skully or Dogtown and their
families got assistance, a shameful thing; in those shabby rows of
houses on mud roads they kept their babies in cardboard boxes.
But that was just a story, Mitch said; they were trying to get
along like anyone. *You'd say that about any man who worked
on a road, wouldn't matter if he was a lunatic,* and Jean turned
back to the stove, always; she stood by the stove, the kitchen
cabinets, the sink, the whole house moored to earth by her solid
stance, just as the world outside went with Mitch in the car. He
carried the world in and out in the deep khaki pockets of his
workman's pants. When Danner and Billy were with him and the
road crews were out, Mitch waited with no complaint for the
flagman's signal and kept the windows rolled down. Yellow dust
filled the car and caked everything with a chalky powder. Big
machines, earth-movers and cranes, turned on their pedestals

with a thunderous grinding as two or three shirtless men pulled thick pipes across the asphalt with chains. Mitch held both children on his lap behind the steering wheel, the three of them crushed together in a paradise of noise. Jackhammers and drills were louder than the heat, louder than sweat and the shattered ground and the overwhelmed voices of the men. Mitch smoked and talked to the foreman, yelling each sentence twice while the children coughed from the dust and excitement. Jean made them stay in the back seat if they had to stop near the construction; she nodded politely to the flagman, kept the car windows rolled up in the stifling closeness *just another minute,* and locked all the doors. At home they weren't allowed to lock doors: *children are safe at home, you should never be doing anything you don't want Mama to see,* but Danner and Billy closed themselves secretly into adjacent closets and stayed there until the dark scared them, tapping messages with their fists on the plyboard between them. Pressed back against clothes and stacked shoe boxes, Billy wore a billed khaki cap like his father's and Danner kept a navy blue clutch purse her mother no longer used; it smelled of a pressed powder pure as corn, and the satin lining was discolored. Danner unzipped it and put her face in the folds; she held her breath just another minute and that made everything lighten: the fields surrounding the house were full of light, scrub grass grew tall, and the milkweed stalks were thick as wrists. Wild wheat was in the fields and the crows fed, wheeling in circular formations. Milk syrup in the weeds was sticky and white; the pods were tight and wouldn't burst for weeks. Where did the crows go at night? They were dirty birds waiting for things to die, Danner was not to go near them; when the black night came she was in her bed to wake in the dark and pretend she saw the birds, rising at night as they did at noon, their wingspan larger, terrifying, a faint black arching of lines against the darker black; even the grasses, the tangled brushy weeds, were black. Danner heard the house settle, a nearly inaudible creaking, ghostly clicking of the empty furnace pipes; her mother, her father, walking the hall in slippers. They walked differently and turned on no lights if it was late. Danner lay listening, waiting, fighting her own heavy consciousness to hear and see them as they really were. Who were they? The sound of her father was a wary lumbering sound, nearly fragile, his heaviness changed by the slippers, the dark, his legs naked and white in his short robe, the sound of his walking at once shy and violent. Danner heard him ask one word and the word was full of darkness: *Jean?* At night her mother was larger, long robe dragging the floor, slide of fabric over wooden parquet a secretive hush. Danner heard her mother up at night. Doors shut in the dark. The bathroom door, click of a lock. Hem of the long robe gliding, a rummaging in cabinets too high for the kids to reach. Jean finds the hidden equipment and pulls out the white enamel pitcher; the metal is deathly cold, the thin red hose coiled inside is the same one she uses, sterilized before and after, to give the children enemas. "Younger than Springtime" is the song she sings when she rocks Danner to sleep, the child at seven nearly too big to be held like a baby, earaches and sore throats Billy will catch next, and the two of them awake till midnight. She rocks them both at once and reads a thick college text for the classes she takes one at a time. She memorizes everything as though she were a blank slate; next year when Billy's in school she'll do practice teaching and get the certificate, there's never enough money and they meet the bills because she plots and plans, and the smell of her throat and neck as the cane-bottomed rocker creaks is a crushed fragrance like shredded flowers. Danner is the one who won't sleep; she smells her mother and the scent is like windblown seeding weeds, the way the side of the road smells when the State Road mowing machines have finished and the narrow secondary route is littered with a damp verdant hay that dries and yellows. Cars and trucks grind the hay to a powder that makes more dust, swirling dust *softer than starlight;* Danner hears Jean's voice as one continuous sound weaving through days and nights. *Pretty is as pretty does, seen and not heard, my only darling, don't ever talk back to your mother, come and read* Black Beauty, *a little girl with a crooked part looks like no one loves her,* and she cuts Danner's flyaway brown hair to hang straight from the center with bangs, a pageboy instead of braids; that way it takes less time. The chair creaks and Danner is awake until Jean lies in bed with her and pretends she'll stay all night. She calls Danner Princess, Mitch calls her Miss, Billy is called My

Man; *who's my best man?* Danner watches Jean pick him up; he's still the smaller one, hair so blond it's white. He stiffens laughing when his mother burrows her big face in his stomach, and he drinks so much water in the summer that he sloshes when he jumps up and down. Runs in and out of the house all day to ask for more and drinks from the big jug. *How can he have such a thirst? Lifting that heavy jug by himself, looks like a little starving Asian with that round belly;* at five he shimmies to the top of the swing-set poles, a special concrete swing-set their father has brought from the plant and built in the acre of backyard down by the fence and the fields. The poles are steel pipes twenty feet high, sunk into the earth and cemented in place; the swings are broad black rubber hanging by thick tire chains. Billy climbs the tall center pole and the angled triad of pipe that supports the set at either end, but Danner prefers the swings, a long high ride if she pumps hard enough, chains so long the swings fly far out; she throws her head back, mesmerized, holding still as the swing traces a pendulum trajectory. Locusts in the field wheedle their red clamor under her; locusts are everywhere in summer, in daylight; she and Billy find their discarded shells in the garden, a big square of overgrown weeds in a corner of the lot. In the tumbledown plot they dig out roads for Billy's trucks, and the locust shells turn up in the earth: they are hard, delicate, empty. Transparent as fingernails, imprinted with the shape of the insect, they are slit up the middle where something has changed and crawled free. Danner throws the shells over the fence. Billy smells of mud and milk, kneels in dirt and sings motor sounds as he inches the dump trucks along. They make more roads by filling the beds of the bigger plastic trucks, pushing them on their moving wheels to the pile of dirt in the center; when they've tunneled out a crisscross pattern of roads, they simply move the dirt from place to place, crawling in heat that seems cooler when they're close the soil, making sounds, slapping the sweat bees that crawl under their clothes and between their fingers. The stings, burning pinpricks, swell, stay hot, burn in bed at night. Danner sucks her hands in her sleep, and the lights are out, the calls of the night birds are faint, and the dream hovers, waiting at the border of the fields; the dark in the house is black. The bathroom light makes a triangular glow on the hallway floor; the glow hangs in space, a senseless, luminous shape, and disappears. The bedroom door is shut, a lock clicks. Danner lies drifting, hears the furtive sound of the moving bed, the brief mechanical squeak of springs, and no other sound at all but her father's breath, harsh, held back. All sounds stop then in the black funnel of sleep; Danner hears her mother, her father, lie silent in an emptiness so endless they could all hurtle through it like stones. Jean sighs and then she speaks: *Oh, it's hot,* she says to no one. Danner sinks deep, completely, finally, into a dream she will know all her life; the loneliness of her mother's voice, *Oh, it's hot,* rises in the dream like vapor. In the cloudy air, winged animals struggle and stand up; they are limbed and long-necked, their flanks and backs powerful; their equine eyes are lucent and their hooves cut the air, slicing the mist to pieces. The horses are dark like blood and gleam with a black sheen; the animals swim hard in the air to get higher and Danner aches to stay with them. She touches herself because that is where the pain is; she holds on, rigid, not breathing, and in the dream it is the horse pressed against her, the rhythmic pumping of the forelegs as the animal climbs, the lather and the smell; the smell that comes in waves and pounds inside her like a pulse.

# MACHINE DREAMS
## Billy, 1957

Every weekday they went to class; his mother's hands held the letter cards, and she kept her book in front of her so all the kids around the table could see. She had to look at the pictures upside down but she seldom looked because she *knew them by heart:* that meant she had them in her mind, the same way Billy remembered the cement mixers from the concrete company. He wished he could go to the concrete company with his father every day, the way he went to phonics class. Other kids didn't go to school in the summer; Billy knew he and Danner went because their mother was the teacher. Phonics class wasn't really school; it was only two hours a day, not like school he would start in the fall. Then school would be his job, Mom had told him, he would be gone all day like Mitch was gone to the plant, and he would work just as hard at school as his father did on the trucks and in the office with Uncle Clayton. In a year Billy would be reading entire books, like Danner did now; didn't he want to know what words said? Billy didn't care so much;

words were black and hard and flat. But he liked to hear words,
especially the way his mother said them in class. Rhymes were
words and words were letters: letters made the sounds in the
rhymes. There were numbers in rhymes but no numbers in words:
he didn't know why. *Six, seven, go to heaven;* Billy would be
almost seven to start school because last year his birthday was
*not in time.* Billy imagined the birthday far off, alone in the dark
until time traveled toward it. But that was good, his mother had
said, he'd have a head start. So school was like a race.

They were the only class using the school. When they went
there, the building was empty and full of sunlight. The other
rooms were locked, but Billy could see in through the glass panes
in the doors: the desks weren't in even rows but sat jammed
together in a corner. The big reading tables were covered with
sheets, and the shelves were bare. In his mother's room the desks
were in straight rows, and the one table was kidney-shaped, not
really a circle. Twenty kids could all see each other around it and
still have room for notebooks. But there were only eight kids and
no one had a notebook but Danner, who already knew everything
and was only in the class to make enough students.

They played games. Phonics had to be fun because it was
summer. Everyone put their heads down and shut their eyes,
listening for the *a* sound. Billy smelled, near his face, the piney
furniture polish Mom had used to clean the table because the
janitor *did things halfway.* Anything worth doing was worth
doing well, his mother said, and she said it in the same voice she
used for phonics words. Now she was talking and Billy watched
the linoleum floor between his feet. *Apple, animal, atom.* What
was atom? Someone had gouged little holes in the spotted linoleum with a sharp pencil. Under the table, Danner put her san-
daled foot on Billy's shoe. He raised his eyes and Danner was so
close all he saw was her face, so still she seemed to be sleeping,
but she raised one arm at all the right words. Her eye didn't move
under its smooth lid; Billy knew if he touched her there he'd feel
something flutter, alive on its own. Their mother had told them:
the eye is made of water but the water is hard. Hard water. Heads
up. "Listen," she said now in her teacher's voice. "All together."
And they chanted:

*I went away*
*on a trip.*
*In my giant*
*trunk I packed*

"What?" his mother asked. "Billy, a word beginning with *a.* "
"Animal," Billy said.

In the attic Billy's father had a giant trunk. The trunk was from the war. Mitch had taken a trip to the war; Billy knew: there was an animal in the trunk. He'd seen the animal in his mind but he couldn't quite see all of it. Only it was hard and shining and sharp, and the animal wasn't alive. That's why it could stay in the trunk; it was very old and didn't have to breathe. Billy thought the animal was all folded up in the steel trunk, but once Mom had let Billy follow her into the attic, up the long ladder. She let him open the trunk; she had to help him, and when they lifted the heavy lid the trunk was almost empty. It was deep, and stained inside where water had gotten in. The trunk had been somewhere else; now the stains were dry. Billy touched there and the paper was crackly. Don't, his mother had said. Then she found the string to pull and the light bulb above them shone its weak glare. There were things in the very bottom of the trunk: a brown briefcase zipped shut, a green leather scrapbook Mom wouldn't let him open, a folded map. His father's army hat.

*I went away*
*on a trip.*

Billy pleaded; she held it up and said it was a lieutenant's hat. The hat was khaki like Mitch's work clothes, so soldiers were like the men at the plant. But the hat smelled pungently of moth balls and was a strange shape, hard on top, and round as a plate. On the front above the stiff bill and leather strap was a heavy gold pin. Billy touched its sharp prongs and recognized it: the animal, wings spread to fly.

"Danner? Another *a.* "
"Arrow," Danner said. "No, Atlantic. That's the ocean."
"You can't take the ocean on a trip," someone said.

The animal was hard like a jewel, a secret come back. Billy touched the pin to his lips and breathed. Mom took the hat away. That was an eagle, she said, to show who was American while the soldiers were away. But who else was away? Many soldiers, the world was in the war.

"I need everyone's eyes," his mother said. "Watch what I draw on the board." She was wearing her blue and white skirt and one of the white blouses she ironed at night, and the long white chalk in her hand made a squeak like claws. She drew cars that looked like trucks and put letters under them. "Only the ones with *a*'s are real ambulances," she said. "Raise your hand if you see one with an *a.*" In the attic she'd leaned over to say near Billy's face, *move away and I'll shut this up.* Her perfume smelled like warm soap in the dry, cold air from the trunk.

Ambulance was a dark car. Danner drew the first cross to show how. It was a cross like the one at church where the minister stood; their mother erased to show she meant a Red Cross, not a church cross. In church Danner was in a play; she was the lame boy who walked to the angel, down the long red aisle between the pews. Red Cross meant doctors who made people well, but Billy hated doctors and he thought it was dark in an ambulance, dark like the church was dark after they turned off the lights and lit candles. His father and Clayton said church was *a racket*, they took money from you all your life and when you died they said a few words. What words were those? *Great words I'm sure*, the men had laughed, and Clayton was not just an uncle but a great uncle, that's why he was old and lost his hair. *God is great* was a prayer Danner learned at school, and the night of the play had been Christmas; afterward Danner got sick and shivered. She said the dark church made her stomach hurt and she got cold when the angel touched her. That was silly, their mother said, Danner knew the angel was only Ann Gottfried, a high school girl who wanted to be a minister. But Danner had to take a hot bath to get warm, and Mitch let their dog Polly sleep under Danner's bed instead of in the kitchen; he said the Methodists were good at shaming children. In the big dim church, Danner really had looked lame; there were shadows on the red aisle from the candles. At the altar where the angel waited, there were so many candles it

was like day in one small place. Danner was *fanciful* and it
wouldn't hurt her to practice her sounds over summer, then help
Billy at home.

His mother was erasing the board. Chalk dust made a cloud
around her fingers, and the day was warm.

Tomorrow there was no class at school or at home because
it was the Fourth of July and there would be fireworks. His father
would barbecue chicken on the grill and then they would set off
their own fireworks instead of driving into town to see the Armory
show. Mitch had rockets and Japanese lanterns that exploded tails
of sparks. Gladys, his mother's friend, would come for supper and
bring the sparklers that Aunt Jewel always sent home from Ohio.

His mother shucked the corn into a plastic bucket on the
porch, but the yellow silk fell around her feet. Gladys stood beside
her, shaking clods of dirt from the fresh-pulled onions. The garden wasn't really a garden anymore; Gladys said Jean and Mitch
were no farmers except to kids and green onions, which could
grow anywhere. Gladys wore red shoes that were brighter than
her hair, and Billy watched both women through a curtain of
wavering heat. He stood near the barbecue while Mitch cooked.
Mitch never cooked except outside at barbecues, when the grill
was a simple machine rolled out on small wheels, and the metal
rack cranked high or low over coals white-hot because fire had
*burned to the center.*

The coals were flaky and pale as dirty snow, and they lay in
the cradle of the drumlike pit. The chicken crackled and his father
stood still, holding the long fork, his work cap tilted back, one
hand on his hip. He was silent and smoked his cigarette. Billy
waited beside him but Danner had to set the table, a big wooden
picnic table Mitch had been given by the State Road Commission
after a road job. The table had long benches and thick legs bolted
in the shape of an X. In winter it sat in the snow, but every
summer Radabaugh came out from the plant and helped Mitch
move the table onto the porch. The men would lift it, staggering
a little, and when they set the weight down Billy felt a tremor in
the concrete floor of the terrace. The jolt of weight seemed to
please the men; they laughed and shook their heads. Then Mitch

would bring a beer for Radabaugh. Both men sat down and drank
from one bright can, their hands splayed out on the rough wood
of the table. Billy sat with them and Radabaugh always gave him
a drink of the cold, bitter beer. Billy would swallow, serious, his
face expressionless, but Radabaugh grinned anyway and said Big
Man was going to be a Cowboy like Old Mitch, nothing Jean could
do about it. Soon the men would go back to the plant, and Billy
knew his mother would come outside; she put a slick red oilcloth
over the tabletop so no one would get splinters from the old
boards. The oilcloth was as bright as Gladys' shoes or Gladys'
painted toenails. Gladys called the table *a healthy issue* and when
they all sat down there was plenty of room on the benches. The
food steamed and the chicken was hot and reddish on the platter
Mitch had filled. Mom said Gladys was like family since she was
Aunt Jewel's mother, and Billy felt strange eating outside. Sometimes Danner or Billy wouldn't eat and had to sit with full plates
past the dinner hour, watching the day go dark through the screen
of the kitchen door. The green of the ragged grass slanted down-
hill to the tall wire fence and the fields until green turned gray in
the secretive dusk. Now Gladys passed the food while she talked
to Billy's mother.

"Lately your brother wants to be a wholesale shoe salesman," Gladys said. "Jewel told him he could get himself a van and
drive shoes all over Ohio, she wasn't moving again. And if they
split up over shoes, so be it."

Mitch touched the edge of his plate with his fingertips and
looked at Gladys. "It's real trouble trying to find work these
days", he said. "Sounds to me like Jewel might need a good shaking."

"That's a Hampson for you," Gladys said. "I have a mind to
get up from this table right now."

"Gladys, I didn't say he should knock her out."

"If my daughter needs shaking," Gladys said, "I'll do the
shaking. Not some man. Men have got no excuse to beat on
women. I'll tell you, a man might hit me once, but he wouldn't
know where to find me to hit me again."

Mitch smiled. "Gladys, if you pushed him to hitting you, what
makes you think he'd want to find you?"

Billy watched his mother. She was looking at her plate, and she spoke in a quiet, angry voice directed at the center of the table. "Jim wouldn't ever hit Jewel," she said. "He used to have to stand between Mother and Dad when Dad would come in drunk. Now, will you both stop this kind of talk. The kids are right here listening."

"Let them," Gladys said. "Danner and Billy, do you hear your father?"

"Hell," Mitch swore. He put his fork down and pushed the salt and pepper shakers to one side of the table. "I don't think either of you women has been much mistreated," he said. "If I was up there at the Sunset Inn right now with every other man from along this road, you might have reason to complain. Am I right, Billy?" He winked and touched Billy's hair. His hand was big and rough.

"Mitch, if you'd rather be up there, go right ahead. Your son will eat your share."

"No chance," Gladys said. "Mitch cooked this chicken and he's going to eat it. Besides, those men will be splitting each other's skulls when they get roused up tonight. Talk about hitting."

"Why, they're nothing but a bunch of damn yokels," Mitch agreed. "You take your life in your hands in the joints around here. They get out of the mines and they're drinking from first light to last."

Gladys buttered her bread. Her dentures made delicate noises when she chewed. "God knows those miners have reason to drink," she said. "They live thankless lives. When I used to own the shop, they'd come in at Christmas to buy a store dress for their wives."

"Miners make good money," Mitch said, "if they didn't drink most of it."

Gladys sighed. "Well, what would any of us do without the few pleasures we have? People go through times when they'd shoot themselves in the head if it weren't for booze."

"Gladys, for Lord's sake." Billy's mother rolled her eyes at him. She always told Billy and Danner not to listen to half of what Gladys said.

"It's true," Gladys continued. "And some of those people are good people. I've known Clayton Bond to take a few drinks."

Mitch leaned toward Gladys over the table. "Gladys, that's a damn lie. Clayton hasn't touched a drop in years."

"I didn't say he drinks." Gladys smoothed her napkin over her lap. "I said I've known him to."

"Do you mean Uncle Clayton?" Danner asked.

"There, are you satisfied?" Their mother put her silverware down, and her fork clattered on her plate.

"Little pitchers," Gladys said softly. "But it doesn't hurt them to know things."

"I think it does, and I want you to be still."

But Gladys gazed out past the table, over Billy's head. "Clayton is a good soul," she said. "Bess is the iron in that family. He had some hard times."

"Who hasn't?" Billy's mother started to get up from the table.

"Everyone does," Gladys said. "Everyone at this table will."

"We could be a lot worse off. Gladys, come in and help me fix the shortcake."

Mitch was chuckling. "Gladys," he said, "it's a good thing we've got those firecrackers. They're about the only thing that could drown you out when you're wound up."

"I guess you're right," Gladys said. "Now I've got to talk twice as fast to get Jean to forgive me."

Mitch and Gladys were smiling. Billy watched his mother stack dirty dishes, and her tone was steely. "Can we talk about something else now?" she said.

"Yes, Jean," Mitch said. "What would you like to talk about?"

Gladys lifted her napkin to her face and wiped her mouth. "Talk nice to her, Mitch. She's going to be up saving you money tonight, making school clothes for these kids. Why do you think she's got me out here? I bet you've already got those patterns pinned, don't you Jean. And your potato salad was delicious, as usual."

There was silence at the table. Billy swallowed a last mouthful of white meat and turned his head, so Mom wouldn't see him squinting and ask again if he needed glasses. He liked to squint into the distance, out across the fields and the creek, to the hills behind the house. One hill rose conical and forested against the others; Danner said the big hill was a volcano and would blow up sometime in the dark when they were all asleep. Billy squinted harder, his eyes nearly shut, his vision an approximate blur through his lashes. All the shapes were slanted shadows with colors now, and lights shot through them.

"Billy, turn around and finish eating," Mitch said.

At last their father lit the sparklers, held them away in midair just as the flame burst into sprays and stuttered white fire. The sound of the burning was a high-pitched crackling, filling the entire dusk. Danner had grabbed one slender, flaming stick and was down the hill in front of Billy, her white shorts ghostly pale against her skin and the sparkler flaring in one upstretched hand. She always wrote her own name over and over, tracing letters that trailed into one another as they fell away. Billy made ever-widening circles, and slashes that crossed his vision with firey lines. Danner and Billy ran first down the slope of the hill, jumping and screaming, then ran the boundary of the acre lawn, racing along the wire fence and past the square of lumpy ground they called the garden. Just when they were behind the pine trees, hidden from sight of the house, they stopped abruptly and held the sparklers above their heads like lanterns. Billy could feel sparks in his hair, a flare of heat near his face as burning ash fell past his shoulders. "Look," Danner breathed, and he did: the field was darkening in the yellowish dusk. All the way to the fence down by the creek, fireflies were lighting.

The lights were brief and bright and random along the stalks of the grasses and field stubble. Lights were in the briars and the milkweed plants. Then the lights flashed upward, glowing faintly, barely perceptible against whiter sky so they seemed an echo or reflection of those on darker ground. The sparklers began to spit and hiss.

Gladys was sitting on the toilet with the lid down like it was a chair, which made Danner laugh until their mother signaled her

nothing was funny. Gladys went on smoking her cigarette and
looked at a copy of *Upper Room*, a magazine the church gave out.
"I don't know what's so funny about a commode," Gladys said.
"No one can have a conversation with your mother unless they
follow her from room to room."

"I'm not getting out another washcloth. Danner, get through
with that one and let Billy wash." Their mother rested her arms
on the edge of the porcelain tub, then sat back on her haunches
and wiped her wet hands on her skirt. She pushed her sleeves
farther up.

"A person would think two kids six and seven years old could
bathe themselves," Gladys said. She put her cigarette down and
blew the smoke so it made a cloud around her face; in the big
mirror over the sink the smoke looked even bigger and cloudier,
furling into a shape. Billy wanted it to grow even larger and fill
the small room like a fog, like steam did when someone took a
shower. But Gladys had smoked the cigarette to its butt and she
put it out, grinding it hard into the ash tray so the leftover tobacco
would spill out and the filter show. "Right, kids?" Gladys said
now, "and you'd like to, especially if she'd give you back those
water pistols she took away."

"If I did, they'd take forever, and we've got all those patterns
to cut out tonight." Jean rubbed her eyes and frowned, and Billy
saw the part in her dark hair when she bent her head. She wore
her hair long; she kept it pulled back and fastened with a clip, then
folded her hair all around the clip so nothing showed but a thick,
dark, spiral knot.

Gladys' reddish hair was tightly curled all over her head.
She'd been to the beauty parlor that day and told how Mabel had
got her permanent too hard again. Their father had said from his
chair when Gladys first arrived that she didn't look any different
than she ever did. *Mitch Hampson, what would you know about
permanents. I doubt you've ever had one.* Gladys had folded her
pink chiffon head scarf into a square then and touched her head
all over, lightly, as Billy and Danner watched.

Now she squinted over the magazine. "It's a mystery the
Methodists bother to print this thing," she said. "Who reads it?"

"You're reading it, aren't you? Here, Billy, rinse off." His mother gave him the wet cloth and opened her arms wide with a towel for Danner. Danner stood up streaming water.

"That Danner is getting long and stringy. She's tall for her age." Gladys put the magazine down and sat looking, her rouged cheeks pink and her round face nearly expressionless.

"I'm older," Danner said.

"Older every minute," Gladys said, "too old to bathe with boys before long."

"Don't be ridiculous," Jean said, "they're brother and sister." She held Billy's shoulder as he climbed out, then wrapped him up in a towel that covered him to his knees. "Billy," she said then, "get your pajamas on."

Later he heard them, cutting with scissors. He knew they were on their knees, smoothing the patterns with one hand and cutting along a thin line. There was a sound of tissue crinkling against the darker, dull sound of cloth cut steadily. They were cutting the dark wool into shapes with sleeves, shapes to fit big dolls. They were cutting, and his father was sitting at the kitchen table, snapping open the square briefcase that held the plant's account books. He was smoking and coughing and moving a cup across the wooden surface of the table.

His father put bowls in front of them, and Billy poured the cereal. They were going to the plant because it was Saturday morning and business was off this weekend; that meant Billy would not be in the way. "We've just got that one driveway to pour," Mitch said. "One truck will do it easy." Mitch got up to get another cup of coffee. He had his khaki work clothes on but still wore his bedroom slippers; his boots made too much noise, and the work boots he pulled on over his leather boots made even more noise.

All the men at the concrete company wore big rubber boots while they worked. Billy's father wore the boots open until the mixers were actually loading. They were firemen's slick, black boots with metal buckles halfway up. When the boots were open they flopped above the ankle and their black tongues hung to the side. The buckles rattled every step: a sound like someone shaking chains. Now Mitch was stirring orange juice with a long wooden spoon, holding the plastic pitcher away from himself and jabbing at the frozen cylinder of concentrate. When he poured Billy's juice the warmish liquid would still taste of tap water—not like the juice Mom made, which was always very cold and more like oranges. Mitch would pour the juice into the wrong kind of glass, a big milk glass instead of the little cheese-spread containers Mom saved for juice glasses. He did that now and set the still faintly swirling mixture beside Billy's napkin. "Look here," he said, touching the napkin, "I don't want you telling your mother you'd rather be at the plant than at school." But he would rather be at the plant. "That don't matter," his father said, "you've just started the class with your mother and you need to do real well." But could they still go to the plant on Saturdays, every Saturday? "Not every Saturday," his father said, "you know that, but some weekends we will." They were silent and Billy drank his juice. When he dared look over again, his father was watching him. "You sure do like those trucks, don't you?" Mitch laughed quietly, almost to himself. "I guess you sure do."

The big Chevrolet trucks were bright mustard yellow, with black lettering across their huge mixer drums. The big letters said MITCH CONCRETE and Billy had known those words long before he could actually read them. When his father took him up to the plant to be among the men, Billy watched the trucks as though they were live animals, large and ancient. He stood beside the big tires, measuring his own height beside the wheels, then walked around to stand in front, looking up into the massive grill and hood as into a snaggled metallic face. If the men weren't too busy they lifted him into the cab of one of the trucks and let him sit in there by himself. The interiors of the trucks were cracked and brown, with one long brown seat and all the gearshifts coming up out of the floor. The big steering wheels were white and the dashes were brown metal, slightly dented, with a few long scratches where silver showed through. The broad windshields were streaked with dust. Billy would sit looking out. Below him the blond ground was oddly distant and the men gestured toward him, smiling.

Now his father began eating toast, and Billy understood that their conversation was over. Billy drank the juice, holding the glass to his face and drinking slowly until the juice was gone. He could see out the kitchen window; across the road he saw the cows huddled together in one corner of the field. They leaned against each other like they were asleep standing up, and swayed. Later in the day they never stood so close to the road; cars passed and scared them maybe. Or they liked it on the other side of the hill where the big water trough was, and the salt lick. The cows stood so still, Billy wondered about them. When his dog, Polly, slept, she stretched flat on her side and shivered, moving her feet. *Chasing rabbits*, Billy's father always said, *watch her chase them now.* Polly was dreaming. Sometimes Billy dreamed about the cement mixers. Often the Chevrolets were just sitting in his dreams, big and vacant as abandoned houses. There was almost a kind of music near them, like a humming of motors or heat.

Last night Billy had dreamed about the trucks. He'd seen Uncle Clayton in his dream. Billy and his father and some of the men were watching one of the mixers load. The big drum was turning very fast, so fast it looked like a blur. Then Billy's father picked him up and lifted him way high to see inside. Billy had never looked in there before; as his father lifted him higher and higher, he realized he'd always wanted to see. Mitch's hands were very big, but as Billy got higher the hands seemed to go away. The end of the drum was open and Billy peered in. The sides were glowing and going round, grinding out a familiar rumble. Uncle Clayton was in the drum. He was sitting in the metal desk chair from the plant office and the chair floated.

Clayton's face was strange. *Billy?* he said. His voice was almost a whisper. The sides of the drum whirled, shining so bright the air was silver. *Boy*, Clayton said, *go find your father.* He spoke with great effort as though from far away, and his words had a wind behind them. The whirling drum shone painfully bright, so bright Billy could see nothing but the light itself. He had wakened then and looked at the walls of his room, unsure where he was. Then he heard his father in the bathroom, the hiss of the shower and the whine the pipes made as water passed through them.

The kitchen spigot made a similar sound. Billy watched his father rinse out the coffee cup, filling it full of water but no soap

and rubbing the inside once with his hand. "Hurry up now, Billy."
Billy took the bowls to the sink. "Go get your shoes on, and your
jacket. Be quiet though, don't wake up Danner or your mother."

They drove out along the Brush Fork road, past the McCues'
house and the Connors', then past the still fields and across the
narrow stone bridge. Prison Labor was on one side and the old
stables on the other. Billy knew about Prison Labor: rows of big
stone buildings with almost no windows. His father said prisoners
used to live there and build roads, but now the prisoners were
gone and the buildings were full of State Road equipment, bulldozers and buses and trucks. Trucks like the concrete mixers?
"No, no, just dump trucks and rollers. Clayton and me have the
cement plant, you see; State Road hires us to pour concrete for
them. After they've dug out the road and got the surface all
graded and smooth, why we come along."

Everyone was already at the plant, and Radabaugh, who
worked as a driver, was making coffee. All the men called Billy's
father Cowboy, but Uncle Clayton called him Mitch.

Clayton stood by the office door as they pulled up, then
walked out to meet them. He wore khakis like the other men but
never wore a cap. His bald head was shiny and his forehead broad.
When he rode Billy on his shoulders, Billy touched the bald head
with a sense of awe: he could not cover it with his two hands. Now
Clayton leaned in close through Billy's window and smiled his
slow smile. "Here's my big man," Clayton said. "We haven't seen
you around here lately. Where you been keeping him, Mitch?"

"He's been at school with his mother."

"Ah." Clayton pretended he hadn't known, and opened the
car door for Billy. "How do you like having your mother for a
teacher?" Billy explained how his mother wasn't really his
teacher; he'd get his real teacher in the fall when school started.
This was only a phonics class to help kids read.

"Read?" Clayton looked surprised again. "Why you've been
reading everything around here for two years. What's it say on
those big bags over there?" He pointed to the ninety-five-pound
sacks stacked against the truck shelter. Billy knew, of course:
ALPHA READY-MIX. "Ready-Mix what?" Cement, Billy told him.

"You see there," Clayton said. "What other seven-year-old knows that much? And you want to keep knowing, because we old men forget what we're doing half the time. Big Man might be running trucks like these himself someday."

Mitch was looking toward the plant office, a small wooden building built right against the hill. Access roads wound behind the office in a double tier. "Clayton," Mitch said, "we got to get a grader in here and bank up that top road. We got a big load of gravel coming in and Saunder's truck is a lot heavier than ours; liable to slide right down that sand and through the roof of the office."

Clayton straightened. "Can't afford to rent a dozer now," he said. "I phoned Saunders this morning; he'll bring a smaller truck. Just have to pray we don't get a big rainstorm to erode that slant."

They both stood watching the access roads. The first road was level with the office roof and partially obscured by the hills of sand and gravel: aggregates used in the mixing. The higher road was for dump trucks to dump materials into one pile or the other: Billy had seen the big trucks back precariously into position. The big steel beds raised up, straining and clicking until a catch released the tailgate. Then sand fell in cascades, silent and clean, spilling over its own coned shape. Sand fell rapidly, as though it would never stop falling, and the hill of sand grew steeper and larger without ever seeming to change at all. When gravel was dumped, the sound was loud and satisfying. The chips of stone glinted as they poured and the gravel dropped like a hard rain falling all at once, clattering, raising its own brief smoke of dust. The men all stood watching from below, their arms akimbo, and spoke to one another in congratulatory tones. *There she goes*, they'd say amongst themselves. But the dumping of the sand was observed in silence.

Today both piles of aggregate were low; Billy wanted to know when the trucks would come, so he could watch the unloading. But his father and Clayton seemed to have forgotten him. Billy didn't ask, and followed the men into the plant office. Secretly, he liked it better when no one paid attention to him. He felt a little ashamed when the grown men were so friendly; their pleased expressions meant he wasn't one of them.

Inside the office, the big green accounting books were open across the desk. Radabaugh and Pulaski sat on the sofa, which was actually a green vinyl seat from a truck. The seat tipped at an odd angle and rested on rusty metal legs. Beside it was a big ash tray as tall as an end table. The sand in the tray was always full of cigarette butts; the smell of the sand was something like the smell of the whole office—dusty, slightly acrid, a smell of dry, clean dirt mixed with ash.

Pulaski spoke. "Cowboy, Clayton's been up here looking at those books for an hour already. It's enough to make a man nervous."

Clayton said nothing, but Mitch smiled. "Now Pulaski, we don't want you thinking hard enough to get nervous."

"That's right," Clayton said. "Relax. We've been at this five years and we've been in rough spots before."

Radabaugh leaned forward and began rolling a cigarette. He lay the thin paper on his knee and tamped the loose tobacco across it in a straight line. "Rough spots builds character," he said. "That's what my dad always told me. Your dad tell you that, Billy?"

Billy wasn't sure what to answer, so he smiled; slowly all the men smiled, even Pulaski. "What the hell," Pulaski said. And then they were all standing but Clayton, Radabaugh holding the thin cigarette in his mouth and putting on his bulky work gloves, Pulaski buckling his boots. Mitch stood near Clayton and touched the wide page of an account book. "Let me get them going on this engine, and I'll be back in," he said.

The men were out the door. Billy could see them through the big rectangular opening, walking away across the lot.

"Go with them," Clayton said. "Go on, they don't mind. You can learn how to fix an eight-year-old truck that ought to be taken out and burnt."

"Okay," Billy said seriously. But maybe he hadn't said it right, because when he turned around Clayton looked away from him at the books. He put his hand to his head and sat looking so intently that he didn't notice Billy leaving. Clayton didn't notice, and the men at the far end of the lot didn't notice him either; Billy walked in privacy toward them.

Pulaski was in the cab, revving the engine of the Chevrolet. Even this far away, Billy saw the whole truck tremble when Pulaski pressed the gas. Mitch and Radabaugh stood on either side of the big front end, pressing the yellow hood with their hands. They held their heads to the side, listening. What did they hear? "Again," Mitch said loudly. And the motor roared. Mitch waved his hand at Pulaski as Billy reached them, and the motor stopped.

Mitch and Radabaugh stood in place, waiting. Billy waited with them.

"Engine is pulling up," Mitch said. "That right motor mount is near rusted through, and the points have gone again."

"She's rough as a bitch." Radabaugh spat and wiped his mouth on his sleeve. "She ain't firing right or those points wouldn't go so fast."

"We can't put new ones in now unless we have to," Mitch said. "We'll clean these and see how she sounds."

Billy moved to stand nearer his father and he saw, very close, the pale crusted mud that covered the massive inside fender. In there was a hollow that made room for the tire to go round; even with that furious turning, the dried mud was undisturbed, a rumpled interior shell washed of color.

Now his father stroked the back of Billy's neck, the way he did when he was really thinking of something else. "I left my damn gloves in the office," he said. "Run and get them for me, Billy—they're on Clayton's desk, beside the books."

Billy knew the gloves; they were workmen's gloves with hard fingers; even the palms were stiff from getting wet and drying in the sun, or freezing in the winter. The gloves used to be light green but now they were almost white. Billy walked quickly to get them; he knew his father didn't really mean he should run. Mitch wouldn't have run. And besides, Billy knew where the gloves were. They weren't on the desk: they were on the floor, in the corner behind Clayton's chair. Billy saw them in his mind, just the way they lay. He walked watching his feet, wishing he had boots with hard toes that scuffed, and the scuff mark stayed like a scratch that didn't heal. He would tell Clayton he'd come for the gloves, and he would say it matter-of-factly; Clayton would still be *studying the books* and he wouldn't pay attention any more than if one of the men had come back for a moment. Billy stopped at the door of the office and looked up, poised to speak.

Clayton was sitting beside the desk in the chair. He'd said how the chair tilted backward and forward on a big coiled spring; now the chair was tilted slightly and Clayton sat quite still, one long leg stretched before him and the other pulled close. His foot curled strangely near the small gritty wheel of the chair. Clayton's hands were on his thighs, his arms tight to his torso as though he had braced himself. Billy stood watching, arms outstretched to touch both sides of the doorjamb. Under his fingers the wood was minutely gouged and ridged; he touched this splintered surface and waited. Clayton was looking toward the door, but the focus of his blue eyes was not fixed; his gaze was directed far off.

Billy knew not to move. The room was quiet and still; Clayton had changed all the air in it. Billy was cold but his face burned as though some heat approached him. The morning light was behind them both and fell through the door to lighten Clayton's face and Clayton's puzzled eyes. The light moved; Clayton's gaze shifted subtly and grew dimmer. It wasn't like the dream; Clayton didn't say a word, he didn't try to talk.

Billy turned and ran. The ground tilted beneath his feet; the buildings of the plant looked unfamiliar and odd, sheds and garages standing alone like so many big blocks with slanted roofs. Mitch and Radabaugh and Pulaski stood at the far end of the lot as before; the big mixer was still running but now the hood was raised up and all three men stood listening. Billy couldn't see his father's face. Mitch had leaned down to inspect the craw of the opening; he was lost to the waist in dark gears.

Billy never remembered speaking but all three men ran to the office. They were dressed in khaki, like soldiers, and the one mixer kept rumbling in their absence, the empty drum turning. Billy stood where he was until Radabaugh came back and picked him up. He was too old to be carried but Radabaugh lifted him easily;

Billy was pressed close, smelling the engine-oil smell of Radabaugh as they stood in the office doorway. The room had changed
and the stillness was totally gone. The metal chair was pushed far
into a corner where it had rolled when the men bent down together
and lifted Clayton away. The gloves were there, near the wall,
worn palms turned upward; Billy looked at them once and glanced
away. Now he was high up in Radabaugh's arms, and Clayton was
lying on the floor with a jacket folded under his head. Pulaski had
covered him with an army blanket and now he smoothed the green
wool, tucking it under Clayton's shoes. Billy looked for his father
and saw Mitch kneeling beside Clayton. His knees touched Clayton's head and he kept one hand on Clayton's shoulder as though
to hold him still. Clayton's eyes were half-closed the way Danner's
were just as she fell asleep. There was a lot of noise; the men were
all talking at once and Mitch was saying, "Take my car and get
Billy home. I'll ride in the ambulance and Bess will meet us there."
Then Mitch was throwing the ring of keys to Radabaugh; Billy
saw the keys in the air for an instant, and Radabaugh's open hand,
but the keys fell on the floor. Radabaugh bent to get them and the
floor came up fast at Billy; he pulled back and struggled to jump
free. "It's all right," Radabaugh mumbled. His breath was musky
with tobacco, intimate and close.

Radabaugh walked quickly to the Pontiac and they were in
the car, halfway down the dirt road to Route 20, when the ambulance passed them. The siren blared and it was the same sound as
a fire truck. Though the men in the ambulance didn't look at
Radabaugh, he waved them frantically up the hill toward the
plant. Billy felt strange seeing Radabaugh in Mitch's place behind
the wheel, and everything along the road looked wrong. There
were just a few cars at Nedelson's Parkette and someone had left
the neon sign on all night.

The Pontiac shook as Radabaugh went over the railroad
tracks too fast. "You're scared, ain't you Billy."

Billy didn't answer. He watched the road and they drove past
the Mobil station. Soon they would turn onto Main Street and go
past Aunt Bess's house and the hospital and the Dodge Sales and
Service, then out toward Brush Fork and home.

Radabaugh spoke again. "Billy, your dad was too hurried to

say so, but you did just the right thing. You came straight to get us and that was exactly right."

Billy nodded but he didn't want to ask questions. He would wait and ask his father, because his father would know more, wouldn't he? Right now Mitch was with Clayton in the ambulance. Radabaugh lit a cigarette. His khaki sleeves were rolled halfway up, and his wrist was tattooed with a banner folded like flags. *From the service:* Billy knew. The siren had flown past them up the hill to the plant and Radabaugh had waved it faster to make the sound go away. *Keep your mind on your business.* Clayton said that. How still the room had been. Still—but with a floating heat that moved like the chair in the dream. It was like the clock on Saturday afternoons, the long afternoons: when his father was gone to the plant and Danner was in her room and Mom was sewing on the Singer machine in the dinette. There was nothing to do then and television wasn't allowed, and Billy sat at the kitchen table. He sat there with his Tonka trucks—metal trucks so small he could hold all four in his hand at once—and he ran the trucks on the blue-painted surface of the wooden table. But really he only looked at the empty road out the window, and heard the kitchen clock. The clock was round and yellow and it hung on the wall with its white cord snaking down. The clock always ticked but no one heard it really; only on those afternoons was the sound so loud. Billy was quiet and his mother forgot where he was; there was only the steady buzz of the sewing machine, and the clock sound: a gentle and regular knock behind a yellow face, a circle of numbers. Someone wanted in or out but they stayed in between and kept knocking, paid no mind to anything. *Your mind is full of business.* The quiet the clock made leaked into the air, and was only a hint of the quiet Clayton made. Not like ghosts; no one was scared. What was it?

Radabaugh swerved too hard for the turn-off to Brush Fork. The Prison Labor buildings seemed to move their tall stone towers as the car lurched over tracks. They drove across the bridge and up the hill. As the car pulled into the driveway, Billy saw Danner outside with the dog. Danner was out without her shirt, like a boy, and her long hair obscured her face as she whirled in a circle, holding a stick for Polly. The dog leapt in place again and again; they kept a sort of time.

Clayton died that night in the hospital. They dressed up to go to the funeral home. Billy didn't tell anyone about the dream, and he couldn't see in the office again because his father wouldn't take him to the plant. In two weeks the concrete company was sold, though the cement mixers stayed the same bright yellow and continued to bear the legend of his father's name through the town. Radabaugh stayed on to work for the new owners, but Pulaski quit. And now Mitch was going to work for Euclid and sell big machines, like the ones sealed away in the Prison Labor buildings. He would sell dozers and cranes and trucks to construction companies, and to Prison Labor. But why would Prison Labor buy machines when they had so many in their closed stone buildings? Those were scrap machines, Mitch told Billy, used ones saved up for auction. Billy imagined the rows of old machines shut away in the dark, the way they would look from the door of one of the cool stone garages. Giant wound-down toys smelling of aged dust and rock, their separate shapes merged in the twilit far end of the long building. They sat like big, sleeping things. Billy didn't ask to go there and see them. But he still saw the mixers around town that summer; once he was in the car with his mother and they passed a parked MITCH CONCRETE truck. The truck blocked a small side street, and sawhorses had been set up to keep anyone from driving over a strip of newly poured surface. Radabaugh had patched the road where gas lines had been dug up; now he sat on an overturned bucket, low to the ground. He kept his elbows on his knees and hunched over himself, smoking. What was he waiting for? He looked small sitting there and kept the cigarette close his lips. The sawhorses were bright yellow like the still drum of the parked mixer, and they formed a crooked line of demarcation. Radabaugh sat behind them, guardian of a territory under repair.

# REMINISCENCE
# TO A DAUGHTER
## Jean, 1962

Ican't reconstruct things enough to know when I decided. I guess it seems I was working toward the divorce for years, but I was only trying to get to the point where I could support myself. I never even considered divorce—not with kids at home. Maybe I stopped thinking on purpose during those years and lived in the day-to-day. No struggle because every minute was filled.

I try to remember. A few separate days, isolated from each other by months or years, swim up. Then I have to think hard to know what years those were. I know immediately how they *felt*, the weather, the news. How old you and Billy were, your teachers in school, clothes you wore. Your face and Billy's face—exactly how you looked.

You know, I don't remember my own face then. I didn't really see myself. Just the slash of red lipstick and a comb through my hair. There are no photographs of me with you kids from the time you were old enough to be photographed without me. Every year there were school pictures with my first-grade classes, and I always threw them away.

I went back to college when Billy was in kindergarten and took a full course load, but nothing changed at home. I did all the housework and meals and put you kids to bed with stories, then stayed up till two or three reading and memorizing. Long nights, with all the house in darkness and one light burning over the kitchen table. I'd hear sounds outside and the breathing of sleepers.

I'd always been afraid of being alone, but now there was no fear or wondering. I *was* alone, though not surprised, not bitter. My mother had been alone, hadn't she, except for me? I'd borrowed the money to pay for classes and wanted to get straight A's, a perfect record. The one time I got a C on a mid-term, I sat in the rocker in my bedroom and wept. I remember you standing there, trying to reason with me, being very grown-up at eight years old. I suppose my nerves stayed frayed until the degree was finished, and never a word of encouragement from Mitch. No blowups, no fights; he knew it was important I start earning an income, but he grew more silent.

We never fought much. Once, I remember having to stand up to him.

What year was it? The news was full of scary headlines about Cuba, and Mitch maintained we'd never be in this fix if a Catholic hadn't been elected president. People around town were talking about fallout shelters. The VFW organized a Civil Defense League: classes at the post office one night a week for four weeks. Mitch took them in the summer, when those old rooms must have been airless. Then he taught the same class in September. He was working for a construction company then, selling aluminum buildings on commission. Always yelling at you kids, *Get the hell off the telephone! Don't you know I earn a living on this phone?* Things were easier when he was involved in the civil defense work; there were books and pamphlets and construction details Which basements were to be used for town shelters: the courthouse, the high school, all the churches.

It would have been October, and grainy aerial photographs of Cuban missiles were appearing in the newspapers. People were

alarmed and news was broadcast on the hour. I didn't care much;
I remember thinking myself strange. I spent eight hours a day
with six-year-olds bused fifteen or twenty miles from hollows
back in the country. Did they have fallout shelters? They didn't
have mittens or winter coats unless I could find enough at the
Salvation Army. Civil defense seemed crazy to me but it was
important to Mitch, so I kept quiet. He talked about building a
shelter in the little room behind the garage, a utility room where
he kept tools, where the hot-water tank was, and the big cabinet
that held canned goods. A ladder up the wall led to the attic door,
which had to be shoved open from underneath. You kids were
never allowed in the attic—there was no floor except for a narrow
walkway, just insulation between the boards. Every change of
season, I'd find myself up there, opening Mother's big cedar chest
in a corner under the eaves. Packing woolens away with moth
balls or shaking out summer cottons, hoping they weren't all
outgrown.

That night, I was in the attic, trying to find enough winter
school clothes. Dresses with big hems, pants to let out, but there
would have to be new boots and coats. I had a whole pile of
woolens and thought I'd get you both to try everything on while
I finished ironing a basket of Mitch's shirts, and my blouses.
Teaching, I wore skirts and those Ship 'n' Shore cotton blouses
with roll-up sleeves and Peter Pan collars; two white ones, a pale
green one, a blue one. Those are the details I remember, colors
and clothes and the smell of chalk at the blackboard, going over
your homework at night—the red arithmetic book Billy had in the
sixth grade called *Fun with New Math*. No questions about the
meaning of things; you don't think that way if you have children.
The meaning is right in front of you and you live by keeping up
with it. *I have my house and my children* was a phrase I kept
in mind. Piling up clothes, I calculated which would do and which
wouldn't. The light in the attic was dim, one bulb glowing and the
sun setting outside with a gold tinge. Underneath that yellow
color was the cold of the fall coming on. It was a Sunday night
because I was thinking I had the week's lesson plans to do, and
thirty-five big jack-o'-lanterns to cut from orange construction
paper. I loved decorating that classroom and spent hours on a

different display every month. Just that day I'd gotten two big rolls of brown paper so the kids could trace each other's shapes and color their own portraits. I could put the shapes up all around the room, with the movable arms and legs holding vowel sounds, and the jack-o'-lanterns for heads, each with a different expression. In October I was still teaching letter recognition to kids from the country who hadn't seen many books, kids who'd never seen themselves full length in a mirror. At Halloween, a third of the class would be too poor to have costumes; I could take staples and elastic string to school to make masks out of the jack-o'-lantern faces. I'd ask Bess and Gladys for worn-out linens again, and use torn sheets for capes. I stood there in the attic with all these plans, looking at shirts I knew Billy couldn't wear; in the half-finished top of the house, I felt as though I were standing behind the scenes of some production. I couldn't move for a minute, the feeling was so strong. Nothing seemed real. I thought of my mother hemming my dresses on the porch, letting down hems one after another while I sat playing with soap bubbles, a skinny dark sparrow of a kid.

I heard Mitch walking on the concrete floor below. He tapped with his pencil on the water tank, a small reverberating sound that echoed itself. I looked over the edge of the attic opening and saw him figuring on a tablet, holding his OCD manuals and a tape measure. He wore the same khaki clothes at home that he'd worn at the plant, before Clayton died and the business was sold. Now he wore shirts and ties to work and called on customers; I think he hated selling. Too proud not to resent doing it, and at his age. He must have been fifty. I was thirty-five, but I didn't feel young. Looking at him from above, I felt so distant I could have been watching from another planet. He stood inspecting the door to the patio, so involved he was unaware of the light on over his head. He turned abruptly and strode away into the garage.

I stepped back, switched off the light, and took up the bulky clothes in the dark. The ladder was difficult. I held on with one hand and was halfway down when I got stung. Hornets always nested in the attic in summer, but I'd supposed they were gone by now. It was ludicrous; I wasn't willing to drop the clothes on the dirty floor and then sort them all again, and I couldn't move my hand. I called to Mitch but he must not have heard. So I climbed down while the hornet kept stinging me, unable to see over bundled wools and corduroys, and walked into the kitchen where I could put them down.

My hand felt as though it were on fire; there would be some welts. Mitch came in and I stepped behind the heaped ironing board to give him room in the narrow kitchen.

He put a list on the table. "I can make an airtight shelter back there—rig up an air-pipe vent and hand pump through one of the windows, then brick them up with cement block. We've got the water tank we could siphon to supplement the containers, and I'll need about a hundred sandbags to block the doorways."

"Isn't there room for us in the town shelter? We're only two miles away."

"They recommend having your own if you can." He put the manuals on the ironing board in front of me. "You need to read these."

"How can we afford—"

He nodded once. "I'll need your help on this."

What he meant was money. I looked down at the booklet and saw a gray and yellow illustration of a man shoveling dirt onto a door. The door was propped at an angle against an outer wall. His sweater and the dirt were yellow, as though he were already covered with dust. *A Plan But No Time: Pile the dirt from the trench on top of the doors.* I scanned the words, not really seeing them. *Try to get in a shadow; it will help shield you from the heat.* The ironing board was piled high and the supper dishes were still on the table; my hand was throbbing and I felt almost dizzy with frustration. I turned a page and read: *Time But No Plan: Fill buckets, sinks, a bathtub, and other containers with water.*

"I can't read these," I said, "I'll be up until midnight as it is. And the kids need coats this month. I can't give you any help."

For a minute he just looked at me. Then he leaned toward me over the ironing board. He was a lot bigger than me and seemed huge. "Damn it to hell," he said. "I should know better than to expect help from you on a goddamn thing."

The door to the breezeway was behind me, but I wasn't going to turn around and leave my own house. "You've got no right to talk to me like that. For your information, I've paid half the bills in this house and bought all the kids' clothes for two years."

"And don't you think you're goddamn great for every penny you've spent!"

So we started. You remember his short fuse—breathing heavily and shaking with rage in seconds. That's probably why he never raised a hand to you and left all the discipline to me—he got too angry to trust himself. I think I shoved the ironing board against him to get out from behind it. Then we were walking back through the house, just shouting. I was trembling but knew enough not to move too quickly; almost by instinct, he would have reached out and grabbed me.

I realized I was headed toward the back room, our bedroom, and I walked into the bathroom and locked the door. *You'd better stay the hell in there,* he yelled. There was silence except for his voice. I imagined you and Billy in your rooms, listening. I heard you open your door ever so quietly and knew you were afraid.

I told him clearly, *I don't have to stay anywhere. There are laws to protect me from men like you.* The words came out of my mouth as though I'd had them in my mind all along. Later I wondered if I'd heard my mother say them to my father.

You say I planned for years, but there was no plan. He was earning less and less; I had to earn more and more. All those extension classes and summer courses to get the master's, almost a doctorate, then insisting we put that house on the market and move into town when you kids were in high school. Finally he agreed. You know, I told him I'd move out alone if he'd sign an agreement to pay for your college educations. But I would never have left you. I was only gambling.

I couldn't take it anymore, struggling on his ground.

# RADIO PARADE
## Danner, 1963

Danner's family sat in two rows of folding chairs on the wide sidewalk. The parade always passed Bond Hospital and Great Aunt Bess's house at the very beginning, having formed on vacant lots out by the Tastee Freez, where there was room for all the floats to park. Bess sat on the white porch swing under the awning with Aunt Katie; they stayed back from the street so that Katie was out of the sun, but the cousins and the men and nearly everyone stood or sat in the heat. The women wore sunglasses shaped like wings whose transparent frames were pink or blue; Danner's mother wore a red scarf over her black hair. On the high porch of Bond Hospital there were chairs and gliders drawn up for the ambulatory patients, and they began to drift into place guided by nurses. Bess didn't own the hospital anymore and said it had gone down, just an old folks' home, but Danner waited every year to see the patients in their long robes. The old people weren't erectly tense like Bess but seemed weightless, nearly translucent, their skin purely white and their wild hair gauzy. An hour into the long parade, noise and confusion and blasting horns an unremitting din, they fell asleep sitting up, their hands in their laps. Heads fallen back, they dreamed with their mouths wide open.

The air smelled of heat and candy and the parade was heard far off, an invisible blare of cornets and the double-time pounding of drums. Scores of boots clicked taps on pavement, and Danner felt the waiting street shimmer. Candy coins thrown by children were already melting in their gold foil; when the bands fell out at the end of the route, breaking formation past the stone gates of the city park, their bulky uniforms would smell of trampled chocolate and sweat. Danner could almost smell them, when suddenly a first corps of majorettes swung into sight under the big trees of East Main. Their bronzed legs flashed and the crowd rippled, standing and shuffling, raggedly cheering as the girls saluted. The drum majorette wore a tall white fur helmet strapped to her head with a silver strap; behind her the others advanced in perfect double lines, the short skirts of their white uniforms starched nearly horizontal and buoyed by layers of red net crinolines.

These were the Bellington girls from the hometown band, always first in line. The majorettes were the same girls who danced at the pool dances and sat in boys' cars at Nedelson's Parkette, but now they were other-worldly and startling. Gazing straight down the center of the street that wound past the hospital through town to the fraternity houses and mansion funeral homes of Quality Hill, they smiled the same set, perfect smile. College boys would watch them from balconies hung with rebel bunting; watch them, not applauding. *Do you know they set a girl's hair on fire at the May Day Sigma Chi party? Yes, last week.* In the dank basement of the junior high school, girls had stood by rows of battered olive green lockers and speculated. The lockers were ancient, like the rest of the building; Danner's parents, even her father, had gone to high school in the same rooms and hallways. Now there was a new high school just outside Bellington, with a big parking lot where town boys parked their cars. *She was lucky they put it out before her face was burned.* Who put it out? *Danner, how should we know? What a stupid question,* and her eighth-grade compatriots turned away. Danner, reaching into a cluttered metal shelf, found the rouge and the Maybelline eyeliner pencil she kept hidden beside her tattered notebooks; after third period, before noon hour and bag lunches in the gym, she went to the girls' basement bathroom and lined her eyes while the plumbing hissed. Here in the June sunlight of the festival parade, school seemed to have ended years ago. Danner remembered her own surreptitious face, shadowed by yellowish lights of the low cement ceiling and reflected in the cracked mirror. Lined in black, alive in the empty, cell-like room, her eyes had seemed the eyes of an animal. She thought she looked older than she was, but in a secretive, evil way. She didn't belong to her own face; except for her womanish hips, she was skinny and gawky, too tall; her straight brown hair wouldn't curl. She had a reputation for being smart. Boys her age wouldn't talk to her much; she didn't know how to make the kind of conversation they liked. Mornings before classes, older boys from the country had to change school buses to get to the high school; they waited on the massive stone steps of the junior high. They scared Danner; they were like men, big and grown, with shadows on their faces and big hands like her father's hands. They had no money for cars or they wouldn't be riding the buses; they wore shabby coats and laced-up farmers' boots, combed their oily hair forward and then back in out-of-style pompadours, smoked cigarettes in defiance of the rules. Danner walked past them, up the worn steps to the big double doors of the school, stealing glances at their mysterious faces. Always, they were watching her, their expressions guarded, sullen, angry. What did they know about her? No one else ever paid any attention. *Hey*, they sometimes said, softly, appraisingly. Their smiles were sneers. Though she dressed like a girl from town—in penny loafers, full skirt, ankle socks—they watched her openly. She was ashamed and lowered her eyes; the boys looked away then and continued talking as though she were invisible. She heard phrases, snatches of words, as she passed. *How many times she give it up?* or *dead before you know it.* Who was dead? Most of them joined the Army or the mines as soon as they turned eighteen. You never saw them except on the steps—not at dances or the movies, or at the carnival in summer, not at the festival parade. *Son of a fucking bitch* and *she found a train to pull.*

Danner tried to imagine them now, sitting across the street amongst the families, but their faces stayed coldly vaporous in smoke and winter breath. She was sweating and the sun shone in her eyes. The Bellington band had stopped to perform, three minutes of a fancy march-in-step. Horns glinted sideways above shoulders as the band dipped its knees, strutted, retraced its steps, and rocked. Farther up, the majorettes would be doing a routine; from here, Danner saw batons fly into the air above the numberless blue hats of the band. The bobbing hats were like those of wartime soldiers, garrison caps billed in black, the crowns flat. The jackets were dark blue with gold piping and fringed epaulettes; the trousers straight-legged; the shoes black, polished, the flying shine of trombones reflected on their surfaces. The band was beautiful and massive, a well-practiced shock of gold and silver against the mourning of the dark blue. The gold bowls of the tubas turned left to right above it all. In the back row were the boys with chimes and the base drummers, huge blank drums strapped tight to their bodies with belts. Danner felt a pounding in her stomach as the boys marched near her; they stepped in place and beat double time. The rest of the band kept silence and the boys stood pounding with both arms, their bodies vibrating in the center of the noise. Then it was over and the band marched on, "Stars and Stripes Forever" with horns in full and chimes ringing. Relieved, excited, the crowd stood and cheered.

Danner looked for Billy; he'd like the drums, and she thought she heard him yelling. Inclining her head, she saw him farther down the row. He was sitting on the Styrofoam ice chest, slumped forward in his white T-shirt and dirty shorts, his skin sun-beiged and his blond hair bleached almost white. *You kids tan dark as Indians: you can thank your mother's Black Irish blood.* Did that mean Irish Negroes? Last night they'd watched the news on the big Motorola television: police with attack dogs in Birmingham, columns of dark bodies scattering suddenly, as though the film were sped up by mistake. *Those niggers have made a fine mess down there,* Mitch said, and Jean had called from the kitchen, *You don't need to speak that way.* His voice, harsh:

*Don't you try telling me how to speak.* Then silence but for the water running as she rinsed dishes, and the announcer's voice continued. Billy had thrown his leg over Danner's as they lay on the rug; he turned to her and silently mouthed, *Jigaboo.* It was a word that had made them laugh when they were younger, but Danner turned away now contemptuously. The police were the bad ones; they were the ones with the dogs. No one spoke of it in social studies class at the junior high. They were supposed to discuss current events every Thursday when the *Scholastic Readers* were handed out; once the front of the six-page paper was a big murky photo of the marchers. Further on was a photo of President Kennedy in the new Rose Garden, and the teacher discussed the history of the White House. *Hurrah for the red, white, and blue* were the real words of the familiar "Stars and Stripes Forever" march, but the kids at school sang a parody about mothers and ducks. Bored at school, Danner had sung the words to herself, a silent rhythm in her mind, but she thought the word *fuck* instead of *duck.* Fuck was the word written all over basement walls of the old school; it was scrawled even on the big round pipes that were too hot to touch. Scrawled with crayon that melted and left a bright wax thickness, then a pale stain after the janitor scraped the texture off. There were ghostly fucks every few feet along the round steaming pipes; an angry, clinched word, wild. A while ago Danner had mentioned the graffiti to her mother, but Jean wouldn't say the word even to comment. *It's just as bad to curse about sexual matters as to take the Lord's name in vain.* Danner didn't talk about fucking to Billy, but surely he already knew.

The noise of the band moved off and Danner wished she were at home; the Boy Scouts were marching past and she was embarrassed to see them. Her embarrassment, an anxious sadness, confused her. The Scouts were some of the same boys from school, their crew cuts covered by the khaki caps, and the backs of their necks nearly shaved. Their thin necks looked shy and vulnerable; they did nothing but walk, shuffling a little, the sound barely audible. It wasn't easy to walk through the entire parade in the heat; only boys thirteen and up were allowed. Billy wouldn't march with the Scouts until next year, but Danner wished he'd quit before the event took place. Why couldn't he just lose interest? The little cloth merit badges looked like women's jewelry on the sashes they wore across their chests; the yellow scarves seemed feminine too, caught at the throat with metal clasps. She'd seen Billy's up close—it was an eagle like those on Army uniforms or military seals. Painted to look like gold or brass but only iron underneath, dull gray where the wing was scratched. Danner stepped back from the curb and wished them all out of sight as the two leaders, men dressed in drab green and wearing berets, shifted the banner they carried. Of course the men carried it; adults would have felt silly walking along empty-handed. The boys, perhaps fifty of them, were all too warm in their long-sleeved dark shirts. The two Negro boys in the fourth row were wearing Keds instead of leather Buster Browns with laces, but their socks were dark. Danner knew Scouts had to have special black nylon socks with elastic garters; the garters had pleased Jean because they were old-fashioned. *Billy, you will so wear them; they're part of the uniform and I paid good money for them.* Danner stared at her own feet so as not to look; her white sandals were grass-stained and knicked where she'd scuffed them. "Left, Left, Left right left" came the soft voices of the Scouts, meant to be so soft no one could hear.

Danner wiped her face with her hands. She wanted to sit in the shade but the best part of the parade was coming; she looked down the route and saw the first of the Queen's Court floats, vast, shuddering as it moved forward. The biggest floats were constructed over the tractors that pulled them, tractor and driver and hitch hidden in a frame of wood and chicken wire. They were hay wagons decorated in barns, the frames completely covered with crepe paper and thousands of Kleenex roses, colors arranged to make patterns or spell words: MONONGAHELA POWER, ALLEGHENY BELL. But the Queen's Court floats were always purely white, surging constant and slow through the long parade. Hidden teenage boys watched from inside through rectangular peepholes to drive them at five miles per hour. The blockish floats were like an awkward herd of mechanical cakes tiered with girls in gowns and children in white under bowers. The first one always carried part of the Children's Court, six-year-olds who'd participated in the

crowning ceremonies on the lawn of the local college. Little girls
in organdy and gloves, boys in white suits with short pants, bow
ties. Danner squinted up at them against the sun—oh, it was hot
up there—the warm pavement radiating heat, and they felt like
giants.

Danner had been one of those children; somehow Billy
hadn't. She remembered riding in the parade: a confusion of
caretaking by strangers before it began, the frothy dresses and
the heat, *sit just like this and don't move.* Endless slow prog-
ress of the oceanic float, the spell of continuous scattered applause while the street unwound below her. The cool, green-
shaded park where she was lifted off the float by a parade
marshal and fell at his feet as he released her, her legs completely without sensation. *You mean you never moved once in
the whole parade?* His big face above her as he put her under
a tree to wait for her mother, wait for her legs to come alive.
The dreamy, sensual time in which she sat, immobilized, the
green park dense with heavy trees and the parade fallen to wandering fragments across the dappled ground. The coldness of
the shaded grass, her drowsy exhaustion, her legs tingling.
She'd seen Jean walking into the park, wearing a full white skirt
and sleeveless blouse—her hair was long then, pulled back in a
chignon at the nape of her neck; her lipstick was red. Jean
looked beautiful and anonymous, yet deeply familiar. Danner
felt herself alone, unattached and content. Her mother was a
familiar body moving over grass, the way sun moved and
stopped abruptly at the shade of the trees.

Where was Jean now? Danner saw her then, sitting in the
middle of the line in one of the aluminum lawn chairs, pouring a
glass of iced tea from the cooler. She held up the glass and gestured to Danner; Danner approached her, and her mother's dark
face, framed in the red scarf and the line of her black hair, was
calm and steady in the heat. The colors of another band jangled
behind her.

She put her hand on Danner's forehead. "Take a drink of this.
You're so hot your face is flushed. It's that long hair. I don't know
why you won't let me get you a nice haircut for summer."

Danner took the glass. "I don't want short hair."

"All the girls have short hair this summer. Did you see Bonnie Martin's hair?"

Bonnie Martin was a majorette. "No," Danner said.

"Sure you didn't." Jean smiled. "Don't you want me to pull it back for you? Want my scarf?" She touched the scarf to pull it off.

Danner shook her head. The scarf would smell of Jean's hair, a perfume dense and subtle at once, like heavy waxen flowers wilted by warmth. How could her hair smell that way? Danner wanted to touch the scarf and hold it.

Jean sighed. "This parade will go on another two hours. Why not sit on the porch with Katie?" She nodded at Bess's house. "See how cool Katie looks."

Danner turned. Katie didn't see them looking and peered at the street, the porch swing under her moving slightly. Her skin was very pale and she swung absently on the broad white swing, as though the street were empty and she were totally alone. Usually she was alone on her frequent visits; her husband owned a hardware store in Winfield and came to Bellington only a few times a year. Danner turned back to Jean. "Mama, is Gladys coming out for dinner?"

"Yes, and she's bringing the strawberries. Would you rather I have to drive clear up to Hall's field in this traffic and get them?" She waited for an answer; then her expression softened. "Does Gladys bother you so much? She lives all by herself. Who does she have but us, with Jewel clear up in Ohio? It's not like Bess, with Twist and his family right here, and your dad, and Katie coming so often from Winfield."

"I know."

"Go ahead, sit on the porch. Let Katie do French braids. For the dance tonight. Tight as Katie does them, they'd last. Be pretty with your new dress." She stroked Danner's wrist with her warm fingers.

The new dress: Danner's heart sank at the prospect of wearing it. Jean had gone all the way to Winfield to shop and bought the dress as a surprise; it was a tailored white shirtwaist with linen cuffs at the short sleeves. Surely no one wore such clothes at the pool dances; the high school girls would wear full swing skirts and sleeveless rayon shells that clung. The sweaters would be colors like tangerine, aqua, chartreuse; Danner would be the only one in white. Last night she'd lain in bed and heard her parents quarreling in low tones: *You had no damn business* and Jean's bitter *I work for my money* as the dress hung pale and crisp in the darkness of Danner's open closet. *You don't think I work? You need a good slap,* and Danner lay listening, wondering if she could say she planned to swim, and take her real clothes to the dance in a beach bag. Someone would see if she changed in the poolhouse dressing room; suppose she walked into the tall bushes by the railroad tracks? No one would notice. *Just you touch me, go ahead.* The voices stopped then or Danner slept, the dress in her mind's eye veiled with tissue paper, offered in her mother's arms.

"Mama, maybe we should take the dress back."

Jean looked easily away at the parade. "Now why would we do that? You'll look so pretty in it. I can't wait to see you." There was the sound of bells jingling and a steel clack of hooves on cement. "The horses—twice as many this year, and here come the palominos. Oh, roses."

Danner knelt by Jean's chair to look; she saw the closest animals almost from below, and the chests of the horses were beautifully broad. They stepped high in what seemed an effortless gait, but the costumed riders held the reins tense. They prodded the horses sharply, stirrups tight against the veined bellies of the animals. The two palominos, show horses from a stable in Winfield, were always in the parade. This year their ashen manes were plaited and deep red roses sat like knots along their arched necks.

"Someone was careful and took every thorn from those long stems," Jean said.

The wooden floor of Bess's porch was cool and the boards were vaguely uneven; Danner sat cross-legged and waited for Katie to come back with the celluloid brush and comb, and the round white hand mirror, Bess kept on her dressing table. The porch was a big empty rectangle except for the swing; all the other chairs were set up on the sidewalk for the parade. Rhododendron grew shoulder-high around the front of the house, the long waxen leaves so close against the white trellis of the porch they seemed to press the lattice. Danner looked across the wide stone steps of the porch and watched the Shriners march past. They wore skirts and played the bagpipes that were so harsh and sad and melodious; the crowd clapped.

The street, blocked off since the previous night, would have looked completely empty before the parade and the crowds came. Bess would have been up early, sweeping the floor and the thin mats of the porch with a stiff broom. Danner imagined the brushing of the broom in the quiet morning. How would it be to wake up like Katie to that sound; to have a mother so old, nearly seventy; to be an old child nearly thirty and sleep often in the bed you'd always known?

Katie wasn't like other people; Danner wasn't sure why. Katie was thin and willowy and she moved quietly; she wore her dark blond hair in the same pageboy she'd worn in her high school graduation picture, and she wore no makeup. Her face was so fair that the freckles on her cheeks each looked singular and precise, as though someone had painted them on. Her hazel eyes had tiny lines beneath them and in the creases, as if she had to strain slightly to see. Her sweater and sketchbook lay in the empty swing; Danner touched the sweater, a red woolen one. Just touching it made Danner feel too warm, but Katie carried a sweater everywhere, even in the middle of summer. On the hottest days, she wore a white cotton sweater around her shoulders; always, she took a long nap in the middle of the day. Everyone accepted the fact that Katie slept; when she visited Bess, the French doors to the bedroom were pulled shut and Katie lay still, never wrinkling the spread, her arms and chest covered with her sweater. She had been a sickly child, but that wasn't what made her different: Danner thought it was the way Katie slept that signaled her difference. She slept easily and completely, as though some part of her was constantly engaged in serene rest. She had only to give over the wakeful aspects of herself to slip completely into her practiced sleep, her face still, her pale lips delicate as peach-toned porcelain.

Now the screen door banged and Danner felt Katie behind

her. Katie sat down and leaned forward; the swing moved to touch Danner's shoulder.

"Danner, you can't see the parade sitting down so low. Want to sit up beside me?"

"No, it's cool here, and you can reach me better."

Katie lifted Danner's hair as though weighing it in her hand. "Tires you out to see so many colors, doesn't it."

"You mean the parade?"

"Yes, to see so much at once, going by and going by." She combed Danner's hair with her fingers first, to keep the comb from pulling. "I remember the very first festival, in 1949. I think Jean was pregnant with you then; you were going to be born soon. I was—what, thirteen? Just the parade then, much smaller, and a shortcake supper at the firehouse."

"Why do they call it the Strawberry Festival?" Danner sat still as Katie parted her hair down the middle; Katie always stroked the hair apart, petting it into place with strong downward strokes of her wrists.

"They had to call it something," Katie said, "and there have always been big berry crops around Bellington. There were weeks when the berries rotted in baskets before the farmers could sell them. Big baskets they would nearly give away. And when the berries had gone dark and soft, the men made wine. The wine was so light and fragile-tasting, no one valued it much. It was like leftovers, can you imagine?"

"Did you ever drink it?"

"No, they wouldn't let me drink anything like that." She laughed. "I had to drink egg nogs, and raw milk with vitamin tonic."

Recorded music suddenly blared. *O beautiful for patriot dream;* the VFW float was going by. A huge round globe turned on a gold foil axis; the globe was solidly, darkly blue except for a red- and white-striped America on one side. The globe trembled as the float moved, crepe rosettes of the colors ruffling.

"Isn't it pretty?" Katie rested her hands on Danner's back. "Looks unfinished, with no people on it."

"But the empty floats are some of the best ones." Danner felt Katie fasten one braid and begin the second.

"I hear you and Billy are going to the pool dance tonight."

"Well, it's not exactly a dance. You don't have to have a date —it's more of a group activity." Katie didn't have children and her ideas of what they could do seemed liberal to Danner.

"Oh," Katie said. "Is it Billy's first dance?"

"I guess so, except for those church parties. But I'm sure he won't dance. I mean people can swim in the pool or just hang around. Billy doesn't care about dances—he's just waiting for the air show tomorrow. He's been riding his bike out to the airport every morning to look at the planes."

"I see." Katie began running the comb through Danner's tangled hair. Danner hardly ever used a comb, but somehow Katie did it quickly and lightly, pushing with her cool hands on Danner's scalp. "You should never take a brush to your hair, it's so fine and soft."

"It's terrible hair."

"Danner, it isn't, and it's a lovely color." Quickly she braided the other plait, holding Danner's head against her knees and sectioning long pieces. "I'm making them tight, to last. You'll squeak when you blink."

Danner leaned her full weight against Katie and closed her eyes. The white hands in her hair moved light and hard, fast. "Feels like you could pull my eyes wide open," Danner said.

"All the better," Katie said softly.

The bands sounded farther away and people on the street were a continuous, restful hum. The yelling and shouting were only sound; even the line of chairs, when Danner looked, seemed foreign. Danner watched her mother's back, the familiar set of Jean's shoulders. Mitch was farther down the row with Doc Reb Jonas and Uncle Twist, Katie's brother. All three men stood with their arms crossed, in shirt sleeves. Twister was gaunt and thin and gray and drank bourbon even in his iced tea.

"Do you like dances?" Katie's voice was startlingly close against the other faraway noises. She had leaned down to pull the crown hair tight, and Danner felt her breath, a silvery tickling.

"They're all right," Danner said.

"You know, your father used to dance with me when I was

your age and a little younger. He seemed like a giant then. He was
a wonderful dancer."

"He was?" Danner supposed she should be quiet. "He sure
gets mad easy now."

"Does he?" Katie looked out toward the street. "Yes, I suppose he does."

Danner said nothing.

"There," Katie said. She leaned over Danner from above,
picked up the hand mirror and held it, keeping her face close
beside Danner's so that both images were reflected in the glass.
"Let's see if we look alike," she said.

Far off, sirens wailed, marking the end of the parade. Danner
looked into the mirror. "I don't think so," she breathed.

"Look closer. Hold the mirror." Danner took the wide handle
of the mirror and Katie lifted both hands. Forefingers touching
where their faces met, she drew one cool finger across Danner's
brow, one across her own. "Here," she said, "we're the same."

The strawberries were ripe and juicy and left a pink tinge on
Danner's fingers. She sat on the edge of the concrete patio with
Gladys and Jean while Mitch stood at the far side of the yard,
pouring charcoal briquets into the barbecue. The fields around the
house were still brightly yellow in the sun of the late afternoon,
but the grasses had begun to move and show their pale under-
sides; later it might rain. Danner and Jean held the bowls of
berries and capped them with small knives. Danner moved her
knife automatically and watched Billy ride his bike at the far
perimeters of the lawn; he rode around and around, the silver
fenders of the bike shining. Every time he made the hill past the
barbecue, he stood to pedal and moved by with a blast of sound;
he'd taken Danner's transistor radio and hung it from the handlebars. The volume was turned way up and strains of Top 40 songs
twisted in the air.

"Billy's got my radio," Danner told Jean.

Gladys looked up from the bowl of beans she held. "He won't
hurt it, unless he wrecks and hurts himself, and then you'll feel
justified."

"He went in my room and took it, Mom." Danner heard

strains she almost recognized as Billy disappeared around the front of the house; the songs, high wails, seemed to drift behind him.

Gladys and Jean ignored Danner; they were discussing Katie. Katie couldn't get pregnant.

"She's strung too tight, that's why." Gladys broke the beans with a snap. "She looks half-starved, like she'd break in half doing what's necessary."

"I don't know what that would be," Jean said. "All I ever had to do was lie there."

"Not so. It has to do with a state of mind."

"Gladys, that's ridiculous. I got pregnant so easy—all he ever had to do was look at me."

Danner imagined Mitch looking. In the home movies there were always a few dim frames of his face as he held the movie camera in his hands and pondered it, filming himself as he pushed the wrong button. His head filled the frame, lit on one side by tentative light. In the fish-eye view of the camera, his broad forehead curved in near darkness like the smooth plain of an awesome, lonely planet. His chin, his nose, all the features of his face, became a strange, enlarged geography. His eyes were nearly closed as he peered down, his expression wondering.

"Exactly," Gladys told Jean, "he looked at you."

"Oh, Gladys. People don't have to be happy together for the woman to get pregnant."

"Not saying they have to be happy. Happens faster lots of times if couples don't get along. It's a state of mind in the woman before the man even touches her."

"So men have nothing to do with it?" Jean arched her brows at Danner to signal that this was another of Gladys' nutty conversations.

"Sure they do." Gladys looked unconcerned and shook the pot of strung beans. The beans rattled and she smoothed them level with her hand.

Jean smiled. "I hope you're listening to this, Danner. Gladys is going to tell you her version of what makes women pregnant."

"What?" Danner asked.

Gladys leaned closer. "Desperation," she said, "suddenly satisfied." She held up her hand for silence as Jean began to laugh. "Not always desperation for children—could be desperation about something else. But for a few minutes, the desperation is gone, and that's when women get pregnant. *After* they do what's necessary, of course." Gladys nodded once, decisively.

"Most people don't have any trouble getting pregnant," Jean said. "It's hard to believe so many people are desperate."

"Almost everyone is desperate," Gladys said. "Katie is desperate, too. But a hard case like Katie has to have exactly what she *needs*—" Gladys paused for emphasis "—to forget what she *wants*, and have her desperation satisfied."

"Well, what does she want?" Danner asked.

"Something else besides what she has," Gladys answered.

"But that's human nature, Gladys," Jean said. "Everyone wants what they don't have."

"Not as bad as Katie does."

"Gladys," Jean said sarcastically, "maybe you'd better have a talk with Katie right away."

"Not me. You can't talk to a hard case." Gladys placed the bowl of beans in her lap with deliberation, pleased with herself.

"What do you mean by 'satisfied?' " Danner sat hugging her knees, gazing down the expanse of lawn to the fence. Billy was rounding the bottom boundary of the grass, pedaling evenly. The whispering radio swung, veering its music closer in a shimmered falsetto: *in the jungle, the mighty jungle, the lion sleeps tonight*©. The high-pitched words were not loud across the distance, but carried audibly; Billy passed the flaming barbecue in a stop-time and moved out of sight as a shuffled *wee mah wettah, wee mah wettah* faded with him.

"And they call that music," Gladys said, brushing at the front of her skirt. "As for *satisfied*, I'm not saying people *stay* satisfied. You'd be crazy to stay satisfied in this life."

"I'll sugar these berries," Jean said, and she took Danner's bowl. "Danner, go ask your dad what time we'll eat."

"Jean and Gladys will just have to wait. These coals are still burning down." Mitch held the clean grill of the barbecue in one hand and looked into the fire.

"How long does it take?" Danner asked, studying the heat. She stared into the coals as the fire flickered in jagged orange pieces, then disappeared. The briquets glimmered, disintegrating slowly, each piece growing a white ashen fur that looked as though it would be soft to the touch. How could he have danced with Katie? Danner's eyes burned from looking at the warmth.

"Stand back a little," her father said gently, and touched her shoulder.

Danner moved back as music approached, and she saw Billy riding fast across the bottom of the lawn. "Daddy, I want my radio. Will you tell Billy to stop and give it to me?"

"I don't know if he can stop, Miss. He's glued to that bicycle." But he put the grill down and walked a bit to the side, gesturing to Billy. He wore his khaki work clothes when he cooked on the barbecue; from behind he looked big and blockish, and Billy swerved near him, showing off. Mitch walked back toward Danner, shaking his head good-naturedly as Billy stopped.

"You shouldn't go in my room unless you ask," Danner said loudly.

Billy kicked the kickstand down in the soft grass and tilted the bike at a safe angle as the radio swung perilously; Billy caught it as it dropped from the handlebars, and he turned the volume down. "You know you go in my room," he said. His white T-shirt was stretched and grass-stained; he was sweaty and smelled of grass. His lips were slightly swollen and his eyes teary; every spring he had allergies that lasted into summer.

"You're better off if he keeps that radio," Mitch said to Danner. "Doc Reb tells me that crap they play is bad for your mind."

"I'm not hurting her radio," Billy said, walking close. "How could I hurt it?"

"Give your sister the radio." Mitch reached out and took it, then tousled Billy's hair. "You need yourself a crewcut. Hungry?"

Billy nodded. "Why can't I have my own radio?"

"You could have had," Danner said. "You asked for a new bike instead." She opened her palm for the radio, then held it close to her ear and shook it. She turned it off and on. "So don't complain," she said softly.

Billy moved next to her. "Can I give her a little shove?" he asked Mitch.

"You give her a shove and I'll give you a crack on the head. You don't horse around near these hot coals. How many times do I have to tell you?" He frowned and shifted his weight, holding the long meat fork.

"You have to tell him one hundred times, for one hundred years." Danner held the radio to Billy's cheek. "You have to tell him from an airplane."

"I'm talking to both of you," Mitch said. "Billy, put your bike away and go wash up. And I don't want you riding out to the airport again tomorrow. It'll be busy before the show."

"But the air show isn't until afternoon," Billy said, his hands in his pockets.

"They don't want kids out there. Reb said they've had break-ins at the hangar, and they've hired a guard till the festival's over. You stay away from the airport."

Billy looked at the fire a moment, then turned and walked toward the house. Danner and Mitch were silent until he was out of earshot; then Mitch said quietly, "You put the bike away."

"Okay."

He fastened the grill to the barbecue, turning it with the tines of the fork. "How old will you be at the end of this summer, Miss? Fourteen?"

Danner stood watching his heavy face through the curtain of heat. "Yes, fourteen."

"Don't seem possible," he said. "Pretty soon you'll be fifty-three and won't know where the time went."

"I guess so," Danner said. She knew he was sorry about getting mad over the dress. She wished Jean had listened to her and taken it back.

"Well." He stuck the fork through the rings of the grill so it stayed fast, then bent to close the sack of charcoal. "Tell your mother it'll be twenty minutes, and Gladys should bring the meat out now."

"I will. I'm just going to take the bike, and put my radio in my room."

o    o    o

She liked it as a box, as an object, so neat in its leather case with snaps. Brown leather like a woman's purse, with perforations over the palm-sized speaker and cutouts for the volume and tuning buttons; a rectangular strap that folded one way to hug the body of the radio and another for use as a short handle. Without the case the radio was a simple plastic block, red and white, with the white grill in the front. Rather flat, a compact shape, it sat on a tabletop like any other meaningless thing, but the quick click of one tiny wheel (OFF-ON) made it more than itself. *Without a warning you broke my heart,* the sound actually shaking in her hand if she turned it up. *You took it, darling,* tinny, as though trapped in small space but vibrating and pounding. Every sigh, every inflection, echoed a haunting, a push that was sexual and desirous, a promise to *get a little lonely in the middle of the night.* The slow songs, the ones that whimpered and questioned, came across like secrets and confession, the whisper of conscience. *I don't like you but I love you,* the seduction building to a surrender composed of simple facts: *you do me wrong now.* Noon hours at school, student council boys had played scratchy 45s on a record player, and girls jitterbugged on the basketball court. When a slow song crackled over the speakers and the lights dimmed, Danner had stood frozen in place, ashamed no one asked her to dance, terrified someone would. Now she listened to her transistor: the words were different in the privacy of summer; she didn't have to wait to be chosen. She turned the radio over in her hand so the words were lost in her palm, or held it to her throat below her ear while it buzzed against her skin, almost alive. She could turn the sound off then and the lines came unbidden, heard in her head with their nuance and growl intact: *my love is strong now.* \*
She loved the songs especially at night; she wished it were night now, all the words drifting off like air. At night, sounds replaced the words, sounds rose and fell. In bed, she held her knees in her arms, dead man's float, how it felt in water to sink and tilt while the dark came yawning up like liquid around the solid bed. Her room, solid, and the shelves in the wall with their stacked spaces

---

\*"I don't like you but I love you . . . you do me wrong now . . . my love is strong now" from "You Really Got A Hold On Me." Words and music by William "Smokey" Robinson. Copyright © 1962 by Jobete Music Co., Inc. Used by permission. International copyright secured. All rights reserved.

linear and deep. The shelves were filled with books and stacked games in cardboard boxes: Chutes and Ladders, Combat!, Candyland. Below them the trunk dolls were snapped shut in their tumbled wardrobes; *shine on your love light (I wanna know)*. Above and below lay cast-off stuffed animals and fan magazines. Mitch had designed the shelves and ordered them made at the local lumber store: they were walnut, stained dark to match the closet. Danner and Billy had watched their father tear a hole in the wall between their rooms; the hole was the size of a door and extended from floor to ceiling. Radabaugh and Pulaski from Mitch Concrete —Danner remembered them—had carried the ten-foot unit into the house: shelves on both sides, built just the thickness of the wall. The space was perfectly filled. Danner still sometimes pressed her ear to the back of the empty shelf near the floor and heard Billy walking in his room: creak of a chair as he sat at his desk building model airplanes, humming to himself. The sound was muffled, soft, inexact. Different from the radio in the dark: *Come on baby, baby please.* She imagined her mother's room: the big antique bed, the L-shaped bank of windows, the Victorian bureau and its tall mirror bordered with knobs and spires. In Billy's room, just the other side of the shelves, there were twin beds on opposite walls. Usually Mitch slept in one of them and Danner heard her father's snoring behind the sound of the radio. His sleep was labored, oblivious. The sounds didn't seem like her father at all but became instead the rhythmic workings of the house, the blind labor that got them all through the night. He caught his breath and held it, exhaling with a long high sigh that ended in a groan so deep it was nearly a word. In the old photographs at Bess's house he was a blond heavy-lidded baby in a girl's white dress: whose baby was he, orphaned, raised by Bess? The high cheekbones; the blue, long-lashed eyes in a graduation picture; the lips sensual, a little hard. The face too beautiful before his nose was broken, broken twice, fighting. *I'm begging you, baby:* often Danner put the radio inside her pillowcase and tried to fall asleep on it, her own breathing nearly silent. Listening, she knew the look of the larger bedroom: Billy turned on his side, legs drawn up, in the bed under the windows. Mitch asleep on his back, big in the other twin bed. Above them both, Billy's model planes lined up on the windowsill. He built them behind his closed door in the afternoons, moving the smallest wheels and wing fittings to their proper places with a spot of glue on the end of a toothpick. When he finished a plane, he ceremoniously applied a decal of numbers to the tops of the wings, like a name. He put the planes on his windowsill, which was wide and covered with a patchwork of cotton from Jean's jewelry boxes: long, narrow cotton from necklace boxes; square cotton from bracelet boxes. Danner is the one listening at night, imagining shapes: each airplane impervious and gray on cotton snow. Some of them have plastic men at the controls—tiny, frozen men with billed caps, looking out through cockpit windows. *Let it shine on me* while Mitch sleeps with the sheets folded down to his waist, arms at his sides; sleep such work that he spends part of each night awake. Smoking a cigarette at the kitchen table in the glow of a night lamp. Even sitting on the porch, smoking, looking at the dark fields. Sitting in the bathroom on the toilet, smoking cigarettes and reading paperbacks. Danner hears him get out of bed, clearing his throat, coughing. *Oh let it shine shine shine:* the whisper of the radio no longer really heard but felt, beating near her hand, *I feel all right I feel all right I feel all right.*

Danner and Billy sat in the back seat on the way to the dance; Jean and Gladys sat up front.

"I think it's nice the Raffertys have made a dance floor at the pool." Jean stopped for the light on Main Street, her hands dark against the white steering wheel of the Mercury.

"They can well afford a few lights and some poured concrete, the way they've bought up all those old houses near the college. Rent them all out to college students who tear them up, and make plenty. Rafferty will keep on until they own the whole town."

"Got a lot of mouths to feed." Jean smiled.

"Feed?" Gladys snorted. "They work those kids like slaves."

Danner wondered about the dance at the pool; she'd never been there at night before. Mayor Rafferty owned the Mobil station and some real estate, and he owned the pool. Over the double doors of the poolhouse hung a long sign with black letters: S.T. AND VIRGIE, STEVE, SAMMY, SONNY, SUSIE, SALLY, NICK AND

NATHAN. Nick and Nathan were their cousins who lived with them; Danner supposed that's why their names were listed last, even though they were older than Susie and Sally, who were just little girls, not in school yet. The boys were always at the pool, running the office or being lifeguards. *You're benched! Ten minutes!* The shrill of the whistle signaled rest periods, and then the Rafferty boys swam in the empty pool. Steve and Sonny were in high school and they'd teased Danner last summer when she rented her basket from the window on the girls' side: *You sure you just got out of seventh grade?* they'd said, and, *Where do you live?* Confidential laughter at her answer; then, *They grow them tall out there on Brush Fork.* Danner pushed her wire basket forward on the shelf and took the pin with the number, embarrassed, flushed with pleasure. She wasn't so sorry then that Jean had sewn a bra into the top of her two-piece bathing suit, though the cups were a hard rubber that pinched, pressing her small breasts to a barely discernible cleavage. Everyone laughed about Brush Fork; boys took girls to the country roads to park. Would the Rafferty boys remember her this summer? Probably not; her hair was longer, and she had a different bathing suit. But she'd watched the Raffertys for years: sweeping up, strutting on the sidewalk that ran around the edge of the pool, sitting in the lifeguard chairs with their long legs hanging down. She'd gone to the pool nearly every afternoon in summer, a quarter to get in, noon to six.

"You noticed they raised the price to fifty cents a kid this summer," Gladys said.

"Still," Jean answered, "you can't get a baby sitter for fifty cents an afternoon."

The poolhouse was a long low building, cement block, painted pale blue and white, and the dark office was just inside the door. The walls were lined with shelves and baskets, and everyone paid admission at the big window. Boys went to one side and girls to the other; Danner wondered if both sides were the same. The girls' was always damp, the concrete floor cold, and one of the two shower stalls had no door. The dressing rooms were wooden cubicles with a curtain strung across on string; even inside, you could smell a pungence of chlorine, and the heady scent of the honeysuckle that grew by the wire fence. The fence was six feet tall and enclosed the property on both sides, all the way back to the bushes and trees that concealed the railroad tracks.

Gladys turned around in the front seat to look at Danner. "You sure look nice. Why are you taking your beach bag?"

"I might go swimming," Danner said.

"Silly, no one will be swimming at a dance." The turn signal clicked as Jean made the turn by the post office, down Sedgwick Street to the pool. "Anyway, you'd ruin your braids, and you look so pretty in your dress. Why would you wrinkle it all up in one of those dirty baskets?"

"You couldn't pay me to swim in that pool," Gladys said. "All that chlorine."

"They have to use it," Billy said helpfully, "because everyone pees in the water."

"I don't," Danner said. But sometimes she did, and it felt wonderful.

"That's enough, Billy," Jean said.

There were cars parked on both sides of the street; the dance would be crowded. Would everyone look different at night? Danner glimpsed lights in the back, on the side lawn of the pool, and there was such a crowd! She'd heard the concrete dance floor was in the shape of a heart, then a clover leaf, then someone said it was just round. The band hadn't started yet. Oh, Danner wanted it to be nice; she'd change her clothes quickly, before any of her friends saw her and she'd have to explain. What would the high school girls wear? Danner had never seen them at a dance. Probably they'd dress just like they did at school, and not wear anything special.

Summer days the older girls wore their two-piece swimsuits and leaned languidly against the wire fence, talking through wire mesh to boys who stood in the alley. The boys had jobs and drove down on lunch break or came for the last hour, from five to six. The girls had lain in the sun all day, talking and eating ice cream from the snack bar, oiling each other and sleeping. They grew darker and smoother, and let a strap fall off one shoulder to show the dead white strip where it had been. The breasts held in their suits were that white, and their stomachs below their navels.

Bonnie Martin was always at the pool, and Ruthie Bennett, the cheerleader, a red-head who wore freckle cream on her face until the boys came. Dawn Marie Kasten, who dated Steve Rafferty, bleached her hair even though her father was a college professor; she was the only girl who had a car and she drove all her friends to the pool. When Danner had walked past their towels last summer with the grade school girls, she'd tried to listen, hear what they talked about. But she could never tell. They turned up their radios or lay speaking secretly, their heads together like lovers. They swam once all afternoon or not at all, only spraying their arms and legs with water from a bottle, the way Danner's mother dampened clothes before she ironed them on the ironing board. Afternoons they washed their hair under the one outdoor shower, suds streaming down their legs, then sat on their towels to open overnight cases. They took out curlers and pins. The round plastic rollers were bright pink or purple, fastened with long rubber-tipped bobby pins. Some girls didn't need a mirror and were very fast, sectioning off each little strand of hair with the sharp end of a rat-tail comb. The curlers were arranged in patterns and perfectly placed, as though they were a hairstyle in themselves. Heads bristling with cylinders, the girls lay on their stomachs with their faces to the side, tanning while their curls dried. Later, hoping, they went inside to the dank dressing rooms to comb out and put on lipstick. The ones who were going steady could leave their curlers in all day; they talked to their boyfriends like confident wives, leaning against the fence and rerolling a curler that had come loose. Their simple gestures looked intimate. They touched their heads as they talked, flashing their certainties and their alliances in public. Some of them went all the way. The younger girls wondered which ones and played games of Crazy Eights, keeping score on gum wrappers; they swam all day and did underwater somersaults in the deep end.

Danner wished she'd called her friends on the phone to be sure some were coming to the dance. A few were on vacation already with their families; others would be too shy.

"Billy," Jean said, "I'm going to give Danner the spending money, and anytime you want something, just ask her for whatever you need."

Billy groaned. "Why don't you give me my own money?"

"Because I want you to get it from Danner, that's why."

"She wants you two to keep in touch," Gladys said liltingly.

Billy grimaced and looked out the window. Danner touched him across the seat, signaling with a glance that she'd give him his entire share as soon as they got inside.

Jean pulled into the gravel driveway of the poolhouse. The alleyway was full of parked automobiles; lanky teenage boys stood in clusters among them, smoking cigarettes. "Have a good time," Jean said. "I'll be here to pick you up right at ten."

"Okay," Billy said, resigned. He got out of the car and walked up the sidewalk to the entrance.

"Look at him," Gladys said softly. "Walks just like his father, little as he is."

Danner got out of the Mercury and hitched the beach bag to her shoulder. As she stood by the driver's side, Jean beckoned her closer, and she pressed three dollar bills into Danner's hand. "Keep an eye on your brother."

"Mom, Billy will be fine."

Jean smiled and shook her head. "You look so lovely, it makes me sad."

Gladys spoke from inside the car. "Jeannie, let the kid go to the dance. I promise, she'll come home to you."

"Yeah," Danner agreed, "I will."

"Have to," Jean said. "Can't get far on three dollars, can you." She sat still, looking, blocking Gladys' view of Danner's face.

"Not too far." Danner said.


She walked through the narrow concrete corridor of the pool-house that was the girls' side, and stepped out onto the back porch. Dawn Marie Kasten and Bonnie Martin stood quite near her, leaning on the shelf of the snack bar. Danner smiled tentatively; just as she was about to lower her gaze, Dawn Marie spoke to her.

"Aren't you a little old to wear your hair in pigtails?" she asked flatly.

For a moment Danner didn't answer. Her face was burning, but she wouldn't let herself walk away. "These are French braids," she said.

The older girls exchanged glances, and Bonnie Martin smiled. "I think your braids are rather pretty."

Dawn Marie looked off coolly. "Prettier than pedal pushers and a rhinestone tiara, certainly."

"She's talking about our queen," Bonnie Martin said to Danner, raising her eyebrows and nodding toward the lawn.

It was just twilight and growing darker quickly. The queen this year was a co-ed at the local college who'd graduated from Bellington High two years before, and she was walking with Steve Rafferty past the pool. She was a tall girl who'd been head majorette; her white pedal pushers were tight, and the tiara sat securely in her bouffant hairdo. Farther on, lights strung in the tree above the dance floor looked bright against dark leaves. Light bulbs strung on wire across the floor itself looked pale and wishful, glowing in midair.

"Is the dance floor nice?" Danner asked.

The girls had already turned away, but Bonnie Martin looked back quickly. "Yes, dear, it's nice," she said.

"Though the drain in the middle is a bit tacky," Dawn Marie added.

"Dawn Marie is a little tacky herself tonight," Bonnie Martin said, and put her arm around Dawn affectionately. "Steve Rafferty has the bad taste to like pedal pushers."

Dawn Marie laughed, and winked at Danner.

Danner smiled, hoping it was the right response, and walked out the sidewalk toward the pool and the lawn. She looked for Billy and saw him standing at the edge of the dance crowd with two boys his age. He wouldn't want her to give him the money in front of them; she'd have to wait. Why had Dawn Marie winked at her? She was meant to know something she didn't know. The band was tuning up and Danner walked toward the sound. The whines of the guitars were plaintive, punctuated with show-off riffs from the drummer. All around, leaves in the trees were lifting gently. The breeze didn't smell of rain though; and the expanse of grass looked so unbroken, beautifully green. Danner walked twice around the pool, curious and pleased because she'd never seen it so empty of swimmers.

The dance had become a spot of brighter light on the big lawn. Danner moved toward it and realized she didn't see anyone she knew, so she sat down on a bench near the dance floor. When she heard voices and looked up, Steve Rafferty stood close beside her, with Dawn Marie.

"I remember you," he said, looking down. "What a nice white dress; you just get cuter all the time. Now, where was it I used to see you?" He crossed his arms and regarded her.

Dawn Marie stepped closer to him, glaring at the side of his face. "Maybe in a French convent, or in that eighth-grade gym class you impregnated. That's what she is you know, an eighth grader."

He turned to her with a measured movement and put his hands hard on either side of her face. "Poor Dawn," he said, sarcastic, "always jealous of the unspoiled and the innocent." Holding her, he put his lips on hers and kissed her for a long time, turning his face a little to the side and pressing against her as though he were drinking from her mouth, slowly and deeply. Danner sat motionless, scared, afraid to move. When Steve pulled away from Dawn, he still held her and looked at her levelly, daring her to try to resist.

She stared back at him, her eyes wet, and didn't try to move. "Big man," she said, her voice shaking, "you'll end up running a gas station in this hick town."

"Just as long as you're running it with me, sweetheart." His tone was practiced but his fingers slid down her throat almost helplessly, and he touched the ribbed neck of her thin sweater.

Danner stood then and brushed past them, heading across the lawn toward the trees and the tracks. Behind her the dance had actually started. Music rang out loudly but Danner wasn't conscious of which song, which words. She walked quickly toward the cover of the brush, and the music grew less noticeable. Far away, she heard the faintly shuddering rumble of a train approaching. She didn't care anymore about changing her clothes; she just wanted to stay away from the dance until it was time to go home. Now, away from the lights, it was really almost dark; she could sit near the tracks by the river and the train shack. She liked the shack, a dilapidated second-story room on stilts. The dangerously wobbly foundation was nothing but boards nailed around the outer supports to make a high-ceilinged space over the earthern floor. No one went there because it might be full of snakes, but the upper room had a door and windows, and rickety metal stairs with a railing. When the train thundered by, the little room shook; the tops of boxcars flashed by just beneath the windows.

The train moaned again now, still a ways off. As Danner emerged from the bushes near the tracks, she saw the round light of the engine, the small glow approaching through the trees. She heard brush rustle behind her and turned; it was Billy.

"What are you doing following me?" She held the beach bag tighter as though he might intuit its contents.

"I want my money, to get a coke. I yelled at you as you walked off, but you didn't turn around."

"How could I hear you over the band?" She relaxed her grip on the bag and said more softly, "I wish you wouldn't yell out my name in front of everyone."

"No one heard," Billy said. He looked down the track past the train shack to the bend in the rails where the trees were thick. Big limbs hung lushly over the track. "Anyway," he said, pleased, "the train is coming."

"I hate this dance," Danner said. "Don't you hate it?"

Billy shrugged. Unconsciously, they'd kept their voices low. Now he whispered and nodded up at the train shack. "Who's that at the shack?"

In the moonlit dark, they saw the block shape of the old building and the silhouette of the stairs. A line of boys stood on the steps, four of them; then the door of the shack half-opened and a boy came out, wordlessly taking his place at the end of the line. The first boy went inside. Again, four of them stood waiting.

"Stay right here so they won't see us," Billy said. "We can watch the train up close."

Danner barely heard his words as the sound of the train grew louder; once the engine was in sight at the bend, the train came so fast it seemed to fall toward them. Danner and Billy stood perhaps ten feet back, and the boxcars made a clattering wind, blurred words stenciled on their sides, their individual boundaries gone. Danner didn't look directly at the cars but felt the air of the train at the side of her face—smokey, racing air that pulled at her. She saw Billy squinting straight ahead, arms crossed, feet spread as though to hold his ground. Danner looked past him, down the length of the rails. The roar was deafening and the train shack vibrated, the metal steps shaking. The whistle blew again, hooting a long bellow; one boy leaned over the wobbly railing and a ribbon of vomit snaked noiselessly through the air. Danner looked away, watching the building; the two windows glowed faintly as though the interior were lit by flashlights or a dim lantern. Danner had been inside before, sneaking in with girlfriends to look at the forbidden place. But the train shack was just empty and dirty, barnlike but small, with random straw and disintegrating rope on the floor. Burlap bags piled in one corner were stiff, stuck together, and there was a rank, tantalizing smell the summer daylight hadn't quite dispelled. Danner pressed her arms to her sides; the memory of how the room had looked, the memory of the smell, came back to her powerfully. She turned her back on the old building and faced the receding train, past them so fast.

"Oh, that was great," Billy said.

She saw the other boy then, standing farther down the tracks, where he must have been all along. At first she thought he was an adult—he was tall and stood so silently—but he walked closer and she saw his rumpled shirt, the shirttail out, and his jeans. He wore his sleeves rolled up above his biceps but he didn't look country; maybe he was from Winfield or one of the other large towns near Bellington. He smoked his cigarette attentively, holding it with his thumb and forefinger like someone in the movies. The burning ash of the cigarette moved in the dark, a small red ember near his lips, at his side. A shock of thick, dark hair fell over one eyebrow; he shook it back.

"You two lost?" He spoke to Danner, his voice deep but not menacing. "Don't you mean to be at the dance?"

"No. It's a crummy dance."

"Yeah." The older boy leaned slightly forward, looking past Danner at Billy. "Who's he?"

"He's my brother." Danner felt Billy near her, cautious and watchful.

The boy said nothing, then averted his gaze, looking out across the tracks to the brushy riverbank opposite. The water was sluggish, so low and brown, and across the river was the old river road, hardly traveled anymore. There were lights in some of the houses but the lights were scattered; most of those ramshackle places were abandoned now.

"What are they doing in the train shack?" Danner asked.

"What do you think?" He paused. "They got a girl in there."

"How do you know?"

"Never mind how I know." He turned and looked at her then, full face. "You get on out of here now, and take your kid brother."

"Come on," Billy said.

"Are they hurting her?" Danner looked up at the boy. In the light of the moon she saw a stubble of beard on his cheeks. He squinted in the smoke of his cigarette, and past his shoulders the railroad tracks curved out of sight in trees.

"Nah. You can't hurt girls like her." He shook his head and gave a sad half-laugh. "You don't know nothing, do you? Younger than you look, I guess." He threw the cigarette down and ground it under his heel, the pocked gravels of the tracks crunching. "Go on now," he said then, not looking at them, "get going."

Billy took Danner's wrist and moved off, pulling her; then they were walking fast through the leafy brush and Danner saw him dimly ahead. He was several paces in front by the time they broke through the cover of the bushes to cross the lawn; beyond him the swimming pool was an illusory rectangle that glistened, framed in a concrete rim. They passed the still water and Danner ran to catch up. As though by agreement, they neared the lights and noise of the dance floor together, joining the crowd slowly.

They stood safely camouflaged at last, comforted by the rustle of voices, when the band began a slow song.

Too late, Danner caught her breath and tried to back off the floor toward the darkness of the grass. All around her, the crowd dissolved into slowly moving couples, all anonymous, their faces hidden in each other's throats. The girls held the boys around the neck with both bare arms, spellbound, as though suddenly possessed of a sensual fatigue. Danner turned, looking for a way through the dancers. Billy was near her and she thought he was following; then she felt the pressure of his arm around her waist. He pressed close and his heart beat against her. Carefully, they danced, taking small steps, and it was not so difficult. Lights strung on wire above them glimmered, and Billy held one of her hands correctly to the side, as though they kept a breakable object in their clasped hands. His brow came just to her chin and she felt his smooth forehead against her mouth.

# THE AIR SHOW
## Billy, 1963

He saw the planes at slanted angles, looming up snub-nosed with the line of the horizon tilting behind them. The Piper Cub looked gargantuan as it began bumping slowly over ground, the spinner conical and stationary, with the moving propeller a striped blur. Above it the windscreen was clear and reflective like a blank, unfaceted eye. Billy could see the motion of the ailerons in the wings, a machine movement supple as the ripple of a gill in something live. The noise of the engine increased and the nose trembled as the plane moved so close it was nothing but silver. Engine roar faded to the low buzz of an electric razor: his father, shaving in the bathroom. Billy lay still, listening. It was very early and the razor stopped. Light slaps as Mitch applied after-shave, snap and latch of cabinet doors. All the sounds were distinctly male and private, assured of an ownership that was unchallenged. Billy kept his eyes shut, trying to make the time last. Just outside the bedroom windows, scratch of birds on the concrete breezeway. He heard his father coughing, then the sound of his tread in the hall past the bedroom, his soft-soled shoes quiet. He would be going into town to have pancakes with Bess and Katie at seven, as on every Sunday morning, but this was the day of the air show.

Billy looked: on the other side of the room, where his father slept, the twin bed was made, the red bedspread perfectly turned down under the pillow. *You learn in the Army, private: make your bed as soon as you stand up; then it's done, see, for the day.* The engine of the Chevrolet revved, then purred as he backed out the driveway. The house was silent, but if Billy listened hard he could hear the others sleeping: Danner in the small room next to his, and his mother in the bigger room at the end of the hallway.

He stood and pulled the covers up, then walked to the bathroom. His father's leather toilet kit was zipped shut; the razor was put away. Out the window Billy saw crows circling over the field, over the tall seed corn that was choked with wild grass. He peed, thinking. He was twelve, almost thirteen. Three years until his learner's permit, then his license—he'd have a car. He'd have to buy it himself but Mitch would help him. Billy looked again into the fields; near the fence the mown grass was glinting with dew that caught the sun. The sky was already blue. When he was a man, he'd have an airplane of his own—a Cessna, he figured, with floats so he could land on a lake. He tried to imagine a lake appearing far below him, a flat blue shape neat as the lakes on maps. But the blue would spread as he got closer, and the water would look rougher; there would be pine trees all around like there were in Canada. And snow on mountains in summer. He'd seen pictures of fishing trips in his father's *Sports Illustrated* magazines. Could they ever go to Canada in an airplane and catch trout? *Takes money*, Mitch had replied shortly.

How would Billy get money? He'd begun to consider working for an airline. Students filled out information sheets on the first day of seventh grade; in September Billy planned to write *commercial pilot* under "possible career interests." But you had to be a certain height to pilot a passenger jet, and maybe he wouldn't make it. Mom said it was silly to worry; anyway, seventh graders had no business filling out forms about careers, and the school system should concentrate on algebra. All last winter, they'd sat at the kitchen table over his math homework. Long division. Billy did one problem after another while Jean checked them laboriously. He had the numbers in his mind, but all the while he was aware of her face over his shoulder, her attention completely focused. His father watching television, Danner playing 45s on her record player, were only background noise. Daytimes and evenings, the house belonged to Jean; the kitchen was hers, the sink, the stove, the table; the garage, where she kept the washer and dryer, the overflowing baskets of shirts and clean underwear; the living room, where she sat at night to grade papers from her first-grade class, endless mimeographed sheets of clowns and numbers. She taught at the same grade school he and Danner had attended; he was accustomed to seeing her in the lunchroom, drinking coffee with the other women at the teachers' table, or on the playground with her class. He wouldn't be seeing her at the junior high next year. The big old building was so crowded he'd seldom see Danner; she was two grades ahead of him. Classes changed according to bells; he liked the idea of being anonymous in the wide hallways while the bells rang like alarms. Still, some evenings when he built models in his room, the look of his mother's face as she'd counted numbers came back to him. He sat wrapped in a familiar calm, handling plastic pieces that, unassembled, seemed a series of small, meaningless fragments. His collection of model airplanes ranged from Japanese Zeros to Spitfires to F-14s, and they were all to scale; Billy built them slowly and carefully, applying clear viscous glue with the tip of a toothpick. The tiny pilots were frozen in the act of fastening caps or tightening straps; they were already seated on nothingness, knees bent to fit into a cockpit. Billy looked closely at the details of their molded uniforms and remembered the short, black lashes of his mother's unadorned eyes.

Standing now outside the bathroom door, he saw Jean sleeping. She lay on her side in the high antique bed, her hand at her mouth. Her dark hair had loosened and fell back from her face. Her lips were still reddened; there was a faint rose smear on her pillow. She slept so soundly she barely moved with her breath. He could wake Danner up; they could ride out to the airfield on their bikes and be back before their mother woke. By nine-thirty she'd want them dressed for church. Billy grimaced; if he said he was staying home she'd never let him spend the whole afternoon at the air show. There'd be planes from all over the state, taking off in succession and circling, flying banners, or performing simple stunts.

He walked back up the hallway, watching wooden strips of the parquet floor under his bare feet. He knew approximately what Jean did every day. While he and Danner were riding back from the airfield, she'd be waking up; she'd pour herself two cups of coffee, one right after the other. On summer Saturdays she worked in the flower beds before cleaning the house and doing laundry, but on Sundays she slept in until nine and went to church at ten. Weekdays during school semesters, he guessed she did exactly what the other teachers did, only for little kids: reading and social studies before noon, science and math after. What Mitch did was almost a mystery. His work was a vinyl-covered notebook filled with order forms and diagrams of the metal buildings he sold to construction sites. He'd shown Billy the notebook, just as he'd once shown him the engines of concrete mixers. He'd owned the concrete company with Uncle Clayton then. The trucks were no mystery, their hoods thrown up to reveal hard interiors of throbbing blocks and hoses. The parts were crusted with age and smelled of cooked dirt. The notebook his father carried now smelled clean, barely disturbed, like a new text. Danner had probably never even looked inside.

He walked into her room. The pink-checked curtains were drawn, the small room dim in the bright morning. For a moment the bed was only a high dark shape in tangled space. *Stirred with a stick,* his mother called Danner's room. Billy walked over magazines and books and cast-off clothes and stood waiting. She'd wake up if he stared at her, unless she was only pretending to sleep.

She lay on her stomach, limbs outstretched as though she'd reached the bed in free-fall and clung to what she occupied. Her hands held the curved edges of the mattress.

"Danner," he whispered, certain she was awake, "get up."

She opened her eyes immediately. "Why?"

"Ride out to the airfield with me before Mom is awake."

She turned over and pulled the sheet up to her chin. "The hangar isn't even open yet. There won't be anything to see."

"I can get into the hangar," Billy told her, "but we have to hurry."

"You can?" She paused, considering. "Dad told you not to go out there again until after the air show. Is it true there's a guard with a gun at the hangar now?"

"Just old Cosgrove. He's always had a gun—he shoots groundhogs on the landing strip." Billy leaned closer to her. Somewhere near them he heard a minute whispering. He reached under her pillow and held up the transistor radio. "Do you sleep with your radio?"

She smiled, embarrassed, and took it from him. "I forgot. I fell asleep." She turned the sound off and on to make sure the batteries still worked, then held it to her ear. "Last night after we got home from the pool dance, I heard WLS. Now there's only air."

"What's WLS?"

"Chicago. Hundreds of miles away." Her eyes moved to the obscured windows above her bed. "I hated that dance," she said then, almost to herself.

"You told Mom it was okay."

Danner turned the radio off. "Well, it wasn't. I'm not going anymore." She looked at him quizzically. "You never told me you know how to slow-dance."

"I don't. I just moved my feet." He shifted his weight, remembering uncomfortably the crowded floor, the lights strung up above like carnival lights. "It doesn't matter now. Hurry and get up. We have to leave right away, and don't make noise."

Crickets sounded up and down the road in the fields, as though it were still night. The wheels of the bicycles skimmed along the smooth cement. He rode beside Danner, wishing she'd go faster but observing a tacit etiquette.

"Listen how loud the crickets are," Danner said. "They're down in the thick grass near the dirt and don't know it's daylight."

"Sure they do. The sun just isn't hot enough yet to make them stop."

She glanced at him, leaning more forward on her bike. "You don't know why they don't stop."

"I know how to get into the hangar. I'll show you, but you have to do like I say so Cosgrove won't see us."

"Doesn't he live beside the airfield, in that white house?"

"That's why he's the caretaker. He's just an old retired guy." Billy leaned back, steering with one hand. "We go around the other side of the hangar—he can't see from the house."

They rode, without talking, up the hill. There were no cars on the road and no movement around the infrequent houses, but the fields themselves looked alive. Their colors brightened in swatches as the sun got higher. Crows flew. The hoarse calls of roosters ricocheted.

"When Polly got lost, Cosgrove was the old man we talked to at the airfield." Danner spoke without turning her gaze from the road.

"Did Dad bring us out here? Are you sure?"

Their dog, Polly, a retriever mix, had disappeared two years before. Jean had announcements made on the local radio; Mitch had driven up and down dirt roads branching off Brush Fork, while Danner and Billy called the dog's name from the car. Months later, Billy found an animal skeleton in a ditch, deep into the field behind the house. He'd almost stumbled into a depression where the bones lay, creamy-colored, their sheen dull. The perfect fan of the ribs held an oval egg-shaped space in the concave bed of the ditch; the long tail was stretched out, each vertebrae particular and unbroken. The bones were a stencil of a vanished dog. If it was really Polly, where was her collar? But the bones themselves seemed to finalize her disappearance. Billy never told anyone he'd found them. He covered them with long grass. Sometimes men found things with airplanes—they flew over vast lands looking for signs from the air. But even with an airplane he couldn't have found Polly.

"I would have remembered the airfield," Billy said.

Danner smiled, a little out of breath. "You didn't like airplanes yet, so you don't remember."

The sky was brightening to a sharp indigo. Dew still dried in the fields, and the rich smell of the ground was barely evident.

Later on, the heat would fill the air with the weedy odor of soil and plants and pollen. Now, far off, there was the high whine of a locust.

"It's a perfect day," Billy said. "I don't want to go to church."

Danner sighed. "She can't go by herself. No one goes tc that church alone except old ladies whose husbands are dead."

The road leveled; Billy pedaled faster. He hated wearing a coat and tie; he hated seeing all the seated, hushed people. He'd sat through hour-long Methodist services since the age of six, watching his mother's gloved hands. If he was fidgety she'd let him work the short, tight gloves off her hands, finger by finger, then put them back on.

"We can't spend long at the hangar," Danner said. "We have to be back before she wakes up."

Over the crest of the last hill, the weathered tin of the big hangar stood out against the field, the silver roof painted with a giant white circle.

"Ride a little past the airfield," Billy told Danner. "Stop when I do and we'll put the bikes down flat, off the road. We can walk across the meadow on the other side of the hangar—even if Cosgrove is awake, he won't see us." Billy passed her and rode farther ahead.

The old hangar was dilapidated. The wood frame was covered with tin sheeting; the ribbed sheets were dented, pocked in places with BB holes. The sharply sloping metal roof had been patched, but swallows had gotten in under the sheeting and nested under the eaves. Billy led Danner across the high-grown meadow to the side of the building. Behind it was the empty landing strip: long, yellow dirt the width of a two-lane road. Billy stepped close to the hangar and touched a piece of the metal sheeting near a seam, pressing it in. He rattled the big panel until it slipped slightly, then pulled one edge out a couple of feet.

"Go through sideways," he said. "Watch me first." He wondered if she could do it; she was bigger than he was.

Inside there was a smell of damp earth. The light was gray. Long, dim beams slanted from two high windows. Billy stood still as his eyes adjusted, and Danner stumbled behind him, rattling the panel. The planes were parked closer together than he'd ever seen them, in two shadowed rows. The numbers on the wings were clearly legible even in near darkness. He crouched and turned to his sister. "Bend over so you stay below the wings."

"Wait, I can't see. It's so big in here." She bent down, feeling the ground. "There's no floor, just dirt."

"Water comes in when it rains," Billy whispered. "Come on now." He moved quickly, scuttling under wings, and heard Danner behind him trying to keep up. He'd always been alone in the hangar before; hearing her made him feel he was leading an expedition. One of the oldest planes was never locked and seemed never to be flown; he could show her that one, he was sure, and the special box on the copilot's side.

"Don't go so fast," she called after him.

He could have walked down the middle of the two rows but he led her in and out, weaving around and circling the planes. Finally he stopped near the rear of the hangar, beside the old Beechcraft. Danner stood, watching. He opened the door of the airplane and stepped up. She was below him then, looking up expectantly. "Get in. On your side." He shut the door gently and heard her moving under the nose of the plane, then the smooth click of the other door opening. She looked in, pleased, and stepped up. After she latched the door shut, they both sat still.

The Beech was a two-seater in good condition. The seats were specially covered in dark, cracked leather and the instrument panel was wooden. Billy imagined Cosgrove polishing the glossy surface, rubbing it with a rag. Once, the plane had been used often; though the wood of the panel gleamed, the clocks and dials set into it looked old, their metal rims dull. Billy touched the pilot's stick. The room within the plane was completely familiar; Billy knew every detail.

"It's so small in here," Danner said, "like being in a tent."

Billy pointed. "There's a box strapped underneath. Look inside."

She felt under the instrument panel without bending to see; Billy heard the leather straps unsnap. The box was in her hands then; she held it level in her palm, as though afraid the contents would spill.

"It's okay," Billy said. "Open it."

The brown leather of the box was thick; it was neat and square, and the top fit tight like the lid of a cigar box. Danner lifted it. Inside was a narrow, cut-glass flask with a silver base and cap, and a silver goblet on either side; all three objects were held snug by molding covered in dark fabric. Danner lifted the flask carefully. The base was inscribed in small block letters: BEHIND STANDS THE GENERAL NAVIGATOR—COURAGE. 1949.

"What does it mean?" Danner whispered, staring at the letters.

"Navigator is the name of the plane," Billy said, "Beechcraft Navigator."

She turned the bottle from one side to the other, touching the ridges of the textured glass. High up in the rafters of the hangar, swallows called. Their calls were high, drawn-out whistles, echoing, ending on high notes like repeated questions. Danner looked up, then closed the box, smoothing the leather cover with her hand. She took care to replace it exactly. "I don't know if we should be sitting here," she said.

The metal hangar doors rumbled then, sliding back on runners. Billy saw Cosgrove and another, younger man at the entrance, leaning with their shoulders to push the old doors. "Get down," Billy said, and they leaned flat across the seats of the Beech, their bodies overlapping. "It's just a pilot coming to get a plane."

A voice spoke. "Sorry to get you up so early."

Cosgrove answered. "Don't matter. Doing some shooting anyway."

"Get any raccoon?"

"Not in the field here. Not till you cross the creek."

Silence as the men walked. They must have come after one of the Piper Cubs near the front; they stopped not far from the entrance. "I'll help you pivot her," Cosgrove said.

Billy heard them turn the plane; then Cosgrove walked back outside. Now the pilot would be attaching a tow bar to the nose gear so he could pull the plane slowly out of the hangar to the runway.

"Let's get out of here," Danner whispered.

Billy signaled her to stay quiet. She nodded. They listened as the Cub moved, creaking, the sound growing more faint. Billy sat up and looked. "He's outside. We can hide in the field at the end of runway and see him take off."

"You're going to get us in trouble."

"They won't see us, the grass is high. Slide out on my side."

They were out quickly. Billy remembered to latch the door of the Beech. The hangar was lit now with daylight, and they squeezed out through the same opening between the tin panels of the siding. They ran straight across the field, hidden from sight by the hangar itself until they cut over to the far end of the airstrip and threw themselves down on their bellies. They were just in front of the dirt runway, several feet back into the tall field. Billy saw Cosgrove and the pilot talking near the hangar. The Cub was in position to take off and the pilot was paying Cosgrove. He turned and got into the Cub; Cosgrove walked back toward the hangar, holding his rifle low against his leg.

"The plane will taxi straight toward us," Billy told Danner. "Don't move. Promise."

The engine coughed and caught, the single propeller turning seven or eight slow turns. The Cub was moving, picking up speed, the whirring propeller a flash of motion radiating outward from the spinner. The plane came on fast. Billy pressed himself flatter against the ground, staring intently to see through the grass. He stopped thinking then as the Cub approached, the grind of the engine heightened in pitch, smoothing out. There was a sensation of noise and the ground itself slanting, as the nose of the plane honed in.

Then it was airborne.

He'd never seen a plane in flight so close. Streaks of rust were on the underside, and the small wheels of the landing gear still turned. Billy rose up; the plane was perhaps thirty feet above them as it passed over, lifting off, roaring. He stood into the roar, Danner grabbing his arm hard. Then she was on top of him, yelling into his neck as the sound of the plane was everywhere, rumbling through the tall grass. As the plane banked left, Billy saw the pilot look down at them, a shock of surprise on his face. Billy looked back elated as he sank to his knees in the spongy dirt.

He knelt and the field was eye level, glossed with the yellow tassels of the blooming weeds. He could see Cosgrove at the other end of the runway, standing blocklike in overalls and work hat, his back to them.

"Get down," Danner said urgently.

"No, he isn't facing this way." Billy craned his neck to keep the plane in sight as it gained altitude, then grabbed Danner's wrist. "Come on. We'll run. He won't see us now."

"No, wait!" She stayed crouched, trying to pull Billy into the cover of the grass.

Billy tightened his grip on her arm and stood; then he let go and ran. He knew she'd follow him. He ran, hearing the swish of grass against his legs. He ran flat out and saw her beside him, a peripheral moving image. He smiled, running. The plane had gone up just above him, so loud and so close. The pilot had seen him: it was like a pact.

# AMAZING GRACE
## Danner, 1965

Mitch took her to work in the big white Chevrolet. She had a job that summer as a banquet waitress at the local Methodist college, carrying eight heaped plates to conference tables of ministers. The girls piled the plates on oval trays in the kitchen, squatted, balanced the weight on one shoulder, and held it with both hands as they stood. The manager kept the swinging door open as the waitresses, all fifteen and sixteen years old, walked to their assigned places and squatted again, straight-backed, sliding the trays onto stands. Amazed at their own feats of strength, they smoothed their dark skirts and delivered roast beef. Danner hated their uniforms: white blouses, black straight skirts, nylons, and dark shoes. August was so hot that if Jean took her to work, the black '59 Ford having baked in the sun until the seats smelled of hot rubber, Danner's legs were clammy with sweat by the time they arrived. Mitch's car had an air conditioner, and if he was in a good mood he'd turn the engine on and cool the car before Danner got in. She sat in the encapsulated coolness and watched the landscape while they drove to town; the fields by the Brush Fork road seemed to steam with heat, and the edge of the sign that marked the city limits shone sharp and brilliant.

Mitch smoked a cigarette, leaving his window open a sliver to take the smoke. "What time do you want me to pick you up?"

"You don't have to pick me up, it's Friday." Riley always picked her up on Fridays after he got off work at the A&P. Without looking at Mitch, Danner knew her father was shaking his head and frowning. "I won't be late tonight. Eleven was just too early—the drive-in doesn't even start until eight or nine. Mom said I could come in at midnight until school starts."

"I've told Jean what I think of that, but she doesn't give a damn what I say." He glanced over at Danner, then scowled at the road. "I know Riley's father and I like Riley, but he's eighteen and he's a little too old for you."

"I'm almost sixteen," Danner said, and fell silent. After work she and Riley would go to Nedelson's Parkette to eat, then to the drive-in, where Danner would fall asleep exhausted midway through the first feature. The sound of the movie close to her face filled her mind with pictures. Usually she woke in an hour or so, happy, with Riley drinking a beer beside her.

"I know how old you are," Mitch said. "You know that's not what I'm talking about."

Danner knew, but what difference did the time of night make? Riley had taken her parking since last winter, when her curfew was earlier. Now their rituals were established. What moved her most was the moment when he said her name involuntarily; then she was sliding down on the seat under him, and it was like the soundtrack at the drive-in—a surface closed over her. What was near and solid drifted far off and sounds came indescribably close; his breathing was all she heard. They lay down fully clothed and he moved against her until he came, so hard in his pants that she could move her legs slightly apart and feel the shape of him. Danner had still never touched a man. Riley stroked her thighs, moving his hands higher in subtle circles until she clasped his fingers. He would major in business at Lynchburg

State, forty miles away; already, Danner knew she couldn't stay with him. She didn't confide in him, not really.

"What do you think about this moving idea of your mother's?" The cigarette smoked in the ash tray. Mitch drove with one hand and kept the other on the back of his neck, as though to cushion some blow.

"Well, the house she's picked out is nice."

"There's nothing wrong with our own house. It was good enough for her when I built it. I don't know what your mother is doing. She needs a good slap."

Danner turned to look at him. He'd combed his gray hair back with water; under the band of his hat it had dried in the teeth marks of the comb. The hat was a summer baseball hat with a green bill. In the shadow of the bill, his face was profiled. "Don't you ever hit her," Danner said evenly.

Mitch tilted the hat back on his head and raised his voice. "I said a slap. I didn't mean I was going to break her jaw."

"It doesn't matter what you break. A man shouldn't hit a woman." Danner smoothed her skirt nervously, then asked, less assured, "Don't you think I'm right?"

"Hell," Mitch said quietly.

"Think how you'd feel if Riley hit me."

Mitch stubbed the cigarette out. The smell of ash mingled with the odor of mechanical air. "Riley shouldn't be having anything to hit you about. If he could get that mad at you, you're way too involved."

"We aren't too involved." Danner drew a deep breath, and she could taste a tinge of tobacco. "Why don't you ever say these things to Billy? He goes out on dates."

"Your brother is just a kid, and that girl is his age. Riley is going off to college. I wasn't born yesterday. If you're going to go out, you should go out with someone in your own class."

Danner sat back in the seat and said nothing. Now he'd have words with Jean, a cold tense scene, while Gladys Curry sat at the kitchen table pretending not to listen. Danner knew the look on her mother's face exactly: she would keep her expression impassive, her lips set hard. Danner felt the expression stealing over her own face, and she focused only on the road. The concrete glistened in the noon heat, a bright white band bending away toward Bellington.

There was silence between them.

Finally she said to her father, "You don't have to worry about Riley, and that's the truth."

He didn't reply, but they drove along and the atmosphere gradually lightened. Danner dreaded working another ministers' banquet, and the voyage to work became an interlude of privacy. Her father's cars were always big and luxurious, not quite new, impeccably clean and cared for. The motor of the Chevrolet hummed evenly; they rode so smoothly that Danner felt lulled, almost sleepy. She leaned her head back on the seat. "Dad," she said, "do you remember your dreams?"

"Well, yes, don't you?"

"What do you dream about?"

He looked out the window to his left, considering, then said slowly, "Haven't remembered any in a long time."

Danner touched the air-conditioning vent and turned it toward her knees, then left her hand in the stream of cold. The heat outside was thick and fluid like clear paint. Bellington's wooden frame houses flowed by, their big porches shaded and still with heat. "What's the last dream you remember?" Danner asked.

He tipped his hat back and ran his fingers along the curve of the bill. "Dreamed I was in a snowstorm," he said.

"Alone?"

He was hesitant, or maybe responding to the pull of silence that punctuated most of his remarks in conversation. He looked over at Danner, half-frowning, half-smiling, as though she should already have known the answer. "I was driving in a snowstorm along a road," he said, "and snow was flying at the windshield so fast you couldn't see where you was going."

"Were you in this car?"

"I don't know. I was only watching the road." He laughed. "Couldn't see a damn thing."

"What happened next?"

"Nothing, Hon. That's all there was to it."

They had turned down Sedgwick Street to the back campus of the college. Mitch pulled over while Danner gazed at the dining hall. Red brick, with a concrete porch and white columns, the hall matched all the other buildings on the densely green lawns. The small campus ended here; behind the dining hall stretched the railroad tracks and the athletic field.

"You should see the ministers running," Danner said. "It's so hot, you'd think they'd drop dead. Afternoons while we're cleaning, we see them running circles around the field."

Mitch chuckled. "Damn right. Ministers should run, that's about all they're good for."

The banquet hall was full of smooth clatter and murmuring talk while the ministers ate. They didn't raise their voices and weren't boisterous, but their combined noises were like those of a flock of serious, famished birds. They were all in their forties or older; Danner imagined them to be veterans of some sort—veterans of no less than six southern churches, for instance, or of thirty years' service with merit. They ate with studious attention and talked intently. Immediately, they made the room hotter. The air conditioning in the hall didn't work well, and the ministers sat moistly at long tables in their dark suits, eating roasted meat and mashed potatoes. The noon meal was the large one; for supper, the ministers ate hamburgers and french fries with ketchup. Danner thought them a sad lot and could almost be sad herself as she stood by the silverware cart, watching them chew. Automatically, she read the placard again.

Each day there was a placard with the title of the afternoon colloquium, and the titles were always questions about current events. The big card was displayed on a music stand at the back of the room. Today it said: RIOT IN WATTS. IS GOD THERE? The TV news had run pictures of Watts all week. Danner made remarks about the placards to the other waitresses. Today in particular, the question struck her as horrible and pathetic and funny, and she had to walk past the hand-lettered words every time she went into the kitchen. Now she stole a glance at the clock above the entrance doors, then gazed around the hall.

Waitresses stood at various points in the room, camouflaged in their uniforms. Most of them were pretty, and they signaled each other flirtatiously. Everyone was bored at the prospect of cleaning stainless-steel counters and milk machines and floors all afternoon, while the ministers talked about Watts. Finally the men would arrive for their hamburgers or grilled sandwiches. Later the waitresses would clear again, replenish condiments, and do an abridged version of the cleaning they'd just finished. Danner looked at the windows behind the ministers; sunlight assaulted the glass. She wanted to be at Rafferty's Public Pool where girls with no summer jobs tanned themselves all day. Lee Ann Casto, Danner's best friend, worked beside her in the banquet hall. She'd given Danner a gift-certificate admission to Rafferty's Pool. The certificate was worth one dollar, it admitted them both for one afternoon, and it was dated several years in the future.

Lee Ann caught Danner's eye now and gave her characteristic half-shrug. During meals, she often stared at one minister after another, directing Danner's gaze to especially strange specimens. Danner had cracked her up in the kitchen by explaining exactly where God was during the Watts riot: gleaming, black and taut as a leopard, he glided along carrying a huge silver radio. Price tags still flew from the radio and God was all in gold, blasting James Brown amidst sirens and fire. Danner sighed. The ministers ate for a full hour. To pass the time, she dropped ice cubes from the Styrofoam bucket into her water pitcher, one by one, with tongs. She wondered how many of the ministers had even been to California. None of the waitresses had; Danner had asked.

Riley wasn't interested in California. This summer he'd gone to Florida with the guys. For honeymoons, he said, it was a toss-up between Florida and Acapulco. Jean had heard him joking and told him he shouldn't be thinking about honeymoons until he got himself through college. Riley had saluted, and grinned at Danner. He wasn't very excited about college; mostly, he wanted to have a good time, avoid the draft, and stay close to Bellington. He wanted to pick Danner up from school on Fridays this fall, take her to school on Monday mornings, then drive back to Lynchburg and participate in panty raids all week. Riley spoke of Lynchburg as a draft dodger's last resort. Then, seriously, he'd say he wouldn't mind serving his country and planned to enroll in ROTC at Lynchburg. He would have gone to school in Bellington if his grades had been good enough. Danner wasn't sure he'd stick to it.

She touched the sides of the globular metal pitcher. The metal was ice-cold and sweating; Danner concentrated on the feel of it. Sometimes she sat on the back patio of her house alone and looked at the fields, wondering how far she'd travel from this exact place. She didn't talk about such feelings to Riley. His mind just wasn't like hers. He acted so sure of himself, yet he was capable of crying in front of a girl, and begging. Once he'd gone out with someone else, and Danner had refused to see him again. Riley had talked her into going for a drive, then he pulled off the road in a deserted spot and wept as though beside himself with grief. The scene went on nearly an hour. She should forgive him, he said; no one would ever love her again as much as he did. Thinking of the episode always made Danner uneasy. If she ever told Riley she wanted to stop seeing him, he wouldn't accept it. He'd say she was wrong, he didn't believe her, that they belonged together. More and more, Danner felt protective toward him, and guilty. Just a year ago, he'd seemed so powerful. Dressed well, in soft V-neck sweaters and madras shirts that smelled of clean cotton, he was a smooth dancer. A basketball player, popular with girls. With his friends he was cocky, a good-natured braggart. But he wasn't like that with Danner. Sometimes he was considerate in the extreme, as though she were special or different from other people. Twice they'd gone to formal dances. Riley had actually covered a path through the garage, and the floor of his shining Mustang, with white sheets so Danner wouldn't dirty the hem of her gown. Mitch had watched, shaking his head in pleased amusement. Danner blinked, remembering her father's expression in the car. *Nothing, Hon.* When Danner was a little kid, Mitch had called her Princess.

"Excuse me, Miss?" The head minister beckoned Danner.

She walked close to him and bent over to hear. He smelled strongly of Old Spice, the same scent her father and brother wore.

"Right after the dishes are cleared," he said, "before dessert, we're going to present a little performance."

"A performance?"

"Yes, it'll just take a few minutes. You might tell the other girls." He smiled into her eyes and touched the edge of his plate. "It's an entertainment, a sort of farewell."

"Oh." A farewell to whom? Danner nodded as though she

understood, and took his plate. He smiled again, as if he'd confided
a secret. Behind his slightly spotty glasses, his eyes were light
blue and long-lashed. He was energetic and broad-shouldered,
probably one of the men Danner had watched running, but she
could never tell one minister from another if they weren't dressed
in their suits.

The other girls, seeing Danner clear the head table, began to
gather plates. Some of the ministers weren't finished eating; they
lowered their heads discreetly and ate faster as the waitresses
worked their way closer. Danner looked around for the manager;
luckily, he was in the kitchen. She tried to signal Lee Ann to go
more slowly but it was no use; well, best to keep going. When the
manager came out, the tables would already be cleared and the
ministers waiting quietly for dessert. A good thing about ministers was that they seldom complained.

Danner had taken all the plates and was stacking them when
the head minister stood, tapping his glass with his spoon.

"Attention, troops," he said, and glanced in Danner's direction. "Since this is our last big meal together and the conference
ends tomorrow, we'd like to take this opportunity to thank the
kitchen crew and the waitresses for their excellent service."

Danner looked down, embarrassed, and hurried to finish loading the tray. It all had to be loaded carefully or the dishes would
topple when she tried to stand. The other girls kept working as
well, and the minister held up both hands. "Stay where you are,
girls, please. Since we're told financial compensation isn't in order,
we'd like to thank you for your hard work by offering a bit of
entertainment." The four men nearest him stood. There was a
hush in the room and the waitresses looked at each other confusedly. One of the men sounded a note on a pitch pipe. Then, in
the silence, they began to sing. Their voices were strong and
perfect. Behind them the air conditioner whirred, its steady labor-
ing their only accompaniment.

The men stood in a semicircle behind their table, their bodies
attentive, watching each other's lips.

*Amazing grace*, they sang slowly, *how sweet the sound.*

The waitresses stood still, surprised. The song filled the hall
and was somehow reminiscent of childhood; the same plaintive

melody was sung at countless day camps and night sings, at reunions and revivals, at funerals and YWCA and Rainbow Girls. But the ministers didn't sound plaintive; their voices were stalwart and definite. They were breaking bad news and offering comfort, and the words seemed ancient, confessional, inarguable. *I once was lost. But now. I'm found.* Their powerful voices made Danner a little afraid. Were they really found, and what did it mean? Lost. She imagined her father sealed into his dream like a figure in a fluid-filled paperweight, the ones in which snow flew when the globe was shaken. *Snow was flying at the windshield so fast you couldn't see where you was going.* Men sat listening. Row after row, the long, nearly empty tables were covered with white cloths. The old fabrics were worn to a pearly sheen. Suppose they were cold, inches deep. Every winter, the old picnic table her father had been given by the State Road Commission sat out back, covered with even snow that froze unbroken like a thick, cold cloth. *I was blind but now I see.* Danner had a sudden wintry vision of the house from above, the roof a snowy butterfly shape, the yard and fences and surrounding fields all white, deep, silent with snow. Her father had built that house. How could someone else ever live there?

She heard applause. The other girls were smiling and clapping; belatedly, Danner joined in. The ministers held their places a moment as though spellbound by their last clear note, then took their seats. The men all began applauding their compatriots as the waitresses stooped to shoulder trays. Danner stood under the heavy weight, glad the day was half over. She turned toward the kitchen. As she steadied her tray, she saw the minister who had spoken to her. He was sitting, his hands folded, watching her. Quickly, she averted her eyes. He must have seen her face during the singing; always, her face betrayed her.

They stood at the metal counter with trays of ketchup bottles, while the other girls filled salt and pepper shakers or wrapped silverware.

"I thought for sure they'd sing again at supper," Lee Ann said.

"Not over hamburgers, not somber enough." Danner wiped

her forehead with a napkin. "Jesus, wasn't it hot this afternoon? And from now on we have to keep the air conditioner on 'low' unless there are guests eating."

Ketchups were the worst cleanup; the emptiest bottles had to be poured into fuller ones and the empties replaced. The refilled bottles were greasy and their streaked labels had to be wiped clean with a hot rag.

"Let's do this fast," Lee Ann whispered.

"Throw the caps in here." Danner pushed forward a bowl of hot water. "It's easier than wiping the gunk off."

"Riley picking you up tonight?"

"At eight. I guess we're going to the drive-in."

"I saw Rhonda Thompson at the intramural basketball games last night. She's dating some guy from the University, and he drives a Corvette." Lee Ann smirked for emphasis.

"You're kidding." Lee Ann had to report any fact about Rhonda. Rhonda and Riley had been a hot item their first two years of high school; everyone knew they'd slept together. Riley had practically lived with her; her parents had let him stay overnight several times in Rhonda's bed. "I don't want to hear about Rhonda." Danner paused. "Was Riley around?"

"You sure you want me to tell you?" Lee Ann looked up from the ketchups, smiling. "He was there with some senior boys. He spoke to her, but in a snide way. He's probably still telling them stories about her."

Danner untwisted bottle caps, throwing them one by one into cloudy red water. "He shouldn't tell those stories. I've told him that myself."

"Oh, come on. Rhonda is ahead of her time. Everyone tells stories about Rhonda."

"Well, Riley shouldn't. Here, this is clean." She wrung out a hot dishrag and handed it to Lee Ann, who began wiping the wet bottle caps. Danner watched her. "Riley will never tell stories about me, I'll tell you that."

"Why not, Danner? Riley could make you famous, too." She laughed. "Can I finish these while you start pouring? Your aim is better. Listen, suppose he tells stories on you anyway, for things you never even got to do."

"He won't," Danner said, "he wouldn't dare."

"I think you're right," Lee Ann said seriously. "He's really crazy about you. You don't know how crazy." Lee Ann was well informed. Riley phoned her regularly to talk about Danner.

"He was probably crazy about Rhonda as well."

"Yeah, but it's not the same."

Danner poured ketchup and said nothing. Watching ketchup drip was the most pointless activity in the world. Last week they'd rushed through cleanup and cracked the lip of a bottle; the manager had insisted they strain the entire contents for glass shards. As disciplinary action, Danner and Lee Ann had to do ketchups for the next two weeks of conferences. "Who's coming next week?"

"Methodist women's clubs from North Carolina."

"They ought to stay in North Carolina," Danner said. She watched Lee Ann's face. Lee Ann was sweating in the warm kitchen, and her glasses had slid halfway down her nose. They'd been friends since elementary school. Lee Ann had dated an older boy last year, a friend of Riley's, but now she was going steady with someone her age. He was a quiet boy who hadn't been one of their crowd; he'd moved to Bellington from out of state and didn't play sports because he had a regular after-school job. "How are you and Mike doing?" Danner asked.

"Oh, just fine," Lee Ann said.

Danner kept her eyes on the ketchups. It hurt her that Lee Ann didn't tell her things much anymore. Last spring they'd shared a desk in typing class. Lee Ann was reading a note from Mike one day; Danner had turned casually on the swivel seat of her chair, and her gaze fell on a line over Lee Ann's shoulder: *There's nothing wrong with what we did. Don't feel bad.* Danner had looked away, painfully conscious of Lee Ann's grave expression.

It had to be a total secret. You couldn't even tell your best friend.

Lee Ann glanced up suddenly, as though aware of Danner's thoughts. "Billy was at the intramurals."

"I know. He rode his bike in to meet Kato."

"Why weren't you there?"

"New rule. My parents won't let me see Riley more than four

nights a week." Danner twisted clean caps onto the bottles she'd filled.

"Brother," Lee Ann said. "I'll hear all about this from Riley, I'm sure. He must be going nuts."

Danner loaded clean bottles onto one big tray. The tray would be so heavy that she and Lee Ann would have to carry it into the dining room as a team. "I don't know why Riley has to call you so often. What does he ask you?"

"He asks me how much you care about him," Lee Ann said patiently. "He says sometimes he wonders, can't get past first base, etc." Lee Ann raised her eyebrows, smiling. Again, the understood half-shrug.

Danner returned the shrug like a co-conspirator, surprised at her own relief. Good, then Riley hadn't told anyone what they did, not even Lee Ann. Afterward, he always pulled his shirttail out to cover the wetness on his jeans, and they drove around the dark country roads, holding hands like a married couple and telling jokes while the radio played. Thinking about him, she felt a flash of longing.

"Billy is really getting good-looking," Lee Ann went on. "The older girls all notice him now. You know, Kato is supposed to be pretty wild."

"Oh, Kato is fourteen," Danner said dismissively.

"That never stopped Rhonda, when she and Riley were going together. Actually, it was Riley that told me about Kato. He said the high school boys already call her Rhonda Two." Lee Ann stopped talking abruptly, aware she'd said too much. "Look, Riley didn't tell me as a joke. He was kind of concerned, but he didn't want you to hear about it and worry."

"I don't believe stories about Kato. People only talk about her because she's pretty and comes from a poor family."

Lee Ann nodded. Shinner Black, Kato's father, was a some-times drunk.

Together, both girls stepped back and surveyed the big tray of ketchup bottles.

Lee Ann held up her hands, displaying red-smeared finger-nails. "Watts," she deadpanned. "Is God there?"

"Don't be silly," Danner laughed. "These ketchups are beautiful. Ketchups are always a great career, even in Watts."

When she rode through Bellington with Riley, Danner felt beautiful. She was relaxed and tired when she left work; she'd taken a shower and put on makeup in the employees' bathroom, and thrown away her nylons, cheap ones inevitably ruined by the end of the day. The college banquet service had a reputation for hiring "personable" girls, and there was a kind of status about the anonymous-looking uniform; girls sometimes wore them on dates with steady boyfriends when there wasn't much time to change. Riley's car, a canary yellow Mustang with a black top and oversized tires, was well-known around town. He was always early, waiting for her, lounging against the Mustang. By the time they met, the heat had broken and Danner walked toward the bright car, the campus shade trees around her rippling a little with wind. He stood with his arms crossed, in a sport shirt and clean white Levi's, smelling of men's cologne and smoking a cigarette. They drove down Main Street on the way to the Parkette, with the evening cooling and all the windows down. Danner sat close beside Riley, trying to see the street as though she'd never been there before. The brick and clapboard buildings were twilit, the colors deep. Main Street looked too pretty to be real.

Riley steered with one hand. "Baby, what are you thinking about?"

"Nothing, really." She didn't like to be asked what she was thinking.

The courthouse sat back on its big lawn across from the fire station, the gold spire bright against the dark blue dusk. The huge evergreen, used every winter as a town Christmas tree, stood like a backdrop behind the high school football scoreboard. Names of scheduled opponents and game dates were in blue; WON or LOST would be painted on each white line in red. The street was nearly empty. Parking meters along the sidewalk looked decorative. All the small businesses—Liberty Lunch, the Casualaire, HP Hardware—were closed, their windows lit.

Tomorrow morning Main Street would be different, crowded and hot. Saturdays, miners cashed checks in their hard hats and

rumpled clothes; country families stood in line at the welfare office
before shopping at Woolworth's. They choked the three blocks
that were Bellington's downtown. Their children were numerous
and pale, dressed in ill-fitting clothes. They wore muddy shoes
with no socks, or they were barefoot. Their ankles looked battered, scratched and mosquito-bitten. The women were very thin
or very fat, their faces middle-aged and set as though frozen.
Their hair was never styled but hung past their shoulders, occasionally restrained with a child's cheap barrette too small to have
much effect. They were dirty and smelled of dirt, despite the cakes
of harsh yellow soap dispensed by the County. The children were
usually clean except for their feet; their once-a-week cleanliness
made them look even paler. Grade schools and the junior high
were full of country kids, but many dropped out by high school.
Danner remembered looking at them intently on the school bus
from Brush Fork when she was a child. She would stare at them
in profile, afraid but fascinated. Their eyelashes were flaky with
the dust of sleep or neglect.

Riley pulled up at a stop light and put his arm around her
shoulders. "Mr. Losch asked me if you were going to enter the
Miss Jaycees contest."

Danner gave him a surprised look. Losch ran the A&P where
Riley worked. He was a member of the Jaycees, merchants and
professional men who sponsored the contest every fall for high
school girls.

"Why not?" Riley asked. "You'll be sixteen by September.
You could win a scholarship for college, a thousand dollars."

Danner shifted a little away from him. Last year, Rhonda
Thompson had been runner-up as a senior entrant. Danner supposed Riley wanted her to do better.

"Danner, you're one of the prettiest girls they'd have, and
you're smarter than anybody who'd enter."

"Thanks a lot. Anyway, they don't care if you're smart."

"Losch thinks you'd have a good chance. I didn't ask him—
he mentioned it to me." Riley looked at her pointedly, still im-
pressed. "Doc Reb Jonas is one of the judges. Isn't he an old
friend of your father's?"

Danner shrugged, looking straight ahead. "They don't see

each other much now." Mitch certainly wasn't a member of the Jaycees. He still belonged to the Elks', who kept a dim lunchroom down by the tracks. "Riley, you know I wouldn't enter that contest."

He made the turn onto the Winfield road, easing past the Mobil station and picking up speed. "Boys win money for sports. Why shouldn't girls win money for looking good?"

"I don't know, but I don't want to. Think about standing on a stage in a bathing suit while Mr. Losch asks you what your goals are."

Riley smiled. "You could talk for a half hour about your goals, and you only need to come up with three minutes."

"How do you know anything about my goals?"

"I know," he said, entertained. He slowed as they neared Nedelson's, checking out the parking lot for friends. The parking spaces were defined by metal posts fitted with intercoms and bright yellow menus fastened behind plastic. Riley parked on the far side of the lot and leaned out to press the intercom button. A warble of static came through the speaker.

"Hello?" Riley yelled.

"Yeah, yeah, go ahead."

"Two double burgers with tomato, one plain cheeseburger, one large fries, two vanilla shakes." He leaned back and lit a cigarette. "What if Lee Ann was in the contest. Would you enter then?"

Danner frowned. "No. Forget it, will you?"

He smiled. His eyes were extremely blue.

Food came quickly at the Parkette. Within five minutes, a girl brought the car tray, hooked it onto the half-open window, and collected money. Riley passed Danner her shake and cheeseburger. From across the lot they could hear someone's loud radio. They shared the french fries and ate comfortably, without talking. Danner loved just sitting there with him; he felt so familiar, like family.

The horseshoe circle between the rows of cars was constantly filled with slowly moving automobiles. Boys with girls simply wheeled into a spot, but the ones who were alone drove around and around, yelling to each other and whooping before turning

onto the highway again. Danner watched them. In a year or so,
Billy would have a car. He'd get his learner's permit in the fall;
he had a job with State Road this summer cutting brush, already
saving money. Danner couldn't imagine seeing him in his own car,
like Riley. She remembered Kato then.

"Riley, what is all this about Kato?"

For a moment he didn't answer. "Oh, hell. Lee Ann can't keep
her mouth shut. It's a good thing I don't tell her anything important."

"I call it important," Danner said, "and telling people only
spreads the story."

Riley regarded her, irritated. "I didn't even tell the story."

Danner gazed out the windshield of the Mustang, the straw
of her milkshake in her mouth. The frothy liquid was so cold and
sweet it stung her teeth. She swallowed. "What is the story?"

"There isn't any." He picked up his second foil-wrapped
burger, pretending the subject was closed.

"You might as well tell me."

He ate the sandwich as though considering. "A few months
ago, a couple of guys went over to Kato's house. She was home
alone and they had a few beers and played around a little. Nothing
really happened, nothing serious." He paused. "It's just that it
was two guys."

Danner said nothing, waiting.

"I guess she was tipsy. Must have been." He crumpled the
foil and put the paper and empty cups on the Parkette tray. "It
was before Billy was going out with her. Besides, he can probably
handle himself." Riley sat looking at the steering wheel. "I'll talk
to him if you want me to."

"No, don't say a word." She wrapped her sandwich back up
in the foil and handed it to him. "I don't want this. Let's go."

"Okay." He moved closer, then kissed her. "You have to
understand that not everyone is as virtuous as you."

"I'm not virtuous."

Riley grinned, trying to coax a smile from her. "You're not?
You mean it's all an act?"

She did smile. "What do you want? Am I supposed to act like
I'm twenty-five when I'm sixteen?"

"You're not sixteen yet. And by the time you're twenty-five, we'll have three kids." He took the tray off the window and propped it on the intercom box, then turned the ignition key of the Mustang. "Since Mitch is so nervous lately, I'm taking you home early. But first let's skip the drive-in and visit his namesake."

Mitch Concrete was an ideal place to park and they'd discovered it by accident. Danner hadn't been to the plant her father once owned since she was a child, but one night the previous winter she and Riley had driven past the entrance. Curious, Danner asked Riley to drive up the steep dirt lane to the yard. They sat looking, then stayed for an hour. The plant wasn't too far from Nedelson's Parkette, on the highway to Winfield; it was off a side road called Graveyard Road, and up a hill. There was an office building and two prefab garages, and the tipple structure where materials were poured from above into the rolling barrels of the trucks. What materials? Sand? Gravel? Danner wasn't sure, but she had a vague memory of seeing it happen. Now the mixers sat haphazardly around the lot as though their drivers had left them abruptly. They were big rugged trucks, worn and snaggled. A few might be the same trucks her father had owned. Since the year before, he'd sold cars at the Chevrolet garage in Bellington, and little mention was made of his work at home.

Last winter, the snowy plant had looked ghostly and beautiful by night. The piles of dirt were white mounds, the trucks dusted, the tipple a square snow-hung tower with the sheer white mountain of gravel above and behind it. Riley and Danner could see the lights of the town from the plant, and the Winfield road snaking past the Parkette. Cars had moved on the road, long beams of their headlights played out across falling snow. Always, the plant was deserted. Graveyard Road led only to the cemetery; no police patroled it, no one drove by.

Danner and Riley were so sure of their privacy that sometimes, in summer, Riley spread a cloth and they lay down so they could see the stars. The plant was a kind of moonscape by August —not a scrap of green. The dirt of the yard was blond and dry, and puffed like smoke when Riley skipped stones across it. Still, after dusk and into the night, there was the same private quiet as in winter. Tonight they stayed in the car, and the crickets made a staccato chiming in the brush. Danner thought of Mitch Concrete as a distant planet still revolving in the past. Hymns should sound in the background of the emptiness, very low, wisps of hymns. Riley kissed her forehead, her temples, her throat; she remembered the ministers, their bodies so attentive, singing to each other.

"Well," Riley said. He had pulled away and was watching her when she opened her eyes. He touched the bridge of her nose and the lines of her lips. "I bet your parents did a little spooning here. Maybe they still do, on the sly."

Danner shook her head. "They were already married when he started the plant. Anyway, my parents haven't slept together in years."

"You don't know what your parents have done." He put one arm along the back of the seat and bunched her straight hair in his hand. "Jean and Mitch are all right. Parents always make it seem they don't have a sex life."

"They're all right to you—they like you. That doesn't mean they're all right to each other."

"You're wrong," Riley said.

She wasn't, but there was no point explaining. Danner supposed she knew more than most daughters; her mother had no one else to talk to. It was curious—Riley never wanted to admit that her parents didn't get along, as though they were his parents.

He was looking at her. "Listen," he said, "I have a present for you. I'm not going to give it to you until your birthday, but I have to show it to you now so you won't be too surprised."

Danner smiled. "Riley, if it's for my birthday, don't give it to me now."

"I have to," he said. He took a small white box out of his pocket. "Put out your hand."

She did. He put the box on the flat of her palm, then opened it for her. Inside was a gold ring cushioned in white velvet; the center of the ring was a small gold heart set with a diamond chip. "Oh," she said, "it's beautiful."

He circled her wrist with his fingers. "Danner, I want us to be engaged."

"I can't," she said, nearly whispering, "you know I can't."

He put his finger gently against her mouth. "I don't mean we should tell your parents. As far as they know, it's just a present. That's why it's a small diamond—when we tell them, I'll give you a different ring."

She looked at the ring in confusion. The chip of diamond glittered. Riley kept talking. How could he see her face and just keep talking?

". . . You've got two more years of high school. When you graduate I'll give you a real diamond, and we'll tell them together. I'll be halfway through college by then." He looked searchingly at her, trying to pinpoint her reservations. "I know you want to go to school. You can go to Lynchburg with me, or we can go here in town when I get my grades up, or to the University—"

"It's not that," she said slowly. "I can't say I'll get married."

"What are you talking about?"

"I can't say so. I can't." She shook her head.

He held her wrist tightly. "You don't really love me, do you? Why don't you tell me?"

"I do love you, I do so." She turned her hand to grasp his arm, pleading. "Let's not say it's an engagement. What if my parents find out?"

"How would they find out?" he asked, sarcastic. "I suppose you'd tell them, so they'd keep me from seeing you." He took the box from her angrily and put it on the dash in front of them. "Okay. To you it's not an engagement ring. But to me it is. You just remember, when I'm at school. I'll be away, but I'll be thinking you're mine."

Miserably, she put her face in her hands.

He shook her gently, pulling her toward him. "You are," he said, "you are mine. Don't you know that yet?" He unbuttoned her blouse and put his hands inside, pushing the blouse apart and slipping her straps down over her shoulders. She arched up to move away and he put his arm around her waist, holding her tight against him.

She felt the hard buckle of his belt on her pubic bone and then he moved so it was just against her. He slipped his arm down under her hips. She put her hands at his shoulders, pushing him away, but she'd lost her balance and his weight forced them down on the seat. They were both wordless, tense with exertion; he held her legs, flinging his thigh over them, and leaned across her upper chest, his entire weight on his arm. Danner heard herself panting. "You're stronger than me," she said bitingly. "Is that what you're trying to prove?"

"You think I'm trying to rape you, Danner? Jesus, you can be stupid and tight-assed." He tried to quiet his breathing. "Look, I'm not trying to fuck you. I'm not going to lose control and ram it into you—like I don't know you, like I don't care about you."

Danner, so angry she was trembling, didn't answer.

"Now you're not going to talk to me." Her skirt had worked up high around her hips. He pushed it gently higher. "Fine, don't talk."

"Don't hold me down, Riley." She had started to feel sick and weak inside, and her heart was pounding. "If you do, I won't feel anything, I swear."

"No?" He touched her very lightly, with the tips of his fingers, through the thin cotton of her underpants. She stopped struggling. He stroked her and there was silence, as though they'd both begun holding their breath in the same instant. He was watching her face. "Let me," he whispered, "just with my hand. Let me show you."

She couldn't speak. Her eyes had filled with tears.

He shifted his body and pulled her skirt back down to cover her legs, then he lay on top of her as she embraced him. He moved against her and made no sound; tonight it took a long time but he kept pushing and pushing. It seemed to Danner they'd gone on like this for hours. Under him, she was sore from his hardness and she hated herself. She held him and wondered what would ever happen in her life: nothing could be worse than this, than what was happening to him and to her. He stiffened, still silently. When he moved away from her they looked at each other, defeated, then at his pants. He had chafed himself until he bled; the wetness on his white jeans was tinged with pink.

"It doesn't matter," he said, and hugged her.

MOONSHIP
Danner, 1969

Danner waited for Billy on the stone steps of Women's Hall. The old dormitory was situated on a hill overlooking the Student Union; she'd see his Camaro approach from the bottom of the street. Even in Labor Day weekend traffic, his car was obvious—a shiny, four-year-old soft-top, white, with an orange racing stripe down the hood. No wonder he got so many speeding tickets. Cops expected a car like his to speed. Danner wouldn't even smoke a joint in the Camaro; she was scared they'd get stopped. She wished Billy had gotten a room in town, but almost all the freshmen roomed at Towers, a new high-rise complex on South Campus.

She paced, restless. How would thay get through the next three days with their father? He would be moving out and Jean would be gone, to visit relatives in Ohio. She'd filed for divorce in mid-August, as soon as Billy and Danner had left for college. Danner had been urging her to go ahead all summer, and Billy wasn't surprised.

No sense thinking about it now. She would have to go see Aunt Bess tomorrow, too. Bess wouldn't even speak to Jean on the street anymore. How could Jean Hampson do such a thing? Put him out when he was nearly sixty, disabled, with nothing but a pension from the Veterans' Administration. Jean had been over it all with Danner again and again. Nothing in common anymore but children; he'd contributed so little to the household for years; the new house was Jean's responsibility anyway, since he'd refused to sign the papers. Besides, Jean would say, her voice shaking, she just couldn't go on.

Guiltily, Danner was glad she didn't live in Bellington anymore. She looked at rooftops. Across the street, starting at the top of the hill and running all the way to the bottom, was Fraternity Row. The houses were mostly turreted stone mansions; banners printed with rush slogans hung from the windows. Danner was glad she didn't have a brother who'd join a fraternity. Then again, if he joined a frat he'd live across the street from her and never fail a test, because they all cheated. Billy would never cheat. He was too stubborn to cheat—or do much of anything he didn't want to do. How would he manage in college? Required courses for freshmen were mostly big survey courses, one or two hundred students to a class. Danner had made a 3.9 her freshman year, but she'd sat in front rows of the big rooms and taken voluminous notes, then memorized them. She was afraid Billy wouldn't go through all that just for grades, or answer questions in rooms so full of people.

"Danner!" He was standing beside the parked Camaro in the street below her, blond and solid, squinting against the sun. "You ready?" He was back behind the wheel by the time she was down the steps.

Danner got in. "Gee," she said, pretending to look closely at him, "you're cute. Are you a college guy?"

"Not me," Billy said, comically stoic. He smelled faintly of a men's cologne, and his skin was evenly golden. He'd let his hair grow during the summer and it hung just below his ears, wavy and fine-textured. Already it receded a little over his broad forehead. His hands on the steering wheel were square and capable, and the car itself was very clean. Blue tassels from his high school cap-and-gown ceremony still hung from the radio knob. He opened and slammed his door, then locked it. "Lock your door, my sister."

"Why? Are you going to fly all the way to Bellington like a maniac?"

He leaned toward her and placed one hand on her shoulder. "Look, if you ride with the chief, you side with the chief. I don't like to lose passengers."

She rolled her eyes in pretended exasperation but locked the door as he started the engine. "How was your first week at Towers, and registration? Wasn't that a zoo?"

Billy nodded, checking his rearview mirror for a chance to ease into traffic. He found a spot and pulled out, then shifted in his seat, getting ready to thread between lanes and make it to the highway.

"Do you think you'll like it here all right?" Danner looked down the hill and saw long lines of cars streaming onto High Street, the main thoroughfare that led downtown.

He shrugged. "The University is okay, but I just got out of school. If it weren't for the draft, I wouldn't be going to college. Not yet."

She smiled. "What would you be doing?"

"Oh, bartending maybe. At some beach town where there's a lot of girls in the summer and the winters are warm." He grinned.

"Billy, keep your deferment while it lasts. Maybe your number in the lottery will be 365."

"In December. A little Christmas present from Uncle Sam." They were in the downtown crush now, and Billy drove slowly. "Did I tell you I got a letter from your old boyfriend? I was surprised. I bet I haven't seen him since he went over there."

"Riley? He wrote to you?" Danner wondered if Riley's friends stayed in touch with him. Surely they did. "What did he say?"

"Nothing much. Hello to everyone and jokes about the rice paddies. He said to punch a peacenik for him." Billy hit her playfully in the arm. "Maybe he meant you."

"Probably did. But he couldn't be mad at me anymore. Someone told me he's engaged to a girl from Lynchburg." She shook her head. "Just think, Riley wasn't even drafted. He enlisted and thought he was heroic. I don't think it takes much to sign yourself up as cannon fodder."

Light glanced off bright cars all around them. Horns honked. "That depends," Billy said. "Might take about everything."

Danner was silent a moment. "I know. I didn't mean that." She clinched her hands, remembering a box of Riley's letters she'd put away in her closet at home. Four years ago he'd been a freshman himself, at Lynchburg, and wrote her every day. "I just meant it was easier for Riley, in a way, to join the army than to do well at school. He skipped most of his classes and drank beer with his buddies."

"He's not drinking much beer now."

"That's what's awful. If he could have just marched and drunk beer, the whole thing would have been fine." She glanced at Billy. He had his hand on the stick shift, and she reached to touch his wrist. "Billy, I hope you're going to keep your grades up. Maybe they won't do the lottery and the deferments will stay."

They'd stopped at the last red light on High Street. Billy took his eyes from the road and looked at her. "You sound like Mom, except for the bit about deferments."

"I am Mom," Danner said teasingly.

Billy raised one eyebrow. "I wouldn't tell Mitch if I were you, especially this weekend."

"No, I won't." She crossed her arms and leaned back in the bucket seat. Suddenly she was tired.

"Mom went away this weekend, didn't she?"

"She and Gladys went up to see Aunt Jewel in Ohio. If Mom were going to be around for this, I wouldn't even be going home."

Billy didn't seem to be listening. "Christ, we're out of that," he said, accelerating and pulling onto the highway. "It takes half as long to get out of this traffic as it does to get to Bellington." He rummaged in a box beside the driver's seat. "Time to fire up the old tape deck. Now we're going to cruise with Jimi Hendrix." He clicked the 8-track into the player. "Hendrix is a vet. He jumped out of airplanes."

Hendrix's "Star Spangled Banner" vibrated through the car as they left the emptying town behind. The Camaro moved fast and smoothly in the passing lane. Danner felt totally safe with Billy. She shut her eyes and heard the loud song: a translation into a language deciphered in darkness. How could anyone play an instrument like that? Even the silences between notes were full. The peals of the lone guitar were shaped like words, and each shrilled its own tremolo, a sound coming back and coming back.

She slept dreamlessly, and when she woke they were in Bellington. She sat up slowly, disoriented. "What happened to Hendrix?"

"Gone a long time ago," Billy said. "I was tempted to drive to Myrtle Beach and surprise you, but instead we're home."

They were driving up Quality Hill, and Danner saw red-tipped leaves in the crowns of the overhanging oaks. Lower, greener limbs moved slightly upward as cars passed a few feet under them. The street was pretty and made her sad. "You want to go to the ocean? Maybe we should."

"It's not too late. We could drive as far as the car will go, then get out and walk until we see surf."

"Sounds good."

He turned onto their street. Mitch's big Chevrolet was parked in front of the house, the trunk open. Inside were two big cardboard boxes, neatly taped shut, and a set of golf clubs.

"I never knew he had golf clubs," Danner said softly.

Billy pulled up at the house. A 1950s torch song spilled out of the radio. He put the car in neutral and they sat still, the engine idling.

Danner gazed up at the brick house. Her father must have packed his clothes that morning. How long had it taken? Two hours? Tomorrow Billy would borrow a pickup from a friend and move Mitch's desk and file cabinet out of the basement to a bedroom in Bess's house.

"We may as well go in," Billy said. He turned the ignition off. In front of them the blacktopped street was sunny and well kept. The lawns of the houses were trimmed. Everything was in place.

Danner turned and looked at her brother. "This weekend won't always matter the way it does now," she said.

Danner had made supper and done the dishes. They hadn't talked about the divorce over dinner; Mitch made only a few short, bitter references. Mostly they talked about Billy's car and his car insurance payments, food at the dorms, University parking fees. Mitch said he wasn't surprised at the fees—they were out to make money off kids at the University any way they could. Billy and Danner exchanged glances; Jean was paying their tuition and fees. Billy mentioned that home football games were free for freshmen. After they finished eating, he left to meet friends at the Tap Room.

Danner stayed in the kitchen and dried silverware. She wondered what her mother was doing right now—talking to Aunt Jewel? Jean would be rubbing her hands; she got a painful rash on her hands when she was upset. She'd had blisters on her fingers for weeks. Danner wiped the counter clean and hung the damp dish towel over a cabinet door. The house was quiet. The evening had only started. She heard Mitch moving about in the bedroom, putting things in a box, and felt she was sealed into some inviolable space with her father: everyone else was miles away. She heard him behind her then and turned.

"Do you want this, Miss?" Mitch held out a folded newspaper, then opened it to display the top of the front page. The headlines were in caps: TWO STEP ON MOON, ARMSTRONG PILOTS BEYOND BOULDERS. "I was saving it in there," he said, nodding toward the bedroom.

Danner took the paper. "You sure you don't want to keep this?"

"Well, you keep it." He turned, walking back to the bedroom.

"Okay, if you want me to."

She sat down at the kitchen table. July 20. The yellowing edges of the paper were already beginning to curl, and the colors of the photo were altering. Danner had watched the moon launch with her parents. Where had Billy been—hadn't he and Kato broken up in the spring? Apollo 11 took off and the cameras had zoomed in on the wafting explosion of the Saturn rockets under it. The smoke was white on color TV, thick and rippling; it filled the screen like a close-up of a furious waterfall. Then a shot from far away: the silent, conical shape ascending, chased by flame. No one in the room had spoken.

Danner opened the paper. There was a picture of *Eagle* descending for a landing, a metallic beetle with four red legs drawn up at the knees, and silver discs on each foot. Danner scanned the type. She'd been interested in the moon landing but not fascinated; it was just machines. Instead, she'd kept track of details the astronauts told reporters later, small things. The dark moon dust, when you held it in your hands, was heavy and fine like black flour. In the capsule, they could smell the dust and it smelled like gunpowder or—Danner remembered the exact phrase—"spent cap-pistol caps." Also, Neil Armstrong's mother had said he'd had a recurrent childhood dream of hovering over the ground.

Danner had repeated that story to a boy she was dating. He'd smirked. "I wonder if all the guys flying Hueys in Nam had the same dream."

In the bedroom, drawers opened and shut softly. Mitch walked back through the short hall to Danner, holding a set of coasters. He spread three of them out over the newspaper; they were white plastic coasters imprinted with antlered deer. The deer were unearthly and colorless, a memory of deer. He touched one of the raised images.

"These are from over at Blackwater Lodge, where I used to go hunting with Clayton. You have any use for these?"

"Sure," Danner said. She heard him breathing, standing over her. His breath sounded labored. "They're real pretty," she told him, "I'll take them up to school with me."

He nodded once. "Well then, that takes care of that."

# NOVEMBER AND DECEMBER

## Billy, 1969

## NOVEMBER

Riding the bus in from South Campus, Billy looked at the University's new indoor athletic stadium. Its overhanging roof dominated an expanse of green field like the giant fluted cap of a cement mushroom. Long sidewalks led over the hill to the med school, to married students' housing, to the four towers of the dorm complex where he'd lived for two months. He balanced his biology text and spiral notebook on his knees. Touching the face of the notebook, he thought about his parents' handwriting on birthday cards he'd opened that morning. Words in his mother's cursive hand contained modest loops, the writing was large, and the sentences ran on to comprise one form, one image. It was a funny card, a dog on the front with big eyes and a gap-toothed grin; couldn't picture it exactly but the thought bubble referred to some pun on doggone it etc. your birthday. Inside, a check for twenty dollars and her message, which he remembered exactly:

*I wish I could do more, honey, but things are a little tight this month. When you come home next, I'll make you a special birthday dinner. Things all right? Need anything? Love, Mom.* Mitch had sent him fifty dollars. Since the divorce he'd tried to give Billy too much money; Billy would have to persuade his father to take half the fifty back. The card was a money envelope from Central National Bank in Bellington. A paper flap lifted to reveal an oval cutout and the face of Andrew Jackson; near it Mitch had printed *Happy Birthday* and underlined the words. At the bottom, under the money, *Love, Mitch.* And he underlined his name. Lately he signed himself "Mitch" in letters, one every couple of weeks, Bess's address printed in the top left corner of the envelopes as return. Each letter was neatly typed and nearly telegraphic in nature. *Fall has arrived here, nights are cold and fog of a morning. Better to winterize your car before snow, here is a check. Upshur Drill bought the County Bldg. & are adding on, tore hell out of East Main.* He typed one-fingered on the big manual Billy had moved from the basement on Labor Day weekend; the typewriter sat on top of his metal desk just as before. His bedroom at Bess's easily held all his possessions: his clothes, the Formica-topped desk in the corner. A swivel desk chair, a file cabinet. His construction manuals, loose-leaf in vinyl-covered notebooks, displayed between steel bookends. Small graduation photos of Billy and Danner in a plastic frame Mitch must have bought at the five and ten on Main Street. A metal nameplate that read MITCH HAMPSON in white letters on fake wood. This was his father's room and it had existed all along, unacknowledged by anyone, in the basement—in the same cement-block room as the ironing board and the single bed where Jean used to sleep.

Despite the awkward pain of his father's anger, Billy was glad Jean and Mitch finally lived apart. Purposefully, Billy stayed out of the cross fire. Bess was his father's ally, silently, constantly, in companionship, in their familial bickering over when to bring in more coal, over how warm to keep the fire that had burned in the grate of the sitting room since October. Mitch sat in front of the color television in a big-seated upholstered rocker, stoking the fire with a poker. He sat forward, elbows on his knees, feet flat on the floor, his hands touching contemplatively. Or he leaned back, the chair in motion, one arm extended on the broad oak armrest, the other crooked as he stroked the back of his neck. Bess sat in the corner in a small white rocker with her handwork, out of viewing range of the picture constantly beamed by the TV. *I don't watch anyway,* she confided to anyone, telling a joke on herself, *I only listen to the stories*—the stories being several afternoon soap operas. She sat in near darkness doing cross-stitch, a kind of touch braille, Billy thought, since she couldn't possibly see the patterns. Her glasses were thick and their lenses made her eyes seem too large for her thin face. If Billy stood close enough he saw pale blue whorls in her brown irises, a milky flaring of age near the tight dots of her pupils. She stood up from her chair carefully, touching the top of the warm television for support.

They didn't talk about the divorce in front of Billy. *Lord save us,* Bess would comment good-humoredly while Mitch complained about potholes on Main Street or prices at the grocery store. When Billy went by the house on weekends home, they had Saturday lunch in the kitchen: chicken baked in the oven until it was hard and salty, mashed potatoes, soup beans. Flour gravy Bess made at the stove, Mitch pouring the milk into the pan as she stirred. Afterward she insisted on cleaning up alone. *You go on and visit with your father.* Back to the sitting room, Billy rolling his sleeves up in the warmth. Mitch taking his usual seat, then talk, generalities with specific meanings. Long pauses, expected, not uncomfortable. Crackling of the coal fire. Billy never mentioned his mother; Mitch never asked. Jean did discuss the divorce; Billy knew it was final in February.

They all wanted to put Billy somewhere safe while things settled and time passed, but he couldn't cooperate any longer. He'd thought carefully and wondered for weeks; this was the day to go ahead. Withdrawal from the University wasn't difficult. He'd fill out the form and decide what to do next. At home they'd think it was the divorce, or Vietnam and the times, or Kato—or maybe they thought she was out of the picture. *Gone but not forgotten.* Whose phrase was that really, who first said it? The bus pulled at a crawl across crowded Stadium Bridge, a one-way wooden lane, and the Student Union was in sight.

Yesterday he'd taken most of the money out of his checking account at a downtown bank—$400. Tuition at the state school was inexpensive, less than two hundred, but Jean must have paid nearly a thousand for room and board at the dorm. He'd get a job here or in Bellington and pay the rest before he went south, or into the army. The army. Supposedly the first few minutes of the lottery drawing in December were going to be broadcast on television. Just like TV, catch it on film up to about number 30.

Well, numbers were pure if television wasn't. Now it was a matter of numbers, published in a newspaper list. No more dodg-'em plans or 1S deferments: fuck up, drop your grades, and you're gone. He'd know once and for all in December; he wouldn't have to argue it out in his head. It was a joke, really. His birthday—today—written on a white plastic ball and bounced around in a machine. Exactly whose hand would touch the machine? Sometimes Billy dreamed about the lottery, a close-up interior view: hundreds of days of white balls tumbling in a black sphere, silent and very slow, moving as though in accordance with physical laws. A galaxy of identical white planets. No sun. Cold, charged planets, simple, symmetrical, named with months and numbers. *Nov. 1, no. 305 of 365.* Universe stops. Hand reaches in. Suddenly everything in color, and the black sphere turns midnight blue. Crazy dream. The black and white beginning, when the balls moved around and through each other slowly, must be a Bio I flash: all those films of microorganisms, bacteria, swimming shapes.

Billy wasn't worried about the lottery, he wasn't hassled. The lottery was an ingenious system, better than the draft. Having your birthday picked early in the countdown was a completely coincidental happening, like being struck by lightning. Your birthday had been all those cakes and bicycles and new shirts: now pay up. The government could claim near innocence. Of course, they'd set up the system. Supposedly they'd set up the war, too, but Billy wasn't sure. He didn't know histories or politics—he didn't need to know. Knowing wouldn't change what was going to happen. It had no more to do with him than this bus ride, but maybe it would hurt him a lot worse. And it was two years.

His roommate joked over beer and pretzels. *December 1*

*you're going to see me drop acid and park in front of the tube in Towers Lounge, watch it all on the big screen.* Then, more seriously: *Look, Vietnam is practically over. Suppose we do get drafted, might not even go to Nam. Might go to Hawaii. Be fun. Surfboards.* That was DeCosto, the loony Italian from Scranton, Pa.

Some of Billy's friends had talked to draft counselors. Various tables were set up every weekend outside the Student Union: sorority and fraternity rush sign-ups (GO GREEK), Environment Club ski trip sign-ups (PRAY FOR SNOW), Mobilize Against Strip Mining sign-ups, Draft Counseling (PLAN NOW). DeCosto said he planned every Friday so he could get dates with older women on Saturday nights: most of the draft counselors were women grad students. They wore baggy clothes; they looked pale and studious in their wire-frame glasses, or they were clean and energetic, like campers. Occasionally the counselors were men, a hippie law student or a vet. The Vets were usually skinny, long-haired, never glossy. One guy sat there in a wheelchair at the side of the table. Always—in the milling of students, honking of traffic, barking of mutt dogs wearing bandannas—short, intense conversations took place at the draft-counseling tables. Billy never went near them. He would take his cue from the numbers. He thought he would. Numbers were his plan while the holding pattern held.

The bus pulled up to the Student Union steps. Billy knew that General Studies students had to withdraw from the Dean of Students offices upstairs in the Union. As he left the bus and walked into the building, he wished himself a happy birthday. This might not be his best birthday—not like his sixteenth, the day he took his driver's test in a blue secondhand Falcon he already owned. Or his eighteenth, when Kato made him a chocolate cake full of melted M&Ms and gave him a watch she must have saved all year to buy. He checked the watch on the way upstairs: one o'clock. But this birthday would be okay; he was doing exactly what he wanted to do. He opened the door marked DEAN OF STUDENTS.

The woman behind the counter looked up expectantly. She was alone in the room. Behind her a carpeted hallway led out of sight. "Can I help you?"

"I want to withdraw from school," Billy said.

"You want to withdraw now, in November? There's no re-fund on tuition this late."

"I know. Which form do I use?"

She put both hands flat on the counter. "Wait a minute. Mind if I ask—it's my job to ask—why you're withdrawing? Are your grades bad?"

"They're not good, but they're not bad." He didn't think his grades were any of her business. "I'm withdrawing for personal reasons."

She folded her hands and smiled. "Perhaps I can help you."

"No, I don't think so. I'd just like the form, please." He put his books on the counter near her hands and stood waiting, watching her. He wouldn't let himself look away.

"Would you like to come into the office? If you're so sure about doing this, would it hurt to talk it over?"

"I don't want to talk it over, thanks. If you'll just give me the form, I'll fill it out right here."

She gave him the form, one white sheet in triplicate. He filled in the blanks, signed it, and handed the form back to her.

She looked at his name. "You'll receive official notification in the mail, Mr. Hampson."

He nodded. At least she hadn't called him Billy. "I wanted to ask—will I have to move out of the dorm right away?"

"Well, you're paid up. If you don't turn in your key, I suppose you're free to stay until the end of the term." She paused. "Look, I hope you'll re-enroll at some point. Please phone here at the Dean of Students office if we can assist you in any way."

He thanked her and walked back downstairs, then out the double doors of the Student Union to the street. He waited for some precise feeling to wash over him, but nothing came. Almost out of habit, he crossed the street and entered Sumner Hall for bio class. He was a little late.

The room was a sort of tiered concrete arena, with semicircu-lar rows of desks bolted in place on descending levels all the way to the bottom. There, a graduate proctor sat silently behind a long table, reading a book. Far above him, suspended in both forward corners of the ceiling, were the two thirty-inch televisions that taught the course. MITOSIS, said the screens in black and white.

Notebooks shuffled open, lights dimmed slightly. The screens were brighter now, more exclusively boring. Billy resolved to pay close attention, not to "mitosis" but to the room, the people, what they did. He'd watch the screens as well. Maybe bio was interesting and he hadn't noticed because he hated the whole setup—or didn't hate it, thought it was silly. He always sat in the back row; now and then he smoked a joint, which didn't prevent him from taking notes. Actually, he took more explicit notes when he was a little stoned.

He fixed his gaze on the screen. Here came the definition, printed out a few words at a time. *Usual method of cell division. Resolving of the chromatin. Of the nucleus. Into a threadlike form.* It was a wierd language really; they should have someone reciting in a sci-fi thriller voice. Instead, a taped professorial drone pronounced the words as they appeared, or lagged a little behind the pictures; the bio department filmed the lessons themselves and narrated the course. Every freshman at the University had to take Bio I and II, and the big room seated five hundred. But it was never full. Billy envisioned the wonderful confusion if all freshmen, each carefully assigned a numbered section of Bio I, showed up for the same class. Billy listened to the scratching of pens and pencils, the ripping open of cellophane bags of junk food. A few students were sleeping. Innumerable others sat doing nothing, watching. He watched. The illustration, cells dividing under the scrutiny of a microscope, proceeded jerkily, in silence. Maybe if they synced in music, rock music, even classical music. Maybe if the films were in color. What color were cells? Billy thought the endless tones of gray were sad as hell.

His thoughts drifted. Last night Danner had come out to Towers to bring him a birthday cake. She brought a boyfriend with her, Jim his name was, a nice enough guy, and two pints of ice cream. The cake was chocolate with white icing, and Danner put twenty candles on it, one to grow on. They'd set the cake up on the only table in his dorm room, all of them laughing, and when she leaned over, lighting matches, the ends of her long hair had caught fire. Billy put it out fast with his hands, but a few strands near her face were scorched. Danner made a joke about Buddhist protests; no harm was done and they ate cake until most of it was gone. This morning, pulling on his jeans, he'd thought he smelled the acrid odor of burnt hair, and he remembered the scared look on her face as she'd pulled back from the candles. Billy shifted in his seat. There was no smell at all in the bio classroom of Sumner Hall.

The bell rang. All around him books slammed shut, bodies shuffled. Everyone got up at once and moved, a bored herd on its way to cafeteria lines. He sat and let them pass, watching the tiers of seats reassert their emptiness. All summer, he'd waited to come to college. After he was in college, it seemed he was waiting for something else. What was he waiting for now?

He figured he would drive to Bellington. It wasn't fair if he didn't tell Jean right away.

The summer before he started college, Billy worked as a lifeguard at the State Park, a wilderness of rhododendron and pine crossed with trails. The trails were steep and rocky above the winding river, dotted with bridges, picnic tables, stone-hewn barbecue pits, fireplaces built in the Depression by CCC men. The river wound or rushed according to season; every spring someone drowned in the rapids, the river twisting violently around boulders and big rocks that created deep pools in the current. Teenagers from nearby towns went camping or tubing; they hiked the trails back along the river, toting beer and food far from the park entrance. They waded out to favorite rocks, awkwardly carrying ice chests, blankets, radios. Couples staked space on a flat rock and swam off the side in summer when the river was calm; they grew drunk slowly and necked in the sun.

Families stayed farther up where there were guards, where the river was cordoned off near the refreshment stand and restrooms. Billy sat there in his tall white chair, a silver whistle on a chain around his neck, and watched dragonflies skim across the water. Weekends the park was crowded, the stretch of paved riverbank spread with towels and bathers. Transistor radios blared pop legends. Young mothers, high school girls a few years before, lay insensate, their faces blank. They listened to Top 40 and oiled their thighs. Sometimes they started conversations. *Hey there, aren't you Billy Hampson? What class was it you were in—two years ago, right?* Or *I knew your sister, she was just three years behind me. Where was it she went off to?* Billy watched toddlers in the wading pool, a shallows roped off with plastic cord and multicolored floats. Even on weekends, the young mothers were alone. They were girls whose husbands worked Saturdays or watched TV ballgames; they bought new bathing suits every summer at K-Mart and read romance paperbacks. Already they seemed transformed into an isolated species; groups of boys who came to the park in such numbers never glanced at them. *You're a Hampson. Aren't you Billy Hampson? I thought you were.* They pulled piles of plastic toys from beach bags, watched their charges wade into the water, then lay down and abandoned consciousness for a semiwakeful trance. The older women, whose children were eight and ten and twelve, came in couples and played cards. They refereed their kids' quarrels, drank iced tea from a thermos, smoked endless cigarettes; they were stolid, asexual, and self-contained. They didn't notice Billy unless he reprimanded their children, blowing the whistle and signaling them back to the bank for dunking or straying too far. Then the women stood up in their solid-color, one-piece suits, shouting threats and directions, snapping down the legs of the suits to cover a half-moon of sagging derriere.

Weekdays were long, lazy, the park nearly empty and the swimming area frequented only by a country family or two. The men were present then: they were truckers between hauls, or miners or plant workers on night shift, or they were out of work. Never less than five or six kids, and the parents middle-aged on wool blankets. The kids wore shorts and T-shirts; the babies went naked. They brought big rubber intertubes and tires instead of toys. No radios, no plastic bottles of oil. There was little talk and easy silence; the kids could all swim and were usually obedient, and the older ones took care of the younger. Billy sat all day in the swoony heat. By four in the afternoon everyone was gone from the swimming area; he put away life jackets and guard poles, checked the bathrooms, picked up litter. He would lock up at five. Just before, he knelt by the river with a set of corked vials to take a water sample. The river was getting dirtier; mine drainage striped the rocks orange just a few miles up. In a year, two

years, swimming would be officially disallowed. Billy held the vials
to the sun, watched the water cloud, then wrote dates and acidity
registration in the record book. The days smelled of pollen. Close
insects sounded, faint stirrings, dollop of a fish breaking. Billy
would dump the vials, rinse them, put them back in the case and
shut the lid. He stood looking at the water and then went in,
swimming underwater. He cleared the river to the opposite bank
in five powerful strokes and long glides, surfaced, and moved
back across with a regular butterfly stroke, hearing only the
quick, flat impact of his limbs cutting water.

Often on the way home he stopped at a small beer joint called
Bartley's. It was a peaceful red-neck bar not big enough for fights
or dancing. The interior was just nine bar stools, the bar itself, and
five square tables arranged across the slanted wood floor in front.
A closet to the right of the bar held a stained toilet. The insulbrick-
sided building had been some worker's shanty house back in the
days when there were lumber mills. Narrow secondary roads near
the park were dotted with such houses, some of them fallen away
to frames and inverted roofs, the struts pointing into air. Trees
grew up through the floors where there was sun enough.

At Bartley's the sun was muted by brown paper blinds; the
blinds were old and faded and strained the light to a dull gold.
Unhurried conversations continued at the tables. The patrons
were mostly men in their fifties or sixties who lived nearby in
Hampton or Volga, rural settlements begun as mill towns along
the river. Billy's grandfather had built Hampton, had owned a
mill. But the man, his mother's father, had died when Jean was
a girl; Hampton had died before he did. Even then, it must have
been steamy in summer. Country near the State Park was brushy
and still forested, valleys overhung by hills. The old air conditioner at Bartley's wheezed over the entrance, and a small rotat-
ing fan, its face no bigger than a pie plate, stood on the bar. Billy
drank one or two cold beers in tall Stroh's glasses, and wondered
about Kato with little urgency. He thought in terms of 'getting
rid of her,' getting her out of his mind. But four years back, things
referred to her. Summers, winters, high school, movie houses. His
car reminded him of her. His friends reminded him. Girls he went
out with now reminded him; even the best ones seemed coy and

mannered. They were willing to different degrees but wanted something in exchange for their loyalty, their favors—some assurance. They all had plans, secretarial school or college, and they believed in their plans as though the future were cast in iron. His sister, Danner, was a little like that too, but Danner was smart enough it seemed reasonable she have plans. And she could veer off course suddenly. Most girls around Bellington didn't. And to Billy, who'd been sleeping with Kato for nearly two years, the proceeding and backing off in parked cars, the lines drawn, the expectations, seemed a waste of time. He wouldn't make any promises.

Kato hadn't needed promises. He guessed they might have slept together even sooner if he'd tried. Somehow his getting a car had started them off. He wasn't the first; Kato told him candidly she'd been with another boy before, twice. She attached no judgments and neither did Billy. He took her to school every morning and took her home in the afternoon, except during football season, when he was team manager and stayed late. Afternoons, she worked with her father in the billiard room, doing food orders for customers while Shinner poured drafts and saw to the tables. Billy played pool or shot the bull with Shinner until he had to go home to supper. Later, he phoned. Saturday nights they went to the movies at the Colonial, then walked across the street and upstairs to Kato's room. They were always alone then and they didn't have to hurry. Sometimes Billy fell asleep afterward, as though her bedroom were his own, then got up and left after midnight.

He supposed they'd acted grown-up long before they really were. But in some ways Kato was never a kid. Her mother had died a long time before, and she and her brothers had raised themselves. Shinner didn't impose many rules, and he drank. Billy had cleaned him up a few times to save Kato's doing it. Shinner wasn't a mean drunk but he was fairly dependable; twice a month he'd drink himself into a stupor. One of the brothers or even Kato ran the billiard room then, though it meant she served beer. She hadn't turned drinking age until recently, but the cops knew the story and looked the other way.

Billy had gotten used to it all gradually, so nothing had

seemed odd. Only now he wondered, because he wondered about
everything. Shinner had bought the building outright with an
inheritance years before, and the family lived upstairs. He had no
overhead and a pretty good business; there weren't money problems but the rooms upstairs looked impoverished. A rug, one long
couch, a cheap maple coffee table, and a color TV console in the
living room. Arrangement of blue plastic flowers on the console.
The kitchen with its Formica table and chairs, its prefab cabinets
and old sink. A dishwasher, outcast and new, off by itself on one
wall. A low ceiling full of pipes. Kato's bedroom: white child's
bureau, big stuffed animals, presents from Billy, on the floor. A
double bed on a frame. Dimestore full-length mirror he'd helped
her mount on the back of the door, the closed door. They kept a
box of rubbers under the bed, though Shinner would never have
bothered looking.

He liked Billy well enough. Sundays, Billy ate dinner with
them in the kitchen, Rice-a-Roni and pork chops Kato cooked in a
big frying pan. The two brothers, three and four years older than
Kato, ate when they passed through the kitchen. The boys more
or less roomed above the billiard hall and kept no particular hours.
The older one was 4F—*basketball, hell,* Shinner said, *he messed
up that elbow leaning on too many pool tables*—and worked in
the mines near town. The other played football at Lynchburg
State. Weeknights, whoever was around ate downstairs at the
counter: hot dogs, fries, hamburgers made at the grill, and beer.
Sundays, anytime, Billy loved being with Kato above the billiard
hall. He liked all the nearly empty rooms. He loved how she
looked, like she didn't need anything else around her.

Last spring, senior year, when it was certain he'd go away to
college, things had gotten bad between them. She flirted with
other guys and went out with some. He wasn't about to ask her
why or yell at her; he just got his class ring back and stayed away.
Now she was going out with some city cop who hung around the
billiard room; cops ate lunch there. Billy saw her now and then,
not much; she didn't hang around with the high school crowd
anymore. The cop was seven or eight years older—apparently
they went to Winfield to supper clubs, and skeet shooting. Maybe
it wasn't so strange; cops around town had always gone easy on

Shinner, and the whole family had reason to be nice to them. But what did she think was happening to her?

Danner had asked Billy, around graduation, if he'd thought of marrying Kato. He hadn't. He didn't want to be married. He couldn't see Kato married either, to anybody. But nothing was right anymore.

His parents were glad when it ended, especially Jean. She'd talked to him about it in July or so. She was sorry, she told him, but after all, he and Kato were so young. And Kato might be a nice person—her father and Jean had gone to high school together and, no matter what anyone said, there wasn't a better person in this town than Shinner Black—but Kato had never had a mother to teach her certain things. Would she ever have made the kind of home Billy had grown up in, the kind he might someday want?

Billy didn't know what he wanted. Jean had gone on speaking softly, with such worry in her voice that Billy didn't say anything back, only nodded. But all he could think of while she talked was the sound of her footsteps, every early morning all summer, up the stairs from the basement. Ever since they'd moved from the house on Brush Fork, almost two years ago, she'd slept down there in a single bed. Billy hadn't paid much attention before, but that summer he began to notice everything. He got up early, drove the fifteen miles to his job, opened the swimming area by nine. But before he could drive to the park, where it was quiet and lush, he had to listen to his mother's footsteps. He lay in bed, waking up, and listened. Her steps were heavy with a resignation he couldn't fathom. Later he sat by the river and heard the rush of water. He stared at the moving surface, and finally all other sounds left his mind.

After he went away to school, he missed the river badly.

He was in Bellington by four in the afternoon. November light went fast and it was already dusk. On impulse, he drove through an alley off Main Street and pulled up behind the billiard room. The barbecue grill he'd bought the previous spring was still on the fire escape landing; it would rust in the winter if she didn't take it inside soon. Didn't seem right to use the fire escape steps, so he went around front. He didn't want to walk through the billiard room and see people and talk, so he went in the other door, up the dark, narrow stairs that led to the upstairs apartment. His walking was loud in the enclosed hallway. Before he got to the top to ring the bell, she opened the door and looked down. He stopped, waiting.

Dressed in a T-shirt and jeans, barefoot, she hugged her arms in the chilly hallway. "Billy."

He thought he must seem like a fool. He said nothing and leaned against the wall. She looked like she'd been sleeping, her hair tousled. It occurred to him she might be with someone. "Anyone here?"

"No. I was taking a nap." She walked down two steps. "Billy, is anything wrong?"

He shook his head. "Just wanted to talk to you. Haven't seen you in a while. How you doing?"

"Okay."

"Can I come in, or do you want me to go?"

"You want to come in?" She shrugged, flustered. "Sure. Come in."

He followed her inside. She shut the door behind them and he looked around. After the carpeted dorm with its modernistic furniture, the square room looked even more spare. She sat down on the couch a little nervously; he sat beside her but not too near. "So," he asked, "how have you been?"

"Pretty good. I've been working downstairs, but last week I got a job at the newspaper."

"Yeah? Reporting?" *Keep talking*, he thought, *it'll get better.*

"Just typing, but maybe later they'll let me do more. I mean, at least write up birth announcements and things."

"Kato, that's good."

She nodded and took a cigarette from a pack on the table. She tamped it down and lit it, then picked up an ash tray and put it on the cushion between them. She tucked her legs under her and turned toward him. "So. You met any nice people up there?"

At first he thought she was mocking him, then understood again that she was nervous. He didn't want her to be, but it encouraged him. She was asking him about girls. "Well, yeah, I mean it's real easy. But no one special."

Her face betrayed no relief. "How is school?"

"I quit school this morning." It was the first time he'd said it. He leaned a little forward and put his hands on his knees, then clasped them. He realized he was sitting as his father did, and he sat back. "Maybe I shouldn't have come by, but I wanted to talk to someone before I told my parents. I guess I wanted to talk to you."

She didn't answer right away but looked across the room at the window. Then she tapped the ash of the cigarette and looked at him. "Why did you quit?"

"I didn't want to be there. I was just waiting until December really, to find out what my number was. Like, if I did what I was supposed to do and sat through all the classes, my number would be high, and then I could quit." He shook his head. "Stupid. The number is going to be the same, whatever. If it's low, there's no deferment anyway. School isn't going to help. And later, I don't want these grades on my record. I haven't really tried. I couldn't get myself to care."

"You thought about what you're going to do?"

"Maybe stay up there, get a job. I've got the dorm room anyway until the term ends. Or I could come back here. I might go south after Christmas. I could always get a job tending bar in a resort town."

"What would you do if you stayed in Bellington?"

He felt flushed, listening to her simple questions. He heard her talk with an almost physical ache of pleasure. "Would you like it if I stayed around?" He asked uncertainly; he was sure she'd tell him the truth.

She raised her brows in puzzlement and spoke slowly. "I don't know. It would be kind of complicated for me."

"You mean because of this guy you're going out with."

She held the cigarette high in her hand and the smoke, a thin, constant smoke, disappeared into the room. "You know, it wasn't like things were great for me over the summer, when you never even came around. I used to just talk to him once in a while, when he came in for lunch. He was new around here and kind of quiet, old-fashioned. Finally he asked my father if he could take me out sometime."

Billy imagined Shinner's befuddlement and smiled. "What did Shinner say?"

"He said, 'It's no business of mine. Ask her.'" Kato laughed.

Billy nodded. He said, after a pause, "I kept wondering if it wasn't strange, going out with a cop. Does he get upset about some of your habits?"

She put the cigarette out. "I don't do dope in front of him. I don't smoke much dope at all anymore. Turning into a drinker, I guess."

"What?"

"Not like that, Billy. I'm not that dumb."

Maybe Shinner was worse. "I never thought you were dumb at all," Billy said softly.

Far off, they heard a siren. Fire truck barreling up Quality Hill and on out. The corners of her mouth tightened. "Sorry. It's just that Dad is driving me crazy lately. Soon as I save up some money at the paper, I might get my own place."

"He drinking more?"

She opened one hand in a dismissive gesture. "Anyway. You ought to stay around if you want to. Don't let it depend on me, but I mean, maybe the Park Service would hire you back."

Billy let himself imagine it. "I liked the Park Service, even if the pay was bad. I guess they need people in winter. Be nice there in the snow."

She nodded. "They patrol the park in jeeps. You have to have four-wheel drive on those roads."

"Yeah." He touched her shoulder, then moved his hand away. "You could ride around with me and help put out hay for the deer. Or maybe not. Your friend would get mad."

"He doesn't tell me what to do," she said flatly.

"That would be a mistake," Billy agreed.

She smiled a little and leaned forward to touch the edge of the ash tray.

"Does he try to tell you what to do?" Billy watched her hand, her long fingers.

"Not exactly. He just . . . expects me to be more, like, ladylike, than I am. He seems surprised sometimes. I don't know, he's nothing like me. He says most girls he knows only sleep with the one they're going to marry. I told him I was kind of married to you, if he wants to think of it that way."

"Is that how you thought of it?"

She looked up guiltily, as though she'd admitted too much. "No. Not until lately anyway."

It was dark outside. The room had gotten dark, and it was cold. The small neon light that advertised Black's Billiards blinked on and off downstairs, throwing up a muted rosiness that came and went beyond the living room windows. They could hear, through the floor, the soft clicks of pool cues, the thumps of balls dropping into pockets. The sounds were so known and so familiar, so comforting. Billy felt an edge release inside him. "Quiet down there," he said. "No jukebox?"

"Broken," Kato said. "Dad hasn't got it fixed yet."

"Well, I better go." He started to stand but she stood first.

She walked over and said, from above him, very near, "I don't mean we should change things, but I wish you wouldn't leave yet."

He stood to meet her halfway but they were on the couch again and he couldn't hold her close enough, hard enough, his face pressed tight against her, sounds of surprise and relief in his throat. She felt more real than anything had felt in all these months.

Though it was only ten, his mother's house was in darkness. He stood on the stoop and considered sleeping in his car but, no, he'd driven here to tell her. He rang the bell. Inside, the hallway light went on. As the doorknob turned and the door swung open, he realized she might have wakened out of sleep to loud and unexpected sounds. "Mom," he called, "it's just me, Billy."

"Billy?" She was at the door, her face in shadow. "What's wrong?"

"Nothing's wrong. Everything is fine."

"What do you mean? Don't you have classes tomorrow?" She opened the door wide and stepped back to let him enter.

"No, not tomorrow. I'm sorry I woke you up." He took his

jacket off and hung it over the newel post, and hugged her.
"You're turning in early these days."

"I wasn't really sleeping." She looked at him confusedly.
"Did you eat dinner? Are you hungry?"

"No, I'm not hungry."

She drew her robe closer around her, the long red woolen
robe he remembered from last year and other years. She'd worn
it every night, sitting in a straight-backed chair in the small den,
reading or knitting while the television droned low in a corner.
Last winter, Billy had come in late to find his father asleep in the
downstairs bedroom, and Jean in the den with both doors of the
little room shut, *to keep the heat in.* Sometimes he sat down with
her to watch the last of the eleven o'clock news or a few minutes
of a late movie. She was quiet and relaxed; Billy felt as though
they were alone in the house. Later he walked upstairs soundlessly on the carpeted steps; Danner was at college and the whole
upstairs was his domain.

"I don't even have a bed made for you," Jean said. "I'll have
to get some sheets out of the closet." She turned.

"Mom," he said, and waited until she faced him. "I withdrew
from school today."

"You what?" She sat down on the piano bench in the living
room.

"Here's the refunded tuition, and I'll pay you back for the
dorm costs." He took two hundred-dollar bills from his pocket
and, standing beside her, put the money on top of the piano.

She made no move and only stared at him, bewildered.

He sat down on the couch opposite her. "I knew during the
summer that I'd made plans for school because there was really
no other choice, with the draft. I was accepted and I thought I
should go, give it a chance. The longer I went to classes, the surer
I was—that I don't know what I want to do."

"Billy, no nineteen-year-old kid has to decide in the first semester of college what he wants to do. You're there to take your
time and find out what you want to do."

"I found out I don't want to be in school."

"When you find yourself in basic training you may wish you
were in school."

He smiled at her. "That doesn't work anymore, Mom. No more school deferments after December. Wouldn't matter if I was number one on the honor roll. Quitting school doesn't affect my draft status one way or the other." He paused, watching her. He didn't want to sound fresh. "Listen, it's a waste of money for me to go to college right now."

The tick of the kitchen clock was loud in the house. She looked at him angrily. "Since it's my money, why don't you let me decide when it's wasted. And I know they didn't give you any refund this late."

He didn't answer.

She sighed. "Isn't it a waste to quit now, when the semester is nearly over?"

His eyes were tired and he fought the impulse to touch them. He felt as though he'd been en route to this house for weeks. "When I really decide, for myself, that I want to go to school, I want to start clean. These grades, these courses some adviser signed me up for at registration, mean nothing to me."

His mother looked at him levelly. "Were you failing, Billy? Why didn't you tell me if you were having trouble? You always said you were doing fine."

"I was. My grades weren't good but I wasn't failing." Now he did rub his eyes, and he touched his forehead. He could smell Kato on his hand, the perfumed, musky smell of her neck and throat. He didn't want to think about her now; he wanted to talk to Jean and make her understand. "Mom, if it turns out my number is high, I want to work for a year. I'll get a job, either here or maybe farther south, and save some money. If my number is low and I go into the army, I don't want to have spent these weeks going to classes. Either way, I did the right thing."

Jean's hands were open in her lap. She looked down at her palms and said slowly, "Is this my fault? Have I made things so confusing?"

"No, Mom. Maybe I went along with going to school because I didn't want to cause trouble when everyone was upset anyway. But keeping on with that mistake isn't going to help—"

"With my mistakes?" she asked gently.

"I don't think you made a mistake. You did what you had to

do. I just wish you'd understand—I did, too. I'm in a bind like yours, in a way." He looked up at her, as though for help with words. "I guess that doesn't make any sense."

"No, it does." She looked at the floor and bent over to pick up a bit of fuzz from the carpet. Absently she held a blur of gold threads, her fingers touching lightly. "Lord," she said, "I hope you haven't given yourself a terrible birthday present."

"I don't think I have."

She nodded. Across the gulf of the floor between them, her gaze was direct and quietly frightened. She looked more vulnerable than he'd ever seen her. Billy suddenly wondered if he'd ever sit across some room listening to his own kid and get scared.

"It's going to be all right," he told his mother now. "Things will turn out."


## DECEMBER

Billy picked his sister up at the courthouse the night of December 2nd. Near evening the day-long drizzle had turned to constant rain. There was no bus station anymore in Bellington, and Trailways let people off on Main Street at the courthouse steps. Billy drove up and saw Danner standing under the portico of the domed building, alone, hems of her jeans wet to the ankles, collar of her denim jacket turned up. *After all the money she spent on clothes in high school,* Jean had said as Billy left the house, *Danner dresses like a bum.* Danner had no raincoat, no umbrella, but she had a larger suitcase than was necessary for a visit of a few days. Billy got out of the car to help her, but before he could cross the street she was halfway to him, the rain drenching her. They threw the suitcase in the back seat and pulled both doors shut; then he handed her a towel.

"You look drowned," he told her as she dried her face. "I can't believe you rode the bus to Bellington in a storm like this. They must have stopped at every little podunk on Route 20. No wonder it took three hours."

Danner laughed. "At least it wasn't snow. The bus would have ended up in a drift in Peel Tree."

"You want to go down by Shinner's and have a beer with Kato before we go home?"

She looked up as Billy started the car, a little surprised. "Sure, I guess. You seeing Kato again since you came home?"

"Some." There were no cars on Main Street. Billy ran a red light and turned the corner down past the movie house. "Why didn't you wait until the weekend to come home?"

She threw the towel in the back seat. "I saw the lottery list this morning and I got the first bus that came through Bellington. I want to talk to you, Billy. Before we go inside."

Billy parked opposite the billiard room, then pointed across the street. "Take a look at Shinner's new sign." The long horizontal sign snapped lazily off and on behind the downward slant of the rain. B I L L I A R D S, it said in alternate hot pink and blue, waves of the colors rippling, muted in rain.

"Big," Danner said. "Not exactly classy, but very noticeable. Billy, can you turn the heat on?"

Billy did. "All right, I want a beer. What do you want to tell me?"

"Just hear me out, okay?" She looked down at her bare hands, her long hair dripping onto her jacket. With the heat on, Billy could smell the dampness on her, almost smell rain. She looked back up at him. "Billy, you've got to make some plans. You don't have to let them send you over there."

"You mean Fort Knox? Basic training?"

"You know what I mean, Billy. Don't make fun of me. This is not funny."

"I'm not laughing, Danner." The motor of the Camaro idled and the windshield wipers thwacked, regular as metronomes.

"I've brought some money with me, a thousand dollars. And an address in Canada. Saturday you're supposed to drive me back to the University. We'll say you're staying overnight with some school friends, and when we get to Montreal, we'll phone and say where we are. I'll stay a couple of days and take a bus back."

"Where did you get a thousand dollars?"

"Emergency Student Loans."

"You got the money that fast, in one day?"

"No. I applied last week, just in case." She gazed out the windshield, then turned to him. "Oh God, please listen to me. One way or the other, they're going to fuck you up. Look, if you're standing on a railroad track and a locomotive is coming closer, very fast, don't you step off the track? Don't you get the hell out of the way?"

"Not until the last minute." He looked away from her and switched off the wipers. Rain immediately runneled on the windshield, distorting the street to colors on a black shine.

"You can't wait, Billy. If you leave after you're inducted, you're AWOL, you're a criminal. If you leave now, you're a resister. A lot of people think resisters will be pardoned, maybe in just a few years."

"You mean the draft counselors at the University think so."

She didn't miss a beat. "Draft counselors everywhere think so. But I didn't get the address from them. A girl in my dorm has a sister in Montreal."

He smiled at her. Lighten it up. "A pretty sister?"

But she looked at him, frustrated, fearful, her face open and naked, and bit her lips. "Please," she said, "please think about this."

"What the fuck, Danner," he said quietly, "don't you know I've thought about it? I thought before I quit school and I've thought all month, selling trousers up there at Rossing's. Hardly anyone comes into Rossing's. I had time to think about it a lot."

Danner looked past his face at the billiards sign, but he knew she wasn't seeing it. She was planning her next remark, some way to convince him.

"Listen," he said, "if it was possible to avoid the army, I would. But my number is nineteen. I'm not going to Canada for ten years, I'm not going to Canada at all. I decided I'd go with the numbers."

"Don't be an idiot," she said angrily. "They're not your numbers."

"I don't feel that way," he said, raising his voice. "Things are in the cards. I could buy it right here in Bellington, crack up my car on the Winfield road, like that college kid did last weekend."

"That's stupid reasoning," she yelled back. "You don't put yourself where bad things happen."

"Bad things can happen anywhere!" He caught himself then and sat back. "You don't reason through these things. The best way to be lucky is to take what comes and not be a coward." He looked silently into the rain. "I'm going to go. It's in the cards."

"What cards?" She was almost whispering.

"Everyone's cards." He looked over at her. "It'll be different for you after I go."

"Jesus, I'm not worried about me."

Billy touched her hands and they were cold. He held both her hands hard between his. "The fuckers won't do me in. I'll stay off the ground if they send me, get into an air crew. I'll keep my ass in the air."

"Great. Then you'll have farther to fall." Danner had slumped down in the seat beside him. and she moved her legs toward the heating vent.

"Please," he said, encircling her forearm with his hand, "take the money back to Student Loans, and don't give me any more suggestions. Not about Canada and not about Nam. And don't mope around all through Christmas. Weren't you going to go to Florida for New Year's with your pals? I want you to go ahead and go."

She looked away from him, her eyes wet.

"Don't be a pain," he said gently. "You're not the one with the number. It's not your show."

"All right, all right. Let's go have a beer." She caught his arm as he turned off the ignition. "But if you change your mind, you'll tell me."

"I will." He opened the door of the car and the rain asserted its steady patter. "When we get inside, be sure to tell Shinner you like the sign."

The first heavy snow blanketed Bellington on Christmas Eve. Billy sat in the living room. He listened to his mother and Danner in the kitchen and gazed at the tree, a six-foot pine decked out in lights and ornaments and gold trim. The thing had been hell to get through the kitchen door and into the holder, since Danner wasn't

strong enough to help much. Jean had swathed the metal holder
with a wide length of hemmed red corduroy. Billy and Danner had
marked the change silently; always before there had been a simple white bedsheet under the tree, to look like snow. But the
dining room table was familiar, set with the white damask cloth,
the silver service, the Havilland china. Billy knew the name because Jean had always referred to the white, gold-scalloped plates
as *my mother's Haviland,* washed before and after use each
Christmas and Easter. The kitchen radio played carols and the
house was filled with the smells of roast turkey and yams. The day
felt long and slow and full; since he'd left school, each day had
seemed completely separate from any other.

Jean was doing pretty well. She'd wept easily the first couple
of weeks after the lottery, but then she determined they'd have
a normal Christmas. Well, not exactly normal. Dinner on Christmas Eve, since he and Danner would eat the big noon meal tomorrow with all the relatives at Bess's, with Mitch.

"Billy, you want another egg nog?" Danner leaned out of the
kitchen doorway. "Or straight bourbon?"

Jean's voice, from the vicinity of the stove: "Don't you dare
give him straight bourbon."

"No thanks," Billy told them. "Since you two are drinking so
hard, I believe I'll stay sober."

Danner looked nice in black velvet. Jean's reproof: *I haven't
seen you in a dress since Billy's high school graduation.* Now
his sister smiled and disappeared again. Billy knew she'd made
careful preparations for tomorrow; a special joint rolled in red and
green papers to smoke in the car on the way to Bess's house. But
he wasn't sure he'd partake. Though he didn't leave for basic until
January 5th, the relatives would all feel they had to mention his
going into the army. Only Mitch would not refer to it. *Damn it,*
was all he'd said to Billy, his face grave, the morning the lottery
list was published.

Radio music in the kitchen increased slightly in volume; Danner came into the living room and sat with Billy on the couch.
"How do you think Mom is doing?" she asked in a low voice.

"Good."

Danner nodded. "I think I may go to Florida, but I'll leave on the 26th and be back on the 2nd. Then stay a few days after you have to go. She shouldn't be alone then." She took a drink of her bourbon and coke. "You and Kato exchanging presents?"

"Tomorrow night. I got her a gold necklace, a chain. Something she can keep. Real pretty."

"Want me to wrap it for you?"

"They wrapped it at the store. Otherwise, I would have already asked you."

Danner looked at the tree. "What ever happened to that cop of hers?"

"I guess he's biding his time. Kato must have told him I'm on my way to foreign parts, though so far it's only Kentucky." He touched Danner's arm. "You look cold, you've got goose bumps."

"It's colder out here than in the kitchen." She looked down at her drink.

"Kato told me he was in Nam in '65. He's only been a cop for a year."

"Gee, Kato's turning into a real heartbreaker. First you, now him."

"That's not how it is, Danner. We don't advertise things. I don't stay over there. Now we're like all the other couples in Bellington, we make it in my car."

She smiled. "Cars aren't bad."

"Takes flexibility."

A pause.

Danner frowned. "Do you think she's sleeping with both of you?"

Billy shook his head and gave his sister a sideways glance. "I don't worry about those details. I don't ask her if she sleeps with him. That's her business, and his."

"I bet she isn't," Danner said slowly, and folded her arms, "not now."

"I think you're right," Billy said.

"Right about what?" Their mother stood by the dinner table, holding the big platter of roast turkey.

"Mom," Danner reprimanded, "you should have let me bring that in for you."

"Who do you think carried it home from the store? It's not

much heavier now." She smiled, pretty in her white wool dress.
Billy had given her a corsage, a white gardenia, and she'd kept it
in the refrigerator until five minutes ago. The white flower was
just opening, ribboned with red satin and a sprig of holly. Billy
knew she'd keep the ribbons in a drawer for years.

They put the rest of the food on the table together: potatoes,
peas, yams, gravy, bread dressing with walnuts, relishes, all in
china serving dishes. Finally they sat down.

"Enough for a party of eight," Danner said. "Mom, maybe we
didn't need quite such a big turkey."

"We count for eight," Jean responded, "and this is a celebration. Besides, these leftovers will last until the army comes for
us."

Billy caught Danner's warning glance. "Right," he said, "and
then you can always ship crates of turkey sandwiches to Fort
Knox."

Jean handed Billy the carving knife and fork. She'd put the
platter of meat near his plate. "Really, there are things to celebrate. We're together, you don't have to leave until after the
holidays, and your sister—did you know she'll make the dean's list
this semester?"

"Mom," Danner said, "it's not for sure."

"A toast." Billy raised his glass, then asked in a stage whisper, "Who *is* the dean, anyway?"

"Bob Hope," Danner answered.

"Danner," Jean said seriously, "you should go ahead and go
to Florida, since your friends are going and you have a ride.
You've worked hard, and you've been such a help to me, too—."
She stopped talking, her voice quavering.

"Come home with a tan like Bob Hope's," Billy injected
quickly. "I'll supervise here in Bellington."

Danner unfolded her napkin. "You mean you'll supervise
Black's Billiards."

"Exactly. But first I'll eat my dinner." He picked up the
carving knife and made ready.

"Wait." Jean held up one hand. "Let's say the blessing."

"Good idea." Danner fixed Billy with an encouraging look.
"Billy, the floor is yours."

"Do I know a blessing?" Billy put the knife down. "I'll make one up."

Their mother shook her head. "You act as though you were raised as heathens."

"We'll hold hands for luck." Danner crossed her wrists as though taken captive.

But they did hold hands, Jean at one side of the square table, Billy and Danner at either end. Danner couldn't quite reach Billy; she moved her chair closer and arched one arm over the steaming food. Their fingertips met in a pyramid.

"Secret signal," Billy said, and stood to grasp her hand. Pewter bells on the front door moved in the wind; he remembered the snow outside, drifting along the street. When they were children, in the country on Brush Fork, the snow drifted magically high. They'd worn bulky mittens impossible to lose, mittens strung on yarn around their necks and through the sleeves of their snowsuits.

"Start talking," Danner said, "it'll come to you." She and Jean bowed their heads and waited, smiling.

Billy spoke, words from one of the old prayers, but behind his closed eyes played a memory of startling clarity: watching the snow plow with Danner, both of them small, standing in snow to their knees. The big yellow machine rumbling by, slow, all-powerful. Engine roar, shrill jangling of chains. The powdery snow thrown up in fanned continuous spray as the heavy machine pressed on.

December 31st. Snow on his boots, stamping his feet on the back porch of the white house beside the hospital. Chains of the dismantled swing moved in the wind, and the lattice of the porch roof was built up with thick snow so wet that the square spaces of the lattice work were solidly snowed in. Snow made the gray light whiter; he stamped his feet and heard them inside—his father and Aunt Bess moving from their chairs to the kitchen door: Mitch coughing, his tread heavy; and Aunt Bess moving stiffly, laced into her corsets. The coal bucket was full beside the door and laced with snow, the black lumps jagged and big, showing snow like a powder. Billy took off his gloves and brushed the snow away; the coal was so cold it left no smear on his fingers. By now they were at the door and the sound of the knob turning was loud. Aunt Bess was there, behind the screen, his father hovering beyond her like a wall. Her face wore that pleased, surprised expression, the thick eyeglasses exaggerati..g her inquiring gaze.

"Well hello, Mister," she said. "You're up early."

Mitch motioned for Billy to come inside. "Get on in here, let's not let Bess get cold." He shut the door behind them all and clapped a hand on Billy's shoulder. "Got some spuds cooking. You want some eggs?"

"No thanks." Billy put his snowy gloves in his pocket and unzipped his jacket.

"Big mistake," Mitch said, "I make good eggs." He nodded at Bess. "Even Bess eats them, and she's hard to please."

"Your father is a wonderful cook," Bess told Billy. "Now, there's no question about it, we all know I can't cook." She went to the stove to pour hot water into two cups of instant coffee.

Mitch gave Billy an amused look, then sat down again.

Billy stood awkwardly in the small room as Bess brought the coffee to the table. He took a breath. He would just have to go ahead and tell them. "Mitch, Danner called last night from Florida. She got into some trouble. She got arrested for possession."

"Possession of what? What are you talking about?"

"Possession of marijuana. Danner got busted."

His father looked at him, incredulous. Behind him Aunt Bess touched the back of his chair.

"You mean drugs," Mitch said. "Is Danner in jail?"

"Yes. Mom went down to the bank this morning to borrow the money for bail. She had to borrow two thousand dollars."

"Jesus Christ." His father bowed his head and leaned his elbows on the table. He turned his head to one side and touched his forehead, then covered his eyes with his hand. For a strange moment Billy thought he was praying.

Aunt Bess still stood, gripping the back of Mitch's chair as though holding it in place. "But Danner is all right, she's not hurt."

"No, no, she's okay. She should be out of the jail by tonight."

Billy stepped closer to the table but kept his hands in his pockets. His father sat silently, with no movement in his body. He moved his hand now to support his forehead and tears fell on the checked tablecloth. Billy felt very warm, as though he were going to be dizzy. Snow was falling past the kitchen windows in big wet flakes; the yard and bushes on the other side of the glass were a smooth, unbroken white. The kitchen was lit with snow light, indirect and off-white. The warmth of the room was inconsistent with the light and the consciousness of snow; Bess was baking bread, that was it—Billy hadn't smelled it till now.

He looked at his great aunt and she faced him from behind his father, unblinkingly. She seemed to be looking straight through Billy, through the walls of the house as well, sadly and evenly. She was very thin and held her rounded shoulders high, of some long habit; her stance lent the front of her body a concave aspect from chest to knees. Now she moved to give Mitch her white handkerchief, taking the small square from the pocket of her sweater, unfolding it, placing it near him. Her gesture was deliberate and unobtrusive. She sat down, very straight, on the tall stool beside the hoosier.

Mitch refolded the handkerchief, his eyes wet. "I hope your mother is satisfied now," he said.

"It's not her fault," Billy said.

Mitch continued as though Billy hadn't spoken. "This would never have happened."

They were all quiet. Snow was falling and a car moved through the alley, its motor muffled and sputtering. There was the sound of chains on ice as tires spun for traction. New snow would be flying up all around the wheels.

"You never know what can happen," Bess said.

Her words were so heavy in the room that Billy found himself saying more than he'd intended. "Dad, they only had a couple of grams between the four of them."

"Grams? What the hell do you mean? What do you know about grams?"

"I mean they only had a small amount."

His father made no response.

"I think she has to stay in the state about a week," Billy said, "until the arraignment. The father of one of the boys flew down last night. I guess he's arranging things. They already have a lawyer, and rooms in a motel."

"What motel?"

"A place called the Sea View. In Naples." Billy dropped his voice, uncertain how much Danner would want Mitch to know. "They were camping out on a beach in Naples."

Mitch stood, scowling. "You get me the phone number of that motel. I want to talk to Danner."

Billy nodded. "Mom has it. I'd better get back, she's pretty upset."

His father didn't answer. Billy gestured at Bess apologetically. "I'll call or come down as soon as I hear anything."

"Yes," Bess said, "of course you will."

He turned and let himself quietly out the house, pulling the door tight behind him and closing the screen door so it latched. The look of the old woman's face stayed with him as he walked through deep snow to his car. He tried to imagine Danner in jail and couldn't. Bail would be arranged by afternoon. They wouldn't send four kids up for three grams of marijuana, especially when the nearly empty box of dope was found at the campsite and none of them admitted to possession anyway. Even though it was a felony charge, getting them off would probably be a technicality. And the lawyers' making some money. But his parents wouldn't see it that way. They thought Billy was going into the army and Danner was going wrong, all in the same week.

When he touched her there, through her clothes, he felt a small hardness throbbing like a pulse point. Her whole body, spread-eagled on the seat of the car, turned on that hardness. Kato draped one leg over the back of the seat and the other over the column of the steering wheel so that Billy was just at the vee of her crotch, leaning back against the door on his side and watching her. She threw her arms out as though floating on water and kept her eyes closed, and Billy watched her with no self-consciousness. She worked up to her own feeling a little shyly, in private; when she couldn't keep her eyes closed any longer that was a signal. If he kept touching her then, it was an unspoken promise he wouldn't stop, and when she came her whole body rippled lengthwise with a delicate vibration that reminded Billy of horses shivering their flanks. Often he didn't let her go that far; he liked to feel the trembling tight around him, from inside her. Her muscles seemed to imitate a spastic lapping of water. It was so gentle and felt so foreign, so mysterious, something fluttering against the inner walls of a cage. To Billy it didn't seem part of either one of them; if he was lost in his own sensation, he missed hers altogether and couldn't tell if she'd felt it. So he tried to wait and while they were touching each other, taking turns and trading off, he was priming himself to wait; they were intent and usually stopped talking except for involuntary sounds. This was a drug between them; there was the weightless high of dope but they were excruciatingly alert and wound tight. They could go on for hours.

Finally they took their clothes off and the heated interior of the car was like a capsule with steamed windows, drifting in space. They lay down in this isolated nowhere and cried out with relief at his first thrust inside her. They made love every way possible in the cramped room of the front seat, one of them changing position when they felt him almost coming. At last they let go and rode their own movement, not thinking, racing: he opened his eyes for an instant and a small shape in the steamy window had teared clear. The snowy hill below the plant lot was a luminous slant in the winter dark. Far below, cars moved on the Winfield road. Billy saw the lit points of headlights in the midnight blue of the cold air, but knowledge of what he was looking at was nowhere inside him.

First he was conscious again of sounds; he heard the hum of the car heater, he heard Kato breathing. "You there?" he whispered.

"I'm here."

He sat up, pulling out of her as she touched him. She'd used their clothes as a pillow; now she gave him his pants and shirt and pulled her coat on over her nakedness. "I'd feel better if we parked behind the drive-in," she said. "It's spooky here, all these old trucks."

Billy zipped his Levi's. "You scared?" He circled her throat with his hands, pulled her closer and kissed her forehead. "I used to come here when I was a kid, same trucks. Doesn't seem spooky to me. Besides, there are always two or three cars parked behind the drive-in—the police swing by. And who knows which police."

"He wouldn't," Kato said. "I'd never speak to him again." She pulled her jeans on under the coat.

"What have you told him, anyway, all this time?"

"I haven't told him anything lately. About a month ago, I just said I couldn't see him for awhile." She reached into her purse for a cigarette.

"Kato, suppose I wasn't getting drafted?"

"We were seeing each other again before you knew you were getting drafted."

"But not as much." He raised his brows, smiling. "Maybe you have a thing for uniforms."

She lit the cigarette. Now he saw her clearly in the glow of the match; her eyes glistened with moisture. What was she feeling? Her eyes always looked wet after they made love, but the wetness seemed an automatic response, like the tears of someone choking or sneezing.

Kato held the cigarette and looked at Billy, her hand shaking a little. "Maybe I do, Billy," she said, and her voice broke.

He touched the steering wheel. It was cold and suddenly he was cold; he felt the cold dark seeping into the car. He leaned forward, switched the heat on higher. The blower hummed.

"I'll write to you, Billy." She pursed her lips when she exhaled smoke.

"Maybe you will at first," he said carefully. "But it's okay. You've already written to me."

She flung her blond hair back from her face and moved over near him. "Anytime you come home, call me. You'll be back on a leave before they send you anywhere, won't you? No matter what people tell you, get in touch with me."

They both sat looking at the patch of night framed in the windshield of the Camaro. It was snowing again. Kato rested one hand on Billy's thigh. There was no sense being jealous, or mad at her. She would always be herself, pretty and tarnished, but honest like a guy was honest. She didn't try to work things around.

"I don't know what will happen," she said. Her hand on his leg moved now, stroking him. "You can always reach me through my father."

Billy gazed into the snow, imagining himself a grunt with a shaved head, buying Shinner Black cups of coffee at the Tap Room or the Rainbow. *Where's Kato, Shinner? Give me a phone number.* Shiner would smell of Rebel Yell and he'd answer with a bleary, good-natured silence. Billy shook his head.

Kato glanced at him. "I know, but eventually he'd tell you."

"I suppose so."

"You heard anything else about Danner?"

"She's staying in a motel. Her arraignment isn't until the day after I leave. I bet she's having a great New Year's Eve."

"I guess." Kato leaned forward and put her cigarette out. "Do you want to go by that party?"

"No, this is my party. 1969 can end right here."

Kato laughed. "I think it already did."

Billy pulled her close and put his face against her hair, smelling a sweetish odor of cream rinse and tobacco smoke. Her hair wasn't usually so light in winter; she must be bleaching it again. She had a kind of sexiness that wouldn't diminish as she grew older. Middle-aged, she would look knowing and tired, he thought, her blondness brassier.

She rubbed her eyes with her hands, like a kid, then looped both arms in his and settled against him. "I wish we could just go to sleep," she said.

The snow blew now in minute flakes that swirled like sand. There must be a long narrow beach behind the Sea View Motel in Naples, Florida; Billy couldn't quite see it but he imagined the sound of surf. Here the wind was a constant murmur with snow inside it. His mother would be lying awake in the dark, listening.

# WAR LETTERS
Billy, 1970

Why have we been able, so many times, to spoil Charlie's whole day? Two reasons: One, the devastating firepower our weapons produce; Two, the rapidity with which we can put out that fire. But—and here's the hooker—we can't do that unless we're on the guns, completely alert and aggressive about starting to fire. We can't do it if, when the first incoming rounds start, we head for cover and wait until things let up. We have to watch for the flashes, spot them, and shoot back with everything we've got.

Don't get me wrong—I know this is the way our crews do it. So, all I'm saying is—keep up the good work!
>—*The Triumverate*, May 1968
>First Infantry Division newssheet
>Lake G. Churchill, Jr.
>LTC, Arty
>Commanding

To ANTI-WAR American Servicemen! We *warmly* welcome American GIs *who*, for the sake of America's honor and human conscience, resolutely oppose the aggressive *war waged* by US Imperialism in South Vietnam! We *warmly welcome* conscientious GIs *who* refuse to obey Inhuman orders forcing you to perform savage acts against the Vietnamese people! We have good *will* for you and don't want to *hurt* you. To help us differentiate you from the stubborn thugs fighting us, you should do as follows. Read all instructions with care!
>—Propaganda pamphlet
>distributed by SVNLF forces

THE VIETNAMESE PEOPLE ARE FIGHTING FOR THEIR INDEPENDENCE AND FREEDOM THAT IS JUST WHAT THE AMERICAN DID IN 18TH CENTURY
>—SVNLF trail leaflet

M-16 Rifle Tips (c.) Clean your rifle every chance you get. 3–5 times a day will not be too often in some cases. Cleanliness is next to godliness, boy, and it may save your life!
>—Defense Department pamphlet,
>1967

## FORT KNOX, KENTUCKY

Pvt. W. Hampson/RA 11949711
Co. E, 16 Bn 4Tng Boe USATCA
Fort Knox, KY

Jan. 20, 1970

Dear Mom. How's life in Bellington? Things here are not too bad. I am fine and have put on some weight even tho the food is terrible. Weight must be all muscle since Basic is one 24 hr. workout. Quarters are okay, I think from WW II, two-story wood barracks with double metal bunks. Weather here a lot better than at home, not near as much snow. You'll be glad to know I'm getting good grades as a draftee, tho no PX privileges for anyone for three more weeks. Training classes are pretty interesting, things like map reading, CPR, marksmanship that are generally useful. Danner will be fine, don't make a big deal of it all, she wouldn't be on the dean's list etc if she were "on drugs," as you say. Not much time to write but like getting your letters. Keep them coming! Will be here until at least end of Feb. when I get reassigned for AIT (adv. indiv. training), I hope somewhere in the south. I did get south after all, so goes to show you, someone is on my side. Take care and write soon.

love, Billy

Feb. 20, 1970

Dear Danner. Mitch already wrote me the case was finally dropped in Florida and you are officially a free woman—too bad, you could have dropped by to see me on your way back to trial in Naples! He took care to check and you don't have a record. Now you can think of the whole thing as a business deal that took some suffering. I don't know about being glad it happened (to see what jail is like? a day and a night don't count)—that's like me being glad I'm here. So far am keeping my head straight, only ones that get harassed real bad are the fat ones who just can't make it. Made a good friend, Rick Singleton from Merrimac, Ky., not too far from here, so we met his girl and her friend on a weekend pass. Had several letters from Kato, sent me clippings of weddings she wrote up, pretty funny. Some of them she just talks to the mothers on the phone. You wanted to know what it's like here—get up at three when it's dark out and cold as hell in the barracks—gets fucking cold in Kentucky no matter what you heard. Make tight beds, 45-degree angle creases the DI measures if he wants to give us shit, sweep, mop, wax floor, line up footgear in rows. Then double time to parade ground for reveille, still dark, damp as hell, no snow but thick white frost on the ground and mist and weird, all these silent guys lined up like tenpins waiting for a giant bowling ball. Uniforms a big deal. Buttons buttoned or the DI pulls them off and hands them to you to sew on again. Later: All you swinging dicks wake up, sleep in Basic, die in Nam. That shit is the fuck of it but they don't get to me much. Truth is I like the physical

stuff—being in top shape and passing all their tests, even the
screwball shit like night infiltration, crawling around under
barbed wire through ditches while they fire machine guns over
our heads. Can't see shit, only tracers. Then everyone gets up at
the end and marches back to the barracks in the dark. It's a real
setup and the DIs are real assholes, but it's hard to believe all
this is really going to lead to anything later, like Nam, you
know? Some guys in the platoon saw your picture and asked me
if you wanted to write them or if you have any girlfriends who
want to write letters. I told them your friends were a bunch of
hippies and they thought that sounded fine.

love, your bro

FORT DIX, NEW JERSEY

Pvt. W. Hampson/RA 11949711
Co. B, 3rd Bn, USATCA
Fort Dix, NJ

March 10, 1970

Dear Mom. Arrived here at AIT about four days ago, assigned to
Weapons Platoon. Similar barracks etc but colder now than was
in Ky in Jan. Some of the same drills and phys. cond. courses but
mostly training on the M-60 since my MOS is machine gunner. Got
your letter about you and Danner coming up—I think that would
be fine, maybe late in the month. Will apply for a pass but anyway
will be able to go off base to dinner, etc. There is a Family Welcome Center that runs tours of the base and some reasonable
motels nearby. Whole unit is doing well so far, so PX privileges
are up. Food about the same as Fort Knox unfortunately, I'm
looking forward to my May leave so I can get a good hamburger.
Hope your job is going well and you are feeling good—may still
be cold there but don't be depressed, spring will be coming before
you know it.

love,
Billy

April 2, 1970

Dear Dad. Sorry no letters back lately, but I have been real busy.
Am real familiar by now with the M-60, step up from the M-16's
at Fort Knox—gun is a 7.62 standard round with an interchangea-
ble lock mechanism, weighs about thirty pounds, heavy sucker to
lug around but have gotten used to the noise and am pretty good
in practice, am developing an affection for the thing. Since it looks
like I will get sent over, am getting used to the idea, have been
thinking of volunteering as a chopper door gunner—carrying the
M-60 through triple-canopy jungle for a year does not appeal to
me much. Have talked to my CO about it and will make up my
mind in two weeks or so whether to put in a request for duty.
Have always wanted to fly tho would rather do it over the Caroli-
nas or Kentucky—actually I could use VA benefits for pilot training after I get out, would get plenty of experience in a chopper
crew. Tell Aunt Bess and Katie thanks for the socks and scarf
they sent last month, but real glad I don't need them anymore. As
for what I do with spare time, not much—nearest towns are
Wrightstown and Sykesville, smaller than Bellington, kind of deserted almost or look that way by nine at night. Mt. Holly a little
bigger but real drab. In the company we call them Cities of Abuse.
Some of the guys wrote up a petition for passes to Saigon as a
joke.

> All the best to
> everyone,
> Billy

April 27, 1970

Dear Danner. Yes I've been getting your letters and I understand,
but this is my thing and you'll have to try to accept it. If you were
me you might do the same. The nightmare is going to be on the

ground, that is clear, no matter what the statistics about gunners (where do you *get* all this shit?), and we hear plenty here based on the real stuff—I want to be up, moving over it with my own gun in front of me. If I get hit I want to get hit with plenty of metal around me. This is not crazy logic—we are not talking about the same world, and there is no way to play it safe. I've hauled the M-60 all over Fort Dix, and any fucker dragging it through paddies and setting it up in hill country is going to be plenty vulnerable—they always go for the gunners, to put them out, whether they're in the air or not—so whatever choice I had was gone when I got assigned Weapons and the M-60 before AIT. My choice is ground or air, and I know I feel less like a sitting chickenshit in the air. I only tell you this because I know you will keep it to yourself. My real feeling is that I'm not so scared of being dead, if it's fast—I'm scared as shit of lying in some jungle all fucked up, waiting for a dustoff that can't get in because the zone is too hot. That's what I have the dreams about. What do you mean, aren't I scared? What kind of fucking question is that? If I go down in a chopper there will be another chopper in fast, to get me and to protect the machine. Now that I know I'm going to Nam, I would just as soon go, stop thinking and waiting. Probably when I get there the only familiar thing will be the gun and I will be feeling like holding on to it. It's nothing like John Wayne or that show we used to watch after school—what was it?—12 O'Clock High. Used to love that show and the bomber jackets. When you get finished firing fourteen rounds on an M-60, you get this vibration in your body that's like the *ack-ack* of the ammo, except it's silent, and a hot flash like a drug hit as you step away. But no bomber jacket. Sorry I hardly ever write, I do read all your letters, some of the best entertainment around here, and I mean that. We can talk more on my leave—I'll be home by the night of the 5th. Mitch is driving up to spare this poor grunt the bus ride.

love,
Billy

PS—Enclosed a Kodak of me and Cindy, the girl from Merrimac I went out with at Fort Knox. She came up and I got a pass & we went to Normandy Beach, ocean still cold but real pretty. She made me give her your address in case I go back on my promise to write from the Nam. See you soon. Hope you ace your finals.

OAKLAND, CALIFORNIA

> Pfc. Hampson/RA 11949711
> US Army Personnel Center
> Oakland CA
>
> May 24, 1970

Dear Danner. You wanted a post card of the Golden Gate, so here it is! I hear it really *is* red but haven't seen it myself. Am flying out of here tonight on a chartered Braniff. Will write on arrival.

> Billy

LONG BINH, SOUTH VIETNAM

> Pfc. Hampson/RA 11949711
> Company C, 227th Aviation Bn.
> 1st Infantry Div.
> APO Frisco, 96490
>
> May 27, 1970

Dear Mom. Arrived in good shape, landed at Tan Son Nhut Airport in Saigon and joined 93rd Replacement Bn at Long Binh Base Camp for reassignment probably to a chopper out of Lai Khe. Don't worry, I will stay light on my feet. Temp. here is 100 plus and real humid, so am glad I'll be in the air, cooler at 1500 ft. If you look at the map on the envelope (I guess the army is trying to explain to parents etc where we are, I sure don't know), I am near Bien Hoa. No address yet, so don't write until my next letter, have told Mitch the same. Talked to some guys waiting to go on R&R (one going home) at the Enlisted Men's Club but haven't seen much except the Base and the land as we came in—even from the air, it didn't look like anywhere I've ever been. Travel broadens the mind—Nam is my first foreign country, will keep you posted. Write often, I like to hear all the news. Unlike the guys on the ground, I will come back to a base every night with the choppers and have an actual workday, will get letters within 2 weeks or so. Don't know what else to say to reassure you, except it's probably better not to watch the news—they show the hot spots. The war is hot in Cambodia as the news says, but combat assaults are rotated and a lot of the days will be mostly routine, mail drops, resupply runs, what is routine here.

                              love,
                              Billy

PS—Mom, I had a real nice time on leave and I want to thank you for all the fine meals and for throwing the party for me. Good to see all the high school crowd, and Kato had a great time, too.


LAI KHE, SOUTH VIETNAM

                    Pvt. W. Hampson/RA 11949711
                    Co. C, 227th Aviation Bn.
                    1st Infantry Div.
                    APO Frisco, 96490

                    June 1, 1970

Dear Danner. Am at Lai Khe, 3 days OJT now, am assigned to a Huey UH1-D chopper crew-chiefed by a guy from Oklahoma named Luke Berringer, short-timer gunner everyone calls The Luke. Pilots and copilots are rotated and I'll be the resident twinkie on any crew for awhile. Berringer will be training me. He goes on about how The Luke is my shepherd etc and calls the chopper Barbarella. This is his second tour & he says he has an understanding with Barbarella. I share a hooch (square shack made out of plyboard & ammo boxes, sandbagged walls) with him and two other gunners, Gonzalez (Texas) and Taylor, a black guy from LA. They've all been here six months or more, know what they're doing. These pilots do some incredible maneuvering and we're all plugged into helmets, earphones, eyeshields, mouthpieces, like some kind of futuristic air riders—better than bomber jackets. Glad I'm not out there humping at night, wrapped in a poncho in the jungle rot. Instead, I come back here if I get my ass thru the day, and drink slightly cold beer. Lot of dope around but too soon to fuck my head up, all of a sudden there's no doubt I'm here. You asked how it was at the very first—got off the plane, these American stewardesses and Muzak behind me, a sergeant checking the bathrooms to make sure no one was hiding in the can. Right out of the air conditioning you step into this furnace, I mean the air is cooked, 105 degrees, but the weight is worse than the heat, the air smells, sort of ripe and spoiled, like rotting vegetation or something burning that was rotten. Turns out they burn all the shit from the latrines. Guess they have to burn shit in this heat or it would get up and walk. Well, that's all the (you guessed it) shit from here. I'm not feeling too bad. Take care of yourself and drop me a line.

love,<br>Billy

June 8, 1970

Dear Danner. Thanks for writing and also for the pictures you sent. Kato sent me some pictures from the going-away party at Mom's. Don't hold it against her for going out with anyone—I don't expect her to be waiting for me like a nun. As for what I'm really doing, right now we're doing combat assaults into Cambodia. Seven or eight a day from sunrise on, as well as resupply and mail runs. At least seven choppers, carrying six grunts or eight ARVN. We go in from Song Be or Brown or one of the other close Firebases. Circle for about ten minutes while the base fires artillery prep, sounds like the finale at a fireworks display. Then the Cobras (AH1 gunships) go in, clear the treeline with rockets. They break off on both sides and we're on short final, quarter of a mile from touching down, gunners firing their asses off. All sounds good but the Cong figured it out a long time ago—they just hide about 20 ft. down in their holes, listen for the prep to stop, listen for the Cobras to drop and pull off, listen for the choppers coming in. Then they crawl up into the trees with their AK-47's & their rpg rockets and fire at us from about 50 ft away. You never see them, you see muzzle flashes. Women's Lib is real big with the NVA and the Cong—sometimes it's women trying to waste us. You're up there in the *chump-chump* of the blades, spotting flashes and firing while the chopper drops low enough to land the grunts. If you're carrying ARVN and the zone is hot, they might lay down on the floor of the chopper and have to be shoved out the fucking door. On the ground it can be hell and crazy and you still never see any Cong but dead ones. It's like they've just been there and turned everything to fuck or they're invisible, raining ammo in. Like cowboys and Indians, except the Indians are ghosts and they can't lose because nothing really kills them. Listen, I write Dad part of this and I don't write it to Mom at all. I'm glad you're staying at home this summer, but I can't do anything about Mom's being depressed. I guess she'll get used to it. Right now her nerves are the least of my problems. I guess I sound pissed. I am pissed but not at you. I don't know. Keep writing to me but don't tell me shit about Mom.

Billy

June 17

Dear Danner. Am at Firebase X-Ray, about midnight here. Funny to get mail from you in the drop we'd brought out to X-Ray since our mail stays at Lai Khe. Your letter was in the bag by mistake. Weird because today was the hottest LZ I'd come into. Air Force prep had blasted out a zone with daisy-cutters, 5000 lbs of bomb that goes off at the treeline and knocks everything down so the choppers can land. Jungle green and waving and charred at the edges, and there were twenty choppers or more, red flares up for the dustoffs, everyone scrambling in or out of machines in this orange air. There were so many wounded we took on WIAs coming back from every run. The Medivacs were filled. Luke had a medic kit & bandaged the ones so fucked up the medics hadn't found all their wounds, while I stayed on the gun. We did four runs into that zone, coming thru fire meant to score choppers before they could land reinforcements, but the last one was the worst. One of the choppers just below us as we lifted off took a rocket and we were close enough to bounce as it blew. Explosion hit in the center and took the whole bird. We were taking pops ourselves and had to pull away. After we got back, Luke told me that was my first day—air hot enough to char the asshole was always the first day. Not much time to sit on my ass here wondering is the war right or wrong—right is getting thru and pulling everyone else thru, getting bodies back if we can't get anything else. I'm with Luke and the crew and we live in the chopper. These guys are the only country I know of and they're what I'm defending—I'm not stupid enough to think my country is over here. Luke and me joke about how clicked in we are to Barbarella. He's been shot down twice but says she's not like those other cunts, etc. Wants to take her back to Oklahoma and fly her over Bluestem Lake until they both die of old age. His grandmother is an Osage & says charms. Luke says B. is an Osage chopper living in the Nam just to save our asses. Can you believe it? Sometimes it seems like I dreamed everything but this, because what I remember was in the World. Well, my ass is beat. Like we said, keep my letters to yourself. See you in 344 days. I'm getting shorter all the time.

love,<br>
Billy

June 24

Dear Dad. Things here status quo. Thank Bess & Katie for writing, okay? Have had a lot of 18 hr days this last week, no chance to write, but today we came back to Lai Khe late afternoon after resupply runs near here, so decided to drop a line. When I get time I try to figure how to describe this place. Monsoons begin in

August but now it never rains, days are just blue and hot. The sunlight is so hot it's heavy. I don't know why I never asked you about the war you went to, I guess I thought I saw it in the movies. They'll never show this one there, pictures don't say how it is. If a whole operation moves across a field out in the bush, the sky can be full of twenty or thirty choppers in formation, and below them just the humped cattle and the villagers looking small in the grass. Even the old women carry long poles over their shoulders, baskets on rope at each end. The people all have the same coloring, and out in the country they dress the same—to me they all look similar, especially the girls and the children. Their faces look perfect in a way. We sweep across windrushing the grass, and they stay where they are. Our guys, the ones I'm up there with, are the best I've met, the best I've been with anytime. Maybe you know what I mean. I think about bringing a couple to lunch at Bess's, then sitting on the porch swing (summer, of course) and watching a few cars go by on East Main. Big ambitions, right? Tell Bess to expect us and don't worry too much.

> love to everybody,
> Billy

<br>

WESTERN UNION
TELEGRAM

MR. AND MRS. MITCHELL HAMPSON
68 PINE STREET
BELLINGTON, WEST VIRGINIA

INFORMATION RECEIVED STATES THAT YOUR SON, PRIVATE FIRST CLASS WILLIAM MITCHELL HAMPSON, HAS BEEN LISTED AS MISSING IN ACTION EFFECTIVE JUNE 1970 WHILE PARTICIPATING IN AN OPERATION AGAINST A HOSTILE FORCE. YOU WILL BE PROMPTLY ADVISED AS ADDITIONAL INFORMATION IS RECEIVED.

> UNITED STATES ARMY
> DEPT. OF THE ARMY
> WASHINGTON, D.C.

Spec. 4 Robert Taylor/RA 21350688
Co. C, 227th Aviation Bn.
1st Infantry Div.
APO Frisco, 96490

July 5, 1970

Dear Miss Hampson. You may not know of me but I shared a hooch with your brother, Billy, and Luke at Lai Khe. Their chopper went down in a night operation west of Tay Ninh and I was in that operation. I was interviewed for the After Action Report, but those aren't released most times and I'm writing because we had agreements, and Billy told me to write to you. He was real fond of you and used to read us some of your letters (the funny parts) out loud. All this is real bad for us here. Your family will want to know as much as possible about what happened. Night of June 30 we were resupplying an 18-man unit, just two choppers. We had no word of a hot zone but we came in very hot. Their chopper took a lot of hits, lifted off, started flaming from the engine at about a hundred feet. Both of us on the right of our machine, the copilot and me, saw the gunners jump more or less simultaneous. The chopper moved forward maybe fifteen feet as the pilot tried to touch down, then fell nose first and exploded. We had to pull off and call in artillery, and the area was not searched until dawn. There was nothing left of the unit, but they were all accounted for, and the pilots were with the chopper wreckage. If Luke and Billy had not got clear of the wreck, we would have found them. If they'd been killed in the ambush, we would have found them. Since they had no weapons or radios, it's likely they hid and were captured as the VC pulled out. If they were not hurt and were trying to evade capture, they might have circled around as the fighting continued, and been captured somewhere between there and the nearest friendlies —which would have been Firebase X-Ray, about 20 clicks east. But there were a lot of VC in the area, doesn't seem likely they would have gotten far. There is no way of knowing. I hope something more definite is learned, but I doubt it. I send you and your family my condolence. We have lost our own in

Billy and Luke, but I hold out some hope for them, at least
for a while. Luke was The Vet and Billy was our new guy,
they were tight. They would have hung together if possible, I
tell you that.

Sincerely yours,
Spec. 4 Robert Taylor

# THE WORLD
Danner, 1972

$M$y father owned a concrete plant. He wore khaki shirts and work pants, the same kind of clothes he wore in wartime photographs when he was building airstrips in New Guinea and teaching the Papuan natives how to operate steam rollers. They could learn a good bit, he told me once. In grade school my brother Billy and I rode the Brush Fork school bus from our house in the country past bus shelters emblazoned with our father's name, and the name of the plant: MITCH CONCRETE. The words were painted on the three-sided shelters in large red letters. The bus driver stopped at each shed to pick up children who had walked as far as a mile or two down dirt roads to the highway. The shelters were well built and didn't leak. They had corrugated fiberglass roofs, concrete floors, and built-in wooden benches painted white. The bus shelters were not actually heated, but when they were under construction my father brought up the possibility of building sliding aluminum doors across the fronts to cut down the wind and rain, the blowing snow

in winter. The school board said no, that some of the kids waiting
in the shelters would be junior high or even high school students,
and it wasn't wise to equip the shelters with privacy. Besides, if
the sheds were built deeply enough, a portion of wind and rain
would be eliminated. My father followed this advice, and there
was no recorded case of sexual activity in the bus shelters.

The shelters are still standing, well kept and newly lettered
with the same two words, because the subsequent owners of the
concrete plant decided to keep the original name. My father sold
the plant after my Great Uncle Clayton, his partner, died of a
stroke in the plant office as one of the mixers was being repaired
outside. The plant was gone, and years before Billy and I entered
high school my father was working first as a salesman for a
heavy-equipment company, then at a desk job for the State Road
Commission. The desk job was short-lived. He became self-
employed, an independent salesman of heavy equipment, aluminum buildings, office supplies, or cars. In the worst of it, shortly
before he retired early and drew a disability pension from the
Veterans' Administration, he was selling a doubtful brand of life
insurance from a makeshift office in the basement of the house
we'd moved to in Bellington. He had a file cabinet and big desk
down there, both pieces of the same metal office equipment he'd
once sold. On the desk sat a lamp, a large manual typewriter, a
row of spiral-bound construction catalogs between metal bookends, a porcelain coffee mug full of pens and sharpened pencils,
and a nameplate with his name on it.

These objects from the room in the basement were the only
ones my father took with him when my parents were divorced.

Also in the room was a single bed in which my mother slept
the last few years of their marriage, boxes of old toys, a washer
and drier, and a discarded couch and chair from an old living room
set. On the wall was Billy's black light poster of Jimi Hendrix; I
don't know why he put it up in the basement, but no one has ever
moved it. The poster is lettered in pale green and rimmed in pink;
both colors are meant to glow. Directly under the poster is the
ironing board on which my mother once folded the family laundry.
The laundry was piled first in a jumbled heap of clean white cotton
on the same single bed where she slept then, hearing the water

pipes and tin furnace ducts make sounds over her at night. The
pipes wind in and out of the basement walls, in and out of the
ceiling, and at night they assume a dominance over the rest of the
room.

The subterranean dominance of the pipes, their silent twists
and turns in the dark, are reminiscent in spirit of the last few
years my family lived in one house, and the year Billy went away.
He was nineteen, the year was 1970, and he went away to Fort
Knox for basic training. Fort Knox is where they keep the gold
and train the kids. I hope they trained him damn well—it's the
least they could have done—but I don't know. I've looked through
Billy's Fort Knox yearbook many times; Charles Hollis, Brigadier
General, USA, Commanding, was right: *This yearbook will help
you, your family, and friends to vividly recall the start of your
military career.* The entrance to Fort Knox is pictured; there is
a tank on a broad stone platform and a sign that says WELCOME
TO THE HOME OF ARMOR. The famous gold is kept in the Gold
Vault, a bunkertype building that looks like a two-layered concrete box cake with barred windows. I think about all those gold
bars sitting inside a well-fortified silence, row after row of gold
bars. Billy was golden, in the summer; he got that kind of tan. I
wonder if someday I'll be forty and think to myself, *Billy was a
beautiful kid.* No, I refuse to ever think that.

Billy didn't fail the first semester of his freshman year at the
state University, but his grades weren't good. He quit school on
the day of his nineteenth birthday, before grades were ever sent
home. Billy didn't feel very involved in college, and he wouldn't
let them grade him. As he pointed out, grades would not have
saved him from the lottery anyway. He didn't resist the fall of the
numbers the way I might have, but he evaluated things on a
personal scale. I realize now that Billy was one of the more deci-
sive souls in Bellington: he would not be moved. He made his own
definitions. I finally begin to understand some of Billy's definitions, but I'm a slow learner. It seems as though Billy, whom I
always tried to instruct, is instructing me. And he isn't even here,
not right now.

The morning of December 3rd, 1969, the day after the lottery
drawing for the draft, I went down to Aunt Bess's to talk to my

father. Billy had already refused my suggestion that he resist the draft and go to Canada, but I was still plotting. Bess and Mitch had just finished breakfast. My cousin Katie, Bess's daughter, had stayed the night but had already left for Winfield. Katie is in her mid-thirties, married and childless, delicate; I was sorry she'd gone. In her quiet way, Katie would have agreed with me. Bess stayed in the kitchen as I followed my father into his bedroom; she knew I wanted to talk to him alone.

"Dad," I said, "aren't you worried about Billy?" I stood on one side of the perfectly made double bed. My father stood on the other.

He looked down at the ribbed bedspread and touched the foot of the wooden frame with one hand. "Course I'm worried. We don't have any damn business over there."

"Dad, I borrowed some money from Student Loans. It's money for Billy to go to Canada, and I have information about places for him to go, people to contact. There are organizations that will help. I want him to go soon, and I would drive up with him."

My father looked across the room and made a sound with his mouth. A click of his teeth, a sighing of air through his pursed lips. Scowling, he shook his head. "That's not right either. He'd never even be able to come back here."

"He doesn't have to live here. It's possible to live somewhere else besides Bellington."

"I'm not talking about Bellington, now you know that. He couldn't live anywhere in this country."

"Does that matter?"

"Well, *hell yes* it matters."

I touched the surface of the bed. The spread was so smooth, the pillows so perfectly covered, I didn't see how anyone could have slept there the night before. "Dad," I said, "I think we should all talk to Billy about going to Canada. Someday he'd be able to come back, surely." I waited, my father made no reply. "If we let them get hold of him, there won't be anything we can do later to help him."

Silently, my father nodded. Then he said, "I don't know, Miss. We'll have to hope they don't send him there."

"Don't send him? Of course they'll send him. Why do you think they want him?"

My voice had taken on a strident tone, and my father leaned a little toward me across the bed. "The government has troops all over the world, they don't just send everyone to Vietnam. Besides, this is Billy's decision. If he's old enough to be drafted, he's old enough to decide what he wants to do."

"Daddy, he's just a kid."

Mitch put his hands in his pockets and shifted his weight to one foot. "So are you." He looked at me straight on. "You know what you think. Don't you think he knows what he thinks?"

I was frightened. Suddenly it all seemed real. "What do you think he should do?" I asked.

My father frowned and shook his head. When he frowned so gravely his blue eyes were nearly hidden in his creased eyelids. "I don't know, Danner. Whatever he decides, I will stand with him."

"Does Billy know that?"

"Yes, I think he knows."

"What would you do if it were you?"

"Why, I guess I'd go in. I did before. Most of us did. Anyone who could."

"But this isn't even a declared war."

"Neither was Korea. Lot of boys went to Korea. Lot of boys from around here."

"But not Billy," I said. "Billy is ours." My voice was shaking, so I whispered, "They weren't."

We heard water running from the tap in the kitchen. Bess, the sleeves of her sweater pulled up, was washing the breakfast dishes. She washed dishes in a tin basin in the deep enamel sink, then put them in the drainer and poured scalding rinse water over them. The water would be heating now in the teapot.

"Godammit it to hell," my father said quietly.

Before he went to Vietnam, Billy had a seventeen-day leave home. Once, late at night, we came back from the Tap Room and sat in his Camaro out in front of our mother's house. We listened to the tape deck, shared a bottle of beer, and smoked a joint.

"This dope isn't bad," I said. "Where did you get it?"

"Kato and I bought an ounce in Winfield."

"Billy, you want to hear my latest idea on how you don't go to Nam?" I took a drag on the joint.

He smiled amiably. "Sure."

"You get busted, like I did, only worse. They hold you here for trial. You're found guilty, of course, and they put you in some nice safe jail for first offenders for a couple of years. By the time you get out, Vietnam is over."

He laughed. The car held a fragrant smoke and the town seemed empty, quiet. Street lamps lit up the leaves of the big trees. Early May, and there was a faint green stirring in the leaves, a gradual wind. "You really think they'd let me off the hook on a drugs charge, after they spent sixteen weeks training my ass?" His voice was soft and easy in the dark. "How was jail, anyway? I never asked you."

I heard him draw in, a sound like a calm gasp. "Not much fun," I said, "but calling Mom long distance to get bail was worse."

A silence, then he exhaled as he passed me the joint. "Telling him was no picnic either. New Year's Eve day, snowing like hell, and I went down to the house. We were in the kitchen with Bess, and I told him." Billy tipped the bottle of beer to his mouth, his throat working in the amber dark of the car. He swallowed. "That man went through some changes. You know that blue and white tablecloth with the little squares? He sat there looking at the tablecloth, with his eyes so wet that tears ran down his face." Billy raised his brows and looked at me. "Changes."

I sighed. The joint was gone and I put the roach in the ash tray. "Billy, if you get in trouble over there, you won't be able to call home." I leaned against the door on my side so I could see him.

He pointed upward. "I'll call the Big Guy."

"Do they have a Big Guy? They're Buddhists. They have Buddha."

"Yeah. I believe someone mentioned Buddha at Fort Dix or somewhere." He smiled. He looked younger with his hair shaved so close his head; I hadn't seen him with such short hair since junior high. "Well," he said slowly, "Buddha is a big guy, isn't he? A short, fat, big guy. Besides, Danner, Big Guy is everywhere, like Santa Claus. Isn't that what they always told us?"

"But look what happened to Santa Claus."

"What happened to him?" Billy was laughing, stoned; we were both laughing.

"He kind of disappeared, didn't he?"

"No, sister, he didn't disappear. He just isn't favoring you with his presence lately. He's got urgent calls elsewhere."

"Urgent calls on the phantom phone. The air zone phone. The phone the faithful talk on."

He nodded, seriously, and passed me the beer. "That's right, absolutely."

The beer bottle was cold, beautifully cold on such a balmy spring night. "You get in trouble, is that the phone you'll call me on? Is the Big Guy going to get you through to me?"

"Exactly," Billy said. "Don't call me, I'll call you."

We shook on it. Billy executed a modest salute, two fingers to his forehead; then we sat silently, looking out the windows of the Camaro at our mother's house. The house was pretty and perfect, white curtains behind the panes of the dormer windows, a white trellis by the red stoop of the wide entrance. The flagstone sidewalk along the hedge to the door was breaking up, and pale grass seeded between the stones and the cracked mortar. Along the walk was the bed of yellow marguerites Mom had planted so carefully. She knelt on these spring evenings and picked beetles off the blossoms, then dusted the plants with fertilizer until the fernish, lacey leaves were pale.

"I've been taking a good look at all these houses," Billy said. "Last night I drove around late after I left Kato's; I parked across from Bess's house on East Main and looked for a long time. Then I drove out Brush Fork and looked at our house. You seen it lately?"

I nodded.

"I don't know who owns it now, but they've got a bunch of junk cars parked in the backyard, down near the field. Parts of motors sitting around."

"I know. Mitch kept it all spotless—the yard. In the home

movies, he used to take as much footage of the yard and the house as of us. We'd be standing there with the Easter baskets or whatever, holding up some chocolate rabbit according to Mom's directions, and Mitch would be doing a long pan of the driveway."

Billy grinned. "And the fence. He filmed the fence all the way around the field so you could see the boundaries of the lot." My brother took the bottle from me and drank the last of the beer. "Last night, the house was all dark except for one light, in the back bedroom, their room. The swing set is still in the backyard, and the trees are getting big."

Near Lai Khe in Vietnam, there are rubber plantations still owned by the Michelin Company of France. The rubber trees are forty feet tall and planted in even rows. The light-colored bark is scarred with diagonal cuts on one side; the slashes begin at about the level of a man's chest. If GIs damage any of the trees in maneuvers, the Michelin Company has to be reimbursed by the US government.

Billy never got around to writing me the facts about trees in Vietnam, but maybe he never took a really good look at Asian trees. Not from ground level the way grunts, the foot soldiers, did. Guys in the Veterans' Caucus at the University talked to me about trees, about Lai Khe, about choppers. They would answer any question and their answers were detailed. The leafy branches of cultivated rubber trees start at about twenty feet up the thick trunks; the leaves are long and shiny, a waxen, glossy green.

Trees in Bellington are oaks, elms, chestnuts, maples. Birches, evergreens. These trees are the green world of Bellington, of the county surrounding the town, of the mountainous state. In California, I live way up north, near the sea. The trees are different there. The land—the beautiful cliffs, the ocean, and the waves of the surf—seems foreign. When I think of home, I think of a two-lane road densely overhung with the deciduous trees of a more familiar world. The real world. I come back two or three times a year, always at Christmas, always late in June, most of July. Both are bad times for my family because Billy's absence is so immediate and felt.

The two bedrooms in the upstairs of my mother's house remain just as they were in 1969, except that the beds are covered with handmade cross-stitched quilts. My mother makes quilts in the long evenings when she is alone with the television set. *It gives me something to do with my hands and keeps me from thinking,* she says. This is the second summer Billy has been gone: I do want to think. Weekdays when Mom is at work, I sit in Billy's room and think. I sit on Billy's bed and don't disturb anything, but I open the windows as far as they will go—to get some air circulating, some ventilation. It is late June now and summer is taking hold in Bellington. Most of the upstairs windows have worn-out screens, and my mother advises me not to open them at all; flies get in the house. *Better not stand on the little balcony porch off the upstairs landing; the roof is weak and the cracks in the plaster ceiling of the dining room below might widen. Wipe up the water that seeps out around the bathtub; it rots the flooring. Dry the tiles with a towel after you take a shower; they'll last longer. Don't sit on the quilts or put books on them; you'll break the stitches. And don't use them for cover; use the old blankets.* Her admonishments are low-key and continuous, as though a war is coming, rationing, proud impoverishment, or a death: something requiring fortitude. Except that a thing more continual than death has already happened, and fortitude is an ongoing process. My mother was ready for anything but this. She lived in fear for months before it happened: then it happened.

My mother can't talk about Billy in the present. Her emotions concerning the present are shaky. She doesn't want to join the National League of Families, as I have in California; she says she can't yet be of help to an organization if she hasn't managed to help herself. Perhaps later. Meanwhile, I am the family representative in a league founded to lobby for government support of MIAs and POWs, to remind the general populace that they exist. My mother can't think of Billy as Missing In Action. She thinks of Billy as himself. Often, with constancy and fidelity. She talks about him in letters to me and on the phone; we talk about him when I visit. Maybe she's working her way into the present, questioning and concluding slowly. Last night she talked about taking Billy and me to the doctor as kids. *Billy hated shots. Remember*

*those wide dark steps to Reb's office above the hardware store,
the medicinal smell as you got halfway up? On Saturdays half
the County was there, poured in from the country. That big
glass frame on the wall was filled with hundreds of snapshots,
all the babies Reb had delivered, whole families. I'd try to get
Billy interested in the pictures. He was so scared of needles, but
he wouldn't give in to being afraid until the last minute. He'd
scream and it took two adults to hold him. Afterward I'd have
to get him into the hallway before he'd seem himself again.* Her
stories about the past seem to comfort her, but they sadden me.
After all, I'm in the stories. I'm here, relating the stories to the
present and to the future, and I'm always looking for hints. *You'd
come trailing after us, having watched Billy and then taken
your own shots in rigid silence while I got him out of the office.
Reb kept a drawerful of candy suckers for kids and you brought
Billy's out to him. Once he got the candy in his mouth, he'd stop
shivering. We'd walk down those dim steps to the glass street
door. Light shone through in that shape in the dark. Billy
strained toward it and you walked down stiffly, holding to the
bannister. I could never figure out why you always seemed
afraid when everything was already over with.*

Even with all the windows open, it is too hot in Billy's room.
I lower the windows, then walk out onto the carpeted upstairs
landing, open the screen door to the forbidden porch balcony. It
is a summer afternoon and much later, in the dark, it will rain. The
warm air smells of the promise of rain. I lock my arms around
myself and prop my feet on the railing, memorizing one angle of
vision: the slope of the shingled roof to my mother's square backyard, clean garbage cans sentinel by the alley, the vacant lot with
its one scrawny birch. Across the lot are the empty sidewalks, the
street, and St. Clair funeral home. The house sits squarely on its
wide, banked lawn, waiting. St. Clair Home is one of the few
Quality Hill mansions left completely intact; most of the other old
homes have been chopped into apartments or defiled by fraterni-
ties. The mortuary trade sign, discreet, glassed-in like a portrait,
stands on two legs in the center of the lawn. The large round clock
attached to the railing of the third-floor balcony is a commercial
touch, illuminated at night, but the black numerals and their con-

stant information are easily visible: a service to the community. The peaked slate roof rises over windows framed in blue glass. The glass is densely blue, like the blue of old medicine bottles, and murky.

Billy would never sit and stare at St. Clair Home. He was as uninvolved with undertakers as he was with grades. But I remember coming home from parking at the concrete plant on weekends when I was in high school. Senior year especially, riding past the funeral home with one of the two boyfriends of my high school career. The big St. Clair clock hung as always in its circle of blue neon from the high balcony. The blue ring glowed around the moonish face of the clock. The minute hand moved with a discernible jerk, accurate, later than I'd thought. Late, I fumbled to button my blouse, straighten my stockings. Then whispering, easing of the car to the curb. Winter: patches of ice in the dark. Kisses, good-byes, picking my way up the broken stone walk to the side door as the boyfriend coasted his car down the hill, soundlessly away. Billy was never home yet; he and Kato slept together in her bed and he seldom came in until one or two. I was female, due in at midnight. Inside, glow of the kitchen night-light and again, the tick of a clock loud in the sleeping house. Moving into the hallway, I saw my face in the small mirror above the message board. The apparition of my own image welled up from shadows and startled me. I would think, *Billy's not here, I'm the only one.* In the bedroom my father snored, the sheets turned down to his waist. From her bed in the basement came my mother's voice, her words angry, afraid, and indistinct. I couldn't answer her. What journey was this, and where were we all going?

Billy got to Vietnam in May of 1970. He said it was so hot there you could barely breathe. I had a job that summer in Bellington, teacher's aide at Project Headstart. It was hot in Bellington, too. Billy was in the air and I was in the ground-floor classroom of the old Central Grade School with Mrs. Smith and twenty poor kids. We kept all the windows open; flies buzzed in and out, but the air never moved. Mrs. Smith was teaching all summer for the money; she was nice, she was patient, but she had no illusions about head starts. I had illusions. I had nightmares, too, about

Billy's letters, but I waited for every one of them and wrote to him twice a week. I even started hanging out with his friends, kids who'd been two years behind me in school and so were just finishing a first year of college or a first year working for the gas company, or whatever. We'd have a few beers at the Tap Room, and I'd write Billy about funny things they said, how they looked, who they were going out with. He mentioned Kato in his letters, but I never mentioned her to him. I knew she was spending time again with the cop she'd stopped seeing for the few months before Billy went into the army, that the cop's name was Buck. I felt an unreasonable dislike for Kato and Buck, whoever he was. Even Billy said I was being unreasonable; he didn't seem to dislike either of them. But I disliked nearly everyone at times. I liked being with Billy's friends down at the Tap Room, but occasionally the music would be on loud and the lights would be down and people would be dancing, crowding up the crummy dance floor; we'd all be slightly drunk and I'd feel a flash of hatred, like someone switching on a light. Why should they be sitting here, when he was there and I couldn't find him anymore? Mostly, I disliked people my age, anyone privileged with possibility and liberty. I didn't realize how much I disliked myself, my liberty and my helplessness.

I liked Project Headstart. The kids at Headstart were not at liberty. They reminded me of everything I didn't know; most of them were frail and jagged, but they had adult eyes, old eyes. Eyes that just watched, expecting little. The kids were scary. I kept trying to find out what they knew, but they didn't know what they knew. If they did, they weren't telling.

One of the boys wouldn't talk at all except for one-syllable noises that resembled "me" or "dog" or "no." He was a five-year-old with a stubborn, beautiful, big-eyed face; even his name, Junior, was an afterthought, no name at all. He wasn't aggressive. Mostly he was silent and stuck to the sidelines, but if pushed past a certain point on the playground he fought wildly, with greater dedication than his tormentors could ever muster. He bloodied noses. Still he wanted approval; he grunted, pointed, grabbed. He answered questions if the question required a yes response; he raised his brows emphatically and nodded, the look in his eyes close to hopeful. I liked him best and he knew it. I think he hated coming to the school. Mornings, I met the bus at the door of Central Grade. Junior would get off last, shy and angry, shirking, frowning, but once he saw me he squared his shoulders and walked forward, determined. At recess he stood near the bushes, nervously fingering the small leaves and woody stems. The tangled forsythia and honeysuckle were unpruned, taller than Junior by several feet.

On the morning of a day I won't forget, Junior came in last from recess. I'd come in early to arrange fingerpaints and he'd probably been searching for me. He found me in the classroom, took my hand, and yanked.

"What, Junior?"

He said something that sounded like a whole sentence. I asked him to repeat it. He did, urgently, and tried to lead me toward the door. Mrs. Smith had noticed our exchange. She nodded that I should do as Junior requested, but I was already on my way; I went with him outside. He stopped beside the bushes, looked up at me, and waited.

I squatted so my face was level with his. "What?" I asked.

He repeated the word "honeysuckle." The word was garbled but understandable; all four syllables were distinct. Again, he waited, unsmiling, one hand lost in foliage.

I looked at the honeysuckle.

He meant the bush was in bloom. That was what he meant. I broke off a branch and gave it to him. He broke one for me. And so on. We might have harvested the entire bush if Mrs. Smith hadn't come outside then and stood beside us on the cracked sidewalk.

"I don't think they're going to approve of your breaking these bushes," she said, "but my lips are sealed." She looked down at me. "There's a phone call for you, Danner."

"For me?"

"Yes, in the office. You go ahead. I'll take Junior back, before they bring the building down." She turned, taking him by the hand as they went in. "Junior," she said, "we'll have to put these branches in some water, won't we?"

He nodded but he was finished talking. I followed them as far

as the classroom and went farther back into the wide hallway to
the principal's office. The office was empty; no principal in summer. The big desk was dusty and cleared of papers. The blinds on
the tall windows were drawn. It was the second day of July and
the air in the room was old, hot air. The phone was the only object
on the desk; the curled black cord was strung across the desktop
toward me.

I picked up the receiver. "Hello?"

"Danner, this is Gladys. I'm with your mother. Come home
right away, dear. Your mother needs you."

"What's wrong?"

"A man is here, a sergeant from the army," Gladys said
rapidly. "He brought a telegram. It's not as bad as it could be,
Danner—they say Billy is missing."

"Missing?"

"Yes."

Silence. *Secret signal.* My thought was, *he ran away. He
ran away from the army.* I held onto the black receiver hard with
one hand, and I put my other hand flat on the big desk.

"Since Jean was taking her vacation time and staying home,"
Gladys said, her voice low and rushed, "I came by to bring the
pattern for that skirt she wants to make you. While I was here,
he came to the door. Just a minute ago. Danner?"

"Gladys," I said, "what exactly did he tell you about Billy?"

"He says Billy is listed Missing In Action."

"I'll be right home."

I faded into some automatic zone; I only had it in mind to
hurry. I walked back to the classroom—I had my mother's car and
the keys were in my purse. My thoughts moved along meaning-
lessly, like words flowing by on a screen. Did my father know yet?
What did the army do with divorced parents? *Kill them, like they
kill everyone.* I opened the door of the classroom. The room was
in a sort of friendly chaos. Mrs. Smith was putting the honeysuckle branches into a mason jar and Junior was watching her
carefully, keeping his own counsel. He looked up at me. I said to
his eyes, "I came back to get my purse. I have to go home now."

Mrs. Smith must have assented in some manner, but I didn't
hear her. I found the purse, walked outside past the broken

bushes, unlocked my mother's big blue Buick. I got in, breathing
the heat, shivering, and rolled down one window as I started the
engine. I drove the nine blocks to my mother's house and parked
in front of Gladys' old Chrysler, behind an unmarked Ford with
a Hertz rental sticker. I got out of the car and stood up, looking
at the house, at what was in the house. Back when we lived in the
country on Brush Fork, Billy and I tried to stay in the summer
fields way past dusk, catching lightning bugs in jars. Glass jars,
the metal lids punched through with air holes. Mom called and
called but we wouldn't come in. Finally she would yell at us from
the cement back porch: *I want you home this minute. Right now.*
She couldn't see us; she just yelled into the dark.

I walked up the sidewalk and into the house. My mother was
sitting on the couch; when she saw me she burst into tears. I sat
beside her and put my arm around her and held her. Her body was
shaking and the telegram was in her lap. I read the words
through, black words, yellow paper. *A hostile force*. I thought of
the dark-haired women crawling into the trees with their heavy
guns.

Gladys stood over us. "Danner, this is Sergeant Dixon."

She moved away and the soldier stood behind her. Green
dress uniform with gold buttons, tan shirt, black tie. In his hand,
a billed cap with a green, saucer-shaped top. In the center over the
black bill, a brass medallion with an eagle.

"Miss Hampson," he was saying, "I'm deeply sorry to inform
you. . . ." He went on to repeat the contents of the brief telegram,
his voice soft and southern.

"Are you from Fort Knox?"

"No, ma'am, I've come from Fort Meade, in Maryland, but I
grew up in Georgia."

Did he think I cared where he grew up? Somehow, I thought
they would have sent someone who'd known Billy.

Gladys sat down beside me. "I've called Reb Jonas."

"Why?"

"For some medicine for Jean." Gladys tilted her head to one
side. She looked very old, powdered and faded. "She may need
some medicine, later."

"My mother doesn't need any medicine," I said. "She needs

them to tell her what they've done with Billy." I took the telegram
out of her lap. *"Information Received.* What information? Whoever wrote this out wasn't even there, they don't even know."

"Honey," Gladys said, "I doubt anyone knows."

"Gladys, someone has to know." I looked at Sergeant Dixon.
My mother held my wrist tightly. "No one we can talk to,"
she said, weeping. "He might as well be on the moon."

Gladys gave my mother a Kleenex. We heard someone on the
steps at the door, and Gladys stepped over to open the screen door
for Dr. Jonas. He walked in empty-handed, without his doctor's
bag, inclining his head a little as though the ceiling were too low.

"Gladys," he said.

"Reb." She nodded.

I think Sergeant Dixon introduced himself and they shook
hands. Reb walked over near Mom and me, pulled a chair close to
the couch, and sat down. He touched my mother's shoulder firmly
and left his hand there. "Gladys tells me we've had bad news
about Billy."

My mother gestured toward the telegram in my hand.

"He's missing," I said, not volunteering the piece of paper.
"They must know more, but that's all the telegram says." I
steeled myself against Reb Jonas' voice; he was our doctor, always; when my mother's babies were born, when we got our
vaccinations and flu shots, always. He made me want to be comforted, but no one should be comforted. Billy was the one in
trouble, not us. Why should we be comforted?

Reb looked at me. "We'll have to try to find out what we can.
Your dad and I will make some calls." His gaze shifted from my
mother to Gladys and back to me. "Does Mitch know yet?"

"No," my mother said. "Billy gave this as his only address,
so Sergeant Dixon came here."

"I'll go directly to Mr. Hampson's residence now," Dixon said
softly.

"I'll go with you," I said.

"Yes, you go," my mother told me, drying her eyes. "Gladys
will stay here with me until you get back."

"Certainly," Gladys said, "I'll be right here."

Reb took a bottle of pills from his pocket. "Jean, these will help you sleep. You'll need them. Won't help anything for you to fall ill." He put the pills on the table, then looked at me. "Danner, I'll come by to see your father and Bess in a few minutes."

Sergeant Dixon stood politely and approached me. "Miss Hampson, may I have the telegram? I am required to deliver it into your father's hands."

I held the piece of paper up to him. "Yes, you do that."

"Danner," my mother said, "don't be rude to this man. It won't help."

I touched her hand. "Mom, I'll be back as soon as I can."

I headed for the door and Sergeant Dixon followed me. We went down the front walk toward the cars and I heard his black shoes taking the steps behind me. When we got to the cars, I turned to look at him. "I don't want you to tell my father. I wish you would give me the telegram and just leave. Your superiors didn't even know my parents are divorced, and they won't know the difference."

There was a band of sweat on his upper lip. His chest was broad but he wasn't much taller than me; he was perhaps twelve years older. "I am here as a gesture of respect and condolence and deep concern on the part of the United States Army. I'm required by regulation to tell your father, personally."

"Yes, in the same words you used to us, like a tape recording."

"They're the only words we have, ma'am. They're all we know right now, and it's important they be repeated exactly."

"Don't tell me what's important."

He moved back a step and blinked. His eyes were brown. "Miss Hampson, it is my duty to tell your father, and I will do so to the best of my ability. Are you certain you wouldn't rather stay with your mother?"

I stared into his face. "I won't allow you to tell him without me. He might be alone." I moved to get into the rental car but the door was locked. I think I stumbled on the curb. "You don't know how fucking alone he is," I said. "You don't know anything about this family." Sergeant Dixon opened the door for me with his keys and walked across in front of the car as I got in.

The car was spotless, a machine that belonged to no one, and it smelled new. Sergeant Dixon was beside me; he turned the key in the ignition and adjusted the blower of the air conditioner. Both hands on the wheel, he sat erect and looked at me with care. "Would you please direct me, ma'am?"

For a moment I didn't understand what he meant. There was a ringing in my ears and my heart was pounding. "What?"

"To your father's house," he said quietly.

I looked away at the length of Pine Street. Everything looked normal. "My father lives with his aunt," I said, "since the divorce." This couldn't really be happening. "Back up and turn right, to the big street called Quality Hill. Straight down till you come into downtown past the Fire Department, and Main Street. You must have driven in that way. You turn east on Main. East Main. A white one-story house beside the old hospital."

He put the car in motion. "Miss Hampson, it isn't regulation for me to say so, but my own brother was captured in North Vietnam two years ago. His name has been released as one of those captured. I can appreciate what you're feeling."

I didn't know whether to believe him. Maybe they were supposed to make a non-regulation remark, especially to hostile family members. The houses of Quality Hill were floating into my vision; they were passing. I had to make an effort to speak clearly. "Was your brother drafted, Sergeant Dixon?"

"No, ma'am. He was a career military officer, a pilot, and he requested combat duty."

"Well, Billy didn't," I said flatly. I wanted to keep talking, to keep us from arriving at Bess's so quickly. "Why did you join the military?"

"I come from a military family, ma'am."

"Then your family should be in Vietnam, not my family." I couldn't talk very loudly, but the windows were up and he could hear me clearly over the quiet hum of the air conditioner. "You shouldn't be here. Billy should be here. You should be there."

"I have been ma'am." We had turned onto East Main. He kept talking. "The military owes a great debt of allegiance to every American fighting man in Vietnam, and will do everything in its power to find your brother, to ascertain whether your brother was captured. Men in his own company, men he knew, will make the initial search. They are searching for him now."

"Then what?"

"The matter is never dropped. The matter is turned over to Intelligence."

"Intelligence?" Bess's house was in sight. "I hate you," I said softly. "I hate all of you for taking him."

"I understand, ma'am." He had stopped the car across from the hospital, but the cool air continued humming. His voice was calm and neutral. "Do you feel faint, Miss Hampson? You look pale."

"We should walk up the alley," I said. "If we go to the front, my great aunt will answer the door, and she's past eighty."

We got out of the car and crossed the street into the alley, walking the length of the clapboard house to the concrete walk that went to the small back porch. We came around the side of the house; Katie and my father were there. Katie was sitting in the porch swing. She must have just arrived; her car was on the carport and her purse was beside her. My father sat near her in an aluminum folding chair, cloth strips of the seat sagging with his weight. He looked up at me quizzically as I walked forward with Dixon beside me. He wasn't wearing his glasses. He would misunderstand; he would think I was bringing a friend to meet him.

But I wouldn't have a boyfriend in uniform. Katie knew that. She leaned back in the swing as though pressed backward. Her mouth opened slightly, her hand went to the center of her chest.

Now we were close enough that my father saw my expression. I had such terror in my face that he stood and walked toward me. He reached me and grabbed my upper arm and pulled me closer, as though out of harm's way. Quickly, my voice certain, I said, "Dad, Billy is missing. He's not dead."

Many times that summer, I sat in the sitting room with Bess while my father talked on the phone in the hallway to this or that person in Charleston or Washington. He is a little hard of hearing and speaks loudly, especially over long distance. He called our state senator by his first name and called the congressman from our district "sir." He sounded deferential and I hated hearing that tone in his voice.

"Why," he would begin, not questioning but stating, "we still haven't received an official account of the incident in which my son, William Hampson, was listed as Missing In Action. Do you remember speaking with me last week, sir? [pause] Yes, sir. Private First Class [slowly now, as though the world is hard of hearing and the name must be understood] William, Mitchell, Hampson, 227th Aviation Battalion. We've had unofficial word from a Specialist 4th Class Taylor, a letter to my daughter, but the army still hasn't confirmed the information."

And so on.

Bess sat in her chair with her sewing in her lap, her hands folded across hooped cross-stitching. Once, early on, she turned her birdlike head to me and said, with no fear of being overheard, "You know, your father doesn't sleep at night. He hasn't in all these weeks since. In the afternoon, he falls asleep in his chair."

"I know, Bess. I don't think any of us is sleeping much."

"But your father—" She paused and her hands moved once. "His son, and he's a man. Danner, I think he feels ashamed. That he can't do more. That he should, and he can't."

I listened to his voice, its hesitations. He was asking these faraway, successful men to intercede. He was asking for help.

Bess waited a moment before going on. "It's a terrible thing to think of losing a child. So many times I was afraid about Katie. If you outlive your own child, well, I suppose you go on, but I don't know if you ever really live."

I was alone in the house on the day Robert Taylor's letter came. In two weeks, we'd had no word except that the army had no other information. My mother had gone back to her administrative job in the school system. She said she wept easily and embarrassed herself at work, but working was better than being at home, where that man had stood in her living room and told her about Billy. I hadn't wept at all. The blue envelope with the familiar miniature map of Vietnam lay on my mother's gold carpet under the mail slot, and I thought at first it was a message from Billy. My father had received a letter just a few days ago, written about a week before Billy was MIA. I hadn't let myself read it. But this wasn't his handwriting, and then I saw the name on the return address and sat on the steps to the upstairs and read. Many times, without moving. Then I took the letter to my room and cried loudly, horribly, hearing my own sounds. The letter was a miracle. My first reaction was thankfulness and inordinate hope. I'm still thankful. No matter what happened when they got on the ground, he wasn't alone. *The Luke is my shepherd:* not my phrase, Billy's, Billy's joke. He hadn't been alone, that was it. The image in my mind was of Billy in the air with Luke, both of them poised to land, arms extended.

My father couldn't seem to quite believe the letter at first. I showed it to him that same afternoon and said Billy had mentioned Taylor to me, I did remember the name.

"You say this is a black fellow, from Los Angeles?"

"What difference does that make, Dad?"

My father shook his head impatiently. "Don't make any difference, but the government ought to make this information official. If this is the truth, why haven't they told us this? They ought to back up this man's story. Right now, this is still hearsay."

I was completely puzzled by his reaction. Did he think the set of facts made things seem worse for Billy? "Hearsay?" I took the letter back and looked through it again. "What are you talking about? This man was there. He kept his agreement with Billy and wrote to me. Don't you see what he says here? He saw Billy jump."

My father went inside to phone Reb Jonas, to phone the state senator who'd promised to help. I sat on the porch swing and put the letter carefully back into its thin blue envelope.


When the army wouldn't confirm Robert Taylor's letter, I decided the men Mitch was phoning needed some reminder Billy was real, that Taylor's letter existed. I made a list of men in charge: President Nixon, the Secretary of Defense, the Secretary of the Army, our Congressmen, members of the House Armed Services Committee, the Governor, assorted others. I sent them, along with a typed copy of Taylor's letter, a Xerox of the original, and my own request for information, two 8″ x 10″ photos of Billy. I drove back and forth to Winfield to have the photographs printed in two days by a color lab. They were, in effect, before and after pictures.

The first, taken the summer of '69 when Billy worked for the Park Service at the river, shows him in cutoffs, bare-chested, his hair still long, about to dive from a boulder into green water. The water is very clear and you can see outlines of submerged rocks in the water itself.

The second is Billy in uniform, at the going-away party Mom had for him when he was home on leave in May. Kato took the picture and I went down to Black's Billiards to get the negative from her. It was a hot evening in August; I parked in the alley and walked up the fire escape steps to the back door of the apartment. She gave me the negative in an envelope, and we sat on the ribbed metal landing that served as the Black's porch. We drank iced tea. Kato brought out a box of pretzels but neither of us ate. She told me she'd always keep Billy's letters, made me promise to tell her any news we heard of him. And she gave me an address. Buck had been transferred to a town in western Pennsylvania and she was leaving soon to go and live with him.

"He's so old-fashioned," she said, "he'll start telling me we ought to get married."

I looked over at her. "Are you going to?"

"I don't know." She wore no makeup and her eyes looked tired. There were beads of moisture along her hairline. "It's hard to think. This whole summer—knowing about Billy, my dad drinking so much, the heat—I want to sleep all the time, it seems. If I hadn't already given notice at the paper, they'd probably fire me." She looked down at the cold glass she held.

That's how I remember her. Her face in profile, her eyes lowered. *It's hard to think.* She must have already known she was pregnant; in two weeks, she married Buck in Pennsylvania. She asked to see the other picture I was going to use, and I showed her the snapshot of Billy at the river.

She held the image near her face and looked closely. "Even

if it's twenty years, I'll think of him as gone. I can't think of him as not alive."

Years were on everyone's mind. My mother helped me pay for the photographs and the mailings. We sat in the living room, assembling the packages. "If we had enough money to make these pictures even bigger," I said, "say, billboard size, and pasted them by the hundreds on signs in every major city in the country, I bet we'd find out something."

Jean put down the package she'd just sealed. "Danner, we don't have that kind of money. Even if we did, what is it you expect to happen? If the government paid attention to us and asked personally and especially for Billy, do you think the people who might have him would listen?"

I said nothing, and she looked away from me into the room.

"They're the ones he was taught to shoot at," she said. "They don't care what we want. They won't ever. No matter if the war ends, no matter how many years."

Two days after I mailed the packages, before any of the addressees had seen the pictures, a Family Services Assistance Officer visited my father and mother again. He brought an official telegram from the army that confirmed, five weeks after Billy was listed MIA, most of the information in Robert Taylor's letter. But there was no mention of anyone actually seen jumping from the chopper, only a "supposition that Pfc. Hampson and Sgt. Berringer jumped or otherwise escaped" from the aircraft. There was no mention of an ambush or of an eighteen-man unit lost. I never got a reply to either of my letters to Robert Taylor, thanking him and asking for any other news. Our FSAO told me Luke Berringer's only next of kin was a grandmother who didn't wish her address given out.

I don't know why the army took so long to tell us most of the story Taylor told me. *We had no word of a hot zone but we came in very hot.* Suppose the army had made a mistake, suppose their Intelligence was mistaken. Did they think my family would make trouble in some way? *Blame* them, maybe?

o   o   o

I did blame them. I went back to college in the fall of '70 because I didn't know what else to do. I blamed the army for what I felt, and sought out veterans; I began working as a liaison volunteer for the Veterans' Caucus that had been set up on campus. They had no vote in student government, such as it was. They were self-designated spokesmen for veterans' issues, acknowledged by the administration but not funded. I stopped spending time with nice liberal guys interested in organic farming or tenants' rights, and started seeing veterans. They were who I talked to, listened to, argued with. Finally, in alliances of a few weeks' duration, they were who I slept with. Some of them were kind to me. Kindness is not always a specialty with Vietnam vets, not in the beginning, and I wasn't much interested in getting past beginnings. Some of them weren't kind; they were guys Billy wouldn't even have drunk beer with. But they'd stood on the same ground he had or they'd flown in the same kinds of machines; they knew subtle facts about the military, and they were angry. In the first year Billy was missing, that was all I needed.

One night that winter I went over to Lynchburg State with three vets, to talk to a student committee interested in veterans' programs. The students were straight and uninformed; the men I was with were impatient and resented my attempts at mediation. The meeting went badly and they walked out; I followed them. We went to a bar in Lynchburg and started drinking. There was a feathery tension between us—I'd slept with two of the three and it wasn't clear who I was with. It wasn't clear to Riley either. I looked up from my third or fourth drink to see him standing near me.

"Danner? Could I talk to you for a minute?"

I'd known he was back in school at Lynchburg, that his wife worked in a bank there, but I was so surprised at seeing him, at the look on his face, that I said nothing.

"Who's he?" someone said.

"He's an old friend," I answered. I stood and realized I was dizzy.

Riley and I went out to the parking lot. It was cold and we got into his car. Finally I said, "How long have you been back?"

"Not long." He turned to me in the dark of the car. His hair was close-cropped and he seemed even thinner, more angular. He had a mustache. "You don't look too good, Danner."

"No?"

"I don't mean your looks, I mean the way you act." He glanced out the windshield nervously. Snow was beginning to pelt the glass. "It's no good for Jean and Mitch if you rack yourself up in a car with three drunk vets."

I didn't say anything.

Riley put one hand on the dash. His wedding ring was a plain gold band, unmarked and narrow. "Hell," he said slowly, "I'm sorry about Billy. I'm sorry."

"I know. Your mom came over to the house."

"Have you heard anything?"

"No. I mean we hear, but it's always nothing." I kept watching Riley's face, his eyes. He was really here. Someone real had come back. "I haven't seen you since way before Billy left."

"Danner, I want you to let me drive you back to the University. You stay here, all right? Don't get out of the car. I'll just go back inside and tell your friends we're leaving."

"Yes," I said, "okay." My own voice sounded distant to me. Riley sounded so familiar, when the world was full of strangers.

He came back and I heard him slam the door of the car; he said I should lie down and rest while he drove. I lay down across the seat with my head on his thigh. We didn't talk and I fell asleep. I hadn't slept so easily and quickly since it happened. Sometimes in my sleep I felt the turning of the car in the dark, the winding of the slick road as my body shifted, Riley's hand steadying my shoulder.

I wakened as he pulled up behind a University bus at a red light. I gave him directions to my apartment and asked him in, but he said he had to get home. Before the roads got any worse. "Take better care," he said, holding my face in his two hands. "Will you?"

After that I stopped sleeping with anyone. I stopped going to classes much. One of my honors professors told me I should see a psychiatrist and gave me a name. I started talking to a shrink at Student Health Services. On the eighth visit, the shrink said I had a lot of blocks against talking to him or talking to myself; he suggested I try to talk to Billy. Write him a letter. If I could say things Billy would hear, what would I say? I was to work on the letter a while every day, and I was given a week to complete it.

I wrote the letter. It contained no greeting and was unsigned. The words came into my mind as though carved in stone, and I don't think they will alter. This is the letter in its entirety: *They'll never convince me I won't see you again—I just don't feel alone.*

The psychiatrist wasn't pleased. "That's the whole letter?"

"Yes."

A silence. Then he said, from his chair five feet away, "Who's trying to convince you, Danner?"

"Everyone."

"Who, exactly?"

"The world, the war still going on and on, people I know, guys, time—all the time going on, piling up like evidence against him, that he's just—"

"Just what, Danner?"

*"Dead* over there," I shouted, "you *fucker,* you made me say it—" And I leaped toward him, into him, striking out with my fists. How many times I hit him is a blur. I remember he got me back into my chair. The matronly receptionist was in the room, very nervous, and the shrink was bending down to pick his glasses up off the carpet. He signaled the receptionist to go. She did, but left the office door ajar.

"Well," he said, putting his glasses back on and sitting down, "I think we got somewhere today."

I was sobbing. He tried to hand me a box of Kleenex.

"I'm not coming back here again," I said.

He looked at me resignedly. "I think it's advisable you come twice a week for a while. You have a great deal of anger and sorrow to express."

"I know," I said. "I'll have to express them somewhere else."

I got up and put my coat on and left. An orderly in a white uniform was leaning against the wall just outside the office door. Reinforcements, just in case. He looked me over blankly. "Go fuck yourself," I said.

o   o   o

I had to make appointments with several professors to quit college in the last weeks of an English honors program but, like my determined brother before me, I managed. I spent half the summer in Bellington, until I realized I was only making things worse for my parents. Worse for myself, watching them in such constant, low-profile pain.

My father keeps Billy's Camaro in Bess's wooden garage, and he takes good care of it. After I told him I'd decided to go to California, we walked out to look at the car.

The narrow old garage was just a kind of shed, and the Camaro looked bright and cherished, hidden in a place almost too small for it. Mitch asked if I'd like to drive the car, take it West.

"No," I told him, "I think Billy's car should stay with you."

He nodded, leaning on the white hood of the Camaro. "How is your mother doing?"

"Not good."

"Sweet Jesus," he said, in the pale-lit garage, "we should have gotten him the hell out of the country. I'll never forgive myself."

"Dad, Billy didn't want to leave the country. He'd already decided."

My father looked out the narrow garage window at the alley. "Honey, I hate to see you go so far away."

"I'll come back."

Kato was in town that July before I left; she heard I was leaving and phoned me. I went down by the billiard hall to see her. The baby was five months old and she looked like Kato. Blond, blue-eyed, with the same shape face. I think Kato must have been honest with Buck and they'd both accepted whatever possibilities existed. She told me things were better for her now, that a baby made things better and Buck was a good husband. She asked if we'd heard any news about Billy.

I went to California on the bus and arrived like a refugee, knowing no one. I found an inexpensive apartment in a rundown house on a bay in a northern coastal town. I got a job in an insurance office. All I do there is type letters, pour coffee, post the mail. I have no diversions from thinking, and the thinking has stretched out.

Billy told me, during the summer he worked at the river, that some types of pollution actually clarify the appearance of water. The water grows more and more polluted but becomes clearer and clearer because things that are living in it die.

Maybe that's what's happening. I feel very clear, almost transparent. My next move will come to me.

*The best way to be lucky is to take what comes and not be a coward.* In the beginning, my thoughts were murderous. I fantasized about killing Nixon, someone killing Nixon. I thought about money, trying to get money—how could I get money? Hire some weird mercenary to sink into the morass of Vietnam and find out what happened to Billy, actually bring him back. The North Vietnamese took care of pilots; pilots were officers, political leverage to be exchanged, they possessed information. But the NVA wouldn't realize Billy had information, so much information. *These guys are the only country I know of, they're what I'm defending.* I felt betrayed by my government but I'd expected betrayal: I just hadn't expected betrayal to such a degree. That it would go on so long, that I would have to live with it. If I hated my government, shouldn't I go and live in some other country? Not use the supermarkets, where there was more harvested, neatly wrapped, germ-free food than they'd ever seen at one time in Lai Khe? But my parents are my country, my divided country. By going to California, I'd made it to the far frontiers, but I'd never leave my country. I never will.

For weeks one winter on Brush Fork, Billy came to my room after our parents were asleep. They still slept in the same room, so we were young—seven and eight or so. Each night we shoved my bed away from the wall and surveyed the floor with a flashlight, brandishing two stolen dinner knives and a screwdriver. "It's under there," Billy said, "I can tell." We were looking for a secret passage, a trapdoor. Every night we moved the parquet squares already pried loose and went to work on another, exposing a black gummy surface underneath. The squares of flooring were alternating strips of oak, maple, walnut, ash. We worked at each strip until the whole parquet square came up, an hour, two hours, quietly, breathing dust. "If I find it," Billy whispered, "I'm the king." "King of what?" I asked. "King of the World," he said, "king of everything that's down there." "You are not," I told him, "it's my floor." "Doesn't matter," he said, "I told you the secret. I knew it was there."

My mother discovered the project one Saturday while vacuuming. She had moved the bed away from the wall to do a thorough cleaning, and then she called my father into the room. She called us in from outside.

Mitch stood in my small bedroom, his hands in the deep pockets of his work pants. "What the hell were you kids doing here?" he said.

Billy knew we were in trouble. He explained about the trapdoor.

Mitch knelt down on one knee to get a closer look. He'd already moved all the loose flooring slightly aside. The dismantled work area was about two foot square and looked impressive in daylight. "You two must have worked on this pretty hard," he said respectfully.

I know my father reglued the flooring and Billy helped him. Mitch probably did actually tell us there were no secret passages, that a trapdoor couldn't lead anywhere because the house didn't have a basement—but I don't remember any remarks, only that his lack of anger seemed miraculous.

Now I know his reaction had partly to do with the house. He knew all about the Brush Fork house; he'd contracted the labor and built it himself. He'd designed the heating system, radiant heat piped under the floor so the parquet squares were always warm. He knew how well the floor was built; the parquet had been specially made. Billy's investigation of the house was exploration my father understood: the house was my father's, what he'd made, what he owned. Information he wanted Billy to have.

I think about the past now in terms of what Billy knew. The information he took away with him, his training, what he knew before he ever got to Fort Knox. The world, so to speak, how much he knew. What he'd practiced, what he'd perfected before he ever laid hands on an M-60. Because when he jumped from the chopper, he didn't have the gun anymore. Robert Taylor's letter said Billy hid.

"Cover me," Billy said, "cover me all up."

I piled leaves on top of him until only his face showed, like a face in a hole.

"No," he said, "that too."

"What, you don't want to see?"

"No, I don't want to know where you're running from."

Maybe we were nine and ten. In autumn we went down into the field and crossed the creek, walked up into the woods to a clearing where the leaves were layers deep. Our game was to pile the leaves up very high: one of us got inside, buried to the shoulders, while the other ran and jumped on top. The buried one watched the attacker run forward, screaming like a kamikaze. If the buried one made any sound, the jumper won and got to jump again. Sometimes it didn't matter but occasionally we played the game in earnest.

"Bury me way down deep," Billy said. "You're still bigger than me and you won't be able to tell where I am."

I covered him, piling on more leaves. The wind rattled faintly in the naked trees of the woods, leaves scuttling, dipping and turning in the air. The more leaves I gave him, the better chance he had. I wanted him to win, to stay hidden, stay silent. I kept piling leaves, alone in the clearing, hiding him deeper and deeper, the mound of leaves higher than my chest. I kept working until he was secret, buried, warm. Until he was nowhere.

I dream about Billy. At first I liked having the dreams because I didn't think about what they meant. And I got to see Billy, his face, so clearly. I still see his face, usually his young face, his kid face more real than any photograph or memory. My sense of him is so strong I think he must be coming through from some completely foreign zone, a zone free of interference and boundaries. A zone that is out of this world. I wake up sweating, scared. Then I tell myself the clarity may be a direct correlative of how alive Billy is, how desperate he feels, how hard he's trying to get through.

But in the dreams, Billy isn't desperate. He's just himself. I'm the one who is afraid, who knows something terrible might happen, has happened, will happen. I'm the one who can't stop it from happening.

*You watch your little brother,* Mom would say to me. He was walking, but barely. She would hang clothes out on the line in summer, big baskets of clothes, the sheets flapping and hiding her from view. We were way down in the yard, far from the road, and Jean's radar was finely tuned. She probably didn't take my abilities as Billy's protector all that seriously, since I was only about three myself. But I was very serious. I wouldn't even let him stand up. I kept him entertained with the ball or the block or whatever he was fooling with; if all else failed, I held him down by main force. She'd come back to see why he was crying.

MACHINE DREAM
Danner

Danner and Billy are walking in the deep dark forest. Billy makes airplane sounds. Danner, oblivious to her brother's play, is stalking the magic horse. There are no cloven tracks, but the dust on the path is disturbed and the horse seems to be circling. Occasionally Danner looks over her shoulder and sees the animal watching them through thick leaves. The mare's eyes are large and certain. Certain of what? Billy pays no attention and seems to have followed his sister here almost accidentally. They walk on, and finally it is so dark that Danner can't see Billy at all. She can only hear him, farther and farther behind her, imitating with a careful and private energy the engine sounds of a plane that is going down. War-movie sounds. *Eeee-yoww, ach-ack-ack.* So gentle it sounds like a song, and the song goes on softly as the plane falls, year after year, to earth.